THE MONEYCHANGERS

THE STORY-TELLERS

Arthur Hailey
The Moneychangers

SOUVENIR PRESS

First published in Great Britain 1975
by Michael Joseph Ltd.
in association with Souvenir Press Ltd.

This edition first published 2000 by
Souvenir Press Ltd.,
43 Great Russell Street, London WC1B 3PA

Reprinted 2012

ISBN 9780285635531

Printed and bound in Germany by Bercker, Kevelaer

If thou art rich, thou'rt poor;
For, like an ass whose back with ingots bows,
Thou bear'st thy heavy riches but a journey,
And death unloads thee.

Shakespeare, *Measure for Measure*

Foul-cank'ring rust the hidden treasure frets,
But gold that's put to use more gold begets.

Venus and Adonis

part one

one

Long afterwards, many would remember those two days in the first week of October with vividness and anguish.

It was on Tuesday of that week that old Ben Rosselli, president of First Mercantile American Bank and grandson of the bank's founder, made an announcement – startling and sombre – which reverberated through every segment of the bank and far beyond. And the next day, Wednesday, the bank's 'flagship' downtown branch discovered the presence of a thief – beginning a series of events which few could have foreseen, and ending in financial wreckage, human tragedy, and death.

The bank president's announcement occurred without warning; remarkably, there were no advance leaks. Ben Rosselli had telephoned a few of his senior executives early in the morning, catching some at home at breakfast, others soon after their arrival at work. There were a few, too, who were not executives, simply long-time employees whom old Ben thought of as his friends.

To each, the message was the same: Please be in the Headquarters Tower boardroom at 11am.

Now all except Ben were assembled in the boardroom, twenty or so, talking quietly in groups, waiting. All were standing; no one chose to be first to pull a chair back from the gleaming directors' table, longer than a squash court, which seated forty.

A voice cut sharply across the talk. 'Who authorized that ?'

Heads turned. Roscoe Heyward, executive vice-president and comptroller, had addressed a white-coated waiter from the senior officers' dining room. The man had come in with decanters of sherry which he was pouring into glasses.

Heyward, austere, Olympian in FMA Bank, was a zealous teetotaller. He glanced pointedly at his watch in a gesture which said clearly: not only drinking, but this *early*. Several who had been reaching out for the sherry withdrew their hands.

'Mr Rosselli's instructions, sir,' the waiter stated. 'And he especially ordered the best sherry.'

A stocky figure, fashionably dressed in light grey, turned and said easily, 'Whatever time it is, no sense passing up the best.'

Alex Vandervoort, blue-eyed and fair-haired with a touch of grey at the temples, was also an executive vice-president. Genial and informal, his easygoing, 'with-it' ways belied the tough decisiveness beneath. The two men – Heyward and Vandervoort – represented the second management echelon immediately below the presidency and, while each was seasoned and capable of cooperation, they were, in many ways, rivals. Their rivalry, and differing viewpoints, permeated the bank, giving each a retinue of supporters at lower levels.

Now Alex took two glasses of sherry, passing one to Edwina D'Orsey, brunette and statuesque, FMA's ranking woman executive.

Edwina saw Heyward glance towards her, disapproving. Well, it made little difference, she thought. Roscoe knew she was a loyalist in the Vandervoort camp.

'Thank you, Alex,' she said, and took the glass.

There was a moment's tension, then others followed the example.

Roscoe Heyward's face tightened angrily. He appeared about to say something more, then changed his mind.

At the boardroom doorway the vice-president for Security, Nolan Wainwright, a towering, Othello-like figure and one of two black executives present, raised his voice. 'Mrs D'Orsey and gentlemen – Mr Rosselli.'

The hum of conversation stopped.

Ben Rosselli stood there, smiling slightly as his eyes passed over the group. As always, his appearance seemed to strike a median point between a benevolent father figure and the strong solidity of one to whom thousands of fellow citizens entrusted money for safekeeping. He looked both parts, and dressed them: in statesman-banker black, with the inevitable waistcoat, across its front a thin gold chain and fob. And it was striking how closely this man resembled the first Rosselli – Giovanni – who had founded the bank in the basement of a grocery store a century ago. It was Giovanni's patrician head, with flowing silver hair and full moustache, which the bank reproduced on passbooks and travellers' cheques as a symbol of probity, and whose bust adorned Rosselli Plaza down below.

The here-and-now Rosselli had the silver hair and moustache, almost as luxuriant. Fashion across a century had revolved full circle. But what no reproduction showed was the family drive which all Rossellis had possessed and which, with ingenuity and boundless energy, raised First Mercantile American to its present eminence. Today, though, in Ben Rosselli the usual liveliness seemed missing. He was walking with the aid of a cane; no one present had seen him do so before.

Now he reached out, as if to pull one of the heavy directors' chairs towards him. But Nolan Wainwright, who was the nearest, moved more quickly. The security chief swung the chair around, its high back to the boardroom table. With a murmur of thanks the president settled into it.

Ben Rosselli waved a hand to the others. 'This is informal. Won't take long. If you like, pull chairs around. Ah, thank you.' The last remark was to the waiter from whom he accepted a glass of sherry. The man went out, closing the boardroom doors behind him.

Someone moved a chair for Edwina D'Orsey, and a few others seated themselves, but most remained standing.

It was Alex Vandervoort who said, 'We're obviously here to celebrate.' He motioned with his sherry glass. 'The question is – what?'

Ben Rosselli again smiled fleetingly. 'I wish this were a celebration, Alex. It's simply an occasion when I thought a drink might help.' He paused, and suddenly a new tension permeated the room. It was evident to everyone now that this was no ordinary meeting. Faces mirrored uncertainty, concern.

'I'm dying,' Ben Rosselli said. 'My doctors tell me I don't have long. I thought all of you should know.' He raised his own glass, contemplated it, and took a sip of sherry.

Where the boardroom had been quiet before, now the silence was intense. No one moved or spoke. Exterior sounds intruded faintly; the muted tapping of a typewriter, an air-conditioning hum; somewhere outside a whining jet plane climbed above the city.

11

Old Ben leaned forward on his cane. 'Come now, let's not be embarrassed. We're all old friends; it's why I called you here. And, oh yes, to save anyone asking, what I've told you is definite; if I thought there was a chance it wasn't, I'd have waited longer. The other thing you may be wondering – the trouble is lung cancer, well advanced I'm told. It's probable I won't see Christmas.' He paused and suddenly all the frailty and fatigue showed. More softly he added, 'So now that you know, and as and when you choose, you can pass the word to others.'

Edwina D'Orsey thought: there would be no choosing the time. The moment the boardroom emptied, what they had just heard would spread through the bank, and beyond, like prairie fire. The news would affect many – some emotionally, others more prosaically. But mostly she was dazed and sensed the reaction of others was the same.

'Mr Ben,' one of the older men volunteered. Pop Monroe was a senior clerk in the trust department, and his voice was wavering. 'Mr Ben, I guess you floored us good. I reckon nobody knows what the hell to say.'

There was a murmur, almost a groan, of assent and sympathy.

Above it, Roscoe Heyward injected smoothly, 'What we can say, and must' – there was a hint of reproof in the comptroller's voice, as if others should have waited to allow him to speak first – 'is that while this terrible news has shocked and saddened us, we pray there may be leeway and hope in the matter of time. Doctors' opinions, as most of us know, are seldom exact. And medical science can achieve a great deal in halting, even curing . . .'

'Roscoe, I said I'd been over all that,' Ben Rosselli said, betraying his first trace of testiness. 'And as to doctors, I've had the best. Wouldn't you expect me to?'

'Yes, I would,' Heyward said. 'But we should remember there is a higher power than doctors and it must be the duty of us all' – he glanced pointedly around the room – 'to pray to God for mercy, or at least more time than you believe.'

The older man said wryly, 'I get the impression God has already made up his mind.'

12

Alex Vandervoort observed, 'Ben, we're all upset. I'm especially sorry for something I said earlier.'

'About celebrating? Forget it! You didn't know.' The old man chuckled. 'Besides, why not? I've had a good life; not everyone does, so surely that's a cause to celebrate.' He patted his suit coat pockets, then looked around him. 'Anybody have a cigarette? Those doctors cut me off.'

Several packs appeared. Roscoe Heyward queried, 'Are you sure you should ?'

Ben Rosselli looked at him sardonically but failed to answer. It was no secret that while the older man respected Heyward's talents as a banker, the two had never achieved a personal closeness.

Alex Vandervoort lighted the cigarette which the bank president took. Alex's eyes, like others in the room, were moist.

'At a time like this there are some things to be glad of,' Ben said. 'Being given a little warning is one, the chance to tie loose ends.' Smoke from his cigarette curled around him. 'Of course, on the other side, there're regrets for the way a few things went. You sit and think about those, too.'

No one had to be told of one regret – Ben Rosselli had no heir. An only son had been killed in action in World War II; more recently a promising grandson had died amid the senseless waste of Vietnam.

A fit of coughing seized the old man. Nolan Wainwright, who was nearest, reached over, accepted the cigarette from shaking fingers and stubbed it out. Now it became evident how weakened Ben Rosselli really was, how much the effort of today had tired him.

Though no one knew it, it was the last time he would be present at the bank.

They went to him individually, shaking his hand gently, groping for words to say. When Edwina D'Orsey's turn came, she kissed him lightly on the cheek and he winked.

two

Roscoe Heyward was one of the first to leave the boardroom. The executive vice-president-comptroller had two urgent objectives, resulting from what he had just learned.

One was to ensure a smooth transition of authority after Ben Rosselli's death. The second objective was to ensure his own appointment as president and chief executive.

Heyward was already a strong candidate. So was Alex Vandervoort and possibly, within the bank itself, Alex had the larger following. However, on the board of directors, where it counted most, Heyward believed his own support was greater.

Wise in the ways of bank politics and with a disciplined, steely mind, Heyward had begun planning his campaign, even while this morning's boardroom session was in progress. Now he headed for his office suite, panelled rooms with deep beige broadloom and a breathtaking view of the city far below. Seated at his desk, he summoned the senior of his two secretaries, Mrs Callaghan, and gave her rapid-fire instructions.

The first was to reach by telephone all outside directors, whom Roscoe Heyward would talk to, one by one. He had a list of directors on the desk before him. Apart from the special phone calls, he was not to be disturbed.

Another instruction was to close the outer officer door as she left – in itself unusual since FMA executives observed an open-door tradition, begun a century ago and stolidly upheld by Ben Rosselli. That was one tradition which had to go. Privacy, at this moment, was essential.

Heyward had been quick to observe at this morning's session that only two members of First Mercantile American's board other than the senior management officers, were present. Both directors were personal friends of Ben Rosselli – obviously the reason they had been called in. But it meant that fifteen members of the board were uninformed, so far, of the impending death. Heyward would make sure that all fifteen received the news personally from him.

He calculated two probabilities: first, the facts were so sudden and shattering that there would be an instinctive alliance between anyone receiving the news and whoever conveyed it. Second, some directors might resent not having been informed in advance, particularly before some of FMA's rank and file who heard the announcement in the boardroom. Roscoe Heyward intended to capitalize on this resentment.

A buzzer sounded. He took the first call and began to talk. Another call followed, and another. Several directors were out of the city but Dora Callaghan, an experienced, loyal aide, was tracking them down.

A half hour after he began phoning, Roscoe Heyward was informing the Honourable Harold Austin earnestly, 'Here at the bank, of course, we're overwhelmingly emotional and distressed. What Ben told us simply does not seem possible or real.'

'Dear God!' The other voice on the telephone still reflected the dismay expressed moments earlier. 'And to have to let people know personally!' Harold Austin was one of the city's pillars, third generation old family, and long ago he served a single term in Congress – hence the title 'honourable', a usage he encouraged. Now he owned the state's largest advertising agency and was a veteran director of the bank with strong influence on the board.

The comment about a personal announcement gave Heyward the opening he needed. 'I understand exactly what you mean about the method of letting this be known, and frankly it did seem unusual. What concerned me most is that the directors were not informed first. I felt they should have been. But since they weren't, I considered it my duty to advise you and the others immediately.' Heyward's aquiline, austere face showed concentration; behind rimless glasses his grey eyes were cool.

'I agree with you, Roscoe,' the voice on the telephone said. 'I believe we should have been told, and I appreciate your thinking.'

'Thank you, Harold. At a time like this, one is never sure exactly what is best. The only thing certain is that someone must exercise leadership.'

The use of first names came easily to Heyward. He was old family himself, knew his way around most of the power bases in the state, and was a member in good standing of what the British call the old boy network. His personal connections extended far beyond state boundaries, to Washington and elsewhere. Heyward was proud of his social status and friendships in high places. He also liked to remind people of his own direct descent from one of the signers of the Declaration of Independence.

Now he suggested, 'Another reason for keeping board members informed is that this sad news about Ben is going to have tremendous impact. And it will travel quickly.'

'No doubt of it,' the Honourable Harold concurred. 'Chances are, by tomorrow, the press will have heard and will be asking questions.'

'Exactly. And the wrong kind of publicity could make depositors uneasy as well as depress the price of our stock.'

'Um.'

Roscoe Heyward could sense wheels turning in his fellow director's mind. The Austin Family Trust, which the Honourable Harold represented, held a big block of FMA shares.

Heyward prompted, 'Of course, if the board takes energetic action to reassure shareholders and depositors, also the public generally, the entire effect could be negligible.'

'Except for the friends of Ben Rosselli,' Harold Austin reminded him dryly.

'I was speaking entirely outside the framework of personal loss. My grief, I assure you, is as profound as anyone's.'

'Just what do you have in mind, Roscoe?'

'In general, Harold – a continuity of authority. Specifically, there should be no vacancy in the office of chief executive, even for a day.' Heyward continued, 'With the greatest of respect to Ben, and not withstanding all our deep affection for him, this bank has been regarded for too long as a one-man institution. Of course, it hasn't been that way for many years; no bank can achieve a place among the nation's top twenty and still be individually run. But there are those, outside, who think it is.

That's why, sad as this time is, the directors have an opportunity to act to dissipate that legend.'

Heyward sensed the other man thinking cagily before answering. He could visualize Austin, too – a handsome, ageing playboy type, flamboyant dresser and with styled and flowing iron-grey hair. Probably, as usual, he was smoking a large cigar. Yet the Honourable Harold was nobody's fool and had a reputation as a shrewd, successful businessman. At length he declared, 'I think your point about continuity is valid. And I agree with you that Ben Rosselli's successor needs to be decided on, and probably his name announced before Ben's death.'

Heyward listened intently as the other went on.

'I happen to think you are that man, Roscoe. I have for a long time. You've the qualities, experience, the toughness, too. So I'm willing to pledge you my support and there are others on the board whom I can persuade to go the same route with me. I assume you'd wish that.'

'I'm certainly grateful . . .'

'Of course, in return I may ask an occasional *quid pro quo*.'

'That's reasonable.'

'Good! Then we understand each other.'

The conversation, Roscoe Heyward decided as he hung up the phone, had been eminently satisfactory. Harold Austin was a man of consistent loyalties who kept his word.

The preceding phone calls had been equally successful.

Speaking with another director soon after – Philip Johannsen, president of MidContinent Rubber – another opportunity arose. Johannsen volunteered that frankly he didn't get along with Alex Vandervoort whose ideas he found unorthodox.

'Alex *is* unorthodox,' Heyward said. 'Of course he has some personal problems. I'm not sure how much the two things go together.'

'What kind of problems?'

'It's women, actually. One doesn't like to . . .'

'This is important, Roscoe. It's also confidential. Go ahead.'

'Well, first, Alex has marital difficulties. Second, he's involved with another woman, as well. Third, she's a left-wing

17

activist, frequently in the news, and not in the kind of context which would be helpful to the bank. I sometimes wonder how much influence she has on Alex. As I said, one doesn't like to . . .'

'You were right to tell me, Roscoe,' Johannsen said. 'It's something the directors ought to know. Left-wing, eh?'

'Yes. Her name is Margot Bracken.'

'I think I've heard of her. And what I've heard I haven't liked.'

Heyward smiled.

He was less pleased, however, two telephone calls later, when he reached an out-of-town director, Leonard L. Kingswood, chairman of the board of Northam Steel.

Kingswood, who began his working life as a furnace melder in a steel plant, said, 'Don't hand me that line of bullshit, Roscoe,' when Heyward suggested that the bank's directors should have had advance warning of Ben Rosselli's statement. 'The way Ben handled it is the way I'd have done myself. Tell the people you're closest to first, directors and other stuffed shirts later.'

As to the possibility of a price decline in First Mercantile American stock, Len Kingswood's reaction was, 'So what?'

'Sure,' he added, 'FMA will dip a point or two on the Big Board when this news gets out. It'll happen because most stock transactions are on behalf of nervous nellies who can't distinguish between hysteria and fact. But just as surely the stock will go back up within a week because the value's there, the bank is sound, and all of us on the inside know it.'

And later in the conversation: 'Roscoe, this lobbying job of yours is as transparent as a fresh washed window, so I'll make my position just as plain, which should save us both some time.

'You're a topflight comptroller, the best numbers and money man I know anywhere. And any day you get an urge to move over here with Northam, with a fatter pay cheque and a stock option, I'll shuffle my own people and put you at the top of our financial pile. That's an offer and a promise. I mean it.'

The steel company chairman brushed aside Heyward's murmured thanks as he went on.

'But good as you are, Roscoe, the point I'm making is – you're not an over-all leader. At least, that's the way I see it, also the way I'll call it when the board convenes to decide on who's to follow Ben. The other thing I may as well tell you is that my choice is Vandervoort. I think you ought to know that.'

Heyward answered evenly, 'I'm grateful for your frankness, Leonard.'

'Right. And if ever you think seriously about that offer, call me anytime.'

Roscoe Heyward had no intention of working for Northam Steel. Though money was important to him, his pride would not permit it after Leonard Kingswood's biting verdict of a moment earlier. Besides, he was still fully confident of obtaining the top role at FMA.

Again the telephone buzzed. When he answered, Dora Callaghan announced that one more director was on the line. 'It's Mr Floyd LeBerre.'

'Floyd,' Heyward began, his voice pitched low and serious, 'I'm deeply sorry to be the one to convey some sad and tragic news.'

three

Not all who had been at the momentous boardroom session left as speedily as Roscoe Heyward. A few lingered outside, still with a sense of shock, conversing quietly.

The old-timer from the trust department, Pop Monroe, said softly to Edwina D'Orsey, 'This is a sad, sad day.'

Edwina nodded, not ready yet to speak. Ben Rosselli had been important to her as a friend and he had taken pride in her rise to authority in the bank.

Alex Vandervoort stopped beside Edwina, then motioned to his office several doors away. 'Do you want to take a few minutes out ?'

She said gratefully, 'Yes, please.'

The offices of the bank's top echelon executives were on the same floor as the boardroom – the thirty-sixth, high in FMA Headquarters Tower. Alex Vandervoort's suite, like others here, had an informal conference area and there Edwina poured herself coffee from a Cona. Vandervoort produced a pipe and lit it. She observed his fingers moving efficiently, with no waste motion. His hands were like his body, short and broad, the fingers ending abruptly with stubby but well-manicured nails.

The camaraderie between the two was of long standing. Although Edwina, who managed First Mercantile American's main downtown branch, was several levels lower than Alex in the bank's hierarchy, he had always treated her as an equal and often, in matters affecting her branch, dealt with her directly, bypassing the layers of organization between them.

'Alex,' Edwina said, 'I meant to tell you you're looking like a skeleton.'

A warm smile lit up his smooth, round face. 'Shows, eh ?'

Alex Vandervoort was a committed party-goer, and loved gourmet food and wine. Unfortunately he put on weight easily. Periodically, as now, he went on diets.

By unspoken consent they avoided, for the moment, the subject closest to their minds.

He asked, 'How's business at the branch this month ?'

'Quite good. And I'm optimistic about next year.'

'Speaking of next year, how does Lewis view it ?' Lewis D'Orsey, Edwina's husband, was owner-publisher of a widely-read investors' newsletter.

'Gloomily. He foresees a temporary rise in the value of the dollar, then another big drop, much as happened with the British pound. Also Lewis says that those in Washington who claim the US recession has "bottomed out" are just wishful thinkers – the same false prophets who saw "light at the end of the tunnel" in Vietnam.'

'I agree with him,' Alex mused, 'especially about the dollar. You know, Edwina, one of the failures of American banking is that we've never encouraged our clients to hold accounts in foreign currencies – Swiss francs, Deutsche marks, others – as European bankers do. Oh, we accommodate the big corporations because they know enough to insist: and American banks make generous profits from other currencies for themselves. But rarely, if ever, for the small or medium depositors. If we'd promoted European currency accounts ten or even five years ago, some of our customers would have gained from dollar devaluations instead of lost.'

'Wouldn't the US Treasury object?'

'Probably. But they'd back down under public pressure. They always do.'

Edwina asked, 'Have you ever broached the idea – of more people having foreign currency accounts?'

'I tried once. I was shot down. Among us American bankers the dollar – no matter how weak – is sacred. It's a head-in-sand concept we've forced upon the public and it's cost them money. Only a sophisticated few had the sense to open Swiss bank accounts before the dollar devaluations came.'

'I've often thought about that,' Edwina said. 'Each time it happened, bankers knew in advance that devaluation was inevitable. Yet we gave our customers – except for a favoured few – no warning, no suggestion to sell dollars.'

'It was supposed to be unpatriotic. Even Ben . . .'

Alex stopped. They sat for several moments without speaking.

Through the wall of windows which made up the east side of Alex's office suite they could see the robust Midwest city spread before them. Closest to hand were the business canyons of downtown, the larger buildings only a little lower than First Mercantile American's Headquarters Tower. Beyond the downtown district, coiled in a double-S, was the wide, traffic-crowded river, its colour – today as usual – pollution grey. A tangled latticework of river bridges, railway lines, and freeways ran outward like unspooled ribbons to industrial complexes and suburbs in the distance, the latter sensed rather than seen in an all-pervading haze. But nearer than the industry and suburbs, though beyond the river, was the inner residential city, a labyrinth of predominantly sub-standard housing, labelled by some the city's shame.

In the centre of this last area, a new large building and the steelwork of a second stood out against the skyline.

Edwina pointed to the building and high steel. 'If I were the way Ben is now,' she said, 'and wanted to be remembered by something, I think I'd like it to be Forum East.'

'I suppose so.' Alex's gaze swung to follow Edwina's. 'For sure, without him it would have stayed an idea, and not much more.'

Forum East was an ambitious local urban development, its objective to rehabilitate the city's core. Ben Rosselli had committed First Mercantile American financially to the project and Alex Vandervoort was directly in charge of the bank's involvement. The big main downtown branch, run by Edwina, handled construction loans and mortgage details.

'I was thinking,' Edwina said, 'about changes which will happen here.' She was going to add, *after Ben is dead . . .*

'There'll be changes, of course – perhaps big ones. I hope none will affect Forum East.'

She sighed. 'It isn't an hour since Ben told us . . .'

'And we're discussing future bank business before his grave is dug. Well, we have to, Edwina. Ben would expect it. Some important decisions must be made soon.'

'Including who's to succeed as president.'

'That's one.'

'A good many of us in the bank have been hoping it would be you.'

'Frankly, so was I.'

What both left unsaid was that Alex Vandervoort had been viewed, until today, as Ben Rosselli's chosen heir. But not this soon. Alex had been at First Mercantile American only two years. Before that he was an officer of the Federal Reserve and Ben Rosselli had personally persuaded him to move over, holding out the prospect of eventual advancement to the top.

'Five years or so from now,' Old Ben had told Alex at the time, 'I want to hand over to someone who can cope efficiently with big numbers, and show a profitable bottom line, because that's the only way a banker deals from strength. But he must be more than a top technician. The kind of man I want to run this bank won't ever forget that small depositors – individuals – have always been our strong foundation. The trouble with bankers nowadays is that they get too remote.'

He was making no firm promise, Ben Rosselli made clear, but added, 'My impression, Alex, is you are the kind of man we need. Let's work together for a while and see.'

So Alex moved in, bringing his experience and a flair for new technology, and with both had quickly made his mark. As to philosophy, he found he shared many of Ben's views.

Long before, Alex had also gained insights into banking from his father – a Dutch immigrant who became a Minnesota farmer.

Pieter Vandervoort Sr had burdened himself with a bank loan and, to pay interest on it, laboured from pre-dawn until after darkness, usually seven days a week. In the end he died of over-work, impoverished, after which the bank sold his land, re-covering not only arrears of interest but its original investment. His father's experience showed Alex – through his grief – that the other side of a bank counter was the place to be.

Eventually the route to banking for young Alex was a Har-vard scholarship and an honours degree in economics.

'Everything may still work out,' Edwina D'Orsey said. 'I pre-sume the board will make the choice of president.'

'Yes,' Alex answered almost absently. He had been thinking of Ben Rosselli and his father; his memories of the two were strangely intertwined.

'Length of service isn't everything.'

'It counts.'

Mentally, Alex weighed the probabilities. He knew he had the talent and experience to head First Mercantile American but, chances were, the directors would favour someone who had been around here longer. Roscoe Heyward, for example, had worked for the bank for almost twenty years and despite his occasional lack of rapport with Ben Rosselli, Heyward had a significant following on the board.

Yesterday the odds favoured Alex. Today, they had been switched.

He stood up and knocked out his pipe. 'I must get back to work.'

'Me, too.'

But Alex, when he was alone, sat silent, thoughtful.

Edwina took an express lift from the directors' floor to the main floor foyer of FMA Headquarters Tower – an architec-tural mix of Lincoln Centre and the Sistine Chapel. The foyer surged with people – hurrying bank staff, messengers, visitors, sightseers. She acknowledged a security guard's friendly salute.

Through the curving glass front Edwina could see Rosselli Plaza outside with its trees, benches, a sculpture court, and gushing fountain. In summer the plaza was a meeting place and downtown office workers ate their lunches there, but now it appeared bleak and inhospitable. A raw autumn wind swirled leaves and dust in small tornadoes and sent pedestrians scurrying for indoor warmth.

It was the time of year, Edwina thought, she liked least of all. It spoke of melancholy, winter soon to come, and death.

Involuntarily she shuddered, then headed for the 'tunnel', carpeted and softly lighted, which connected the bank's headquarters with the main downtown branch – a palatial, single-storey structure.

This was her domain.

four

Wednesday, at the main downtown branch, began routinely.

Edwina D'Orsey was branch duty officer for the week and arrived promptly at 8.30, a half hour before the bank's ponderous bronze doors would swing open to the public.

As manager of FMA's flagship branch, as well as a corporate vice-president, she really didn't have to do the duty officer chore. But Edwina preferred to take her turn. Also it demonstrated that she expected no special privileges because of being a woman – something she had always been careful about during her fifteen years at First Mercantile American. Besides, the duty only came around once in ten weeks.

At the building's side door she fumbled in her brown Gucci handbag for her key; she found it beneath an assortment of lipstick, purse, credit cards, compact, comb, a shopping list, and other items – her handbag was always uncharacteristically disorganized. Then, before using the key, she checked for a 'no ambush' signal. The signal was where it should be – a small yellow card, placed inconspicuously in a window. The card would have been put there, minutes earlier, by a porter whose job was to be first in the big branch each day. If all was in order inside, he placed the signal where arriving staff would see it. But if robbers had broken in during the night and were waiting to seize hostages – the porter first – no signal would be placed, so its absence became a warning. Then, later arriving staff not only would not enter, but instantly would summon aid.

Because of increasing robberies of all types, most banks used a 'no ambush' signal nowadays, its type and location changing frequently.

On entering, Edwina went immediately to a hinged panel in the wall and swung it open. In sight was a bell push which she pressed in code – two long, three short, one long. The Central Security operations room over in Headquarters Tower now knew that the door alarm, which Edwina's entry had triggered a moment ago, could be ignored and that an authorized officer was in the bank. The porter, also on entering, would have tapped out his own code.

The ops room, receiving similar signals from other FMA branch banks, would switch the building's alarm system from 'alert' to 'stand by'.

Had either Edwina, as duty officer, or the porter failed to tap out their correct code, the ops room would have alerted police. Minutes later the branch bank would have been surrounded.

As with other systems, codes were changed often.

Banks everywhere were finding security in positive signals when all was well, an absence of signals if trouble erupted. That way, a bank employee held hostage could convey a warning by merely doing nothing.

By now other officers and staff were coming in, checked by the uniformed porter who had taken command at the side door.

'Good morning, Mrs D'Orsey.' A white-haired bank veteran named Tottenhoe joined Edwina. He was operations officer in charge of staff and routine running of the branch, and his long, lugubrious face made him seem like an ancient kangaroo. His normal moodiness and pessimism had increased as compulsory retirement neared; he resented his age and seemed to blame others for it. Edwina and Tottenhoe walked together across the bank's main floor, then down a wide, carpeted stairway to the vault. Supervising the vault's opening and closing was the duty officer's responsibility.

While they waited by the vault door for the time lock to switch off, Tottenhoe said gloomily, 'There's a rumour that Mr Rosselli's dying. Is it true?'

'I'm afraid it is.' She told him briefly of the meeting yesterday.

Last night at home Edwina had thought of little else, but this morning she was determined to concentrate on bank business. Ben would expect it.

Tottenhoe mumbled something dismal which she didn't catch.

Edwina checked her watch. 8.40. Seconds later, a faint click within the massive chrome steel door announced that the overnight time lock, set before the bank closed the night before, had switched itself off. Now the vault combination locks could be actuated. Until this moment they could not.

Using another concealed push-button, Edwina signalled Central Security ops room that the vault was about to be opened – a normal opening, not under duress.

Standing side by side at the door, Edwina and Tottenhoe spun separate combinations. Neither knew the combination setting of the other; thus neither could open the vault alone.

An assistant operations officer, Miles Eastin, had now arrived. A young, handsome, well-groomed man, he was invariably cheerful – in pleasant contrast to Tottenhoe's dependable glumness. Edwina liked Eastin. With him was a senior vault teller who would supervise transference of money in and out of the vault through the remainder of the day. In cash alone, nearly a million dollars in currency and coinage would be under his control through the next six operating hours.

Cheques passing through the big branch bank during the same period would represent another twenty million.

As Edwina stood back, the senior teller and Miles Eastin together swung open the huge, precision-engineered vault door.

It would remain open until the close of business tonight.

'Just took a phone message,' Eastin informed the operations officer. 'Scratch two more tellers for today.'

Tottenhoe's look of melancholy deepened.

'Is it flu ?' Edwina asked.

An epidemic had swept the city for the past ten days, leaving the bank short of staff, especially tellers.

'Yes, it is,' Miles Eastin answered.

Tottenhoe complained, 'If I could just catch it myself, I could go home to bed and leave someone else to worry about manning the counters.' He asked Edwina, 'Do you insist we open today ?'

'It seems to be expected of us.'

'Then we'll empty an executive chair or two. You're the first elected,' he said to Miles Eastin, 'so get a cash box and be ready for the public. Do you remember how to count ?'

'Up to twenty,' Eastin said. 'As long as I can work with my socks off.'

Edwina smiled. She had no fears about young Eastin; everything he touched he did well. When Tottenhoe retired next year, Miles Eastin would almost certainly be her choice as operations officer.

He returned the smile. 'Not to worry, Mrs D'Orsey. I'm a pretty good utility outfielder. Besides, I played handball for three hours last night and managed to keep score.'

'But did you win ?'

'When I keep score ? Of course.'

Edwina was aware, too, of Eastin's other hobby, one which had proved useful to the bank – the study and collection of currencies and coin. It was Miles Eastin who gave orientation talks to new employees at the branch, and he liked to toss in historical nuggets such as the fact that paper money and inflation were both invented in China. The first recorded instance of inflation, he would explain, was during the thirteenth century when the Mongol emperor, Kublai Khan, was unable to pay his soldiers in coins, so used a wood printing block to produce military money. Unfortunately so much was printed that it quickly became worthless. 'Some people,' young Eastin would quip, 'believe the dollar is being mongolized right now.' Because of his studies, Eastin had also become the resident expert on counterfeit money, and doubtful bills which turned up were referred to him for his opinion.

The three of them – Edwina, Eastin, Tottenhoe – ascended the stairs from the vault to the main banking area.

Canvas sacks containing cash were being delivered from an armoured truck outside, the money accompanied by two armed guards.

Cash arriving in large volume always came early in the morning, having been transferred earlier still from the Federal Reserve to First Mercantile American's own Central Cash Vault. From there it was distributed to branch banks in the FMA system. Reason for the same-day schedule was simple. Excess cash in vaults earned nothing; there were dangers, too, of loss or robbery.

The trick, for any branch bank manager, was never to run short of cash, but not to hold too much.

A large branch bank like FMA's downtown kept a working cash float of half a million dollars. The money now arriving – another quarter million – was the difference required on an average banking day.

Tottenhoe grumbled to the delivery guards, 'I hope you've brought us some cleaner money than we've been getting lately.'

'I told them guys over at Central Cash about your beef, Mr Tottenhoe,' one guard said. He was youngish, with long black hair overflowing his uniform cap and collar. Edwina looked downward, wondering if he were wearing shoes. He was.

'They said you'd phoned in, too,' the guard added. 'Now me, I'll take money clean or dirty.'

'Unfortunately,' the operations officer said, 'some of our customers won't.'

New currency, arriving from the Bureau of Printing and Engraving via the Federal Reserve, was keenly competed for by banks. A surprising number of customers, referred to as 'the carriage trade', rejected dirty bills and demanded new, or at least clean notes which bankers called 'fit'. Fortunately there were others who simply didn't care and tellers had instructions to pass out the worst soiled money where they could get away with it, saving their fresh, crisp bills for those who asked for them.

28

'Hear there's lots of high-grade counterfeit stuff around. Maybe we could get you a bundle.' The second guard winked at his companion.

Edwina told him, 'That kind of help we can do without. We've been getting too much of it.'

Only last week the bank had discovered nearly a thousand dollars in counterfeit bills – money paid in, though the source was unknown. More than likely it had come through numerous depositors – some who had been defrauded themselves and were passing their loss along to the bank; others who had no idea the bills were counterfeit, which was not surprising since the quality was remarkably high.

Agents of the US Secret Service, who had discussed the matter with Edwina and Miles Eastin, were frankly worried. 'The counterfeit money we're seeing has never been as good, and there's never been as much in circulation,' one of them admitted. A conservative estimate was that thirty million dollars of bogus money had been produced the previous year. 'And a lot more never gets detected.'

England and Canada were major supply sources of spurious US currency. The agents also reported that an incredible amount was circulating in Europe. 'It's not so easily detected there, so warn your friends who go to Europe never to accept American bills. There's a strong chance they could be worthless.'

The first armed guard shifted the sacks on his shoulders. 'Don't worry folks! These are genuine greenbacks. All part of the service!'

Both guards went down the stairway to the vault.

Edwina walked to her desk on the platform. Throughout the bank, activity was increasing. The main front doors were open, early customers streaming in.

The platform where, by tradition, the senior officers worked, was raised slightly above the main-floor level and carpeted in crimson. Edwina's desk, the largest and most imposing, was flanked by two flags – behind her and to the right the Stars and Stripes, and on her left the state burgee. Sometimes, seated there, she felt as if she were on TV, ready to make a solemn announcement while cameras dollied in.

The big downtown branch itself was modern. Rebuilt a year or two ago when FMA's adjoining Headquarters Tower was erected, the structure had had design expertise and a fortune lavished on it. The result, in which crimson and mahogany predominated with an appropriate sprinkling of gold, was a combination of customer convenience, excellent working conditions and just plain opulence. Occasionally, Edwina admitted to herself, the opulence seemed to have an edge.

As she settled down, her tall, lithe figure slipping familiarly into a high-backed swivel chair, she smoothed her short hair - needlessly, since as usual it was impeccably in place.

Edwina reached for a group of files containing loan applications for amounts higher than other officers in the branch had authority to approve.

Her own authorization to lend money extended to a million dollars in any single instance, providing two other officers in the branch concurred. They invariably did. Amounts in excess were referred to the bank's credit policy unit over in Headquarters.

In First Mercantile American, as in any banking system, an acknowledged status symbol was the size of a loan which a bank official had power to sanction. It also determined his - or her - position on the organization totem pole and was spoken of as 'the quality-of-initial', because an individual's initial put final approval on any loan proposal.

As a manager, the quality of Edwina's initial was unusually high, though it reflected her responsibility in running FMA's important downtown branch. A manager of a lesser branch might approve loans from ten thousand to half a million dollars, depending on the manager's ability and seniority. It always amused Edwina that quality-of-initial supported a caste system with attendant perks and privileges. In the Headquarters credit policy unit, an assistant loan inspector, whose authority was limited to a mere fifty thousand dollars, worked at an unimpressive desk alongside others in a large open office. Next in the pecking order, a loan inspector whose initial was good for a quarter million dollars rated a larger desk in a glass-panelled cubicle.

An honest-to-goodness office with door and window was the perquisite of an assistant loan supervisor whose quality-of-initial extended higher, to a half million dollars. He also rated a capacious desk, an oil painting on the wall and printed memo pads with his name, a free daily copy of *The Wall Street Journal* and a complimentary shoeshine every morning. He shared a secretary with another assistant supervisor.

Finally, a loan officer-vice-president whose initial was good for a million dollars, worked in a corner office with *two* windows, *two* oil paintings, and a secretary of his own. His name memos were *engraved*. He, too, had a free shoeshine and newspaper, plus magazines and journals, the use of a company car when required for business, and access to the senior officers' dining-room for lunch.

Edwina qualified for almost all the quality-of-initial perks. She had never used the shoeshine.

This morning, she studied two loan requests, approved one and pencilled some queries on another. A third proposal stopped her short.

Startled, and conscious of a bizarre coincidence after yesterday's experience, she read through the file again.

The loan officer who had prepared the file answered Edwina's intercom buzz.

'Castleman here.'

'Cliff, please come over.'

'Sure.' The loan officer, only half a dozen desks away, looked directly at Edwina. 'And I'll bet I know why you want me.'

Moments later, as he seated himself beside her desk, he glanced at the open file. 'I was right. We get some lulus, don't we?'

Cliff Castleman was small and precise with a round pink face and soft smile. Borrowers liked him because he was a good listener and sympathetic. But he was also a seasoned loan man with sound judgement.

'I was hoping,' Edwina said, 'that this application is some kind of sick joke, even if a ghastly one.'

'Ghoulish would be more apt, Mrs D'Orsey. And while the whole thing may be sick, I assure you it's real.' Castleman motioned to the file. 'I included all the facts because I knew you'd want them. Obviously you've read the report. And my recommendation.'

'Are you serious in proposing to lend this much money for *this* purpose ?'

'I'm deadly serious.' The loan officer stopped abruptly. 'Sorry! That wasn't intended to be gallows humour. But I believe you should approve the loan.'

It was all there in the file. A forty-three-year-old pharmaceutical salesman named Gosburne, locally employed, was applying for a loan of twenty-five thousand dollars. He was married – a first marriage which had lasted seventeen years – and the Gosburnes owned their suburban home except for a small mortgage. They had had a joint account with FMA for eight years – no problems. An earlier, though smaller, bank loan had been repaid. Gosburne's employment record and other financial history were good.

The intended purpose of the new loan was to buy a large stainless steel capsule in which would be placed the body of the Gosburnes' child, Andrea. She had died six days ago, at the age of fifteen, from a kidney malignancy. At present, Andrea's body was at a funeral parlour, stored in dry ice. Her blood had been drawn off immediately after death and replaced with a blood-like 'anti-freeze' solution called dimethylsulfoxide.

The steel capsule was specially designed to contain liquid nitrogen at a sub-zero temperature. The body, wrapped in aluminium foil, would be immersed in this solution.

A capsule of the type sought – a giant bottle, really, and known as a 'cryo-crypt' – was available in Los Angeles and would be flown from there if the bank loan was approved. About a third of the intended loan was for pre-payment of vault storage rent for the capsule, and replacement of the liquid nitrogen every four months.

Castleman asked Edwina, 'You've heard of cryonics societies ?'

'Vaguely. It's pseudo-scientific. Not very reputable.'

'Not very. And pseudo indeed. But the fact is, cryonics groups have a big following and they've convinced Gosburne and his wife that when medical science is more advanced – say fifty or a hundred years from now – Andrea can be thawed out, brought back to life and cured. Incidentally, the cryonics people have a motto: *Freeze – wait – reanimate.*'

'Horrible,' Edwina said.

The loan officer conceded. 'Mostly I agree with you. But look at it their way. They believe. Also they're adult, reasonably intelligent people, deeply religious. So who are we, as bankers, to be judge and jury? As I see it, the only question is: Can Gosburne repay the loan? I've gone over the figures, and I say he can and will. The guy may be a nut. But the record shows he's a nut who pays his bills.'

Reluctantly Edwina studied the income and expenses figures. 'It will be a terrible financial strain.'

'The guy knows that but insists he can handle it. He's taking on some spare-time work. And his wife is looking for a job.'

Edwina said, 'They have four younger children.'

'Yes.'

'Has anyone pointed out that the other children – the living – will need money soon for college, other things, and that twenty-five thousand dollars could be put to better use for them?'

'I did,' Castleman said. 'I've had two long interviews with Gosburne. But according to him, the whole family talked that over and they made their decision. They believe the sacrifices they'll have to make will be worth the chance of bringing Andrea back to life some day. The children also say that when they're older they'll take over responsibility for her body.'

'Oh God!' Again Edwina's thoughts went back to yesterday. Ben Rosselli's death, whenever it came, would be dignified. This made death ugly and a mockery. Should the bank's money – in part, Ben's – be used for such a purpose?

'Mrs D'Orsey,' the loan officer said, 'I've had this on my desk for two days. My first feeling was the same as yours – the whole thing's sick. But I've thought about it and I've come around. In my opinion, it's an acceptable risk.'

Acceptable risk. Essentially, Edwina realized, Cliff Castleman was right because acceptable risks were what banking was all about. He was also right in asserting that in most personal matters a bank should not be judge and jury.

Of course, this particular risk might not work out, though even if it failed to, Castleman would not be blamed. His record was good, his 'wins' far greater than his losses. In fact, a perfect win record was frowned on, a busy retail loan officer was expected, almost obligated, to have a few of his loans turn sour. If he didn't he could be in trouble in reverse when a computer printout warned management he was losing business through excessive caution.

'All right,' Edwina said. 'The idea appals me but I'll back your judgement.'

She scribbled an initial. Castleman returned to his desk.

Thus – apart from a loan for a frozen daughter – this day had begun like any other.

It stayed that way until early afternoon.

On days when she lunched alone, Edwina used the basement cafeteria over at FMA Headquarters. The cafeteria was noisy, the food only so-so, but service was brisk and she could be in and out in fifteen minutes.

Today, however, she had a client as a guest and exercised her vice-president's privilege by taking him to the senior officers' private dining-room, high in the executive tower. He was the treasurer of the city's largest department store and needed a three million dollar short-term loan to cover a cash deficit resulting from light autumn sales plus costlier-than-usual purchases of Christmas merchandise.

'This goddamned inflation!' the treasurer complained over a spinach soufflé. Then, licking his lips, he added, 'But we'll get our money back this next two months, and then some. Santa Claus is always good to us.'

The department store account was an important one; nevertheless Edwina drove a tough bargain, with terms favourable to the bank. After some grumbling by the customer, these were agreed by the time they reached peach melba for dessert. The three million dollars exceeded Edwina's personal authority, though she anticipated no trouble getting approval from Headquarters. If necessary, for speed's sake, she would talk with Alex Vandervoort who had backed up her judgements in the past.

It was while they were having coffee that a waitress brought a message to their table.

'Mrs D'Orsey,' the girl said, 'a Mr Tottenhoe is on the phone for you. He says it's urgent.'

Edwina excused herself and went to a telephone in an annexe.

The voice of her branch operations officer complained, 'I've been trying to locate you.'

'Now you have. What is it ?'

'We have a serious cash shortage.' He went on to explain: a teller had reported the loss half an hour ago. Checking had been going on continuously since. Edwina sensed panic as well as gloom in Tottenhoe's voice and asked how much money was involved.

She heard him swallow. 'Six thousand dollars.'

'I'll be down right away.'

Within less than a minute, after apologizing to her guest, she was in the express lift en route to the main floor.

five

'As far as I can see,' Tottenhoe said morosely, 'the only thing all of us know for certain is that six thousand dollars in cash is not where it should be.'

The operations officer was one of four people seated around Edwina D'Orsey's desk. The others were Edwina; young Miles Eastin, Tottenhoe's assistant; and a teller named Juanita Núñez.

It was from Juanita Núñez's cash drawer that the money was missing.

Half an hour had elapsed since Edwina's return to the main branch. Now, as the others faced her across the desk, Edwina answered Tottenhoe. 'What you say is true, but we can do better. I want us to go over everything again, slowly and carefully.'

The time was shortly after 3pm. Customers had gone. The outer doors were closed.

Activity, as usual, was continuing in the branch, though Edwina was conscious of covert glances towards the platform from other employees who knew by now that something serious was wrong.

She reminded herself that it was essential to remain calm, analytical, to consider every fragment of information. She wanted to listen carefully to nuances of speech and attitude, particularly those of Mrs Núñez.

Edwina was aware, too, that very soon she must notify head office of the apparent heavy cash loss, after which Headquarters Security would become involved, and probably the FBI. But while there was still a chance of finding a solution quietly, without bringing up the heavy artillery, she intended to try.

'If you like, Mrs D'Orsey,' Miles Eastin said, 'I'll start because I was the first one Juanita reported to.' He had shed his usual breeziness.

Edwina nodded approval.

The possibility of a cash shortage, Eastin informed the group, first came to his attention a few minutes before 2pm. At that time Juanita Núñez approached him and stated her belief that six thousand dollars was missing from her cash drawer.

Miles Eastin was working a teller's position himself, filling in as he had through most of the day because of the shortage of tellers. In fact, Eastin was only two stations away from Juanita Núñez, and she reported to him there, locking her cash box before she did so.

Eastin had then locked his own cash box and gone to Tottenhoe.

Gloomier than usual, Tottenhoe took up the story.

He had gone to Mrs Núñez at once and talked with her. At first he hadn't believed that as much as six thousand dollars could be missing because even if she suspected *some* money had gone, it was virtually impossible at that point to know how much.

The operations officer pointed out: Juanita Núñez had been working all day, having started with slightly more than ten thousand dollars cash-from-vault in the morning, and she had been taking in and paying out money since 9am when the bank opened. That meant she had been working for almost five hours, except for a forty-five-minute lunch break, and during that time the bank was crowded, with all tellers busy. Furthermore, cash deposits today had been heavier than usual; therefore the amount of money in her drawer – not including cheques – could have increased to twenty or twenty-five thousand dollars. So how, Tottenhoe reasoned, could Mrs Núñez be certain not only that money was missing but know the amount so specifically?

Edwina nodded. The same question had already occurred to her.

Without being obvious, Edwina studied the young woman. She was small, slight, dark, not really pretty but provocative in an elfin way. She looked Puerto Rican, which she was, and had a pronounced accent. She had said little so far, responding only briefly when spoken to.

It was hard to be sure just what Juanita Núñez's attitude was. It was certainly not cooperative, at least outwardly, Edwina thought, and the girl had volunteered no information other than her original statement. Since they started, the teller's facial expression had seemed either sulky or hostile. Occasionally her attention wandered, as if she were bored and regarded the proceedings as a waste of time. But she was nervous, too, and betrayed it by her clasped hands and continuous turning of a thin gold wedding band.

Edwina D'Orsey knew, because she had glanced at an employment record on her desk, that Juanita Núñez was twenty-five, married but separated, with a three-year-old child. She had worked for First Mercantile American for almost two years, all of that time in her present job. What wasn't in the employment record, but Edwina remembered hearing, was that the Núñez girl supported her child alone and had been, perhaps still was, in financial difficulties because of debts left by the husband who deserted her.

Despite his doubts that Mrs Núñez could possibly know how much money was missing, Tottenhoe continued, he had relieved her from duty at the counter, after which she was immediately 'locked up with her cash'.

Being 'locked up' was actually a protection for the employee concerned and was also standard procedure in a problem of this kind. It simply meant that the teller was placed alone in a small, closed office, along with her cash box and a calculator, and told to balance all transactions for the day.

Tottenhoe waited outside.

Soon afterwards she called the operations officer in. Her cash did not balance, she informed him. It was six thousand dollars short.

Tottenhoe summoned Miles Eastin and together they ran a second check while Juanita Núñez watched. They found her report to be correct. Without doubt there was cash missing, and precisely the amount she had stated all along.

It was then that Tottenhoe had telephoned Edwina.

'That brings us back,' Edwina said, 'to where we started. Have any fresh ideas occurred to anyone ?'

Miles Eastin volunteered, 'I'd like to ask Juanita some more questions if she doesn't mind.'

Edwina nodded.

'Think carefully about this, Juanita,' Eastin said. 'At any time today did you make a TX with any other teller ?'

As all of them knew, a TX was a teller's exchange. A teller on duty would often run short of bills or coins of one denomination and if it happened at a busy time, rather than make a trip to the cash vault, tellers helped each other by 'buying' or 'selling' cash. A TX form was used to keep a record. But occasionally, through haste or carelessness, mistakes were made, so that at the end of the business day one teller would be short on cash, the other long. It would be hard to believe, though, that such a difference could be as large as six thousand dollars.

'No,' the teller said. 'No exchanges. Not today.'

Miles Eastin persisted, 'Were you aware of anyone else on the staff, at any time today, being near your cash so they could have taken some ?'

'No.'

'When you first came to me, Juanita,' Eastin said, 'and told me you thought there was some money gone, how long before that had you known about it ?'

'A few minutes.'

38

Edwina interjected, 'How long was that after your lunch break, Mrs Núñez ?'

The girl hesitated, seeming less sure of herself. 'Maybe twenty minutes.'

'Let's talk about *before* you went to lunch,' Edwina said. 'Do you think the money was missing then ?'

Juanita Núñez shook her head negatively.

'How can you be sure ?'

'I know.'

The unhelpful, monosyllabic answers were becoming irritating to Edwina. And the sulky hostility which she sensed earlier seemed more pronounced.

Tottenhoe repeated the crucial question. 'After lunch, why were you certain not only that money was missing, but exactly how much ?'

The young woman's small face set defiantly. 'I knew.'

There was a disbelieving silence.

'Do you think that some time during the day you could have paid six thousand dollars out to a customer in error ?'

'No.'

Miles Eastin asked, 'When you left your teller's position before you went to lunch, Juanita, you took your cash drawer to the cash vault, closed the combination lock and left it there. Right ?'

'Yes.'

'Are you sure you locked it ?'

The girl nodded positively.

'Was the operations officer's lock closed ?'

'No, left open.'

That, too, was normal. Once the operations officer's combination had been set to 'open' each morning, it was usual to leave it that way through the remainder of the day.

'But when you came back from lunch your cash drawer was still in the vault, still locked ?'

'Yes.'

'Does anyone else know your combination ? Have you ever given it to anyone ?'

'No.'

For a moment the questioning stopped. The others around the desk, Edwina suspected, were reviewing mentally the branch's cash vault procedures.

The cash drawer which Miles Eastin had referred to was actually a portable strongbox on an elevated stand with wheels, light enough to be pushed around easily. Some banks called it a cash truck. Every teller had one assigned and the same cash drawer or truck, conspicuously numbered, was used normally by the same individual. A few spares were available for special use. Miles Eastin had been using one today.

All tellers' cash trucks were checked in and out of the cash vault by a senior vault teller who kept a record of their removal and return. It was impossible to take a cash unit in or out without the vault teller's scrutiny or to remove someone else's, deliberately or in error. During nights and week-ends the massive cash vault was sealed tighter than a pharaoh's tomb.

Each cash truck had two tamperproof combination locks. One of these was set by the teller personally, the other by the operations officer or assistant. Thus, when a cash unit was opened each morning it was in the presence of two people – the teller and an operations officer.

Tellers were told to memorize their combinations and not to confide them to anyone else, though a combination could be changed any time a teller wished. The only written record of a teller's combination was in a sealed and double-signed envelope which was kept with others – again in double custody – in a safe deposit box. The seal on the envelope was only broken in the event of a teller's death, illness, or leaving the bank's employ.

By all these means, only the active user of any cash drawer knew the combination which would open it and tellers, as well as the bank, were protected against theft.

A further feature of the sophisticated cash drawer was a built-in alarm system. When rolled into place at any teller's position at a counter, an electrical connection linked each cash unit with an inter-bank communications network. A warning trigger was hidden within the drawer beneath an innocuous appearing pile of bills, known as 'bait money'.

Tellers had instructions never to use the bait money for normal transactions, but in the event of a hold-up to hand over this money first. Simply removing the bills released a silent plunger switch. This, in turn, alerted bank security staff and police, who were usually on the scene in minutes; it also activated hidden cameras overhead. Serial numbers of the bait money were on record for use as evidence later.

Edwina asked Tottenhoe, 'Was the bait money among the missing six thousand dollars ?'

'No,' the operations officer said. 'The bait money was intact. I checked.'

She reflected: so there was no hope of tracing anything that way.

Once more Miles Eastin addressed the teller. 'Juanita, is there any way you can think of that anyone, *anyone at all*, could have taken the money out of your cash drawer ?'

'No,' Juanita Núñez said.

Watching closely as the girl answered, Edwina thought she detected fear. Well, if so, there was good reason because no bank would give up easily where a loss of this magnitude was involved.

Edwina no longer had doubts about what had happened to the missing money. The Núñez girl had stolen it. No other explanation was possible. The difficulty was to find out – how ?

One likely way was for Juanita Núñez to have passed it over the counter to an accomplice. No one would have noticed. During an ordinarily busy day it would have seemed like any routine cash withdrawal. Alternatively, the girl could have concealed the money and carried it from the bank during her lunch break, though in that case the risk would have been greater.

One thing Mrs Núñez must have been aware of was that she would lose her job, whether it was proved she had stolen the money or not. True, bank tellers were allowed occasional cash discrepancies; such errors were normal and expected. In the course of a year, eight 'overs' or 'unders' was average for most tellers and provided each error was no larger than twenty-five dollars, usually nothing was said. But no one who experienced a major cash shortage kept her job, and tellers knew it.

Of course, Juanita Núñez could have taken this into account, deciding that an immediate six thousand dollars was worth the loss of her job, even though she might have difficulty getting another. Either way, Edwina was sorry for the girl. Obviously she must have been desperate. Perhaps her need had to do with her child.

'I don't believe there's any more we can do at this point,' Edwina told the group. 'I'll have to advise head office. They'll take over the investigation.'

As the three got up, she added, 'Mrs Núñez, please stay.' The girl resumed her seat.

When the others were out of hearing, Edwina said with deliberate informality, 'Juanita, I thought this might be a moment for us to talk frankly to each other, perhaps as friends.' Edwina had banished her earlier impatience. She was aware of the girl's dark eyes fixed intently on her own.

'I'm sure that two things must have occurred to you. First, there's going to be a thorough investigation into this and the FBI will be involved because we're a federally insured bank. Second, there is no way that suspicion cannot fall on you.' Edwina paused. 'I'm being open with you about this. You understand?'

'I understand. But I did not take any money.'

Edwina observed that the young woman was still turning her wedding ring nervously.

Now Edwina chose her words carefully, aware she must be cautious in avoiding a direct accusation which might rebound in legal trouble for the bank later.

'However long the investigation takes, Juanita, it's almost certain the truth will come out, if for no other reason than that it usually does. Investigators are thorough. They're also experienced. They do not give up.'

The girl repeated, more emphatically, 'I did not take the money.'

'I haven't said you did. But I o want to say that if by any chance you know something more than you have said already, now is the time to speak out, to tell me while we're talking quietly here. After this there will be no other chances. It will be too late.'

42

Juanita Núñez seemed about to speak again. Edwina raised a hand. 'No, hear me out. I'll make this promise. If the money were returned to the bank, let's say no later than tomorrow, there would be no legal action, no prosecution. In fairness, I'll have to say that whoever took the money could no longer work here. But nothing else would happen. I guarantee it. Juanita, do you have *anything* to tell me ?'

'No, no, no! *Te lo juro por mi hija !*' The girl's eyes blazed, her face came alive in anger. 'I tell you I did not take any money, now or ever.'

Edwina sighed.

'All right, that's all for now. But please do not leave the bank without checking with me first.'

Juanita Núñez appeared on the verge of another heated reply. Instead, with a slight shrug, she rose and turned away.

From her elevated desk, Edwina surveyed the activity around her; it was her own small world, her personal responsibility. The day's branch transactions were still being balanced and recorded, though a preliminary check had shown that no teller – as was originally hoped – had a six-thousand-dollar overage.

Sounds were muted in the modern building: in low key, voices buzzed, papers rustled, coinage jingled, calculators clicked. She watched it all briefly, reminding herself that for two reasons this was a week she would remember. Then, knowing what must be done, she lifted a telephone and dialled an internal number.

A woman's voice answered. 'Security department.'

'Mr Wainwright, please,' Edwina said.

six

Nolan Wainwright had found it hard, since yesterday, to concentrate on normal work within the bank.

The chief of security had been deeply affected by Tuesday

morning's session in the boardroom, not least because over a decade, he and Ben Rosselli had achieved both friendship and mutual respect.

It had not always been that way.

Yesterday, returning from the tower executive floor to his own more modest office which looked out on to a light well, Wainwright had told his secretary not to disturb him for a while. Then he had sat at his desk, sad, brooding, reaching back in memory to the time of his own first clash with Ben Rosselli's will.

It was ten years earlier. Nolan Wainwright was the newly appointed police chief of a small upstate town. Before that he had been a lieutenant of detectives on a big city force, with an outstanding record. He had the ability for a chief's job and, in the climate of the times, it probably helped his candidacy that he was black.

Soon after the new chief's appointment, Ben Rosselli drove through the outskirts of the little town and was clocked at 80 mph. A police patrolman of the local force handed him a ticket with a summons to traffic court.

Perhaps because his life was conservative in other ways, Ben Rosselli always loved fast cars and drove them as their designers intended – with his right foot near the floor.

A speeding summons was routine. Back at First Mercantile American headquarters he sent it, as usual, to the bank's security department with instructions to have it fixed. For the state's most powerful man of money, many things could be fixed and often were.

The summons was dispatched by courier next day to the FMA branch manager in the town where it was issued. It so happened that the branch manager was also a local councilman and he had been influential in Nolan Wainwright's appointment as chief of police.

The bank manager-councilman dropped over to police headquarters to have the traffic summons withdrawn. He was amiable. Nolan Wainwright was adamant.

Less amiably, the councilman pointed out to Wainwright that he was new to the community, needed friends, and that noncooperation was not the way to recruit them. Wainwright still declined to do anything about the summons.

The councilman put on his banker's hat and reminded the police chief of his personal application to First Mercantile American Bank for a home mortgage loan which would make it possible to bring Wainwright's wife and family to the town. Mr Rosselli, the branch manager added somewhat needlessly, was president of FMA.

Nolan Wainwright said he could see no relationship between a loan application and a traffic summons.

In due course Mr Rosselli, for whom counsel appeared in court, was fined heavily for reckless driving and awarded three demerit points, to be recorded on his licence. He was exceedingly angry.

Also in due course the mortgage application of Nolan Wainwright was turned down by First Mercantile American Bank.

Less than a week later Wainwright presented himself in Rosselli's office at First Mercantile American headquarters, taking advantage of the accessibility on which the bank president prided himself.

When he learned who his visitor was, Ben Rosselli was surprised that he was black. No one had mentioned that. Not that it made any difference to the banker's still simmering wrath at the ignominious notation on his driving record -- the first of a lifetime.

Wainwright spoke coolly. To his credit, Ben Rosselli had known nothing of the police chief's mortgage loan application or its rejection; such matters were conducted at a lower level than his own. But he smelled the odour of injustice and sent, there and then, for the loan file which he reviewed while Nolan Wainwright waited.

'As a matter of interest,' Ben Rosselli said when he had finished reading, 'if we don't make this loan, what do you intend to do?'

Wainwright's answer now was cold. 'Fight. I'll hire a lawyer and we'll go to the Civil Rights Commission for a start. If we don't succeed there, whatever else can be done to cause you trouble, that I'll do.'

It was obvious he meant it and the banker snapped, 'I don't respond to threats.'

'I'm not making threats. You asked me a question and I answered it.'

Ben Rosselli hesitated, then scribbled a signature in the file. He said, unsmiling, 'The application is approved.'

Before Wainwright left, the banker asked him, 'What happens now if I get caught speeding in your town?'

'We'll throw the book at you. If it's another reckless driving charge, you'll probably be in jail.'

Watching the policeman go, Ben Rosselli had the thought, which he would confide to Wainwright years later: *You self-righteous s.o.b.! One day I'll get you.*

He never had – in that sense. But in another, he did.

Two years later when the bank was seeking a top security executive who would be – as the head of Personnel expressed it – 'tenaciously strong and totally incorruptible', Ben Rosselli stated, 'I know of such a man.'

Soon after, an offer was made to Nolan Wainwright, a contract signed, and Wainwright came to work for FMA.

From then on, Ben Rosselli and Wainwright had never clashed. The new head of Security did his job efficiently and added to his understanding of it by taking night school courses in banking theory. Rosselli, for his part, never asked Wainwright to breach his rigid code of ethics and the banker got his speeding tickets fixed elsewhere rather than through Security, believing Wainwright never knew, though usually he did. All the while the friendship between the two grew until, after the death of Ben Rosselli's wife, Wainwright frequently would eat dinner with the old man and afterwards they would play chess into the night.

In a way, it had been a consolation for Wainwright, too, for his own marriage had ended in divorce soon after he went to work for FMA. His new responsibilities, and the sessions with old Ben, helped fill the gap.

They talked at such times about personal beliefs, influencing each other in ways they realized and in others of which neither was aware. And it was Wainwright – though only the two of them ever knew it – who helped persuade the bank president to employ his personal prestige and FMA's money in helping the Forum East development in that neglected city area where Wainwright had been born and spent his adolescent years.

Thus, like many others in the bank, Nolan Wainwright had his private memories of Ben Rosselli and his private sorrow.

Today, his mood of depression had persisted, and after a morning during which he had stayed mostly at his desk, avoiding people whom he did not need to see, Wainwright left for lunch alone. He went to a small café on the other side of town which he favoured sometimes when he wanted to feel briefly free from FMA and its affairs. He returned in time to keep an appointment with Vandervoort.

The locale of their meeting was the bank's Keycharge credit card division, housed in the Headquarters Tower.

The Keycharge bank card system had been pioneered by First Mercantile American and now was operated jointly with a strong group of other banks in the US, Canada, and overseas. In size, Keycharge ranked immediately after BankAmericard and Master-Charge. Alex Vandervoort, within FMA, had over-all responsibility for the division.

Vandervoort was early and, when Nolan Wainwright arrived, was already in the Keycharge authorization centre watching operations. The bank security chief joined him.

'I always like to see this,' Alex said. 'Best free show in town.'

In a large, auditorium-like room, dimly lighted and with acoustic walls and ceilings to deaden sound, some fifty operators – predominantly women – were seated at a battery of consoles. Each console comprised a cathode ray tube, similar to a TV screen, with a keyboard beneath.

It was here that Keycharge cardholders were given or refused credit.

When a Keycharge card was presented anywhere in payment for goods or services, the place of business could accept the card without question if the amount involved was below an agreed floor limit. The limit varied, but was usually between twenty-five and fifty dollars. For a larger purchase, authorization was needed, though it took only seconds to obtain.

Calls poured into the authorization centre twenty-four hours a day, seven days a week. They came from every US state and Canadian province, while a row of chattering Telex machines brought queries from thirty foreign countries including some in the Russian-Communist orbit. Whereas builders of the British Empire once cheered proudly for the 'red, white, and blue', creators of the Keycharge economic empire rooted with equal fervour for the 'blue, green, and gold' -- international colours of the Keycharge card.

The approval procedures moved at jet speed.

Wherever they were, merchants and others dialled directly through WATS (Wide Area Telecommunications Service) lines to the Keycharge nerve centre in FMA Headquarters Tower. Automatically, each call was routed to a free operator whose first words were, 'What is your merchant number ?'

As the answer was given, the operator typed the figures, which appeared simultaneously on the cathode ray screen. Next was the card number and amount of credit being sought, this too typed and displayed.

The operator pressed a key, feeding the information to a computer which instantly signalled 'ACCEPTED' or 'DECLINED'. The first meant that credit was good and the purchase approved, the second that the cardholder was in arrears and credit had been cut off. Since credit rules were lenient, with banks in the system wanting to lend money, acceptances by far outnumbered turn-downs. The operator informed the merchant, the computer meanwhile recording the transaction. On a normal day fifteen thousand calls came in.

Both Alex Vandervoort and Nolan Wainwright had accepted headsets so they could listen to exchanges between callers and operators.

The security chief touched Alex's arm and pointed, then changed headset plugs for both of them. The console Wainwright indicated was carrying a flashing message from the computer – 'STOLEN CARD'.

The operator, speaking calmly and as trained, answered, 'The card presented to you has been reported as stolen. If possible, detain the person presenting it and call your local police. Retain the card. Keycharge will pay you thirty dollars reward for its return.'

They could hear a whispered colloquy, then a voice announced, 'The bastard just ran out of my store. But I grabbed the mother's plastic. I'll mail it in.'

The storekeeper sounded pleased at the prospect of an easy thirty dollars. For the Keycharge system it was also a good deal since the card, left in circulation, could have been used fraudulently for a much greater total amount.

Wainwright removed his headset; so did Alex Vandervoort. 'It works well,' Wainwright said, 'when we get the information and can programme the computer. Unfortunately most of the defrauding happens before a missing card's reported.'

'But we still get a warning of excessive purchasing?'

'Right. Ten purchases in a day and the computer alerts us.'

Few cardholders, as both men were aware, ever made more than six or eight purchases during a single day. Thus a card could be listed as 'PROBABLY FRAUDULENT' even though the true owner might be unaware of its loss.

Despite all warning systems, however, a lost or stolen Keycharge card, if used cagily, was still good for twenty thousand dollars worth of fraudulent purchasing in the week or so during which most stolen cards stayed unreported. Airline tickets for long-distance flights were favourite buys by credit card thieves; so were cases of liquor. Both were then resold at bargain prices. Another ploy was to rent a car – preferably an expensive one – using a stolen or counterfeit credit card. The car was driven to another city where it received new licence plates and forged registration papers, and was then sold or exported. The rental agency never saw car or customer again. One more gimmick was to buy jewellery in Europe on a fraudulent credit card backed up by a forged passport, then smuggle the jewellery into the US for resale. In all such instances the credit card company bore the eventual loss.

As both Vandervoort and Wainwright knew, there were devices used by criminals to decide whether a credit card in their possession could be used again, or if it were 'hot'. A favourite was to pay a headwaiter twenty-five dollars to check a card out.

49

He could get the answer easily by consulting a weekly confidential 'warning list' issued by the credit card company to merchants and restaurants. If the card was unreported as hot, it was used for a further round of buying.

'We've been losing a helluva lot of money through fraud lately,' Nolan Wainwright said. 'Much more than usual. It's one of the reasons I wanted to talk.'

They moved into a Keycharge security office which Wainwright had arranged to use this afternoon. He closed the door. The two men were much in contrast physically – Vandervoort, fair, chunky, non-athletic, with a touch of flab; Wainwright, black, tall, trim, hard, and muscular. Their personalities differed, too, though their relationship was good.

'This is a contest without a prize,' Nolan Wainwright told the executive vice-president. He placed on the office desk eight plastic Keycharge credit cards, snapping them down like a poker dealer, one by one.

'Four of those credit cards are counterfeit,' the security chief announced. 'Can you separate the good ones from the bad?'

'Certainly. It's easy. The counterfeits always use different typefaces for embossing the cardholder's name and . . .' Vandervoort stopped, peering down at the group of cards. 'By God! These don't. The typeface is the same on every card.'

'Almost the same. If you know what to look for, you can detect slight divergences with a magnifier.' Wainwright produced one. Dividing the cards into two groups, he pointed to variations between the embossing on the four genuine cards and the others.

Vandervoort said, 'I see the difference, though I wouldn't have without the glass. How do the counterfeits look under ultraviolet?'

'Exactly the same as real ones.'

'That's bad.'

Several months earlier, following an example set by American Express, a hidden insignia had been imprinted on the face of all authentic Keycharge credit cards. It became visible only under ultraviolet light. The intention was to provide a quick, simple check of any card's genuineness. Now that safeguard, too, had been outflanked.

'It's bad, all right,' Nolan Wainwright agreed. 'And these are only samples. I've four dozen more, intercepted *after* they'd been used successfully in retail outlets, restaurants, for airline tickets, liquor, other things. And all of them are the best counterfeits which have ever shown up.'

'Arrests ?'

'None so far. When people sense a phony card is being queried they walk out of a store, away from an airline counter, or whatever, just as happened a few minutes ago.' He motioned towards the authorization room. 'Besides, even when we do arrest some users it doesn't follow we'll be near the source of the cards; usually they're sold and resold carefully enough to cover a trail.'

Alex Vandervoort picked up one of the fraudulent blue, green, and gold cards and turned it over. 'The plastic seems an exact match too.'

'They're made from authentic plastic blanks that are stolen. They have to be, to be that good.' The security chief went on, 'We think we've traced the source of the cards themselves. Four months ago one of our suppliers had a break-in. The thieves got into the strong room where finished plastic sheets are stored. Three hundred sheets were missing.'

Vandervoort whistled softly. A single plastic sheet would produce sixty-six Keycharge credit cards. That meant, potentially, almost twenty thousand fraudulent cards.

Wainwright said, 'I did the arithmetic too.' He motioned to the counterfeits on the desk. 'This is the tip of an iceberg. Okay, so the phony cards we know about, or think we do, can mean ten million dollars loss in charges before we pull them out of circulation. But what about others we haven't heard of yet ? There could be ten times as many more.'

'I get the picture.'

Alex Vandervoort paced the small office as his thoughts took shape.

He reflected: ever since bank credit cards were introduced, all banks issuing them had been plagued by heavy loss through fraud. At first, entire mailbags of cards were stolen, their contents used for spending sprees by thieves – at bank expense. Some mail shipments were hijacked and held for ransom Banks paid the ransom money, knowing the cost would be far greater if cards were distributed through the underworld, and used. Ironically, in 1974 Pan American Airways was castigated by press and public after admitting it paid money to criminals for the return of large quantities of stolen ticket blanks. The airline's objective was to avoid enormous losses through misuse of the tickets. Yet unknown to Pan Am's critics, some of the nation's biggest banks had quietly been doing the same thing for years.

Eventually, mail theft of credit cards was reduced, but by then criminals had moved on to other, more ingenious schemes. Counterfeiting was one. The early counterfeit cards were crude and easily recognizable, but quality improved, until now – as Wainwright had shown – it took an expert to detect the difference.

As fast as any credit card security measure was devised, criminal cleverness would circumvent it or attack a vulnerability elsewhere. As an example, a new type credit card now being marketed used a 'scrambled' photograph of the cardholder. To ordinary eyes the photo was an indistinguishable blur, but placed in a descrambling device it could be viewed clearly and the cardholder identified. At the moment the scheme looked promising, but Alex had not the least doubt that organized crime would soon find a way to duplicate the scrambled photos.

Periodically, arrests and convictions of those using stolen or bogus credit cards were made, but these represented a small portion only of the total traffic. The main problem, so far as banks were concerned, was a lack of investigative and enforcement people. There simply were not enough.

Alex ceased his pacing.

'These latest counterfeits,' he queried, 'is it likely that there's some kind of ring behind them?'

'It's not only likely, it's a certainty. For the end product to be this good, there has to be an organization. And it's got money behind it, machinery, specialist know-how, a distribution system. Besides, there are other signs pointing the same way.'

'Such as ?'

'As you know,' Wainwright said, 'I keep in touch with law agencies. Recently there's been a big increase through the whole Midwest in counterfeit currency, travellers' cheques, credit cards – other cards as well as our own. There's also a lot more traffic than usual in stolen and counterfeit securities, stolen and forged cheques.'

'And you believe all this, and our Keycharge fraud losses, are linked ?'

'Let's say it's possible.'

'What's Security doing ?'

'As much as we can. Every lost or missing Keycharge card that turns fraudulent is being checked out and, where possible tracked down. Recovered cards and fraud prosecutions have increased every month this year; you've had the figures in reports. But something like this needs a full-scale investigation and I don't have either staff or budget to handle it.'

Alex Vandervoort smiled ruefully. 'I thought we'd get around to budget.'

He surmised what was coming next. He knew of the problems under which Nolan Wainwright laboured.

Wainwright, as a vice-president of First Mercantile American, was in charge of all security matters in the Headquarters Tower and at branches. The credit card security division was only one of his responsibilities. In recent years the status of Security within the bank had been advanced, its operating funds increased, though the amount of money allotted was still inadequate. Everyone in management knew it. Yet because Security was a non-revenue-producing function, its position on the priority list for additional funds was low.

'You've got proposals and figures, I presume. You always have, Nolan.'

Wainwright produced a manila folder which he had brought with him. 'It's all there. The most urgent need is two more full-time investigators for the credit card division. I'm also asking for funds for an undercover agent whose assignment would be to locate the source of these counterfeit cards, also to find out where the leakage is occurring inside the bank.'

Vandervoort looked surprised. 'You think you can get someone?'

This time Wainwright smiled. 'Well, you don't begin by advertising in "help wanted" columns. But I'm willing to try.'

'I'll look carefully at what you've suggested and do my best. That's all I can promise. May I keep these cards?'

The security chief nodded.

'Anything else on your mind?'

'Only this: I don't think anyone around here, including you, Alex, is taking this whole credit card fraud problem seriously. Okay, so we congratulate ourselves that we've held losses down to three-quarters of one per cent of total business, but business has grown enormously while the percentage has stayed steady, even increased. As I understand it, Keycharge billings next year are expected to be three billion dollars.'

'That's what we're hoping for.'

'Then – at the same percentage – fraud losses could be more than twenty-two million.'

Vandervoort said dryly, 'We prefer to speak of it in percentages. That way it doesn't sound as much, and the directors don't get alarmed.'

'That's pretty cynical.'

'Yes, I suppose it is.'

And yet, Alex reasoned, it was an attitude which banks – all banks – took. They played down, deliberately, credit card crime, accepting such losses as a cost of doing business. If any other bank department showed a seven-and-a-half-million-dollar loss in a single year, all hell would erupt before the board. But where credit cards were concerned, 'three-quarters of one per cent' for criminality was accepted or conveniently ignored. The alternative – an all-out fight against crime – would be more costly by far. It could be said, of course, that the bankers' attitude was indefensible because in the end it was customers – credit card holders – who paid for fraud through increased charges. But, from a financial point of view, the attitude made business sense.

'There are times,' Alex said, 'when the credit card system sticks in my gullet, or rather parts of it do. But I live within the limits of what I think I can accomplish in the way of change,

and what I know I can't. The same goes for budget priorities.'
He touched the manila folder which Wainwright had put down.
'Leave it with me. I've already promised I'll do what I can.'

'If I don't hear, I'll be along to pound the desk.'

Alex Vandervoort left but Nolan Wainwright was delayed by
a message. It asked the security chief to contact Mrs D'Orsey,
manager of the main downtown branch, at once.

seven

'I've spoken to the FBI,' Nolan Wainwright informed Edwina
D'Orsey. 'They'll have two special agents here tomorrow.'

'Why not today?'

He grinned. 'We've no dead body; there wasn't even any
shooting. Besides, they have a problem over there. A thing
called manpower shortage.'

'Don't we all?'

'Then can I let the staff go home?' asked Miles Eastin.

Wainwright answered, 'All except the girl. I'd like to talk with
her again.'

It was early evening, two hours since Wainwright had responded to Edwina's summons and taken over investigation of
the cash loss. In the meantime he had covered the same ground
the branch officers had gone over earlier, interviewing the teller,
Juanita Núñez, Edwina D'Orsey, Tottenhoe the operations
officer, and young Miles Eastin, the operations assistant.

He had also spoken with other tellers who had been working
near the Núñez girl.

Not wanting to be a focus of attention on the platform, Wainwright had taken over a conference room at the rear of the bank.
He was there now with Edwina D'Orsey and Miles Eastin.

Nothing new had emerged except that theft appeared likely;
therefore, under federal law the FBI must be called in. The

law, on such occasions, was not always applied painstakingly, as Wainwright was well aware. First Mercantile American and other banks often labelled thefts of money as 'mysterious disappearances' and, that way, such incidents could be handled internally, avoiding prosecution and publicity. Thus a member of the bank's staff suspected of theft might suffer dismissal only – ostensibly for some other reason. And since the guilty individuals were not inclined to talk, a surprisingly large number of theft cases were kept secret, even within the bank itself.

But the present loss – assuming it to be theft – was too large and flagrant to be concealed.

Nor was it a good idea to wait, hoping for more information. Wainwright knew the FBI would be angry if called in several days after the event to investigate a cold trail. Until the Bureau agents arrived, he intended to do what he could himself.

As Edwina and Miles Eastin left the small office, the operations assistant said helpfully, 'I'll send Mrs Núñez in.'

A moment later the small, slight figure of Juanita Núñez appeared at the office doorway. 'Come in,' Nolan Wainwright instructed. 'Shut the door. Sit down.'

He made his tone official and businesslike. Instinct told him that phony friendliness would not deceive this girl.

'I want to hear your whole story again. We'll take it step by step.'

Juanita Núñez looked sulky and defiant, as she had earlier, but now there were traces of fatigue. With a sudden flash of spirit, though, she objected, 'Three times I have already done that. Everything!'

'Perhaps you forgot something the other times.'

'I forgot nothing!'

'Then this time will make a fourth, and when the FBI arrive there'll be a fifth, and maybe after that a sixth.' He held her eyes with his own and kept authority in his voice but didn't raise it. If he were a police officer, Wainwright thought, he'd have had to caution her about her rights. But he wasn't, and wouldn't. Sometimes, in a situation like this, private security forces had advantages which police were not allowed.

'I know what you are thinking,' the girl said. 'You think I will say something different this time, so you can prove that I was lying.'

'*Are* you lying?'

'No!'

'Then why worry about that?'

Her voice quavered. 'Because I am tired. I would like to go.'

'I would, too. And if it wasn't for a missing six thousand dollars – which you admit you had in your possession earlier – I'd be finished work for the day and driving home. But the money *is* gone and we'd like to find it. So tell me about this afternoon again – when you say you first saw something wrong.'

'It was like I told you – twenty minutes after lunch.'

He read contempt in her eyes. Earlier, when he began asking questions, he had sensed the girl's attitude as being easier towards him than the others. No doubt because he was black and she was Puerto Rican, she assumed they might be allies or, if not that, that he would be a softer touch. What she didn't know was that where investigative work was concerned he was colour-blind. Nor could he concern himself about any personal problems the girl might have. Edwina D'Orsey had mentioned these, but no personal circumstance, in Wainwright's view, ever justified stealing or dishonesty.

The Núñez girl had been right, of course, about his wanting to catch her out in some variation of her story. And it could happen, despite her obvious caution. She had complained of being tired. As an experienced investigator, Wainwright knew that guilty people, when tired, were apt to make mistakes during interrogation, a small one first, then another and another, until they became trapped in a web of lies and inconsistency.

Wondering if it would happen now, he pressed on.

It took three-quarters of an hour, during which Juanita Núñez's version of events remained identical with what she had stated earlier. While disappointed at having uncovered nothing new, Wainwright was not overly impressed with the girl's consistency. His police background made him realize that such exactitude could have two interpretations: either she was speaking the truth or she had rehearsed her story so carefully that she was perfect in it. The latter seemed a probability because innocent people usually had a few slight variations between one recounting and the next. It was a symptom which detectives learned to look for.

At the end, Wainwright said, 'All right, that's everything for now. Tomorrow you can take a lie detector test. The bank will arrange it.'

He made the announcement casually, though watching for a reaction. What he had not expected was one as sudden or as fierce.

The girl's small dark face flushed red. She shot upright in her chair.

'No, I will not! I will not take such a test!'

'Why not?'

'Because it is an insult!'

'It's no insult. Lots of people take the test. If you're innocent, the machine will prove it.'

'I do not trust such a machine. Or you. *Basta con mi palabra!*'

He ignored the Spanish, suspecting it was abusive. 'You've no reason not to trust me. All I'm interested in is getting to the truth.'

'You have heard truth! You do not recognize it! You, like the others, believe I took the money. It is useless to tell you I did not.'

Wainwright stood up. He opened the door of the tiny office for the girl to go. 'Between now and tomorrow,' he advised, 'I suggest you reconsider your attitude about that test. If you refuse to take it, it will look bad for you.'

She looked him fully in the face. 'I do not have to take such a test, do I?'

'No.'

'Then I will not.'

She marched from the office with short, quick steps. After a moment, unhurriedly, Wainwright followed.

Within the bank's main working area, though a few people were still at desks, the majority of staff had gone and overhead lights were dimmed. Outside, darkness had descended on the raw autumn day.

Juanita Núñez went to a locker room for her street clothes,

and returned. She ignored Wainwright. Miles Eastin, who had been waiting with a key, let her out through the main street door.

'Juanita,' Eastin said, 'is there anything I can do? Shall I drive you home?'

She shook her head without speaking and went out.

Nolan Wainwright, watching from a window, saw her walk to a bus stop across the street. If he had had a larger security force, he thought, he might have had her followed, though he doubted it would do any good. Mrs Núñez was clever and she would not give herself away, either by handing the money to someone else in public or even storing it in a predictable place.

He was convinced the girl did not have the money on her. She was too astute to run that risk; also, the amount of cash would be too bulky to conceal. He had looked at her closely during their talk and afterwards, observing that her clothes clung tightly to her small body and there were no suspicious bulges. The handbag she carried from the bank was tiny. She had no packages.

Wainwright felt certain that an accomplice was involved.

He had little remaining doubt, if any, that Juanita Núñez was guilty. Her refusal to submit to a lie detector test, considered with all other facts and indications, had convinced him. Remembering her emotional outburst of a few minutes ago, he suspected it was planned, perhaps rehearsed. Bank employees were well aware that in cases of suspected theft a lie detector was employed; the Núñez girl was likely to have known that, too. Therefore she could have guessed the subject would come up and been ready for it.

Remembering how she had looked at him with contempt and, before that, her unspoken assumption of alliance, Wainwright felt a surge of anger. With an unusual intensity he found himself hoping that tomorrow the FBI team would give her a hard time and shake her down. But it would not be easy. She was tough.

Miles Eastin had relocked the main street door and now returned.

'Well,' he said cheerfully, 'time to head for the showers.'

The security chief nodded. 'It's been quite a day.'

Eastin seemed about to say something else, then apparently decided otherwise.

Wainwright asked him, 'Something on your mind?'

Again Eastin hesitated, then admitted, 'Well, yes, there is. It's a thing I haven't mentioned to anyone because it could be just a wild pitch.'

'Does it relate in any way to the missing money?'

'I suppose it could.'

Wainwright said sternly, 'Then whether you're sure or not, you have to tell me.'

The assistant operations officer nodded. 'All right.'

Wainwright waited.

'It was mentioned to you – by Mrs D'Orsey, I think – that Juanita Núñez is married. Her husband deserted her. He left her with their child.'

'I remember.'

'When the husband was living with Juanita he used to come in here occasionally. To meet her, I guess. I spoke to him a couple of times. I'm pretty sure his name is Carlos.'

'What about him?'

'I believe he was in the bank today.'

Wainwright asked sharply, 'Are you sure?'

'Fairly sure, though not enough so I could swear to it in court. I just noticed someone, thought it was him, then put it out of mind. I was busy. There was no reason for me to think about it – at least not until a long time later.'

'What time of day was it when you saw him?'

'About mid-morning.'

'This man you thought was the Núñez girl's husband – did you see him go to the counter where she was working?'

'No, I didn't.' Eastin's handsome young face was troubled. 'As I say, I didn't think about it much. The only thing is, if I saw him, he couldn't have been far away from Juanita.'

'And that's everything?'

'That's it.' Miles Eastin added apologetically, 'I'm sorry it isn't more.'

'You were right to tell me. It could be important.'

If Eastin were right, Wainwright reasoned, the presence of the husband could tie in with Wainwright's own theory of an outside accomplice. Possibly the girl and her husband were together again or, if not, had some arrangement. Perhaps she had passed the money over the counter to him, and he had taken it from the bank, to divide it with her later. The possibility was certainly something for the FBI to work on.

'Quite apart from the missing money,' Eastin said, 'everybody in the bank is talking about Mr Rosselli – we heard about the announcement yesterday, his illness. Most of us are pretty sad.'

It was a sudden, painful reminder as Wainwright regarded the young man, usually so full of banter and joviality. At this moment, the security chief saw, there was distress in Eastin's eyes.

Wainwright realized that the investigation had driven all thought of Ben Rosselli from his mind. Now, remembering, he experienced new anger that thievery should leave its ugly mark at such a time.

With a murmured acknowledgment and a good night to Eastin, he walked through the tunnel from the branch bank, using his pass-key to re-enter the FMA Headquarters Tower.

eight

Across the street, Juanita Núñez – a tiny figure against the soaring city block complex of First Mercantile American Bank and Rosselli Plaza – was still waiting for her bus.

She had seen the security officer's face watching her from a window of the bank, and had a sense of relief when the face disappeared, though commonsense told her the relief was only temporary, and the wretchedness of today would resume and be as bad, or even worse, tomorrow.

A cold wind, knifing through downtown streets, penetrated the thin coat she had on, and she shivered as she waited. Her regular bus had gone. She hoped another would come soon.

The shivering, Juanita knew, was partly from fear because, at this moment, she was more frightened, more terror-stricken, than ever before in all her life.

Frightened and perplexed.

Perplexed because she had no idea how the money had been lost.

Juanita knew that she had neither stolen the money, nor handed it across the counter in error, or disposed of it in any other way.

The trouble was: no one would believe her.

In other circumstances, she realized, she might not have believed herself.

How *could* six thousand dollars have vanished? It was impossible, *impossible*. And yet it had.

Time after time this afternoon she had searched her recollection of every single moment of the day to find some explanation. There was none. She had thought back over cash transactions at the counter during the morning and early afternoon, using the remarkable memory she knew she had, but no solution came to her. Not even the wildest possibility made any sense.

She was positive, too, that she had locked her cash drawer securely before taking it to the vault while she had lunch, and it was still locked when she returned. As to the combination, which Juanita had chosen and set herself, she had never discussed it with anyone else or even written it down, relying as usual on her memory.

In one way it was her memory which had added to her troubles.

Juanita knew she had not been believed, either by Mrs D'Orsey, Mr Tottenhoe, or Miles, who at least had been friendlier than the others, when she claimed to know, at two o'clock, the exact amount of money which was gone. They said it was impossible she could know.

But she *had* known. Just as she *always* knew how much cash she had when she was working as a teller, although she found it impossible to explain to others how or why.

She was not even sure herself how she kept the running tally in her head. It was simply there. It happened without effort, so that she was scarcely aware of the arithmetic involved. For almost as long as Juanita could remember, adding, subtracting, multiplying, and dividing seemed as easy as breathing, and as natural.

She did it automatically at the bank counter as she took money in from customers or paid it out. And she had learned to glance at her cash drawer, checking that the cash she had on hand was what it should be, that various denominations of notes were in their right order, and in sufficient numbers. Even with coins, while not knowing the total so precisely, she could estimate the amount closely at any time. Occasionally, at the end of a busy day when she balanced her cash, her mental figure might prove to be in error by a few dollars, but never more.

Where had the ability come from ? She had no idea.

She had never excelled in school. During her sketchy high school education in New York, she seldom achieved more than a low average in most subjects. Even in mathematics she had no real grasp of principles, merely an ability to calculate with lightning speed and carry figures in her head.

At last the bus arrived with an uneven roar and diesel stink. With others who were waiting, Juanita climbed aboard. No seats were available and standing space was crowded. She managed to grab a handhold and continued thinking, straining to remember as the bus swayed through the city streets.

What would happen tomorrow ? Miles had told her that FBI men were coming. The thought filled her with fresh dread and her face set tensely in a bleakness of anxiety – the same expression which Edwina D'Orsey and Nolan Wainwright had mistaken for hostility.

She would say as little as possible, just as she had done today after she found that no one was believing her.

As to the machine, the lie detector, she would refuse. She knew nothing of how such a machine worked, but when no one else would understand, believe, or help her, why would a machine – the bank's machine – be different ?

It was a three-block walk from the bus to the nursery school where she had left Estela this morning on her way to work. Juanita hurried, knowing she was late.

The little girl ran towards her as she entered the small school play-room in the basement of a private house. Though the house, like others in the area, was old and dilapidated, the school rooms were clean and cheerful – the reason Juanita had chosen the school in preference to others, though the cost was higher and a strain for her to pay.

Estela was excited, as full of joy as always.

'Mommy! Mommy! See my painting. It's a train.' She pointed with a paint-covered finger. 'There's a bagoose. That's a *man* inside.'

She was a small child, even for three, dark like Juanita, with large liquid eyes reflecting her wonder at each new interest, at the fresh discoveries she made every day.

Juanita hugged her and corrected her gently. 'Caboose, *amorcito*.'

It was obvious from the stillness that the other children were all gone.

Miss Ferroe, who owned and ran the school, came in primly, frowning. She looked pointedly at her watch.

'Mrs Núñez, as a special favour I agreed that Estela could stay after the others, but this is far too late . . .'

'I really am sorry, Miss Ferroe. Something happened at the bank.'

'I have private responsibilities also. And other parents observe the school's closing time.'

'It won't happen again. I promise.'

'Very well. But since you are here, Mrs Núñez, may I remind you that last month's bill for Estela has not been paid.'

'It will be on Friday. I'll have my pay cheque then.'

'I'm sorry to have to mention it, you understand. Estela is a sweet little girl and we're glad to have her. But I have bills to pay . . .'

'I do understand. It will be Friday for sure. I promise.'

'That's two promises, Mrs Núñez.'

'Yes, I know.'

'Good night then. Good night, Estela dear.'

Despite her starchiness, the Ferroe woman ran an excellent nursery school and Estela was happy there. The money owing to the school, Juanita decided, would have to come out of her pay this week, as she had said, and somehow she must manage until the pay day after that. She wasn't sure how. Her wage as a teller was $98 weekly; after taxes and Social Security deductions, her take-home pay was $83. Out of that there was food to buy for the two of them, Estela's school fees, plus rent of the tiny walk-up flat they lived in at Forum East; also the finance company would demand a payment since she had missed the last.

Before Carlos left her, simply walking out and disappearing a year ago, Juanita had been naïve enough to sign finance papers jointly with her husband. He had bought suits, a used car, a colour TV, all of which he took w th him. Juanita, however, was still paying, the instalments seeming to stretch on into a limitless future.

She would have to visit the finance company office, she thought, and offer them less. They would undoubtedly be nasty, as they were before, but it would have to be endured.

On the way home, Estela skipped happily along, one small hand in Juanita's. In her other hand Juanita carried Estela's painting, carefully rolled up. In a little while, in the apartment, they would have their evening meal and afterwards they usually played and laughed together. But Juanita would find it difficult to laugh tonight.

Her earlier terror deepened as she considered for the first time what might happen if she lost her job. The probability, she realized, was strong.

She knew, too, that it would be hard to find work elsewhere. No other bank would hire her and other employers would want to know where she had worked before, then would find out about the missing money and reject her.

Without a job, what would she do? How could she support Estela?

Abruptly, stopping on the street, Juanita reached down and clasped her daughter to her.

She prayed that tomorrow someone would believe her, would recognize the truth.

Someone, *someone*.

But who?

nine

Alex Vandervoort, also, was abroad in the city.

Earlier in the afternoon, returning from the session with Nolan Wainwright, Alex had paced his office suite, seeking to place recent events in true perspective. Yesterday's announcement by Ben Rosselli was a major cause for reflection. So was the resultant situation in the bank. So, too, were developments, within recent months, in Alex's personal life.

Pacing back and forth – twelve strides one way, twelve the other – was an old established habit. Once or twice he had stopped, re-examining the counterfeit Keycharge credit cards which the security chief had allowed Alex to bring away. Credit and credit cards were additionally a part of his preoccupation – not only fraudulent cards, but genuine ones, too.

The genuine variety was represented by a series of advertising proofs, also on the desk, and now spread out. They had been prepared by the Austin Advertising Agency and the purpose was to encourage Keycharge holders to use their credit and their cards increasingly.

One announcement urged:

WHY WORRY ABOUT MONEY?

USE YOUR KEYCHARGE CARD

AND

LET *us* WORRY FOR YOU!

Another claimed:

BILLS ARE PAINLESS
WHEN YOU SAY
'PUT IT ON MY KEYCHARGE!'

A third advised:

WHY WAIT?
YOU *can* AFFORD TOMORROW'S DREAM TODAY!
USE YOUR KEYCHARGE –
now!

A half dozen others were on similar themes.

Alex Vandervoort was uneasy about them all.

His unease did not have to be translated into action. The advertising, already approved by the bank's Keycharge division, had merely been sent to Alex for general information. Also, the overall approach had been agreed on several weeks ago by the bank's board of directors as a means to increase the profitability of Keycharge which – like all credit card programmes – sustained losses in its initial, launching years.

But Alex wondered: had the board envisaged a promotional campaign quite so blatantly aggressive?

He shuffled the advertising proofs together and returned them to the folder they had arrived in. At home tonight he would reconsider them and he would hear a second opinion, he realized – probably a strong one – from Margot.

Margot.

The thought of her melded with the memory of Ben Rosselli's disclosure yesterday. What had been said then was a reminder to Alex of life's fragility, the brevity of time remaining, the inevitability of endings, a pointer to the unexpected always close at hand. He had been moved and saddened for Ben himself; but also, without intending to, the old man had revived once more an oft-recurring question: should Alex make a fresh life for himself and Margot? Or should he wait? And wait for what?

For Celia?

That question, too, he had asked himself a thousand times.

Alex looked out across the city towards where he knew Celia to be. He wondered what she was doing, how she was.

There was a simple way to find out.

He returned to his desk and dialled a number which he knew by heart.

A woman's voice answered, 'Remedial Centre.'

He identified himself and said, 'I'd like to talk with Dr McCartney.'

After a moment or two a male voice, quietly firm, inquired, 'Where are you, Alex?'

'In my office. I was sitting here wondering about my wife.'

'I asked because I intended to call you today and suggest you come in to visit Celia.'

'The last time we talked you said you didn't want me to.'

The psychiatrist corrected him gently. 'I said I thought any more visits inadvisable for a while. The previous few, you'll remember, seemed to unsettle your wife rather than help.'

'I remember.' Alex hesitated, then asked, 'There's been some change?'

'Yes, there is a change. I wish I could say it was for the better.'

There had been so many changes, he had become dulled to them. 'What kind of change?'

'Your wife is becoming even more withdrawn. Her escape from reality is almost total. It's why I think a visit from you might do some good.' The psychiatrist corrected himself, 'At least it should do no harm.'

'All right. I'll come this evening.'

'Any time, Alex; and drop in to see me when you do. As you know, we've no set visiting hours here and a minimum of rules.'

'Yes, I know.'

The absence of formality, he reflected, as he replaced the telephone, was a reason he had chosen the Remedial Centre when faced with his despairing decision about Celia nearly four years ago. The atmosphere was deliberately non-institutional. The nurses did not wear uniforms. As far as was practical, patients moved around freely and were encouraged to make decisions of their own. With occasional exceptions, friends and families were welcome at any time. Even the name Remedial Centre had been chosen intentionally in preference to the more forbidding 'mental hospital'. Another reason was that Dr Timothy McCartney, young, brilliant, and innovative, headed a specialist team which achieved cures of mental illnesses where more conventional treatments failed.

The Centre was small. Patients never exceeded a hundred and fifty though, by comparison, the staff was large. In a way, it was like a school with small classes where students received personal attention they could not have gained elsewhere.

A modern building and spacious gardens were as pleasing as money and imagination could make them.

The clinic was private. It was also horrendously expensive but Alex had been determined, and still was, that whatever else happened, Celia would have the best of care. It was, he reasoned, the very least that he could do.

Through the remainder of the afternoon he occupied himself with bank business. Soon after 6pm he left FMA Headquarters, giving his driver the Remedial Centre address, and read the evening paper while they crawled through traffic. A limousine and chauffeur, available at any time from the bank's pool of cars, were perquisites of the executive vice-president's job and Alex enjoyed them.

Typically, the Remedial Centre had the façade of a large private home with nothing outside, other than a street number, to identify it.

An attractive blonde, wearing a colourful print dress, let him in. He recognized her as a nurse from a small insignia pin near her left shoulder. It was the only permitted dress distinction between staff and patients.

'Doctor told us you'd be coming, Mr Vandervoort. I'll take you to your wife.'

He walked with her along a pleasant corridor. Yellows and greens predominated. Fresh flowers were in niches along the walls.

'I understand,' he said, 'that my wife has been no better.'

'Not really, I'm afraid.' The nurse shot him a sideways glance; he sensed pity in her eyes. But for whom? As always, when he came here, he felt his natural ebullience desert him.

They were in a wing, one of three running outwards from the central reception area. The nurse stopped at a door.

'Your wife is in her room, Mr Vandervoort. She had a bad day today. Try to remember that, if she shouldn't . . .' She left the sentence unfinished, touched his arm lightly, then preceded him in.

The Remedial Centre placed patients in shared or single rooms according to the effect which the company of others had on their condition. When Celia first came she was in a double room, but it hadn't worked; now she was in a private one. Though small, Celia's room was cosily comfortable and individual. It contained a studio couch, a deep armchair and ottoman, a games table and bookshelves. Impressionist prints adorned the walls.

'Mrs Vandervoort,' the nurse said gently, 'your husband is here to visit you.'

There was no acknowledgment, neither movement nor spoken response, from the figure in the room.

It had been a month and a half since Alex had seen Celia and, though he had been expecting some deterioration, her present appearance chilled him.

She was seated – if her posture could be called that – on the studio couch. She had positioned herself sideways, facing away from the outer door. Her shoulders were hunched down, her head lowered, arms crossed in front, with each hand clasping the opposite shoulder. Her body, too, was curled upon itself and her legs drawn up with knees together. She was absolutely still.

He went to her and put a hand gently on one shoulder. 'Hullo, Celia. It's me – Alex. I've been thinking about you, so I came to see you.'

She said, low-voiced, without expression, 'Yes.' She did not move.

He increased the pressure on the shoulder. 'Won't you turn around to look at me ? Then we can sit together and talk.'

The only response was a perceptible rigidity, a tightening of the position in which Celia was huddled.

Her skin texture, Alex saw, was mottled and her fair hair only roughly combed. Even now her gentle, fragile beauty had not entirely vanished, though clearly it would not be long before it did.

'Has she been like this long ?' he asked the nurse quietly.

'All of today and part of yesterday; some other days as well.'

The girl added matter-of-factly, 'She feels more comfortable that way, so it's best if you take no notice, just sit down and talk.'

Alex nodded. As he went to the single armchair and settled himself, the nurse tiptoed out, closing the door gently.

'I went to the ballet last week, Celia,' Alex said. 'It was *Coppélia*. Natalia Makarova danced the lead and Ivan Nagy was Frantz. They were magnificent together and, of course, the music was wonderful. It reminded me of how you loved *Coppélia*, that it was one of your favourites. Do you remember that night, soon after we were married, when you and I . . .'

He could call back in memory clearly, even now, the way Celia had looked that evening – in a long pale-green chiffon gown, tiny sequins glittering with reflected light. As usual, she had been ethereally beautiful, slim and gossamer-like, as if a breeze might steal her if he looked away. In those days he seldom did. They had been married six months and she was still shy at meeting Alex's friends, so that sometimes in a group she clung tightly to his arm. Because she was ten years younger than himself, he hadn't minded. Celia's shyness, at the beginning, had been one of the reasons why he fell in love with her, and he was proud of her reliance on him. Only long after, when she continued to be diffident and unsure – foolishly, it seemed to him – had his impatience surfaced, and eventually anger.

How little, how tragically little, he had understood! With more perception he would have realized that Celia's background before they met was so totally different from his own that nothing had prepared her for the active social and domestic life he accepted matter-of-factly. It was all new and bewildering to Celia, at times alarming. She was the only child of reclusive parents of modest means, had attended convent schools, had never known the leavening propinquity of college living. Before Celia met Alex she had had no responsibilities, her social experience was nil. Marriage increased her natural nervousness; at the same time, self-doubts and tensions grew until eventually – as psychiatrists explained it – a burden of guilt at failing snapped something in her mind. With hindsight, Alex blamed himself. He could, he afterwards believed, have helped Celia so easily, could have given advice, eased tensions, offered reassurance. But when it mattered most he never had. He had been too thoughtless, busy, ambitious.

'. . . so last week's performance, Celia, made me sorry we weren't seeing it together . . .'

In fact, he had been to Coppélia *with Margot, whom Alex had known now for a year and a half, and who zestfully filled a gap in his life which had been empty for so long. Margot, or someone else, had been necessary if Alex – a flesh and blood man – were not to become a mental case, too, he sometimes told himself. Or was that a self-delusion, conveniently assuaging guilt?*

Either way, this was no time or place to introduce Margot's name.

'Oh, yes, and not long ago, Celia, I saw the Harringtons. You remember John and Elise. Anyway, they told me they had been to Scandinavia to see Elise's parents.'

'Yes,' Celia said tonelessly.

She had still not stirred from the huddled position, but evidently was listening, so he continued talking, using only half his mind while the other half asked: *How did it happen? Why?*

'We've been busy at the bank lately, Celia.'

One reason, he assumed, had been his preoccupation with his work, the long hours during which – as their marriage deteriorated – he had left Celia alone. That, as he now saw it, was when she had needed him most. As it was, Celia accepted his absences without complaint but grew increasingly reserved and timid, burying herself in books or looking interminably at plants and flowers, appearing to watch them grow, though occasionally – in contrast and without apparent reason – she became animated, talking incessantly and sometimes incoherently. Those were periods in which Celia seemed to have exceptional energy. Then, with equal suddenness, the energy would disappear, leaving her depressed and withdrawn once more. And all the while their communication and companionship diminished.

It was during that time – the thought of it shamed him now – he had suggested they divorce. Celia had seemed shattered and he let the subject drop, hoping things would get better, but they hadn't.

Only at length, when the thought occurred to him almost casually that Celia might need psychiatric help, and he had sought it, had the truth of her malady become clear. For a while, anguish and concern revived his love. But, by then, it was too late.

At times he speculated: perhaps it had always been too late. Perhaps not even greater kindness, understanding, would have helped. But he would never know. He could never nurture the conviction he had done his best and, because of it, could never shed the guilt which haunted him.

'Everybody seems to be thinking about money – spending it, borrowing it, lending it, though I guess that's not unusual and what banks are for. A sad thing happened yesterday, though. Ben Rosselli, our president, told us he was dying. He called a meeting and . . .'

Alex went on, describing the scene in the boardroom and reactions afterwards, then abruptly stopped.

Celia had begun to tremble. Her body was rocking back and forth. A wail, half moan, escaped her.

Had his mention of the bank upset her? – *the bank into which he had thrown his energies, widening the gulf between them. It was another bank then, the Federal Reserve, but to Celia one bank was like another.* Or was it his reference to Ben Rosselli?

Ben would die soon. *How many years before Celia died? Many, perhaps.*

Alex thought: she could easily outlive him, could live on like this.

She looked like an animal!

His pity evaporated. Anger seized him; the angry impatience which had marred their marriage. 'For Christ's sake, control yourself!'

Her trembling and the moans continued.

He hated her! She wasn't human any more, yet she remained the barrier between himself and a full life.

Getting up, Alex savagely punched a bell push on the wall, knowing it would summon help. In the same motion he strode to the door to leave.

And looked back. At Celia – his wife whom once he had loved; at what she had become; at the gulf between them they would never bridge. He paused, and wept.

Wept with pity, sadness, guilt, his momentary anger spent, the hatred washed away.

He returned to the studio couch and, on his knees before her,

73

begged, '*Celia forgive me ! Oh, God, forgive me !*'

He felt a gentle hand on his shoulder, heard the young nurse's voice. 'Mr Vandervoort, I think you should go now.'

'Water or soda, Alex ?'

'Soda.'

Dr McCartney took a bottle from the small refrigerator in his consulting room and used an opener to flip the top. He poured into a glass which already contained a generous slug of scotch and added ice. He brought the glass to Alex, then poured the rest of the soda, without liquor, for himself.

For a big man – Tim McCartney was six feet five with a football player's chest and shoulders and enormous hands – his movements were remarkably deft. Though the clinic director was young, in his mid-thirties Alex guessed, his manner and voice seemed older and his brushed-back brown hair was greying at the temples. Probably because of a lot of sessions like this, Alex thought. He sipped the scotch gratefully.

The panelled room was softly lighted, its colour tones more muted than the corridors and other rooms outside. Bookshelves and racks for journals filled one wall, the works of Freud, Adler, Jung, and Rogers prominent.

Alex was still shaken as the result of his meeting with Celia, yet in a way the horror of it seemed unreal.

Dr McCartney returned to a chair at his desk and swung it to face the sofa where Alex sat.

'I should report to you first that your wife's general diagnosis remains the same – schizophrenia, catatonic type. You'll remember we've discussed this in the past.'

'I remember all the jargon, yes.'

'I'll try to spare you any more.'

Alex swirled the ice in his glass and drank again; the scotch had warmed him. 'Tell me about Celia's condition now.'

'You may find this hard to accept, but your wife, despite the way she seems, is relatively happy.'

'Yes,' Alex said. 'I find that hard to believe.'

The psychiatrist insisted quietly, 'Happiness is relative, for all of us. What Celia has is security of a kind, a total absence of responsibility or the need to relate to others. She can withdraw into herself as much as she wants or needs to. The physical posture she's been taking lately, which you saw, is the classic foetal position. It comforts her to assume it, though for her physical good, we try to dissuade her when we can.'

'Comforting or not,' Alex said, 'the essence is that after having had the best possible treatment for four years, my wife's condition is still deteriorating.' He eyed the other man directly. 'Is that right or wrong?'

'Unfortunately it's right.'

'Is there any reasonable chance of a recovery, ever, so that Celia could lead a normal or near-normal life?'

'In medicine there are always possibilities . . .'

'I said *reasonable chance.*'

Dr McCartney sighed and shook his head. 'No.'

'Thank you for a plain answer.' Alex paused, then went on, 'As I understand it, Celia has become – I believe the word is "institutionalized". She's withdrawn from the human race. She neither knows nor cares about anything outside herself.'

'You're right about being institutionalized,' the psychiatrist said, 'but you're wrong about the rest. Your wife has not totally withdrawn, at least not yet. She still knows a little about what's going on outside. She also is aware she has a husband, and we've talked about you. But she believes you're entirely capable of taking care of yourself without her help.'

'So she doesn't worry about me?'

'On the whole, no.'

'How would she feel if she learned her husband had divorced her and remarried?'

Dr McCartney hesitated, then said, 'It would represent a total break from the little outside contact she has remaining. It might drive her over the brink into a totally demented state.'

In the ensuing silence Alex leaned forward, covering his face with his hands. Then he removed them. His head came up. With a trace of irony, he said, 'I guess if you ask for plain answers you're apt to get them.'

The psychiatrist nodded, his expression serious. 'I paid you a compliment, Alex, in assuming you meant what you said. I would not have been as frank with everyone. Also, I should add, I could be wrong.'

'Tim, *what the hell does a man do ?*'

'Is that rhetoric or a question ?'

'It's a question. You can put it on my bill.'

'There'll be no bill tonight.' The younger man smiled briefly, then considered. 'You ask me: *what does a man do in a circumstance like yours ?* Well, to begin, he finds out all he can – just as you have done. Then he makes decisions based on what he thinks is fair and best for everyone, including himself. But while he's making up his mind he ought to remember two things. One is, if he's a decent man, his own guilt feelings are probably exaggerated because a well-developed conscience has a habit of punishing itself more harshly than it need. The other is that few people are qualified for sainthood; the majority of us aren't born with the equipment.'

Alex asked, 'And you won't go further ? You won't be more specific ?'

Dr McCartney shook his head. 'Only you can make the decision. Those last few paces each of us walks alone.'

The psychiatrist glanced at his watch and got up from his chair. Moments later they shook hands and said good night.

Outside the Remedial Centre, Alex's limousine and driver – the car's motor running, its interior warm and comfortable – were waiting.

ten

'Without doubt ' Margot Bracken declared 'that is one crappy collection of chicanery and damn lies.'

She was looking down, elbows aggressively out, hands on slender waist, her small but resolute head thrust forward. She was provocative physically, Alex Vandervoort thought – a 'slip of a girl' with pleasingly sharp features, chin jutting and aggressive, thinnish lips, though the mouth was sensual overall. Margot's eyes were her strongest feature; they were large, green, flecked with gold, the lashes thick and long. At this moment, those eyes were glaring. Her anger and forcefulness stirred him sexually.

The object of Margot's censure was the assortment of advertising proofs for Keycharge credit cards which Alex had brought home from FMA, and which now were spread out on the living-room rug in his apartment. Margot's presence and vitality were providing, also, a needed contrast to Alex's ordeal of several hours ago.

He told her, 'I had an idea, Bracken, you might not like those advertising themes.'

'Not like them! I *despise* them.'

'Why?'

She pushed back her long chestnut hair in a familiar though unconscious gesture. An hour ago Margot had kicked off her shoes and now stood, all five-foot-two of her, in stockinged feet.

'All right, look at that!' She pointed to the announcement which began: WHY WAIT? YOU *can* AFFORD TOMORROW'S DREAM TODAY! 'What it is, is dishonest bullshit – high-powered, aggressive selling of debt – concocted to entrap the gullible. Tomorrow's dream, for anyone, is sure to be expensive. That's why it's a dream. And *no one* can afford it unless they have the money now or are certain of it soon.'

'Shouldn't people make their own judgements about that?'

'No! Not the people who'll be influenced by that perverted advertising, the ones you're *trying* to influence. They're the unsophisticated, the easily persuadable, those who believe that what they see in print is true. I know. I get plenty of them as clients in my law practice. My unprofitable law practice.'

'Maybe those aren't the kind of people who have our Keycharge cards.'

'Dammit, Alex, you know that isn't true! The most unlikely people nowadays have credit cards because you all have pushed them so hard. The only thing you haven't done is hand cards out at street corners, and it wouldn't surprise me if you started that soon.'

Alex grinned. He enjoyed these debating sessions with Margot and liked to keep them fuelled. 'I'll tell our people to think about it, Bracken.'

'What I wish other people would think about is that shylocking eighteen per cent interest all bank credit cards charge.'

'We've been over that before.'

'Yes, we have. And I've never heard an explanation which satisfied me.'

He countered sharply, 'Maybe you don't listen.' Enjoyable in debate or not, Margot had a knack of getting under his skin. Occasionally their debates developed into fights.

'I've told you that credit cards are a packaged commodity, offering a range of services,' Alex insisted. 'If you add those services together, our interest rate is not excessive.'

'It's as excessive as hell if you're the one who's paying.'

'Nobody *has* to pay. Because nobody *has* to borrow.'

'I can hear you. You don't have to shout.'

'All right.'

He took a breath, determined not to let *this* discussion get out of hand. Besides, while disputing some of Margot's views, which in economics, politics, and everything else were left of centre, he found his own thinking aided by her forthrightness and keen lawyer's mind. Margot's practice, too, brought her contacts which he lacked directly – among the city's poor and underprivileged for whom the bulk of her legal work was done.

He asked, 'Another cognac?'

'Yes, please.'

It was close to midnight. A log fire, blazing earlier, had burned low in the hearth of the snug room in the small, sumptuous bachelor suite.

An hour and a half ago they had had a late dinner here, delivered from a service restaurant on the apartment block's main floor. An excellent Bordeaux – Alex's choice, Château Gruaud-Larose '66 – accompanied the meal.

Apart from the area where the Keycharge advertising had been spread out, the apartment lights were low.

When he had replenished their brandy glasses, Alex returned to the argument. 'If people pay their credit card bills when they get them, there *is* no interest charge.'

'You mean pay their bills in full.'

'Right.'

'But how many do? Don't most credit card users pay that convenient 'minimum balance' that the statements show?'

'A good many pay the minimum, yes.'

'And carry the rest forward as debt – which is what you bankers really want them to do. Isn't that so?'

Alex conceded, 'Yes, it's true. But banks have to make a profit somewhere.'

'I lay awake nights,' Margot said, 'worrying if banks are making enough profit.'

As he laughed, she went on seriously, 'Look, Alex, thousands of people who shouldn't are piling up long-term debts by using credit cards. Often it's to buy trivia – drugstore items, LPs, bits of hardware, books, meals, other minor things; and they do it partly through unawareness, partly because small amounts of credit are ridiculously easy to obtain. And those small amounts, which ought to be paid by cash, add up to crippling debts, burdening imprudent people for years ahead.'

Alex cradled his brandy glass in both hands to warm it, sipped, then rose and tossed a fresh log on the fire. He protested, 'You're worrying too much, and the problem isn't that big.'

And yet, he admitted to himself some of what Margot had said made sense. Where once – as an old song put it – miners 'owed their souls to the company store', a new breed of chronic debtor had arisen, naïvely mortgaging future life and income to a 'friendly neighbourhood bank'. One reason was that credit cards had replaced, to a large extent, small loans. Where individuals used to be dissuaded from excessive borrowing, now they made their own loan decisions – often unwisely. Some observers, Alex knew, believed the system had downgraded American morality.

Of course, doing it the credit card way was much cheaper for a bank; also, a small loan customer, borrowing through the credit card route, paid substantially higher interest than on a conventional loan. The *total* interest the bank received, in fact, was often as high as twenty-four per cent since merchants who honoured credit cards paid their own additional bank levy, ranging from two to six per cent.

These were reasons why banks such as First Mercantile American were relying on credit-card business to swell their profits, and they would increasingly in future years. True, initial losses with all credit-card schemes had been substantial; as bankers were apt to put it, 'we took a bath'. But the same bankers were convinced that a bonanza was close at hand which would outstrip in profitability most other kinds of bank business.

Another thing bankers realized was that credit cards were a necessary halfway-house on the route to EFTS – the Electronic Funds Transfer System which, within a decade and a half, would replace the present avalanche of banking paper and make existing cheques and record keeping as obsolete as the Model T.

'That's enough,' Margot said. 'The two of us are beginning to sound like a shareholders meeting.' She came to him and kissed him fully on the lips.

The heat of their argument earlier had already aroused him, as skirmishes with Margot so often did. Their first encounter had begun that way. Sometimes, it seemed, the angrier both became, the larger their physical passion for each other grew. After a while he murmured, 'I declare the shareholders meeting closed.'

'Well...' Margot eased away and regarded him mischievously, 'There *is* some unfinished business – that advertising, darling. You're not really going to let it go out to the public the way it is ?'

'No,' he said, 'I don't believe I am.'

The Keycharge advertising was a strong sell – too strong – and he would use his authority to exercise a veto in the morning. He realized he had intended to, anyway. Margot had merely confirmed his own opinion of this afternoon.

The fresh log he had added to the fire was alight and crackling. They sat on the rug before the fireplace, savouring its warmth, watching the rising tongues of flame.

Margot leaned her head against Alex's shoulder. She said

softly, 'For a stuffy old moneychanger, you're really not too bad.'

He put his arm around her. 'I love you, too, Bracken.'

'Really and truly ? Banker's honour ?'

'I swear by the prime rate.'

'Then love me now.' She began to take off her clothes.

He whispered with amusement, 'Here ?'

'Why not ?'

Alex sighed happily. 'Why not indeed ?'

Soon after, he had a sense of release and joy in contrast to the anguish of the day.

And later still, they held each other, sharing the warmth from their bodies and the fire. At last Margot stirred. 'I've said it before and I say it again: you're a delicious lover.'

'And you're okay, Bracken.' He asked her, 'Will you stay the night ?'

She often did, just as Alex frequently stayed at Margot's apartment. At times it seemed foolish to maintain their two establishments, but he had delayed the step of merging them, wanting first to marry Margot if he could.

'I'll stay for a while,' she said, 'but not all night. Tomorrow I have to be in court early.'

Margot's court appearances were frequent and in the aftermath of such a case they had met a year and a half ago. Shortly before that first encounter, Margot had defended half a dozen demonstrators who clashed with police during a rally urging total amnesty for Vietnam deserters. Her spirited defence, not only of the demonstrators but of their cause, attracted wide attention. So did her victory – dismissal of all charges – at the trial's end.

A few days later, at a milling cocktail party given by Edwina D'Orsey and her husband Lewis, Margot was surrounded by admirers and critics. She had come to the party alone. So had Alex, who had heard of Margot, though only later did he discover she was a first cousin to Edwina. Sipping the D'Orseys' excellent Schramsberg, he had listened for a while, then joined forces with the critics. Soon after, others stood back, leaving debate to Alex and Margot, squared off like verbal gladiators.

At one point Margot had demanded, 'Who the hell are you ?'

'An ordinary American who believes that, in the military, discipline is necessary.'

'Even in an immoral war like Vietnam?'

'A soldier can't decide morality. He operates under orders. The alternative is chaos.'

'Whoever you are, you sound like a Nazi. After World War Two, we executed Germans who offered that defence.'

'The situation was entirely different.'

'No different at all. At the Nuremberg trials the Allies insisted Germans should have heeded conscience and refused orders. That's exactly what Vietnam draft defectors and deserters did.'

'The American Army wasn't exterminating Jews.'

'No, just villagers. As in My Lai and elsewhere.'

'No war is clean.'

'But Vietnam was dirtier than most. From the Commander-in-Chief down. Which is why so many young Americans, with a special courage, obeyed their consciences and refused to take part in it.'

'They won't get unconditional amnesty.'

'They should. In time, when decency wins out, they will.'

They were still arguing fiercely when Edwina separated them and performed introductions. Later they resumed the argument, and continued it while Alex drove Margot home to her apartment. There, at one point, they came close to blows but instead found suddenly that physical desire eclipsed all else and they made love excitedly, heatedly, until exhausted, knowing already that something new and vital had entered both their lives.

As a footnote to that occasion, Alex later reversed his once-strong views, observing, as other disillusioned moderates did, the hollow mockery of Nixon's 'peace with honour'. And later still, while Watergate and related infamies unfolded, it became clear that those at the highest level of government – who had decreed: 'No amnesty' – were guilty of more villainy by far than any Vietnam deserter.

There had been other occasions, since that first one, when Margot's arguments had changed or widened his ideas.

Now, in the apartment's single bedroom, she selected a nightgown from a drawer which Alex left for her exclusive use. When she had it on, Margot turned out the lights.

They lay silently, in comforting companionship in the darkened room. Then Margot said, 'You saw Celia today, didn't you?'

Surprised, he turned to her. 'How did you know?'

'It always shows. It's hard on you.' She asked, 'Do you want to talk about it?'

'Yes,' he said, 'I think so.'

'You still blame yourself, don't you?'

'Yes.' He told her about his meeting with Celia, the conversation afterwards with Dr McCartney, and the psychiatrist's opinion about the probable effect on Celia of a divorce and his own remarriage.

Margot said emphatically, 'Then you mustn't divorce her.'

'If I don't,' Alex said, 'there can be nothing permanent for you and me.'

'Of course there can! I told you long ago, it can be as permanent as we both want to make it. Marriage isn't permanent any more. Who really believes in marriage nowadays, except a few old bishops?'

'I believe,' Alex said. 'Enough to want it for us.'

'Then let's have it – on our terms. What I don't need, darling, is a piece of legal stationery saying I'm married, because I'm too used to legal papers for them to impress me overmuch. I've already said I'll live with you – gladly and lovingly. But what I won't have on my conscience, or burden you with either, is shoving what's left of Celia's sanity into a bottomless pit.'

'I know, I know. Everything you say makes sense.' His answer lacked conviction.

She assured him softly, 'I'm happier with what we have than I've ever been before in all my life. It's you, not me, who wants more.'

Alex sighed and, soon after, was asleep.

When she was sure that he was sleeping soundly, Margot dressed, kissed Alex lightly, and let herself out of the apartment.

eleven

While Alex Vandervoort slept part of that night alone, Roscoe
Heyward would sleep in solitude the whole night through.

Though not yet.

Heyward was at home, in his rambling, three-storey house in
the suburb of Shaker Heights. He was seated at a leather-topped
desk, with papers spread out before him, in the small, sedately
furnished room he used as a study.

His wife Beatrice had gone upstairs to bed almost two hours
ago, locking her bedroom door as she had for the past twelve
years since - by mutual consent - they moved into separate
sleeping quarters.

Beatrice's locking of her door, though characteristically imperious, had never offended Heyward. Long before the separate
arrangement their sexual exercises had grown fewer and fewer,
then tapered into nothingness.

Mostly, Heyward supposed, when occasionally he thought
about it, their sexual shutdown had been Beatrice's choice. Even
in the early years of marriage she made plain her mental distaste
for their gropings and heavings, though her body at times demanded them. Sooner or later, she implied, her strong mind
would conquer that rather disgusting need, and eventually it had.

Once or twice, in rare whimsical moments, it had occurred to
Heyward that their only son, Elmer, mirrored Beatrice's attitude
to the method of his conception and birth - an offending, unwarranted invasion of her bodily privacy. Elmer, now nearing
thirty, and a certified public accountant, radiated disapproval
about almost everything, stalking through life as with a thumb
and finger over his nose to protect him from the stench. Even
Roscoe Heyward at times found Elmer a bit much.

As to Heyward himself, he had accepted sexual deprivation
uncomplainingly, partly because twelve years ago he was at a
point where sex was something he could take or leave; partly
because ambition at the bank had, by then, become his central
driving force. So, like a machine which slips into disuse, his

sexual urgings dwindled. Nowadays they revived only rarely – even then, mildly – to remind him with a certain sadness of a portion of his life on which the curtain fell too soon.

But in other ways, Heyward admitted, Beatrice had been good for him. She was descended from an impeccable Boston family and, in her youth, had 'come out' properly as a débutante. It was at the débutante ball, with young Roscoe in tails and white gloves, and standing yardstick straight, that they were formally introduced. Later they had dates on which chaperones accompanied them and, following a suitable period of engagement, were married two years after meeting. The wedding, which Heyward still remembered with pride, was attended by a Who's Who of Boston society.

Then, as now, Beatrice shared Roscoe's notions about the importance of social position and respectability. She had followed through on both by long service to the Daughters of the American Revolution and was now National Recording Secretary General. Roscoe was proud of this and delighted with the prestigious social contacts which it brought. There had been only one thing Beatrice and her illustrious family lacked – money. At this moment, as he had many times before, Roscoe Heyward wished fervently that his wife had been an heiress.

Roscoe's and Beatrice's biggest problem was, and always had been, managing to live on his bank salary.

This year, as the figures he had been working on tonight showed, the Heywards' expenses would substantially exceed their income. Next April he would have to borrow to pay the income tax he owed, as had been necessary last year and the year before. There would have been other years, too, except that during some he had been lucky with investments.

Many people with much smaller incomes would have scoffed at the idea that an executive vice-president's $65,000 a year salary was not ample to live on, and perhaps to save. In fact, for the Heywards, it was not.

To begin with, income taxes cut the gross amount by more than a third. After that, first and second mortgages on the house required payments of another $16,000 yearly, while municipal taxes ate up a further $2,500. That left $23,000 – or roughly

$450 a week – for all other expenses including repairs, insurance, food, clothes, a car for Beatrice (the bank supplied Roscoe with a chauffeur-driven pool car when he needed it), a housekeeper-cook, charitable donations, and an incredible array of smaller items adding up to a depressingly large sum.

The house, Heyward always realized at times like this, was a serious extravagance. From the beginning it had proved larger than they needed, even when Elmer lived at home, which now he didn't. Vandervoort, whose salary was identical, was wiser by far to live in an apartment and pay rent, but Beatrice, who loved their house for its size and prestige, would never hear of that, nor would Roscoe favour it.

As a result they had to scrimp elsewhere, a process which Beatrice sometimes refused to acknowledge, taking the view she *ought* to have money; therefore to worry about it herself was *lèse majesté*. Her attitude was reflected in countless ways around the house. She would never use a linen napkin twice, soiled or not, it must be laundered after every use. The same applied to towels, so that linen and laundry bills were high. She made long-distance phone calls casually and rarely deigned to turn off switches. Moments earlier, Heyward had gone to the kitchen for a glass of milk and, though Beatrice had been in bed for two hours, every downstairs light was on. He had irritatedly snapped them off.

Yet, for all Beatrice's attitude, fact was fact and there were things they simply could not afford. An example was holidays – the Heywards had had none for the past two years. Last summer Roscoe told colleagues at the bank, 'We considered a Mediterranean cruise, but decided after all we'd prefer to stay home.'

Another uncomfortable reality was that they had virtually no savings – only a few shares of FMA stock which might have to be sold soon, though the proceeds would not be enough to offset this year's deficit.

Tonight, the only conclusion Heyward had reached was that after borrowing they must hold the line on expenses as best they could, hoping for a financial upturn before too long.

And there would be one – satisfyingly generous – if he became president of FMA.

In First Mercantile American, as with most banks, a wide salary gap existed between the presidency and the next rank downward. As president, Ben Rosselli had been paid $130,000 annually. It was a virtual certainty his successor would receive the same.

If it happened to Roscoe Heyward, it would mean *immediate doubling* of his present salary. Even with higher taxes, what was left would eliminate every present problem.

Putting his papers away, he began to dream about it, a dream which extended through the night.

twelve

Friday morning.

In their penthouse atop fashionable Cayman Manor, a residential high-rise a mile or so outside the city, Edwina and Lewis D'Orsey were at breakfast.

It was three days since Ben Rosselli's dramatic announcement of his impending death, and two days since discovery of the cash loss at First Mercantile American's main downtown branch. Of the two events, the cash loss – at this moment – weighed more heavily on Edwina.

Since Wednesday afternoon, nothing new had been discovered. Through all of yesterday, with low-key thoroughness, two FBI special agents had intensively questioned members of the branch staff, but without tangible result. The teller directly involved, Juanita Núñez, remained the prime suspect, but she would admit nothing, continued to insist that she was innocent, and refused to submit to a lie detector test.

Although her refusal increased the general suspicion of her guilt, as one of the FBI men put it to Edwina, 'We can suspect her strongly, and we do, but there isn't a pinhead of proof. As to the money, even if it's hidden where she lives, we need some solid evidence before we can get a search warrant. And we don't have any. Naturally, we'll keep an eye on her, though it isn't the kind of case where the Bureau can maintain a full surveillance.'

The FBI agents would be in the branch again today, yet there seemed little more that they could do.

But what the bank could do, and would, was end Juanita Núñez's employment. Edwina knew she must dismiss the girl today.

But it would be a frustrating, unsatisfactory ending.

Edwina returned her attention to breakfast - lightly scrambled eggs and toasted English muffins - which their maid had served a moment earlier.

Across the table, Lewis, hidden behind *The Wall Street Journal*, was growling as usual over the latest lunacy from Washington where an Under Secretary of the Treasury had declared before a Senate committee that the US would never again return to a gold standard. The secretary used a Keynesian quotation in describing gold as 'this barbarous yellow relic'. Gold, he claimed, was finished as an international exchange medium.

'My God! That leprous ignoramus!' Glaring over his steel-rimmed half-moon glasses, Lewis D'Orsey flung his newspaper to the floor to join *The New York Times*, *Chicago Tribune*, and a day-old *Financial Times* from London, all of which he had skimmed through already. He stormed on about the Treasury official, 'Five centuries after dimwits like him have rotted into dust, gold will still be the world's only sound basis for money and value. With the morons we have in power, there's no hope for us, absolutely none!'

Lewis seized a coffee cup, raised it to his lean, grim face and gulped, then wiped his lips with a linen napkin.

Edwina had been leafing through *The Christian Science Monitor*. She looked up. 'What a pity you won't be around five centuries from now to say, "I told you so".'

Lewis was a small man with a body like a twig, making him seem frail and half starved, though in fact he was neither. His face matched his body and was lean, almost cadaverous. His movements were quick, his voice more often than not impatient. Occasionally Lewis would joke about his unimpressive physique. Tapping his forehead he asserted, 'What nature omitted on the bodywork, it made up behind here.'

And it was true, even those who detested him conceded, he had a remarkably agile brain, particularly when applied to money and finance.

His morning tantrums seldom bothered Edwina. For one thing, over their fourteen years of marriage she had learned they were rarely directed at herself; and for another, she realized Lewis was girding himself for a morning session at his typewriter where he would roar like the righteously angry Jeremiah that readers of his twice-a-month financial newsletter expected him to be.

The high-priced, private newsletter containing Lewis D' Orsey's investment advice to an exclusive list of international subscribers provided him with both a rich livelihood and a personal spear on which to impale governments, presidents, prime ministers, and assorted politicians when any of their fiscal acts displeased him. Most did.

Many financial men attuned to modern theories, including some at First Mercantile American Bank, abhorred Lewis D' Orsey's independent, acidly biting, ultraconservative newsletter. Not so, however, most of Lewis's enthusiastic subscribers who regarded him as a combination of Moses and Midas in a generation of financial fools.

And with good reason, Edwina admitted. If making money was your objective in life, Lewis was a sound man to follow. He had proved it many times, uncannily, with advice which paid off handsomely for those who followed it.

Gold was one example. Long before it happened, and while others scoffed, Lewis D'Orsey predicted a dramatic upsurge in the free market price. He also urged heavy buying of South African gold mining shares, at the time low-priced. Since then, several subscribers to *The D'Orsey Newsletter* had written to say they were millionaires, solely as a result of taking this advice.

With equal prescience he had foreseen the series of US dollar devaluations and advised his readers to put all the cash they could raise into other currencies, notably Swiss francs and Deutsche marks, which many did – to their great profit.

In the most recent edition of *The D'Orsey Newsletter* he had written:

The US dollar, a once proud and honest currency, is moribund, like the nation it represents. Financially, America has passed the point of no return. Thanks to insane fiscal policies, misconceived by incompetent and corrupt politicans who care solely about themselves and re-election, we are living amid financial disaster which can only worsen.

Since our rulers are knaves and imbeciles and the docile public stands vacuously indifferent, it's time for the financial lifeboats! Every man (or woman) for himself!

If you have dollars, keep only enough for cab fare, food, and postage stamps. Plus sufficient for an airline ticket to some happier land.

For the wise investor is the investor who is departing these United States, living abroad and shedding US nationality. Officially, Internal Revenue Code section 877 says that if US citizens renounce their citizenship to avoid income taxes, and the IRS can prove it, their tax liability remains. But for those who know, there are legal ways to thwart the IRS. (See *The D'Orsey Newsletter* of July last year on how to become an ex-American citizen. *Single copies available for $16 or Swiss fr 30 each.*)

The reason for a change of allegiance and scene: The value of the US dollar will continue to diminish, along with Americans' fiscal freedom.

And even if you can't leave personally, send your money overseas. Convert your US dollars while you can (it may not be for long!) into Deutsche marks, Swiss francs, Dutch guilders, Austrian schillings, Krugerrands.

Then place them, out of reach of US bureaucrats, in a European bank, preferably Swiss . . .

Lewis D'Orsey had trumpeted variations on that theme for several years. His latest newsletter continued with more of the same and concluded with specific advice on recommended investments. Naturally, all were in non-US currencies.

Another subject arousing Lewis's rage had been the US Treasury's gold auctions. 'In a generation from now,' he had written, 'when Americans wake up and realize their national patrimony was sold at fire-sale prices to titillate the schoolboy vanity of Washington theorists, those responsible will be branded traitors' and cursed down history's years.'

Lewis's observation had been quoted widely in Europe, but ignored in Washington and by the US press.

Now, at the breakfast table, Edwina continued to read the *Monitor*. There was a report of a House of Representatives bill proposing tax law changes which would reduce depreciation allowances on real property. It could affect mortgage lending at the bank and she asked Lewis his opinion about the likelihood of the bill becoming law.

He answered crisply, 'Nil. Even if it gets through the House, it will never pass the Senate. I phoned a couple of senators yesterday. They don't take it seriously.'

Lewis had an extraordinary range of friends and contacts -- one of several reasons for his success. He kept abreast, too, of anything affecting taxes, advising his newsletter readers on situations they could exploit to their advantage.

Lewis himself paid only a token amount of income tax each year -- never more than a few hundred dollars, he boasted proudly -- yet his real income was in seven figures. He achieved this by utilizing tax shelters of all kinds -- oil investments, real estate, timber exploitation, farming, limited partnerships, and tax-free bonds. Such devices enabled him to spend freely, live splendidly, yet -- on paper -- sustain a personal loss each year.

Yet all these tax devices were totally legal. 'Only a fool conceals income, or cheats on taxes in some other way,' Edwina had heard Lewis declare often. 'Why take that risk when there are more legitimate escape hatches from taxes than holes in a Swiss cheese? All that's needed is the work to understand, and enterprise to use them.'

So far, Lewis had not taken his own advice to live overseas and shed his US citizenship. However, he detested New York where he had once lived and worked and now called it, 'a decaying, complacent, bankrupt bandit lair existing on solipsism and with bad breath.' It was also an illusion, he maintained, 'fostered by arrogant New Yorkers, that the best brains are to be found in that city. They aren't.' He preferred the Midwest where he had moved, and met Edwina a decade and a half ago.

Despite her husband's example in avoiding taxes, Edwina went her own way on that subject, filing her individual return and paying far more than Lewis, even on her more modest income. But it was Lewis who took care of their bills – for this penthouse and staff, their twin Mercedes cars, and other luxuries.

Edwina admitted honestly to herself that the high style of living, which she enjoyed, had been a factor in her decision to marry Lewis and her adaptation to their marriage. And the arrangement, as well as their independence and dual careers, worked well.

'I wish,' she said, 'your insight extended to knowing where all that cash of ours went on Wednesday.'

Lewis looked up from his breakfast which he had attacked fiercely as if the eggs were enemies. 'The bank's cash is still missing? Once more the gallant, fumble-fisted FBI has discovered nothing?'

'I suppose you could put it that way.' She told him of the impasse they had reached, and of her own decision that the teller would have to be let go today.

'And after that, no one else will employ her, I suppose.'

'Certainly no other bank.'

'She has a child, I think you said.'

'Unfortunately, yes.'

Lewis said gloomily, 'Two more recruits for the already swollen welfare rolls.'

'Oh, really! Save all that Birchism for your readers.'

Her husband's face cracked into one of his rare smiles. 'Forgive me. But I'm not used to your needing advice. It's not often that you do.'

It was a compliment, Edwina realized. One of the things she appreciated about their marriage was that Lewis treated her, and always had, as an intellectual equal. And although he had never said so directly, she knew he was proud of her senior management status at FMA – unusual even nowadays for a woman in the male chauvinist world of banking.

'Naturally I can't tell you where the missing money is,' Lewis said; he appeared to have been thinking. 'But I'll give you a piece of advice I've found useful sometimes in conundrum situations.'

'Yes, go on.'

'It's this: mistrust the obvious.'

Edwina felt disappointed. Illogically, she supposed, she had expected some kind of miracle solution. Instead, Lewis had delivered a hoary old bromide.

She glanced at her watch. It was almost eight o'clock. 'Thank you,' she said. 'I must go.'

'Oh by the way, I'm leaving for Europe tonight,' he informed her. 'I'll be back Wednesday.'

'Have a good trip.' Edwina kissed him as she left. The sudden announcement did not surprise her. Lewis had offices in Zurich and London, and his comings and goings were casual.

She went down in the private lift which connected their penthouse with an indoor parking garage.

As she drove to the bank, and despite her dismissal of Lewis's advice, the words *mistrust the obvious* stayed annoyingly, persistently in her mind.

A discussion at mid-morning with the two FBI agents was brief and inconclusive.

The meeting took place in the conference room at the rear of the bank where, over the preceding two days, the FBI men had interviewed members of the staff. Edwina was present. So was Nolan Wainwright.

The senior of the two agents, whose name was Innes and who spoke with a New England twang, told Edwina and the bank's security chief, 'We've gone as far as we can with our investigation here. The case will stay open and we'll be in touch if new facts come to light. Of course, if anything more develops here you'll inform the Bureau at once.'

'Of course,' Edwina said.

'Oh, there is an item of negative news.' The FBI man consulted a notebook. 'The Núñez girl's husband – Carlos. One of your people thought they saw him in the bank the day the money was missing.'

Wainwright said, 'Miles Eastin. He reported it to me. I passed the information on.'

'Yes, we questioned Eastin about that; he admitted he could have been mistaken. Well, we've traced Carlos Núñez. He's in Phoenix, Arizona; has a job there as a motor mechanic. Our

Bureau agents in Phoenix have interviewed him. They're satisfied he was at work on Wednesday, in fact every day this week, which rules him out as an accomplice.'

Nolan Wainwright escorted the FBI agents out. Edwina returned to her desk on the platform. She had reported the cash loss – as she was required to do – to her immediate superior in Headquarters Administration and word, it seemed, had filtered upwards to Alex Vandervoort. Late yesterday, Alex had telephoned, sympathetic, and asking if there was anything he could do to help. She had thanked him, but said no, realizing that she was responsible and must do whatever had to be done herself.

This morning, nothing had changed.

Shortly before noon Edwina instructed Tottenhoe to advise the payroll department that Juanita Núñez's employment would be terminated at the end of the day, and to have her severance pay cheque sent down to the branch. The cheque, delivered by messenger, was on Edwina's desk when she returned from lunch.

Uneasy, hesitating, Edwina turned the cheque over in her hand.

At this moment Juanita Núñez was still working. Edwina's decision about that yesterday had brought grouchy objections from Tottenhoe who protested, 'The sooner we're rid of her, the surer we'll be of no repetition.' Even Miles Eastin, back at his regular operations assistant's desk, had raised his eyebrows, but Edwina overruled them both.

She wondered why on earth she was worrying so much, when obviously the time had come to end the incident and put it out of mind.

Obviously out of mind. The *obvious* solution. Again Lewis's phrase occurred to her – *mistrust the obvious.*

But how ? In what way ?

Edwina told herself: think just once more. Go back to the beginning.

What were the *obvious* facts of the incident as they occurred ? The first obvious thing was that money was missing. *No room for dispute there.* The second obvious thing was that the amount was six thousand dollars. That had been agreed by four people: Juanita Núñez herself, Tottenhoe, Miles Eastin, and, eventually, the vault teller. *No argument.*

The third obvious feature concerned the Núñez girl's assertion that she knew the exact amount of money missing from her cash drawer at 1.50pm, after almost five hours of busy transactions at the counter, and *before* she had balanced out her cash. All others in the branch who knew about the loss, including Edwina, agreed that was obviously impossible; from the start, the knowledge had been a cornerstone of their joint belief that Juanita Núñez was a thief.

Knowledge . . . *obvious* knowledge . . . *obviously* impossible.

And yet was it impossible . . . ? An idea occurred to Edwina.

A wall clock showed 2.10pm. She noted that the operations officer was at his desk nearby. Edwina got up. 'Mr Tottenhoe, will you come with me, please?'

With Tottenhoe glumly trailing, she crossed the floor, briefly greeting several customers en route. The branch was crowded and busy, as usual in the closing hours of business before a weekend. Juanita Núñez was accepting a deposit.

Edwina said quietly, 'Mrs Núñez, when you've dealt with this customer, please put up your "position closed" sign and lock your cash box.'

Juanita Núñez made no response, nor did she speak when she had completed the transaction, or while transferring a small metal plaque to the counter as instructed. When she turned to close the cash box, Edwina saw why. The girl was crying silently, tears coursing down her cheeks.

The reason was not hard to guess. She had expected to be fired today and Edwina's sudden appearance confirmed that belief.

Edwina ignored the tears. 'Mr Tottenhoe,' she said, 'I believe Mrs Núñez has been working on cash since we opened this morning. Is that correct?'

He acknowledged, 'Yes.'

The time period was roughly the same as on Wednesday, Edwina thought, though the branch had been busier today.

She pointed to the cash box. 'Mrs Núñez, you've been insisting that you always know the amount of cash you have. Do you know how much is in there now?'

The young woman hesitated. Then she nodded, still unable to speak through tears.

Edwina took a slip of paper from the counter and held it out. 'Write down the amount.'

Again, visible hesitation. Then Juanita Núñez took a pencil and scribbled $23,765.

Edwina passed the slip to Tottenhoe. 'Please go with Mrs Núñez and stay with her while she balances out today's cash. Check the result. Compare it with this figure.'

Tottenhoe looked at the paper sceptically. 'I'm busy, and if I stayed with every teller . . .'

'Stay with this one,' Edwina said. Recrossing the bank floor, she returned to her desk.

Three-quarters of an hour later Tottenhoe reappeared.

He looked nervous. Edwina saw his hand was shaking. He had the slip of paper and put it on her desk. The figure which Juanita Núñez had written had a single pencilled tick beside it.

'If I hadn't seen it myself,' the operations officer said, 'I might not have believed.' For once his gloom was gone, surprise replacing it.

'The figure was right?'

'*Exactly* right.'

Edwina sat tensely, marshalling her thoughts. Abruptly and dramatically, she knew, almost everything concerning the investigation had changed. Until this moment, all assumptions had been based upon the Núñez girl's inability to do what she had now demonstrated conclusively that she could.

'I remembered something while I was walking over just now,' Tottenhoe said. 'I did know somebody once; it was in a little country branch upstate – must be twenty years or more ago – who had that knack of keeping track of cash. And I remember, then, hearing there are other people like that. It's as if they had a calculating machine right inside their heads.'

Edwina snapped, 'I wish your memory had been working better on Wednesday.'

As Tottenhoe returned to his own desk, she drew a notepad towards her and scribbled summations of her thoughts.

Núñez not yet cleared, but more believable. Possibly innocent victim ?

If not Núñez, who ?

96

Someone who knows procedures, could somehow watch for opportunity.

Staff? Inside job?

But how?

'How' later. Find motive first, then person.

Motive? Someone who needs money badly?

She repeated in capitals, NEEDS MONEY. And added: *Examine personal checking/savings accounts, all branch personnel* – TONIGHT!

Edwina began leafing quickly through an FMA Headquarters phone book, looking for 'Chief of Audit Service'.

thirteen

On Friday afternoons all branches of First Mercantile American Bank stayed open an extra three hours.

Thus, at the main downtown branch this Friday, the outer street doors were closed and locked by a security guard at 6pm. A few customers, still in the bank at closing time, were let out by the same guard, one by one, through a single plate-glass door.

At 6.05 precisely, a series of sharp, peremptory taps sounded on the outside of the glass door. When the guard turned his head in response, he observed a young male figure dressed in a dark topcoat and business suit, carrying a briefcase. To attract attention inside, the figure had tapped with a fifty-cent piece wrapped in a handkerchief.

As the guard approached, the man with the briefcase held an identity document flat against the glass. The guard inspected it, unlocked the door, and the young man stepped inside.

Then, before the guard could close the door, a proliferation occurred, as unexpected and remarkable as a magician's trick. Where there had been one individual with briefcase and proffered credentials, suddenly there were six, behind them six more, with still another phalanx at the rear. Swiftly, like an inundation, they streamed into the bank.

A man, older than most of the others and emanating authority, announced curtly, 'Headquarters Audit Staff'.

'Yes sir,' the security guard said; he was a veteran at the bank who had been through this before, and he continued checking the other credential-holders in. There were twenty, mostly men, four women. All went immediately to various locations in the bank.

The older man who had made the announcement headed for the platform and Edwina's desk. As she rose to greet him, she regarded the continuing influx into the bank with unconcealed surprise.

'Mr Burnside, is this a full-dress audit ?'

'It certainly is, Mrs D'Orsey.' The audit department head removed his overcoat and hung it near the platform.

Elsewhere in the bank other staff members wore disconcerted expressions, while some groaned and voiced aggrieved comments. 'Oh, jeez! A Friday, of all times to pick!' . . . 'Dammit, I had a dinner date!' . . . 'Who says auditors are human ?'

Most were aware of what the visit by a headquarters audit group entailed. Tellers knew there would be an extra counting of their cash before they left tonight, and vault reserve cash would be checked out too. Accountants would be required to stay until their records were listed and balanced. Senior management staff would be lucky to be away by midnight.

The newcomers had already, quickly and politely, taken over all ledgers. From this moment any additions or changes would be under scrutiny.

Edwina said, 'When I asked for an examination of staff accounts I didn't expect *this*.' Normally a branch bank audit took place every eighteen months to two years and tonight's was doubly unexpected since a full audit of the main downtown branch had occurred only eight months earlier.

'*We* decide the how, where, and when of audit, Mrs D'Orsey.' As always, Hal Burnside maintained a cool aloofness, the hallmark of a bank examiner. Within any major bank an audit department was an independent, watchdog unit with authority and prerogatives like the Inspectorate General of an army. Its members were never intimidated by rank, and even senior managers were candidates for reproof about irregularities which a thoroughgoing inspection of a branch revealed – and there were invariably some.

'I know about that,' Edwina acknowledged. 'I'm just surprised you could arrange all this so quickly.'

The audit chief smiled, a trifle smugly. 'We have our methods and resources.'

What he did not reveal was that a surprise audit of another FMA branch had been planned for this evening. Following Edwina's phone call three hours ago, the earlier plan was cancelled, arrangements hastily revised, and additional staff called in for the present expedition.

Such cloak-and-dagger tactics were not unusual. An essential part of the audit function was to descend, irregularly and without warning, on any of the bank's branches. Elaborate precautions were taken to preserve secrecy and any audit staff member who violated it was in serious trouble. Few did, even inadvertently.

For today's manoeuvre, the score of auditors involved had assembled an hour ago in a salon of a downtown hotel, though even that destination had not been revealed until the latest possible moment. There they were briefed, duties allocated; then inconspicuously, in twos and threes, they had walked towards the main downtown branch of FMA. Until the last few crucial minutes they loitered in lobbies of nearby buildings, strolled casually, or browsed shop windows. Then, traditionally, the most junior member of the group had rapped on the bank door to demand admission. As soon as it was gained, the others, like an assembling regiment, fell in behind him.

Now, within the bank, audit team members were at every key position.

A convicted bank embezzler of the 1970s, who successfully concealed his massive defalcations for some twenty years, observed while eventually en route to prison, 'The auditors used to come in and do nothing but shoot the breeze for forty minutes. Give me half of that time and I can cover up anything.'

The audit department of First Mercantile American, and other large North American banks, took no such chance. Not even five minutes passed after the surprise of the auditors' arrival until they were all in pre-assigned positions, observing everything.

Resigned, regular staff members of the branch went on to complete their day's work, then to assist the auditors as needed.

Once started, the process would continue through the following week and part of the next. But the most critical portion of the examination would take place within the next few hours.

'Let's you and me get to work, Mrs D'Orsey,' Burnside said. 'We'll start with the deposit accounts, both time and demand.' He opened his briefcase on Edwina's desk.

By 8pm the initial surprise attending the audit team's arrival had worn off, a notable amount of work had been accomplished, and ranks of the regular branch staff were thinning. All tellers had left; so had some of the accountants. Cash had been counted, inspection of other records was well advanced. The visitors had been courteous and, in some cases, helpful in pointing out mild errors, all of which was part of their job.

Among the senior management staff still remaining were Edwina, Tottenhoe, and Miles Eastin. The two men had been kept busy locating information and responding to queries. Now, however, Tottenhoe appeared tired. But young Eastin, who had responded helpfully and cheerfully to every demand so far, was as fresh and energetic as when the evening had begun. It was Miles Eastin who arranged for sandwiches and coffee to be sent in for auditors and staff.

Of the several audit task forces, a small group was concentrating on savings and checking (current) accounts and, from time to time, one among their number would bring a written note to the Chief of Audit Service at Edwina's desk. In every case he glanced over the information, nodded, and added the note to other papers in his briefcase.

At ten minutes to nine he received what appeared to be a lengthier note with several other papers clipped to it. This Burnside studied carefully, then announced, 'I think Mrs D'Orsey and I will take a break. We'll go out for our coffee and supper.'

A few minutes later he escorted Edwina through the same street door by which the auditors had entered nearly three hours earlier.

Outside the building the audit chief apologized. 'I'm sorry, but that was a small theatrical performance. I'm afraid our supper, if any, will have to wait.' As Edwina looked puzzled he added, 'You and I are on our way to a meeting, but I didn't want it known.'

With Burnside leading, they turned right, walking half a block from the still brightly lighted bank, then used a pedestrian-only street to double back to Rosselli Plaza and the FMA Headquarters Tower. The night was cold and Edwina pulled her coat tightly around her, reflecting that the tunnel route would have been both shorter and warmer. Why all the mystery ?

Inside the bank headquarters building, Hal Burnside signed a night visitors book, after which a guard accompanied them in a lift to the eleventh floor. A sign and arrow indicated SECURITY DEPARTMENT. Nolan Wainwright and the two FBI men who had dealt with the cash loss were waiting for them there.

Almost at once they were joined by another member of the audit team who clearly had followed Edwina and Burnside from the bank.

Introductions were accomplished quickly. The latest arrival was a youngish man named Gayne, with cool alert eyes behind heavy-rimmed glasses which made him look severe. It was Gayne who had delivered the several notes and documents to Burnside while the latter worked at Edwina's desk.

Now, at Nolan Wainwright's suggestion, they moved into a conference room and seated themselves around a circular table.

Hal Burnside told the FBI agents, 'I hope what we've discovered will justify calling you gentlemen out at this time of night.'

This meeting, Edwina realized, must have been planned several hours ago. She asked, 'Then you *have* discovered something ?'

'Unfortunately, a good deal more than anyone expected, Mrs D'Orsey.'

At a nod from Burnside, the audit assistant, Gayne, began to spread out papers.

'As the result of your suggestion,' Burnside stated in a lecturer's tone, 'an examination has been made of personal bank accounts – savings and checking – of all personnel employed at the main downtown branch. What we were seeking was some evidence of individual financial difficulty. Fairly conclusively, we found it.'

He sounds like a pompous schoolmaster, Edwina thought. But she continued listening intently.

'I should perhaps explain,' the audit chief told the two FBI men, 'that most bank employees maintain their personal accounts at the branch where they work. One reason is that the accounts are 'free' – that is, without service charges. Another reason – the more important – is that employees receive a special low interest rate on loans, usually one per cent below prime rate.'

Innes, the senior FBI agent, nodded. 'Yes, we knew that.'

'You'll also realize, then, that an employee who has taken advantage of his or her special bank credit – has borrowed to the limit, in fact – and then borrows other sums from an outside source such as a finance company, where interest rates are notoriously high, has placed himself or herself in a tenuous financial position.'

Innes, with a trace of impatience, said, 'Of course.'

'It appears we have a bank employee to whom exactly that has happened.' He motioned to the assistant, Gayne, who turned over several cancelled cheques which until now had been face down.

'As you'll observe, these cheques are made out to three separate finance companies. Incidentally, we've already been in touch by telephone with two of the companies, and notwithstanding the payments that you see, both accounts are seriously delinquent. It's a reasonable guess that, in the morning, the third company will tell us the same story.'

Gayne interjected, 'And these cheques are for the current month only. Tomorrow we'll look at microfilm records for several months back.'

'One other fact is relevant,' the audit chief proceeded. 'The individual concerned could not possibly have made these payments' – he gestured towards the cancelled cheques – 'on the basis of a bank salary, the amount of which we know. Therefore during the past several hours we have searched for evidence of theft from the bank, and this has now been found.'

Once again the assistant, Gayne, began placing papers on the conference table.

... evidence of theft from the bank ... this has now been found. Edwina, scarcely listening any more, had her eyes riveted on the signature on each of the cancelled cheques – a signature she saw each day, familiar to her, bold and clear. The sight of it, here and now, appalled and saddened her.

The signature was Eastin's – young Miles whom she liked so well, who was so efficient as assistant operations officer, so helpful and tireless, even tonight, and whom only this week she had decided to promote when Tottenhoe retired.

The Chief of Audit Service had now moved on. 'What our sneak thief has been doing is milking dormant accounts. Once we detected a single fraudulent pattern earlier this evening, others were not hard to find.'

Still in his lecturer's manner, and for the benefit of the FBI men, he defined a dormant account. It was an account – savings or checking, Burnside explained – which had little or no activity. All banks had customers who for varied reasons left such accounts untouched over long periods, sometimes for many years, and with surprisingly large sums remaining in them. Modest interest did accumulate in savings accounts, of course, and some people undoubtedly had that in mind, though others – incredible but true – abandoned their accounts entirely.

When a checking account was observed to be inactive, with no deposits or withdrawals, banks ceased mailing monthly statements and substituted an annual one. Even those, at times, were returned marked: 'Moved – address unknown.'

Standard precautions were taken to prevent fraudulent use of dormant accounts, the audit chief continued. The account records were segregated; then, if a transaction suddenly occurred it was scrutinized by an operations officer to make sure it was

legitimate. Normally such precautions were effective. As assist-
ant operations officer, Miles Eastin had authority to scrutinize and
approve dormant account transactions. He had used the authority
to cover up his own dishonesty – the fact that he had been stealing
from such accounts himself.

'Eastin has been rather clever, selecting those accounts least likely to cause trouble. We have here a series of forged with-drawal slips, though not forged very skilfully because there are obvious traces of his handwriting, after which the amounts have been transferred into what appears to be a dummy account of his own under an assumed name. There's an obvious similarity of handwriting there also, though naturally experts will be need-ed to give evidence.'

One by one they examined the withdrawal slips, comparing the handwriting with the cheques they had looked at earlier. Al-though an attempt had been made at disguise, a resemblance was unmistakable.

The second FBI agent, Dalrymple, had been writing careful notes. Looking up, he asked, 'Is there a total figure on the money involved?'

Gayne answered, 'So far we've pinpointed close to eight thou-sand dollars. Tomorrow, though, we'll have access to older records through microfilm and the computer, which may show more.'

Burnside added, 'When we confront Eastin with what we know already, it could be he'll decide to make things easier by admitting the rest. That's sometimes a pattern when we catch embezzlers.'

He's enjoying this, Edwina thought; really enjoying it. She felt irrationally defensive about Miles Eastin, then asked, 'Have you any idea how long this has been going on?'

'From what's been uncovered so far,' Gayne informed them, 'it looks like at least a year, possibly longer.'

Edwina turned to face Hal Burnside. 'So you missed it com-pletely at the last audit. Isn't an inspection of dormant accounts part of your job?'

It was like pricking a bubble. The audit chief flushed crimson as he admitted, 'Yes, it is. But even we miss things occasionally when a thief has covered his tracks well.'

'Obviously. Though you did say a moment ago the hand-writing was a give-away.'

Burnside said sourly, 'Well, we've caught it now.'

She reminded him, 'After I called you in.'

The FBI agent Innes broke the ensuing silence. 'None of this puts us any further ahead so far as Wednesday's missing cash goes.'

'Except it makes Eastin the prime suspect,' Burnside said. He seemed relieved to redirect the conversation. 'And he may admit that, too.'

'He won't,' Nolan Wainwright growled. 'That cat is too damn smart. Besides, why should h ? We still don't know how he did it.'

Until now the bank security head had said little, though he had shown surprise, then his face had hardened as the auditors produced their succession of documents and the evidence of guilt. Edwina wondered if Wainwright was remembering how both of them had put pressure on the teller, Juanita Núñez, disbelieving the girl's protested innocence. Even now, Edwina supposed, there was a possibility the Núñez girl had been in league with Eastin, but it seemed unlikely.

Hal Burnside stood up to go, refastening his briefcase. 'Here's where Audit leaves off and the law takes over.'

'We'll require these papers and a signed statement,' Innes said.

'Mr Gayne will stay, and be at your disposal.'

'One more question. Do you think that Eastin has any idea he's been found out ?'

'I doubt it.' Burnside glanced towards his assistant who shook his head.

'I'm certain he doesn't. We were careful not to show what we were looking for and, to cover up, we asked for many things we didn't need.'

'I don't think so either,' Edwina said. She remembered sadly how busy and cheerful Miles Eastin had been immediately before she had left the branch with Burnside. *Why had he done it ? why, oh why ?*

Innes nodded his approval. 'Then let's keep it that way. We'll pick Eastin up for questioning as soon as we've finished here but he mustn't be warned. He's still at the bank ?'

'Yes,' Edwina said. 'He'll stay at least until we get back, and normally he'd be among the last to leave.'

Nolan Wainwright cut in, his voice unusually harsh, '*Amend* those instructions. Keep him there as late as possible. After that, let him go home thinking he hasn't been found out.'

The others glanced at the bank security chief, puzzled and startled. In particular the eyes of the two FBI men searched Wainwright's face. A message seemed to pass between them.

Innes hesitated, then conceded, 'All right. Do it that way.'

A few minutes later, Edwina and Burnside took the lift down.

Innes said politely to the remaining auditor, 'Before we take your statement, I wonder if you'd leave us alone a moment.'

'Certainly.' Gayne left the conference room.

The second FBI agent closed his notebook and put down his pencil.

Innes faced Nolan Wainwright. 'You've something in mind ?'

'I have.' Wainwright hesitated, wrestling mentally with choices and his conscience. Experience told him that the evidence against Eastin had gaps which needed to be filled. Yet to fill them the law would have to be bent in a way running counter to his own beliefs. He asked the FBI man, 'Are you sure you want to know ?'

The two eyed each other. They had known each other for years and shared a mutual respect.

'Getting evidence nowadays is sensitive,' Innes said. 'We can't take some of the liberties we used to, and if we do it's liable to bounce back.'

There was a silence, then the second FBI agent said, 'Tell us as much as you think you should.'

Wainwright interlaced his fingers and considered them. His body transmitted tension, as his voice had earlier. 'Okay, we've enough to nail Eastin on a larceny rap. Let's say the amount stolen is eight thousand dollars, more or less. What do you think a judge will give him ?'

'For a first offence he'll draw a suspended sentence,' Innes said. 'The court won't worry about the money involved. They'll figure banks have lots and it's insured anyway.'

'Check!' Wainwright's fingers tightened visibly. 'But if we can prove he took that other cash – the six thousand last Wednesday; if we can show he aimed to throw the blame on the girl, and damn near did . . .'

Innes grunted understanding. '*If* you could show that, any reasonable judge would send him straight to jail. But can you ?'

'I intend to. Because I personally want that son of a bitch behind bars.'

'I know what you mean,' the FBI man said thoughtfully. 'I'd like to see it happen too.'

'In that case do it my way. Don't pick up Eastin tonight. Give me until morning.'

'I'm not sure,' Innes mused. 'I'm not sure I can.'

The three of them waited, conscious of knowledge, duty, and a pull and tug within themselves. The other two guessed roughly what Wainwright had in mind. But when, and to what extent, did an end justify the means ? Equally to the point: how much liberty nowadays could a law-enforcement officer take and get away with ?

Yet the FBI men had become involved in the case and shared Wainwright's view about objectives.

'If we do wait till morning,' the second agent cautioned, 'we don't want Eastin to run. That could cause everybody trouble.'

'And I don't want a bruised potato either,' Innes said.

'He won't run. He won't be bruised. I guarantee it.'

Innes glanced towards his colleague who shrugged.

'Okay then,' Innes said. 'Until morning. But understand one thing, Nolan – this conversation never took place.' He crossed to the conference room door and opened it. 'You can come in, Mr Gayne. Mr Wainwright's leaving and we'll take your statement now.'

fourteen

A list of branch bank officers, maintained in the security department for emergency use, revealed Miles Eastin's home address and telephone number. Nolan Wainwright copied down both.

He recognized the address. A medium income residential area about two miles from downtown. It included the information 'Apartment 2G'.

Leaving FMA Headquarters Building, the security chief used a call box on Rosselli Plaza to dial the telephone number and heard the ringing continue unanswered. He already knew Miles Eastin was a bachelor. Wainwright was hoping he also lived alone.

If the phone had been answered, Wainwright would have made an excuse about a wrong number and revised his plans. As it was, he now headed for his car, parked in the headquarters basement garage.

Before leaving the garage he opened the boot of the car and removed a slim chamois case, placing it in an inside pocket. He then drove across town.

He walked towards the apartment building casually but taking in details. A three-storey structure, probably forty years old and showing signs of disrepair. He guessed it contained two dozen or so apartments. No doorman was visible. Inside a hall Nolan Wainwright could see an array of letter boxes and buzzers. Double glass doors opened from the street to the hall; beyond them was a more solid door, undoubtedly locked.

The time was 10.30. Traffic on the street was light. No other pedestrians were near the apartment house. He went in.

Next to the letter boxes were the three rows of buzzers and a speaker-phone. Wainwright saw the name EASTIN and depressed the button beside it. As he expected, there was no response.

Guessing that 2G indicated the second floor, he chose a buzzer at random with the prefix 3 and pressed it. A man's voice on the speaker-phone rasped, 'Yeah, who is it?'

The name beside the button was Appleby.

'Western Union,' Wainwright said. 'Telegram for Appleby.'

'Okay, bring it up.'

Behind the heavy interior door a buzzer sounded and a lock clicked open. Wainwright opened the door and went in quickly.

Immediately ahead was a lift which he ignored. He saw a stairway to the right and went up it, two stairs at a time, to the second floor.

On his way, Wainwright reflected on the astounding innocence of people generally. He hoped that Appleby, whoever he was, would not wait too long for his telegram. This night Mr Appleby would suffer no harm beyond minor puzzlement, perhaps frustration, though he might have fared far worse. Yet apartment tenants everywhere, despite repeated warnings, continued to do exactly the same. Of course, Appleby might grow suspicious and alert the police, though Wainwright doubted it. In any case, a few minutes from now it would make no difference.

Apartment 2G was near the end of the second-floor corridor and the lock proved uncomplicated. Wainwright tried a succession of slim blades from the chamois case he had pocketed, and on the forth attempt the lock cylinder turned. The door swung open and he went in, closing the door behind him.

He waited, letting his eyes adjust to the darkness, then crossed to a window and drew the curtains. He found a light switch and turned it on.

The apartment was small, designed for use by one person; it was a single room divided into areas. A living-dining space contained a sofa, armchair, portable TV, and a small table. A bed was located behind a partition: the kitchenette had folding louvered doors. Two other doors which Wainwright checked revealed a bathroom and a storage cupboard. The place was orderly and clean. Several shelves of books and a few framed prints added a touch of personality.

Without wasting time, Wainwright began a systematic, thorough search.

He tried to suppress, as he worked, gnawing self-criticism for the illegal acts he was committing tonight. He did not wholly succeed. Nolan Wainwright was aware that everything he had done so far represented a reversal of his moral standards, a negation of his belief in law and order. Yet anger drove him. Anger and the knowledge of failure, four days ago, within himself.

He remembered with excruciating clarity, even now, the mute appeal in the eyes of the young Puerto Rican girl, Juanita Núñez, when he encountered her for the first time last Wednesday and began the interrogation. It was an appeal which said unmistakably: *You and I . . . you are black, I am brown. Therefore you, of all people, should realize I am alone here, at a disadvantage, and desperately need help and fairness.* But while recognizing the appeal, he had brushed it aside harshly, so that afterwards contempt replaced it, and he remembered that in the girl's eyes too.

This memory, coupled with chagrin at having been duped by Miles Eastin, made Wainwright determined to beat Eastin at his game, no matter if the law was bent in doing it.

Therefore, methodically, as his police training had taught him, Wainwright went on searching, determined that if evidence existed he would find it.

Half an hour later he knew that few places remained where anything could be hidden. He had examined cupboards, drawers and contents, had probed furniture, opened suitcases, inspected pictures on the walls, and removed the back of the TV. He also riffled through books, noting that an entire shelf was devoted to what someone had told him was Eastin's hobby – the study of money through the ages. Along with the books, a portfolio contained sketches and photographs of ancient coins and banknotes. But of anything incriminating there was no trace. Finally he piled furniture in one corner and rolled up the living area rug. Then, with a flashlight, he went over every inch of floorboard.

Without the flashlight's aid he would have missed the carefully sawn board, but two lines, lighter coloured than the wood elsewhere, betrayed where cuts had been made. He gently pried up the foot or so of board between the lines and in the space between were a small black ledger and cash in twenty-dollar notes.

Working quickly, he replaced the board, the rug, the furniture.

He counted the cash; it totalled six thousand dollars. Then he studied the small black ledger briefly, realized it was a betting record and he whistled softly at the size and number of amounts involved.

He put the book down – it could be examined in detail later – on an occasional table in front of the sofa, with the money beside it.

Finding the money surprised him. He had no doubt it was the six thousand dollars missing from the bank on Wednesday, but he would have expected Eastin to have exchanged it by now, or have deposited it elsewhere. Police work had taught him that criminals did foolish, unexpected things, and this was one.

What still had to be learned was how Eastin had taken the money and brought it here.

Wainwright glanced around the apartment, after which he turned out the lights. He reopened the curtains and, settling comfortably on the sofa, waited.

In the semi-darkness, with the small apartment lighted by reflections from the street outside, his thoughts drifted. He thought again of Juanita Núñez and wished somehow he could make amends. Then he remembered the FBI report about her missing husband, Carlos, who had been traced to Phoenix, Arizona, and it occurred to Wainwright that this information might be used to help the girl.

Of course, Miles Eastin's story about having seen Carlos Núñez in the bank the same day as the cash loss was a fabrication intended to throw even more suspicion on Juanita.

That despicable *bastard*! What kind of man was he, first to direct blame towards the girl, and later to add to it ? The security chief felt his fists tighten, then warned himself not to allow his feelings to become too strong.

The warning was necessary, and he knew why. It was because of an incident long buried in his mind and which he seldom disinterred. Without really wanting to, he began remembering it.

Nolan Wainwright, now nearly fifty, had been spawned in the city's slums and, from birth, had found life's odds stacked against him. He grew up with survival as a daily challenge and with crime – petty and otherwise – a surrounding norm. In his teens he had run with a ghetto gang to whom brushes with the law were proof of manhood.

Like others, before and since, from the same slum background, he was driven by an urge to be somebody, to be noticed in whatever way, to release an inner rage against obscurity. He had no experience or philosophy to weigh alternatives, so participation in street crime appeared the only, the inevitable route. It seemed likely he would graduate, as many of his contemporaries did, to a police and prison record.

That he did not was due, in part, to chance; in part, to Bufflehead Kelly.

Bufflehead was a not-too-bright, lazy, amiable elderly neighbourhood cop who had learned that a policeman's survival in the ghetto could be lengthened by adroitly being somewhere else when trouble erupted, and by taking action only when a problem loomed directly under his nose. Superiors complained that his arrest record was the worst in the precinct, but against this – in Bufflehead's view – his retirement and pension moved satisfyingly closer every year.

But the teenage Nolan Wainwright *had* loomed under Bufflehead's nose the night of an attempted gang-bust into a warehouse which the beat cop unwittingly disturbed, so everyone had run, escaping, except Wainwright who tripped and fell at Bufflehead's feet.

'Y' stupid, clumsy monkey,' Bufflehead complained. 'Now it's all kinds of paper and court work you'll be causin' me this night.'

Kelly detested paperwork and court appearances which cut annoyingly into a policeman's off-duty time.

In the end he compromised. Instead of arresting and charging Wainwright he took him, the same night, to the police gym and, in Bufflehead's own words, 'beat the b'jesus out of him' in a boxing ring.

Nolan Wainwright, bruised, sore, and with one eye badly swollen – though still with no arrest record – reacted with hatred. As soon as possible he would smash Bufflehead Kelly to a pulp, an objective which brought him back to the police gym – and Bufflehead – for lessons in how to do it. It was, Wainwright realized long afterwards, the needed outlet for his rage. He learned quickly. When the time arrived to reduce the slightly stupid, lazy cop to a punished punching bag, he found the desire to do so had evaporated. Instead he had become fond of the old man, an emotion surprising to the youth himself.

A year went by during which Wainwright continued boxing, stayed in school, and managed to keep out of trouble. Then one night Bufflehead, while on duty, accidentally interrupted a hold-up of a grocery store. Undoubtedly the cop was more startled than the two small-time hoodlums involved and would certainly not have impeded them since both were armed. As investigation afterwards brought out, Bufflehead did not even try to draw his gun.

But one robber panicked and, before running, fired a sawed-off shot gun into Bufflehead's gut.

News of the shooting spread quickly and a crowd gathered. It included young Nolan Wainwright.

He would always remember – as he did now – the sight and sound of harmless, lazy Bufflehead, conscious, writhing, wailing, screaming in demented agony as blood and entrails gushed from his capacious, mortal wound.

An ambulance was a long time coming. Moments before it arrived, Bufflehead, still screaming, died.

The incident left its mark for ever on Nolan Wainwright, though it was not Bufflehead's death itself which affected him most. Nor did the arrest and later execution of the thief who fired the shot, and his companion, seem more than anticlimactic.

What shocked and influenced him above all else was the appalling, senseless waste. The original crime was mean, foolish, foredoomed to failure; yet, in failing, its devastation was outrageously immense. Within young Wainwright's mind that single thought, that reasoning, persisted. It proved a catharsis through which he came to see all crime as equally negative, equally destructive – and, later still, as an evil to be fought. Perhaps, from the beginning, a streak of puritanism had been latent, deep inside him. If so, it surfaced.

He progressed from youth to manhood as an individual with uncompromising standards and, because of this, became something of a loner, among his friends and eventually when he became a cop. But he was an efficient cop who learned and rose fast, and was incorruptible, as Ben Rosselli and his aides once learned.

And later still, within First Mercantile American Bank, Wainwright's strong feelings stayed with him.

It was possible that the security chief dozed off, but a key inserted in the apartment lock alerted him. Cautiously he sat up. His illuminated watch dial showed it was shortly after midnight.

A shadowy figure came in; a shaft of outside light revealed it as Eastin. Then the door closed and Wainwright heard Eastin fumble for a switch. The light came on.

Eastin saw Wainwright at once and his surprise was total. His mouth dropped open, blood drained from his face. He tried to speak, but gulped, and no words came.

Wainwright stood up, glaring. His voice cut like a knife. 'How much did you steal today?'

Before Eastin could answer or recover, Wainwright seized him by the coat lapels, turned him and pushed. He fell sprawling on the sofa.

As surprise turned to indignation, the young man spluttered, 'Who let you in? What the hell do you . . .' His eyes moved to the money and the small black ledger, and he stopped.

'That's right,' Wainwright said harshly, 'I came for the bank's money, or what little is left.' He motioned to the notes stacked on the table. 'We know what's there is what you took on Wednesday. And in case you're wondering, we know about the milked accounts and all the rest.'

Miles Eastin stared, his expression frozen, stupefied. A convulsive shudder went through him. In fresh shock his head came down, his hands went to his face.

'Cut that out!' Wainwright reached over, pulled Eastin's hands free and pushed his head up, though not roughly, remembering his promise to the FBI man. No bruised potato.

He added, 'You've got some talking to do, so let's start.'

'Hey, time out, huh?' Eastin pleaded. 'Give me a minute to think.'

'Forget it!' The last thing Wainwright wanted was to give Eastin time to reflect. He was a bright young man who might reason, correctly, that his wisest course was silence. The security chief knew that at this moment he had two advantages. One was having Miles Eastin off balance, the other being unrestricted by rules.

If the FBI agents were here they would have to inform Eastin of his legal rights – the right not to answer questions, and to have a lawyer present. Wainwright, not a policeman any more, had no such obligation.

What the security chief wanted was hard evidence pinning the six-thousand-dollar cash theft on Miles Eastin. A signed confession would do it.

He sat down facing Eastin, his eyes impaling the younger man. 'We can do this the long, hard way or we can move fast.'

When there was no response, Wainwright picked up the small black ledger and opened it. 'Let's start with this.' He put his finger on the list of sums and dates; beside each entry were other figures in a code. 'These are bets. Right?'

Through a muddled dullness Eastin nodded.

'Explain this one.'

It was a two-hundred-and-fifty-dollar bet, Miles Eastin mumbled, on the outcome of a football game between Texas and Notre Dame. He explained the odds. The bet had been on Notre Dame. Texas had won.

'And this?'

Another mumbled answer: Another football game. Another loss.

'Go on.' Wainwright persisted, keeping his finger on the page, maintaining pressure.

Responses came slowly. Some of the entries covered basketball games. A few bets were on the winning side, though losses outnumbered them. The minimum bet was one hundred dollars, the highest three hundred.

'Did you bet alone or with a group?'

'A group.'

'Who was in it?'

'Four other guys. Working. Like me.'

'Working at the bank?'

Eastin shook his head. 'Other places.'

'Did they lose, too?'

'Some. But their batting average was better than mine.'

'What are the names of the other four?'

No answer. Wainwright let it go.

'You made no bets on horses. Why?'

'We got together. Everybody knows horse racing is crooked, races fixed. Football and basketball are on the level. We worked out a system. With honest games, we figured we could beat the odds.'

The total of losses showed how wrong that figuring had been.

'Did you bet with one bookie, or more?'

'One.'

'His name?'

Eastin stayed mute.

'The rest of the money you've been stealing from the bank – where is it?'

The young man's mouth turned down. He answered miserably, 'Gone.'

'And more besides?'

An affirmative, dismal nod.

'We'll get to that later. Right now let's talk about *this* money.' Wainwright touched the six thousand dollars which lay between them. 'We know you took it on Wednesday. How?'

Eastin hesitated, then shrugged. 'I guess you may as well know.'

Wainwright said sharply, 'You're guessing right but wasting time.'

'Last Wednesday,' Eastin said, 'we had people away with flu. That day I filled in as a teller.'

'I know that. Get to what happened.'

'Before the bank opened for business I went to the vault to get a cash truck – one of the spares. Juanita Núñez was there. She unlocked her regular cash truck. I was right alongside. Without Juanita knowing, I watched to see her combination.'

'And?'

'I memorized it. As soon as I could, I wrote it down.'

With Wainwright prompting, the damning facts multiplied.

The main downtown branch vault was large. During the day a vault teller worked in a cage-like enclosure just inside, near the heavy, time-lock controlled door. The vault teller was invariably busy, counting currency, handing out packages of bills or receiving them, checking tellers and cash trucks in or out. While no one could pass the vault teller without being seen, once they were inside he took little notice of them.

That morning, while outwardly cheerful, Miles Eastin was desperate for cash. There had been betting losses the week before and he was being pressed for payment of accumulated debts.

Wainwright interrupted. 'You already had an employee bank loan. You owed finance companies. Also the bookie. Right ?'

'Right.'

'Did you owe anyone else ?'

Eastin nodded affirmatively.

'A loan shark ?'

The younger man hesitated, then admitted, 'Yes.'

'Was the loan shark threatening you ?'

Miles Eastin moistened his lips. 'Yes; so was the bookie. They both are, still.' His eyes went to the six thousand dollars.

The jigsaw was fitting together. Wainwright motioned to the money. 'You promised to pay the shark and the bookie that ?'

'Yes.'

'How much to each ?'

'Three thousand.'

'When ?'

'Tomorrow.' Eastin looked nervously at a wall clock and corrected himself. 'Today.'

Wainwright prompted, 'Go back to Wednesday. So you knew the combination of the Núñez girl's cash box. How did you use it ?'

As Miles Eastin revealed the details now, it was all incredibly simple. After working through the morning, he took his lunch break at the same time as Juanita Núñez. Before going to lunch they wheeled their cash trucks into the vault. The two cash units were left side by side, both locked.

Eastin returned from lunch early and went into the vault. The vault teller checked Eastin in, then went on working. No one else was in the vault.

Miles Eastin went directly to Juanita Núñez's cash truck and opened it, using the combination he had written down. It took seconds only to remove three packages of bills totalling six thousand dollars, then close and relock the box. He slipped the currency packages into inside pockets; the bulges scarcely showed. He then checked out his own cash truck from the vault and returned to work.

There was a silence, then Wainwright said, 'So while questioning was going on Wednesday afternoon – some of it by you, and while you and I were talking later that same day – all that time you had the money on you?'

'Yes,' Miles Eastin said. As he remembered how easy it had been, a faint smile creased his face.

Wainwright saw the smile. Without hesitating, and in a single movement, he leaned forward and hit Eastin hard on both sides of the face. He used his open palm for the first blow, the back of his hand for the second. The double blow was so forceful that Wainwright's hand stung. Miles Eastin's face showed two bright weals. He shrunk backwards on the sofa and blinked as tears formed in his eyes.

The security chief said grimly, 'That's to let you know I see nothing funny in what you did to the bank or to Mrs Núñez. Nothing at all.' Something else he had just learned was that Miles Eastin was afraid of physical violence.

He observed that it was 1am.

'The next order of business,' Nolan Wainwright announced, 'is a written statement. In your own handwritting and with everything in it that you've told me.'

'No! I won't do that!' Eastin was wary now.

Wainwright shrugged. 'In that case there's no point in my staying longer.' He reached for the six thousand dollars and began stowing it in his pockets.

'You can't do that!'

'Can't I? Try stopping me. I'm taking it back to the bank – the night depository.'

'Listen! – you can't prove . . .' The younger man hesitated. He was thinking now, remembering too late that the serial numbers of the bills had never been recorded.

'Maybe I can prove it's the same money that was taken Wednesday; maybe not. If not, you can always try suing the bank to get it back.'

Eastin pleaded, 'I need it now! Today!'

'Oh, sure, some for the bookie and some for the loan shark. Or the strong-arm guys they'll send. Well, you can try explaining how you lost it, though I doubt if they'll listen.' The security chief eyed Eastin for the first time with sardonic amusement. 'You really *are* in trouble. Maybe they'll both come together, then they'll break one of your arms and one leg each. They're apt to do that sort of thing. Or didn't you know?'

Fear, real fear, showed in Eastin's eyes. 'Yes, I do know. You've got to help me! Please!'

From the apartment doorway Wainwright said coldly, 'I'll consider it. *After* you've written that statement.'

The bank security chief dictated while Eastin wrote the words down obediently.

I, Miles Broderick Eastin, make this statement voluntarily. I have been offered no inducement to make it. No violence or threat of violence has been used . . .

I confess to stealing from First Mercantile American Bank the sum of six thousand dollars in cash at approximately 1.30pm on Wednesday, October . . .

I obtained and concealed this money by the following means . . .

A quarter of an hour ago, after Wainwright's threat to walk out, Miles Eastin had collapsed entirely, cooperative and cowed.

Now, while Eastin continued writing his confession, Wainwright telephoned Innes, the FBI man, at his home.

fifteen

During the first week of November, Ben Rosselli's physical condition worsened. Since the bank president's disclosure of his terminal illness four weeks earlier, his strength had ebbed, his body wasted as proliferating and invading cancerous cells tightened their stranglehold on his remaining life.

Those who visited old Ben at home – including Roscoe Heyward, Alex Vandervoort, Edwina D'Orsey, Nolan Wainwright, and various directors of the bank – were shocked at the extent and speed of his deterioration. It was obvious he had very little time to live.

Then, in mid-November, while a savage storm with gale force winds beset the city, Ben Rosselli was moved by ambulance to the private wing of Mount Adams Hospital, a short journey which was to be his last alive. By then he was under almost continuous sedation, so that his moments of awareness and coherence became fewer day by day.

The last vestiges of any control of First Mercantile American Bank had now slipped from him, and a group of the bank's senior directors, meeting privately, agreed the full board must be summoned, a successor to the presidency named.

The decisive board meeting was set for December 4.

Directors began arriving shortly before 10am. They greeted one another cordially, each with an easy confidence – the patina of a successful businessman in the company of his peers.

The cordiality was slightly more restrained than usual in deference to the dying Ben Rosselli, still clutching feebly to life a mile or so away. Yet the directors now assembling were admirals and field marshals of commerce, as Ben had been himself, who knew that whatever else obtruded, business, which kept civilization lubricated, must go on. Their mood appeared to say: *The reason behind decisions we must make today is regrettable, but our solemn duty to the system shall be done.*

Thus they moved resolutely into the walnut panelled boardroom, hung with paintings and photographs of selected predecessors, once important themselves, now long departed.

A board of directors of any major American corporation resembles an exclusive club. Apart from three or four top management executives who are employed full time, the board comprises a score or so of outstanding businessmen – often board chairmen or presidents themselves – from other, diverse fields.

Usually such outside directors are invited to join the board for one or more of several reasons – their own achievements elsewhere, the prestige of the institution they represent, or a strong connection – usually financial – with the company on whose board they sit.

Among businessmen it is considered a high honour to be a company director, and the more prestigious the company the greater the glory. This is why some individuals collect directorships the way some Indians once collected scalps. Another reason is the directors are treated with ego-satisfying reverence and also generously – major companies pay each director between one and two thousand dollars for every meeting attended, normally ten a year.

Particularly high in prestige is a directorship of any major bank. For an American businessman to be invited to serve on a top-flight bank board is roughly equivalent to being knighted by the Queen; therefore the accolade is widely sought. First Mercantile American, as befitting a bank among the nation's top twenty, possessed a board of directors appropriately impressive.

Or so they thought.

Alex Vandervoort, surveying the other directors as they took seats around the long, elliptical boardroom table, decided there was a high percentage of dead wood. There were also conflicts of interest since some directors, or their companies, were major borrowers of bank money. Among his long-term objectives if he became president would be to make the FMA board more representative and less like a cosy club.

But would he be president? Or would Heyward?

Both of them were candidates today. Both, in a short time, like any seeker after office, would expound their views. Jerome

Patterton, vice-chairman of the board, who would preside at today's meeting, had approached Alex two days earlier. 'You know as well as the rest of us, our decision's between you and Roscoe. You're both good men; making a choice isn't easy. So help us. Tell us your feelings about FMA, in any way you like; the what and how, I leave to you.'

Roscoe Heyward, Alex was aware, had been similarly briefed.

Heyward, typically, had armed himself with a prepared text. Seated directly across from Alex, he was studying it now, his aquiline face set seriously, the grey eyes behind rimless glasses unwaveringly focused on the typewritten words. Among Heyward's abilities was intense concentration of his scalpel-sharp mind, especially on figures. A colleague once observed, 'Roscoe can read a profit and loss statement the way a symphony conductor reads a score – sensing nuances, awkward notes, incomplete passages, crescendos, and potentialities which others miss.' Without doubt, figures would be included in whatever Heyward had to say today.

Alex was unsure whether he would use numbers in his own remarks or not. If he did, they would have to be from memory since he had brought no materials. He had deliberated far into last night and decided eventually to wait until the moment came then speak instinctively, as seemed appropriate, letting thoughts and words fall into place themselves.

He reminded himself that in this same room, so short a time ago, Ben had announced, '*I'm dying. My doctors tell me I don't have long.*' The words had been, still were, an affirmation that all in life was finite. They mocked ambition – his own, Roscoe Heyward's, others'.

Yet whether ambition was futile in the end or not, he wanted very much the presidency of this bank. He longed for an opportunity – just as Ben in his time had had – to determine directions, decide philosophy, allot priorities and, through the sum of all decisions, leave behind a worthwhile contribution. And whether, viewed across a larger span of years, whatever was accomplished mattered much or little, the zest itself would be rewarding – the doing, leading, striving, and competing, here and now.

Across the boardroom table to the right, the Honourable Harold Austin slipped into his accustomed seat. He wore a windowpane check Cerruti suit, with a classic button-down shirt and houndstooth pattern tie, and looked like a pacesetting model from the pages of *Playboy*. He held a fat cigar, ready to be lighted. Alex saw Austin and nodded. The nod was returned, but with noticeable coolness.

A week ago the Honourable Harold had dropped by to protest against Alex's veto of Keycharge credit-card advertising prepared by the Austin agency. 'Keycharge marketing expansion was approved by the board of directors,' the Honourable Harold had objected. 'What's more, the department heads at Keycharge had already okayed that particular ad campaign before it got to you. I'm of two minds whether to bring your high-handed action to the attention of the board or not.'

Alex was blunt, 'To begin with, I know exactly what the directors decided about Keycharge because I was there. What they did *not* agree to was that marketing expansion would include advertising which is sleazy, misleading, half-truthful and discreditable to the bank. Your creative people can do better than that, Harold. In fact, they already have – I've seen and approved the revised versions. As for being high-handed, I made an executive management decision well within my authority, and any time necessary I'll do the same again. So if you choose to bring the subject before the board, you can. If you want my opinion, they won't thank you for it – they're more likely to thank me.'

Harold Austin had glowered, but apparently decided to drop the subject, perhaps wisely, because Austin Advertising was going to do just as well financially with the revised Keycharge campaign. But Alex knew he had created an antagonist. He doubted, though, if it would make any difference today since the Honourable Harold obviously preferred Roscoe Heyward and was likely to support him anyway.

One of his own strong supporters, Alex knew, was Leonard L. Kingswood, outspoken, energetic chairman of Northam Steel, now seated near the head of the table, conversing intently with his neighbour. It was Len Kingswood who had telephoned Alex several weeks ago to advise him that Roscoe Heyward was actively canvassing directors for support as president. 'I'm not saying you should do the same, Alex. That's for you to decide. But I'm warning you that what Roscoe's doing can be effective. He doesn't fool me. He's not a leader and I've told him so. But he has a persuasive way which is a hook that some may swallow.'

Alex had thanked Len Kingswood for the information but made no attempt to copy Heyward's tactics. Solicitation might help in some cases but could antagonize others who objected to personal pressure in such matters. Besides, Alex had an aversion to campaigning actively for Ben's job while the old man remained alive.

But Alex accepted the necessity for today's meeting and decisions to be made here.

A hum of conversation in the boardroom quietened. Two late arrivals who had just come in were settling down. Jerome Patterton, at the table's head, tapped lightly with a gavel and announced, 'Gentlemen, the board will come to order.'

Patterton, projected into prominence today, was normally self-effacing and, in the management echelon of the bank, something of a timeserver. Now in his sixties and near retirement, he had been acquired as part of a merger with another, smaller bank several years ago; since then his responsibilities had quietly, and by mutual agreement, diminished. Currently he concerned himself almost equally with trust department matters and playing golf with clients. The golf took priority, to the extent that on any working day Jerome Patterton was seldom in his office after 2.30pm. His title of vice-chairman of the board was largely honorary.

In appearance he resembled a gentleman farmer. Mostly bald, except for a white, halo-fringe of hair, he had a pointed pink head uncannily like the narrow end of an egg. Paradoxically, his eyebrows were matted and fiercely sprouting; the eyes beneath were grey, bulbous, and becoming rheumy. Adding to the farmer image, he dressed tweedily. Alex Vandervoort's assessment of Patterton was that the vice-chairman had an excellent brain which in recent years he had used minimally, like an idling motor.

Predictably, Jerome Patterton began by paying tribute to Ben Rosselli, after which he read aloud the latest hospital bulletin which reported 'diminishing strength and eroding consciousness'. Among the directors, lips were pursed, heads shaken. 'But the life of our community goes on.' The vice-chairman enumerated reasons for the present meeting, principally the need to name, speedily, a new chief executive for First Mercantile American Bank.

'Most of you gentlemen are aware of procedures which have been agreed on.' He then announced what everyone knew – that Roscoe Heyward and Alex Vandervoort would address the board, after which both would leave the meeting while their candidacies were discussed.

'As to the order of speaking, we'll employ that ancient chance which all of us were born under – alphabetical precedence.' Jerome Patterton's eyes twinkled towards Alex. 'I've paid a penalty sometimes for being a "P". I hope that "V" of yours hasn't been too burdensome.'

'Not often, Mr Chairman,' Alex said. 'On some occasions it gives me the last word.'

A ripple of laughter, the first today, ran around the table. Roscoe Heyward shared in it, though his smile seemed forced.

'Roscoe,' Jerome Patterton instructed, 'at your convenience, please begin.'

'Thank you, Mr Chairman.' Heyward rose to his feet, moved his chair well back and calmly surveyed the nineteen other men around the table. He took a sip of water from a glass in front of him, cleared his throat perfunctorily, and began speaking in a precise and even voice.

'Members of the board, since this is a closed and private meeting, not to be reported in the press or even to other shareholders, I shall be forthright today in emphasizing what I conceive to be my first responsibility, and this board's – the profitability of First Mercantile American Bank.' He repeated with emphasis, 'Profitability, gentlemen – our priority number one.'

Heyward glanced briefly at his text. 'Allow me to elaborate on that.

'In my view, too many decisions in banking, and in business

generally, are being excessively influenced nowadays by social issues and other controversies of our times. As a banker I believe this to be wrong. Let me emphasize that I do not in any way diminish the importance of an individual's social conscience; my own, I hope, is well developed. I accept, too, that each of us must re-examine his personal values from time to time, making adjustments in the light of new ideas and offering such private contributions as he can. But corporate policies are something else. They should not be subject to every changing social wind or whim. If they were, if that kind of thinking is allowed to rule our business actions, it would be dangerous for American free enterprise and disastrous for this bank by lessening our strength, retarding growth, and reducing profits. In short, like other institutions, we should once again stay aloof from the socio-political scene which is none of our concern other than how that scene affects our clients' financial affairs.'

The speaker intruded a thin smile into his seriousness. 'I concede that if these words were spoken publicly they would be undiplomatic and unpopular. I will go further and say that I would never utter them in any public place. But between us here, where real decisions and policy are made, I conceive them to be wholly realistic.'

Several of the directors gave approving nods. One enthusiastically thumped his fist upon the tabletop. Others, including the steelman Leonard Kingswood, remained expressionless.

Alex Vandervoort reflected: so Roscoe Heyward had decided on a direct confrontation, a total clash of views. As Heyward was undoubtedly aware, everything he had just said ran contrary to Alex's own convictions, as well as Ben Rosselli's, as demonstrated by Ben's increasing liberalization of the bank in recent years. It was Ben who had involved FMA in civic affairs, across both city and state, including projects like Forum East. But Alex had no delusions. A substantial segment of the board had been uneasy, at times unhappy, about Ben's policies and would welcome Heyward's hard, all-business line. The question was: How strong was the hard line segment?

With one statement made by Roscoe Heyward, Alex was in full agreement. Heyward had said: *This is a closed and private*

126

meeting ... where real decisions and policy are made.

The operative word was 'real'.

While shareholders and public might later be fed a soporific, sugar-coated version of bank policy through elaborately printed annual reports and other means, here, behind closed boardroom doors, was where true objectives were decided in uncompromising terms. It was a reason why discretion and a certain silence were requirements of any company director.

'There is a close-to-home parallel,' Heyward was explaining, 'between what I have spoken of and what has happened in the church which I attend, through which I make some social contributions of my own.

'In the 1960s our church diverted money, time, and effort to social causes, notably those of black advancement. Partly this was because of outside pressures; also certain members of our congregation saw it as "the thing to do". In sundry ways our church became a social agency. More recently, however, some of us have regained control, and decided such activism is inappropriate, and we should return to the basics of religious worship. Therefore we have increased religious ceremonies – our church's primary function as we see it – and are leaving active social involvement to government and other agencies where, in our opinion, it belongs.'

Alex wondered if other directors found it hard, as he did, to think of social causes as 'inappropriate' to a church.

'I spoke of profit as our principal objective,' Roscoe Heyward was continuing. 'There are some, I am aware, who will object to that. They will argue that the predominant pursuit of profit is a crass endeavour, shortsighted, selfish, ugly, and without redeeming social value.' The speaker smiled tolerantly. 'You gentlemen are familiar with arguments along those lines.

'Well, as a banker I profoundly disagree. The search for profit is not shortsighted. And, where this bank or any other is concerned, the social value of profitability is high.

'Let me enlarge on that.

'All banks measure profit in terms of earnings per share. Such earnings – which are a matter of public record – are widely studied by shareholders, depositors, investors, and the business community nationally and internationally. A rise or fall in bank earnings is taken as a sign of strength or weakness.

'While earnings are strong, confidence in banking continues high. But let a few big banks show decreased earnings per share and what would happen? General disquiet, increasing swiftly to alarm – a situation in which depositors would withdraw funds and shareholders their investments, so that bank stocks tumbled with the banks themselves imperilled. In short, a public crisis of the gravest kind.'

Roscoe Heyward removed his glasses and polished them with a white linen handkerchief.

'Let no one say: this cannot happen. It happened before in the depression which began in 1929, though today, with banks larger by far, the effect would be cataclysmic by comparison.

'This is why a bank like ours must remain vigilant in its duty to make money for itself and its shareholders.'

Again there were murmurings of approval around the boardroom. Heyward turned another page of his text.

'How, as a bank, do we achieve maximum profit? I will tell you first how we do *not* achieve it.

'We do not achieve it by becoming involved with projects which, while admirable in intent, are either financially unsound or tie up bank funds at low rates of yield for many years. I refer, of course, to funding of low-income housing. We should not, in any case, place more than a minimal portion of bank funds in housing mortgages of any kind, which are notorious for their low return of profit.

'Another way not to achieve profitability is by making concessions and lowering lending standards as, for example, with so-called minority business loans. This is an area nowadays where banks are subjected to enormous pressures and we should resist them, not with racial motives but with business shrewdness. By all means let us make minority loans when possible, but let terms and standards be as strict as those for any other borrower.

'Nor, as a bank, should we concern ourselves unduly with vague matters of environment. It is not *our* business to pass judgement on the way our customers conduct *their* business vis-à-vis ecology; all we ask is that they be in good financial health.

'In short, we do *not* achieve profitability by becoming our brother's keeper – or his judge or jailer.'

'Oh, at times we may support these public objectives with our voice – low-cost housing, civic rehabilitation, improvement of environment, energy, conservation, and other issues which arise. After all, this bank has influence and prestige which we can lend without financial loss. We can even allocate token amounts of money, and we have a public relations department to make our contributions known – even,' he chuckled, 'to exaggerate them on occasions. But for real profitability we should direct our major thrust elsewhere.'

Alex Vandervoort thought: whatever criticism might be levelled at Heyward, no one could complain later that he had failed to make his viewpoints clear. In a way his statement was an honest declaration. Yet it was also shrewdly, even cynically, calculated.

Many leaders in business and finance – including a good proportion of the directors in the room – chafed at restrictions on their freedom to make money. They resented, too, the need to be circumspect in public utterances lest they draw fire from consumer groups or other business critics. Thus it was a relief to hear their inner convictions spoken aloud and unequivocally.

Clearly, Roscoe Heyward had considered this. He had also, Alex was certain, counted heads around the boardroom table, calculating who would vote which way, before committing himself.

But Alex had made his own calculations. He still believed a middle group of directors existed, sufficiently strong to swing this meeting from Heyward towards himself. But they would have to be persuaded.

'Specifically,' Heyward declared, 'this bank should depend, as it has traditionally, on its business with American industry. By that I mean the type of industry with a proven record of high profits which will, in turn, enhance our own.

'Expressed another way, I am convinced that First Mercantile American Bank has, at present, an insufficient proportion of its funds available for large loans to industry, and we should embark immediately on a programme of increasing such lending . . .'

It was a familiar script which Roscoe Heyward, Alex Vander-voort, and Ben Rosselli had debated often in the past. The arguments which Heyward now advanced were not new, though he presented them convincingly, using figures and charts. Alex sensed the directors were impressed.

Heyward talked for another thirty minutes on his theme of expanded industrial lending against a contraction in community commitments. He ended with – as he put it – 'an appeal to reason'.

'What is needed most today in banking is pragmatic leadership. The kind of leadership which will not be swayed by emotion or pressured into "soft" uses of money because of public clamour. As bankers, we must insist on saying "no" when our fiscal view is negative, "yes" when we foresee a profit. We must never buy easy popularity at stockholders' expense. Instead we should lend our own and our depositors' money solely on the basis of the best return and if, as a result of such policies, we are described as "hard-nosed bankers", so be it. I am one who will be glad to be counted among that number.'

Heyward sat down amid applause.

'Mr Chairman!' The steelman, Leonard Kingswood, leaned forward with a hand raised. 'I've several questions and some disagreement.'

From lower down the table the Honourable Harold Austin riposted, 'For the record, Mr Chairman, I have *no* questions and total *agreement* with everything presented so far.'

Laughter erupted and a fresh voice – that of Philip Johannsen, president of MidContinent Rubber – added, 'I'm with you, Harold. I agree it's time we took a harder line.' Someone else injected, 'Me, too.'

'Gentlemen, gentlemen.' Jerome Patterton rapped lightly with his gavel. 'Only part of our business is concluded. I'll allow time for questions later; as for disagreement, I suggest we save that until our discussion when Roscoe and Alex have withdrawn. First, though, let's hear Alex.'

'Most of you know me well, as a man and as a banker,' Alex began. He stood at the boardroom table casually, shoulders

130

slightly hunched as usual, leaning forward momentarily to catch sight of those directors on his right and left as well as others facing him. He let his tone stay conversational.

'You also know, or should, that as a banker I am tough – hard-nosed, if anyone prefers that word. Proof of this exists in financing I've conducted for FMA, all of it profitable, none involving loss. Obviously in banking like any other business, when you deal from profitability you deal from strength. That applies to people in banking, too.

'I'm glad, though, that Roscoe brought up this subject because it gives me an opportunity to declare my own belief in profitability. Ditto for freedom, democracy, love, and motherhood.'

Someone chuckled. Alex responded with an easy smile. He pushed the chair behind him further back to give himself a few paces of free movement.

'Something else about our profitability here at FMA is that it should be drastically improved. More about that later.

'For the moment I'd like to stay with beliefs.

'A belief of my own is that civilization in this decade is changing more meaningfully and quickly than at any other time since the Industrial Revolution. What we are seeing and sharing is a social revolution of conscience and behaviour.

'A few don't like this revolution; personally I do. But like it or not, it's here; it exists; it will not reverse itself or go away.

'For the driving force behind what's happening is the determination of a majority of people to improve the quality of life, to stop spoliation of our environment and to preserve what's left of resources of all kinds. Because of this, new standards are being demanded of industry and business so that the name of the game is "corporate social responsibility". What's more, higher standards of responsibility *are* being achieved and without significant loss of profits.'

Alex moved restlessly in the limited space behind the boardroom table. He wondered if he should meet another of Heyward's challenges head on, then decided, *yes*.

'In the matter of responsibility and involvement, Roscoe introduced the subject of his church. He told us that those who have – as he puts it – "regained control" are opting out and favouring a policy of non-involvement. Well, in my opinion, Roscoe and his churchmen are marching resolutely backwards. Their attitude is neither good for Christianity nor banking.'

Heyward shot up straight. He protested, 'That's unpleasantly personal and a misinterpretation.'

Alex said calmly, 'I don't believe it's either.'

Harold Austin rapped sharply with his knuckles. 'Mr Chairman, I object to Alex's descent to personalities.'

'Roscoe dragged in his church,' Alex argued. 'I'm simply commenting.'

'Maybe you'd better not.' The voice of Philip Johannsen cut sharply, unpleasantly, across the table. 'Otherwise we might judge the two of you by the company you keep, which would put Roscoe and his church way out ahead.'

Alex flushed. 'May I ask exactly what that means ?'

Johannsen shrugged. 'The way I hear it, your closest lady friend, in your wife's absence, is a left-wing activist. Maybe that's why you like involvement.'

Jerome Patterton pounded with his gavel, this time forcefully. 'That's sufficient, gentlemen. The Chair instructs there will be no more references of this kind, either way.'

Johannsen was smiling. Despite the ruling, he had made his point.

Alex Vandervoort, seething, considered a firm statement that his private life was his own affair, then he rejected the idea. Some other time it might be necessary. Not now. He realized he had made a bad mistake by returning to Heyward's church analogy.

'I'd like to get back,' he said, 'to my original contention : how, as bankers, can we afford to ignore this changing scene ? To attempt to do so is like standing in a gale, pretending the wind does not exist.

'On pragmatic, financial grounds alone we cannot opt out. As those around this table know from personal experience, business success is never achieved by ignoring change, but by anticipating and adapting to it. Thus, as custodians of money, sensitive to the changing climates of investment, we shall profit most by listening, heeding, and adapting now.'

He sensed that, apart from his lapse of judgement moments earlier, his opening gambit, with its practical emphasis, had captured attention. Almost every outside board member had had experience with legislation affecting pollution control, consumer protection, truth in advertising, minority hiring, or equal rights for women. Often, such laws were enacted over angry opposition from companies which these bank directors headed. But once the laws were passed, the same companies learned to live with new standards and proudly touted their contributions to the public weal. Some, like Leonard Kingswood, concluded that corporate responsibility was good for business and espoused it strongly.

'There are fourteen thousand banks in the United States,' Alex reminded the FMA directors, 'with enormous fiscal power in extending loans. Surely, when the loans are to industry and business, that power should involve responsibility on our part, too! Surely among criteria for lending should be the standards of public conduct of our borrowers! If a factory is to be financed, will it pollute? When a new product is to be developed, is it safe? How truthful is a company's advertising? As between companies A and B, to one of which we have funds to lend, which has the better record of non-discrimination?'

He leaned forward, glancing around the elliptical table to meet, in turn, the eyes of each board member.

'It is true these questions are not always asked, or acted on, at present. But they are beginning to be asked by major banks as matters of sound business – an example which FMA will be wise to emulate. For just as leadership in any enterprise can produce strong dividends, so leadership in banking will prove rewarding, too.

'Equally important: It is better to do this freely now than have it forced on us by regulation later.'

Alex paused, took a pace from the table, then swung back. Now he asked, 'In which other areas should this bank accept corporate responsibility?

'I believe, with Ben Rosselli, that we should share in improving the life of this city and state. An immediate means is through financing of low-rental housing, a commitment this board has already accepted with the early stages of Forum East. As time goes on I believe our contribution should be greater.'

He glanced towards Roscoe Heyward. 'Of course, I realize that housing mortgages are not a notably high profit area. Yet there are ways to achieve that involvement with excellent profits, too.'

One means, he told the listening directors, was through a determined, large-scale expansion of the bank's savings department.

'Traditionally, funds for home mortgages are channelled from savings deposits because mortgages are long-term investments while savings are similarly stable and long-term. The profitability we shall gain by volume – far greater than our savings volume now. Thus we will attain a threefold objective – profit, fiscal stability, and a major social contribution.

'Only a few years ago large commercial banks like ourselves spurned consumer business, including small savings, as being unimportant. Then, while we dozed, savings and loan associations astutely seized the opportunity we ignored and forged ahead of us, so now they are a main competitor. But still, in personal savings, gigantic opportunities remain. It's likely that, within a decade, consumer business will exceed commercial deposits everywhere and thus become the most important money force existing.'

Savings, Alex argued, was only one of several areas where FMA interests could be dramatically advanced.

Still moving restlessly as he spoke, he ranged through other bank departments, describing changes he proposed. Most had been in a report, prepared by Alex Vandervoort at Ben's request a few weeks before the bank president's announcement of his impending death. In the pressure of events it had remained, so far as Alex knew, unread.

One recommendation was to open nine new branches in suburban areas through the state. Another was for a drastic overhaul of FMA organization. Alex proposed to hire a specialist consulting firm to advise on needed changes and he advised the board, 'Our efficiency is lower than it should be. The machinery is creaking.'

Near the end he returned to his original theme. 'Our banking relationship with industry should, of course, continue to be close. Industrial loans and commercial business will remain pillars of our activity. But not the only pillars. Nor should they be overwhelmingly the largest. Nor should we be so preoccupied with bigness that the importance of small accounts, including those of individuals, becomes diminished in our minds.

'The founder of this bank established it to serve those of modest means to whom other banking facilities were denied. Inevitably, the bank's purpose and operations have broadened across a century, yet neither the founder's son nor grandson ever lost sight of those origins or ignored the precept that smallness multiplied can represent the greatest strength of all.

'A massive and immediate growth in small savings, which I urge the board to set as an objective, will honour those origins, enhance our fiscal strength and – in the climate of the times – advance the public good, which is our own.'

As they had for Heyward, board members applauded as Alex sat down. Some of the applause was merely polite, Alex realized; perhaps half of the directors seemed more enthusiastic. He guessed that the choice between Heyward and himself could still go either way.

'Thank you, Alex.' Jerome Patterton glanced around the table. 'Questions, gentlemen?'

The questioning occupied another half hour, after which Roscoe Heyward and Alex Vandervoort left the boardroom together. Each returned to his office to await the board's decision.

The directors debated through the remainder of the morning but failed to reach agreement. They then adjourned to a private dining-room for lunch, their discussion continuing over the meal. The outcome of the meeting was still inconclusive when a dining-room steward quietly approached Jerome Patterton, carrying a small silver tray. On it was a single sheet of paper, folded.

The vice-chairman accepted the paper, unfolded and read it. After a pause he rose to his feet and waited while conversation around the luncheon table quietened.

135

'Gentlemen.' Patterton's voice quavered. 'I grieve to inform you that our beloved president, Ben Rosselli, died a few minutes ago.'

Soon after, by mutual consent and without further discussion, the board meeting was abandoned.

sixteen

The death of Ben Rosselli attracted international press coverage and some news writers, reaching for the nearest cliché, labelled it 'an era's end'.

Whether it was, or wasn't, his departure signalled that the last major American bank to be identified with a single entrepreneur had moved into mid-twentieth century conformation, with committee and hired management control. As to who would head the hired management, the decision had been postponed until after the Rosselli funeral when the bank's board of directors would convene again.

The funeral took place on Wednesday in the second week of December.

Both the funeral and a lying-in-state which preceded it were garnished with the full rites and panoply of the Catholic Church, suitable to a papal knight and large cash benefactor which Ben Rosselli was.

The two-day lying-in-state was at St Matthew's Cathedral, appropriate since Matthew – once Levi the tax collector – is considered by bankers as a patron saint. Some two thousand people, including a presidential representative, the state governor, ambassadors, civic leaders, bank employees and many humbler souls, filed past the bier and open casket.

On the morning of burial – taking no chances – an archbishop, a bishop, and a monsignor concelebrated a Mass of the Resurrection. A full choir intoned responses to prayers with reassuring volume. Within the cathedral which was filled, a section near the altar had been reserved for Rosselli relatives and friends. Immediately behind were directors and senior officers of First Mercantile American Bank.

Roscoe Heyward, dressed sombrely in black, was in the first row of bank mourners, accompanied by his wife Beatrice, an imperious sturdy woman, and their son, Elmer. Heyward, an Episcopalian, had studied the correct Catholic procedures in advance and genuflected elegantly, both before seating himself and on departure later – the last a piece of punctilio which many Catholics ignored. The Heywards also knew the Mass responses so that their voices dominated others nearby who didn't.

Alex Vandervoort, wearing charcoal grey and seated two rows behind the Heywards, was among the non-responders. An agnostic, he felt out of place in these surroundings. He wondered how Ben, essentially a simple man, would have regarded this ornate ceremony.

Beside Alex, Margot Bracken looked around her with curiosity. Originally Margot had planned to attend the funeral with a group from Forum East, but last night she had stayed at Alex's apartment and he persuaded her to accompany him today. The Forum East delegation – a large one – was somewhere behind them in the church.

Next to Margot were Edwina and Lewis D'Orsey, the latter looking gaunt and starved as usual and frankly bored. Probably, Alex thought, Lewis was mentally drafting the next edition of his investment newsletter. The D'Orseys had driven here with Margot and Alex – the four of them were often together, not just because Edwina and Margot were cousins, but because they found each other's company agreeable. After the Mass of the Resurrection they would all go to the graveside service.

In the row ahead of Alex were Jerome Patterton, the vice-chairman, and his wife.

Despite his detachment from the liturgy, Alex found tears spring to his eyes as the coffin passed by and was carried from the church. His feeling for Ben, he had realized over the past few days, was close to love. In some ways the old man had been

137

a father figure; his death left a gap in Alex's life which would not be filled.

Margot reached gently for his hand and held it.

As mourners began filing out he saw Roscoe and Beatrice Heyward glance their way. Alex nodded and the greeting was returned. Heyward's face softened in an acknowledgment of mutual grief, their feud – in recognition of their own, as well as Ben's mortality – for this brief moment put aside.

Outside the cathedral, regular traffic had been diverted. The coffin was already in a flower-laden hearse. Now, relatives and bank officials were getting into limousines being brought up under police direction. A police motorcycle escort, engines running noisily, was at the head of the assembling cortège.

The day was grey and cold with eddies of wind raising dust whorls in the street. High above, the cathedral towers loomed, the whole façade immense and blackened by the grime of years. Snow had been forecast earlier but so far had not appeared.

While Alex signalled for his car, Lewis D'Orsey peered over his half-moon glasses at TV and still cameramen, shooting pictures of the emerging mourners. He observed, 'If I find all this depressing, and I do, the reports should depress FMA stock even more tomorrow.'

Alex murmured uneasy agreement. Like Lewis, he was aware that First Mercantile American shares, listed on the New York Stock Exchange, had fallen five and a half points since news of Ben's illness. The death of the last Rosselli – a name which for generations had been synonymous with the bank – coupled with uncertainty about the course of future management, had caused the most recent drop. Now, even though illogically, publicity about the funeral could depress the stock still further.

'Our stock will go up again,' Alex said. 'Earnings are good and nothing's really changed.'

'Oh, I know that,' Lewis agreed. 'It's why I'll cover my short position tomorrow afternoon.'

Edwina looked shocked. 'You shorted FMA ?'

'Sure did. Advised a few clients to do the same. As of right now there's a tidy profit.'

She protested, 'You and I know I never discuss anything confidential with you, Lewis. Others don't. Because of my connection with the bank you could be accused of insider trading.'

Alex shook his head. 'Not in this case, Edwina. Ben's illness was public knowledge.'

'When we eventually take over the capitalist system,' Margot said, 'selling short on the stock market will be one of the first things to go.'

Lewis raised his eyebrows. 'Why?'

'Because it's *totally* negative. Short selling is disruptive speculation that requires someone else to lose. It's ghoulish and a non-contribution. It creates nothing.'

'It creates a handy-dandy capital gain.' Lewis grinned broadly; he had crossed arguments with Margot many times before. 'And that isn't easy to come by nowadays, at least with American investments.'

'I still don't like you doing it with FMA stock,' Edwina said. 'It's too close to home.'

Lewis D'Orsey looked at his wife gravely. 'In that case, my dear, after I've covered my shorts tomorrow I will never trade in FMA again.'

Margot glanced over sharply.

'You know he means it,' Alex said.

Alex wondered sometimes about the relationship between Edwina and her husband. Outwardly they seemed ill-matched – Edwina elegantly attractive and self-possessed; Lewis, scrawny, unimpressive physically, an introvert except with those he knew well, though the personal reticence never showed in his roaring-lion financial newsletter. But their marriage appeared to work well, and each showed respect and affection for the other, as Lewis had just now. Perhaps, Alex thought, it proved that not only did opposites attract; they tended to stay married.

Alex's Cadillac from the bank car pool moved into the lengthening line outside the cathedral and the four of them walked towards it.

'It would have been a more civilized promise,' Margot said, 'if Lewis agreed not to sell *anything* short'.

'Alex,' Lewis said, 'what the hell do you have in common with this socialist broad?'

'We're great in the sack,' Margot told him. 'Isn't that enough ?'

Alex said, 'And I'd like to marry her soon.'

Edwina responded warmly, 'Then I hope you will.' She and Margot had been close since childhood, despite occasional clashes of temperament and outlook. Something they had in common was that in both branches of their family women were strong, with a tradition of involvement in public life. Edwina asked Alex quietly, 'Anything new with Celia ?'

He shook his head. 'Nothing's changed. If anything, Celia's worse.'

They were at the car. Alex motioned the chauffeur to remain seated, then opened a rear door for the others and followed them in. Inside, the glass panel separating the driver from the passenger seats was closed. They settled down while the still-assembling cortège inched forward.

For Alex, the mention of Celia sharpened the sadness of this moment; it also reminded him guiltily that he should visit her again soon. Since the session at the Remedial Centre in early October which had so depressed him, he had paid one other call, but Celia had been even more withdrawn, gave not the slightest sign of recognition, and wept silently the entire time. He remained dejected for days afterwards and dreaded a repeat performance.

The thought occurred now that Ben Rosselli, in the coffin up ahead, was better off than Celia because his life had ended conclusively. *If only Celia would die . . .* Alex quelled the thought with shame.

Nor had anything new developed between himself and Margot, who remained adamantly opposed to a divorce, at least until it became clear the Celia would be unaffected. Margot seemed willing to go on indefinitely with the arrangement they had. Alex was less resigned.

Lewis addressed Edwina. 'I've been meaning to ask what the latest is about that young assistant of yours. The one who got caught with his arm in the cash drawer. What was his name ?'

'Miles Eastin,' Edwina answered. 'He appears in criminal court next week and I have to be a witness. I'm not looking forward to it.'

'At least you got the blame where it should be,' Alex said. He had read the audit chief's report about the embezzlement and cash loss; also that of Nolan Wainwright. 'What about the teller who was involved – Mrs Núñez? Is she okay?'

'She seems to be. I'm afraid we gave Juanita a hard time. Unjustly, as it turned out.'

Margot, only half listening, now sharpened her attention. 'I know a Juanita Núñez. Nice young woman who lives at Forum East. I believe her husband left her. She has a child.'

'That sounds like our Mrs Núñez,' Edwina said. 'Yes, I remember now. She does live at Forum East.'

Though Margot was curious, she sensed it was not a time for further questions.

As they sat briefly silent, Edwina pursued her thoughts. The two recent events – Ben Rosselli's death and Miles Eastin's foolish wrecking of his life – had come too close together. Both, involving people whom she liked, had saddened her.

She supposed she should care more about Ben; she owed him most. Her own rapid rise within the bank had been due to ability; however, Ben had never hesitated – as many employers did – to allow a woman the same opportunity as men. Nowadays Edwina resented the parrot cries of women's lib. As she saw it, women in business were being favoured *because* of their sex, giving them an advantage Edwina had never sought or needed. Just the same, across the years she had known Ben, his presence was a guarantee of equal treatment.

Like Alex, Edwina had been moved to tears in the cathedral as Ben's body passed by on its outward journey.

Her thoughts returned to Miles. He was young enough, she supposed, to build another kind of life, though it would not be easy. No bank would ever employ him; nor would anyone else, in a position of trust. Despite what he had done, she hoped he would not be sent to prison.

Aloud, Edwina said, 'I always get a guilty feeling about ordinary conversation at a funeral.'

'No reason to,' Lewis said. 'Personally, at mine I'd like to think there was something solid being said, not just small talk.'

'You could make certain of that,' Margot suggested, 'by publishing a farewell edition of *The D'Orsey Newsletter*. Pallbearers could hand out copies.'

Lewis beamed. 'I might just do that.'

Now the cortège began to move onwards more purposefully. Up ahead the motorcycle escort had revved up and was moving; two outriders shot forward to halt traffic at intersections. The other vehicles following increased their speed and moments later the procession left St Matthew's Cathedral behind and was passing through city streets.

The snow which had been forecast was beginning to fall lightly.

'I like that idea of Margot's,' Lewis mused. 'A "*Bon Voyage Bulletin*". And I have a headline for it. "*Bury the US Dollar with Me! You Might as Well – It's Dead and Done For.*" Then, in what follows, I shall urge creation of a new unit of currency to replace the dollar – the "US D'Orsey". Based, of course, on gold. Later, when it's happened, the rest of the world will hopefully have the sense to follow suit.'

'Then you'd be a monument to retrogression,' Margot said, 'and any picture of you should have the head facing backwards. On a gold standard, even fewer people than now would own most of the world's wealth, with the rest of mankind left bare-assed.'

Lewis grimaced. 'A distasteful prospect – at least, the last one. But even that price would be worth a stable money system.'

'Why?'

Lewis answered Margot. 'Because when money systems break down, as is happening now, it's always the poor who suffer most.'

Alex, on a jump seat ahead of the other three, half turned to join the conversation. 'Lewis, I try to be objective and sometimes your gloom about dollars and the money system makes sense. But I can't share your total pessimism. I believe the dollar can recover. I can't believe everything monetary is falling apart.'

'That's because you don't want to believe it,' Lewis retorted. 'You're a banker. If the money system collapses, you and your bank are out of business. All you could do would be to sell off the worthless paper currency as wallpaper or toilet rolls.'

Margot said, 'Oh, *come on!*'

Edwina sighed. 'You know this always happens when you provoke him, so why do it?'

'No, no!' her husband insisted. 'With all respect, my dear, I demand to be taken seriously. I neither need nor want tolerance.'

Margot asked, 'What *do* you want?'

'I want the truth to be accepted that America has ruined its own and the world's money system because of politics, greed and debt. I want it clearly understood that bankruptcy can happen to nations as well as to individuals and corporations. I want a realization that the United States *is* close to bankruptcy because – God knows! – there's enough precedent and history to show us how and why it happens. Look at the city of New York! It's bankrupt, broke, patched up with string and Band-Aids, with anarchy waiting in the wings. And that's only the beginning. What's happening in New York will happen nationally.'

Lewis went on, 'The collapse of currencies isn't new. Our own century is littered with examples, each one traceable to the selfsame cause – a government which began the syphilis of inflation by printing fiat money unbacked by gold or any other value. For the past fifteen years the United States has done precisely that.'

'There are more dollars in circulation than there should be,' Alex admitted. 'No one with any sense doubts it.'

Lewis nodded dourly. 'There's also more debt than can ever be repaid; debt that's expanding like a monstrous bubble. American governments have spent billions wildly, borrowed insanely, piled up debits beyond believing, then used the printing presses to create more paper money and inflation. And people, individuals, have followed that example.' Lewis motioned in the direction of the hearse ahead. 'Bankers like Ben Rosselli have done their damnedest, piling crazy debts on debts. You too, Alex, with your inflationary credit cards and easy borrowing. When will people relearn the lesson that there *isn't* any easy debt? I tell you, as a nation and as individuals, Americans have lost what they once had – financial sanity.'

'In case you're wondering, Margot,' Edwina said, 'Lewis and I don't discuss banking much. It's more peaceful at home that way.'

Margot smiled, 'Lewis, you sounded exactly like your news-letter.'

'Or,' he said, 'like the beating of wings in an empty room where no one hears.'

Edwina said suddenly, 'It's going to be a white funeral.' She leaned forward, looking through the car's steamy windows at the snow outside, now falling heavily. The suburban streets which they had reached were smooth with freshly fallen snow and the cortège slowed as the police motorcycle escort up ahead reduced its speed for safety.

The cemetery, Alex realized, was barely half a mile away.

Lewis D'Orsey was adding a postscript. 'So, for the bulk of people, all hope is gone, the money game is over. Savings, pensions and fixed interest investments are becoming worthless; the clock's at five past midnight. Right now, it's every man for himself, a time to survive, for individuals to scramble for financial life belts. And there *are* ways to profit from general misfortune. In case you're interested, Margot, you'll find descriptions in my latest book, *Depressions and Disasters: How to Make Money from Them*. Incidentally, it's selling very well.'

'If you don't mind,' Margot said, 'I'll pass. It seems a bit like cornering vaccine in an outbreak of bubonic plague.'

Alex had turned his back to the others and was peering through the windscreen. Sometimes, he reflected, Lewis became theatrical and went too far. Usually, though, an undercurrent of sense and solid reasoning ran through everything he said. It had today. And Lewis *could* be right about a financial crash ahead. If it happened, it would be the most disastrous in history.

Nor was Lewis D'Orsey alone. A few financial pundits shared his views, though they were unpopular and frequently derided, perhaps because no one wanted to believe an apocalypse of doom – bankers least of all.

But it was coincidental that Alex's own thoughts had been turning of late in two of Lewis's directions. One was a need for greater thrift and saving – a reason Alex had urged emphasis on savings deposits in his presentation to the board a week ago. The second was unease about the swelling debts of individuals resulting from proliferating credit, including, especially, those plastic cards.

He swung around once more, confronting Lewis. 'Believing the way you do – that a crash is coming soon – and assuming you were an ordinary saver or depositor with US dollars, what kind of bank would you want to have your money in ?'

Lewis said unhesitatingly, 'A big bank. When a crash comes small banks are the first to fail. It happened in the 1920s when small banks went down like tenpins, and it will happen again because small banks don't have sufficient cash to survive a panic and a run. Incidentally, forget federal deposit insurance! The money available is less than one per cent of all bank deposits, nowhere near enough to cover a countrywide chain of bank failures.'

Lewis considered, then went on. 'But small banks won't be the only ones to fail next time. A few of the big ones will go under, too – those with too many millions locked into big industrial loans; with too high a proportion of international deposits – hot money which can vanish overnight; with too little liquidity when scared depositors want cash. So if I were your mythical depositor, Alex, I'd study the balance sheets of the big banks, then choose one with a low loan-to-deposit ratio and a broad base of domestic depositors.'

'Well, that's nice,' Edwina said. 'It just so happens that FMA fills all of those conditions.'

Alex nodded. 'At the moment.' But the picture could change, he reasoned, if Roscoe Heyward's plans for new and massive loans to industry were agreed to by the board.

The thought was a reminder that the bank's directors would meet again, two days from now, to resume their interrupted meeting of a week ago.

Now the car slowed and stopped, inched forward, stopped again. They had come to the cemetery and travelled through its roads.

Doors of other cars were opening, figures emerging, carrying umbrellas or holding coat collars tightly, hunched up against the cold and falling snow. The coffin was being lifted from the hearse. Soon it, too, was snow covered.

Margot took Alex's arm and, with the D'Orseys, joined others in the quiet procession following Ben Rosselli to his grave.

seventeen

By prior agreement, Roscoe Heyward and Alex Vandervoort did not attend the reconvened meeting of the board. Each waited in his office until summoned.

The summons came shortly before noon, two hours after the board had begun discussion. Also called to the boardroom was the bank's vice-president of public relations, Dick French, who would release an announcement to the press concerning the new FMA president.

Already the PR chief had had two news releases prepared with accompanying photographs.

Their respective headings read:

ROSCOE D. HEYWARD

IS FIRST MERCANTILE AMERICAN BANK PRESIDENT

ALEXANDER VANDERVOORT

IS FIRST MERCANTILE AMERICAN BANK PRESIDENT

Envelopes were addressed. Messengers had been alerted. Priority copies of one release or the other were to be delivered this afternoon to wire services, newspaper city desks, TV and radio stations. Several hundred more would go out by first-class mail tonight.

Heyward and Alex arrived at the boardroom together. They slipped into their regular, vacant seats at the long elliptical table.

The PR vice-president hovered behind the meeting chairman, Jerome Patterton.

It was the director with the longest service, the Honourable Harold Austin, who announced the board's decision.

Jerome Patterton, he stated, until now vice-chairman of the board, would become president of First Mercantile American Bank immediately.

While the announcement was being made, the appointee himself seemed somewhat dazed.

The PR vice-president mouthed inaudibly, 'Oh, shit!'

*　　*　　*

146

Later the same day Jerome Patterton had separate talks with Heyward and Vandervoort.

'I'm an interim Pope,' he informed each of them. 'I didn't seek this job, as you're aware. You also know, and so do the directors, that I'm only thirteen months from mandatory retirement.

'But the board was deadlocked over you two, and choosing me allows that length of time before they need make up their minds.

'Your guess about what happens then is as good as mine. In the meantime, though, I intend to do my best and I need the help of both of you. I know I shall get it because that's to your best advantage.

'Apart from that, the only thing I can promise is an interesting year.'

eighteen

Even before excavation, Margot Bracken was actively involved with Forum East. First she was legal counsel for a citizens group which campaigned to get the project going and later she filled the same role in a Tenants Association. She also gave legal aid to families in the development who needed it – at little cost to them, or none. Margot went to Forum East often and, in doing so, she came to know many of those living there, including Juanita Núñez.

Three days after the Rosselli funeral – on a Saturday morning – Margot encountered Juanita in a delicatessen, part of a Forum East shopping arcade.

The Forum East complex had been planned as a homogeneous community with low-cost living accommodation – attractive apartments, town houses and remodelled older buildings. There were sports facilities, a cinema, a theatre, as well as shops and cafés. The buildings completed so far were linked by tree-lined arcades and overhead walkways – many of the ideas adapted from San Francisco's Golden Gateway and London's Barbican. Other portions of the project were under construction, with still further additions at the planning stage, awaiting financing.

'Hello, Mrs Núñez,' Margot said. 'Will you join me for coffee ?'

On a terrace adjoining the delicatessen they sipped espresso and chatted – about Juanita, her daughter Estela who this morning was at a community-sponsored ballet class, and progress at Forum East. Juanita and her husband Carlos had been among the early tenants in the development, occupying a tiny walk-up apartment in one of the rehabilitated older buildings, though it was shortly after moving in that Carlos had departed for parts unknown. So far Juanita had kept the same accommodation.

But managing was very difficult, she confided. 'Everyone here has the same problem. Each month our money will buy less. This inflation! Where will it end ?'

According to Lewis D'Orsey, Margot reflected, it would end in disaster and anarchy. She kept the thought to herself, but was reminded of the conversation three days ago between Lewis, Edwina, and Alex.

'I heard,' she said, 'that you had some kind of problem at the bank where you work.'

Juanita's face clouded. For a moment she seemed close to tears and Margot said hastily, 'I'm sorry. Perhaps I shouldn't have asked.'

'No, no! It was just that remembering suddenly . . . Anyway, it is over now. But I will tell you if you wish.'

'One thing you should know about us lawyers,' Margot said, 'is that we're always nosy.'

Juanita smiled, then was serious as she described the six-thousand-dollar cash loss and the forty-eight-hour nightmare of suspicion and interrogation. As Margot listened, her anger, never far below the surface, rose.

'The bank had no right to keep on pressuring you without your having legal advice. Why didn't you call me ?'

'I never thought of it,' Juanita said.

'That's the whole trouble. Most innocent people don't.' Margot considered, then added, 'Edwina D'Orsey is my cousin. I'm going to talk to her about this.'

Juanita looked startled. 'I didn't know. But please don't! After all, it was Mrs D'Orsey who found the truth.'

'All right,' Margot conceded, 'if you don't want me to, I won't. But I'll talk to someone else you don't know. And remember this: if you're in trouble again, about *anything*, call me. I'll be there to help.'

'Thank you,' Juanita said. 'If it happens, I will. I really will.'

'If the bank had actually fired Juanita Núñez,' Margot told Alex Vandervoort that night. 'I'd have advised her to sue you, and we'd have collected – heavily.'

'You might well have,' Alex agreed. They were on their way to a supper dance and he was driving Margot's Volkswagen. 'Especially when the truth about our thieving operations man, Eastin, came out – as it was bound to eventually. Fortunately, Edwina's womanly instincts functioned, saving us from yours.'

'You're being flip.'

His tone changed. 'You're right, and I shouldn't be. The fact is, we behaved shabbily to the Núñez girl, and everybody concerned knows it. I do, because I've read everything to do with the case. So does Edwina. So does Nolan Wainwright. But fortunately, in the end nothing really bad happened. Mrs Núñez still has her job, and our bank has learned something which will help us do better in the future.'

'That's more like it,' Margot said.

They left it there, which, given their mutual love of argument, was an accomplishment.

nineteen

During the week preceding Christmas, Miles Eastin appeared in the Federal Court charged with embezzlement on five separate counts. Four of the charges involved fraudulent transactions at the bank from which he had benefited; these totalled thirteen thousand dollars. The fifth charge related to the six-thousand-dollar cash theft.

Trial was before the Honourable Judge Winslow Underwood, sitting with a jury.

On advice of counsel, a well-meaning but inexperienced young man appointed by the court after Eastin's personal resources had proven to be nil, a not guilty plea was entered on all counts. As it turned out, the advice was bad. A more seasoned lawyer, assessing the evidence, would have urged a guilty plea and perhaps a deal with the prosecuting lawyer, rather than have certain details – principally Eastin's attempt to incriminate Juanita Núñez – revealed in court.

As it was, everything came out.

Edwina D'Orsey testified, as did Tottenhoe, Gayne of central audit staff, and another audit colleague. FBI Special Agent Innes introduced as evidence Miles Eastin's signed admission of guilt concerning the cash theft, made at FBI local headquarters subsequent to the confession which Nolan Wainwright extracted from Eastin at the latter's apartment.

Two weeks before the trial, at discovery proceedings, defendant's counsel had objected to the FBI document and made a pre-trial motion to have it barred from evidence. The motion was denied. Judge Underwood pointed out that before Eastin made his statement he had been properly cautioned about his legal rights in the presence of witnesses.

The earlier confession obtained by Nolan Wainwright, the legality of which might have been challenged more effectively, was not needed and therefore was not introduced.

The sight of Miles Eastin in court depressed Edwina. He appeared pale and haggard with dark rings beneath his eyes. All

150

of his accustomed buoyancy had gone and, in contrast to the immaculate grooming she remembered, his hair was untidy and his suit rumpled. He seemed to have aged since the night of the branch audit.

Edwina's own evidence was brief and circumstantial and she gave it straightforwardly. While being mildly cross-examined by counsel for the defence, she glanced several times towards Miles Eastin, but his head was down and he declined to meet her eyes.

Also a witness for the prosecution – albeit a reluctant one – was Juanita Núñez. She was nervous and the court had difficulty hearing her. On two occasions the judge intervened, asking Juanita to raise her voice, though his approach was coaxing and gentle, since by then her injured innocence in the whole affair had been made clear.

Juanita demonstrated no antagonism towards Eastin in her evidence, and kept her answers brief, so that the prosecuting lawyer pressed her constantly to amplify them. Plainly all she wanted was to have the ordeal over.

Defence counsel, making a belated wise decision, waived his right to question her.

It was immediately following Juanita's testimony that defence counsel, after a whispered consultation with his client, asked leave to approach the bench. Permission was granted. The prosecutor, judge, and defence counsel thereupon engaged in a low-toned colloquy during which the latter requested leave to change Miles Eastin's original 'not guilty' plea to 'guilty'.

Judge Underwood, a quiet-spoken patriarch, with steel not far below the surface, surveyed both lawyers. He matched their lowered voices so the jury could not hear. 'Very well, the change of plea will be permitted if the defendant so wishes. But I advise counsel that at this point it makes little, if any, difference.'

Sending the jury from the courtroom, the judge then questioned Eastin, confirming that he wished to change his plea and realized the consequences. To all the questions the prisoner answered dully, 'Yes, your honour.'

The judge recalled the jury to the courtroom and dismissed it. After an earnest entreaty by the young defence lawyer for clemency, including a reminder that his client had no previous criminal record, Miles Eastin was remanded into custody for sentencing the following week.

Nolan Wainwright, though not required to testify, had been present throughout the court proceedings. Now, as the court clerk called another case and the contingent of bank witnesses filed out from the courtroom, the bank security chief moved alongside Juanita.

'Mrs Núñez, may I talk with you for a few minutes ?'

She glanced at him with a mixture of indifference and hostility, then shook her head. 'It is all finished. Besides, I am going back to work.'

When they were outside the Federal Courts Building, only a few blocks from FMA Headquarters Tower and the downtown branch, he persisted, 'You're walking to the bank ? Right now ?'

She nodded.

'Please. I'd like to walk with you.'

Juanita shrugged. 'If you must.'

Wainwright watched as Edwina D'Orsey, Tottenhoe, and the two audit staff men, also heading for the bank, crossed a nearby intersection. He deliberately held back, missing a green pedestrian light so the others would remain ahead.

'Look,' Wainwright said, 'I've never found it easy to say I'm sorry.'

Juanita said tartly, 'Why should you bother ? It is only a word, not meaning much.'

'Because I want to say it. So I do – to you. I'm sorry. For the trouble I caused you, for not believing you were telling the truth when you were and needed somebody to help.'

'So now you feel better ? You have swallowed your little aspirin ? The tiny pain is gone ?'

'You don't make it easy.'

She stopped. 'Did you ?' The small elfin face was tilted upwards, her dark eyes met his own steadily and for the first time he was aware of an underlying strength and independence. He was also, to his own surprise, conscious of her strong sexuality.

'No, I didn't. Which is why I'd like to help now if I can.'

'Help about what ?'

'About getting maintenance and child support from your husband.' He told her of the FBI inquiries concerning her absent husband Carlos, and tracing him to Phoenix, Arizona. 'He has a job there as a motor mechanic and obviously is earning money.'

'Then I am pleased for Carlos.'

'What I had in mind,' Wainright said, 'is that you should consult one of our lawyers at the bank. I could arrange that. He would advise you how to take action against your husband and afterwards I'd see to it you weren't charged any legal fees.'

'Why would you do that ?'

'We owe it to you.'

She shook her head. 'No.'

He wondered if she had properly understood.

'It would mean,' Wainwright said, 'there would be a court order and your husband would have to send you money to help take care of your little girl.'

'And will that make Carlos a man ?'

'Does it matter ?'

'It matters that he should not be forced. He knows that I am here and that Estela is with me. If Carlos wanted us to have his money he would send it. ¿ Si no, para qué ? she added softly.

It was like a fencing match with shadows. He said in exasperation, 'I'll never understand you.'

Unexpectedly Juanita smiled. 'It is not necessary that you should.'

They walked the remaining short distance to the bank in silence, Wainwright nursing his frustration. He wished she had thanked him for his offer; if she had, it would have meant, at least, she took it seriously. He tried to guess at her reasoning and values. She obviously rated independence high. After that he imagined she accepted life as it came, fortune or misfortune, hopes raised or yearnings shattered. In a way he envied her and, for that reason and the sexual attraction he had been aware of earlier, he wished he knew her better.

'Mrs Núñez,' Nolan Wainwright said, 'I'd like to ask you something.'

'Yes.'

'If you have a problem, a real problem, something I might help with, will you call me?'

It was the second such offer she had had in the past few days. 'Maybe.'

That – until much later – was the last conversation between Wainwright and Juanita. He felt he had done all he could, and had other things on his mind. One was a subject he had raised with Alex Vandervoort two months ago – planting an undercover informer in an attempt to track down the source of counterfeit credit cards, still gouging deep financial wounds in the Keycharge card system.

Wainwright had located an ex-convict, known to him only as 'Vic', who was prepared to take the considerable risk in return for money. They had had one secret meeting, with elaborate precautions. Another was expected.

Wainwright's fervent hope was to bring the credit card swindlers to justice, as he had Miles Eastin.

The following week, when Eastin appeared once more before Judge Underwood – this time for sentencing – Nolan Wainwright was the sole representative of First Mercantile American Bank in court.

With the prisoner standing, facing the bench on the court clerk's orders, the judge took his time about selecting several papers and spreading them before him, then regarded Eastin coldly.

'Do you have anything to say?'

'No, your honour.' The voice was barely audible.

'I have received a report from the probation officer' – Judge Underwood paused, scanning one of the papers he had selected earlier – 'whom you appear to have convinced that you are genuinely penitent for the criminal offences to which you have pleaded guilty.' The judge articulated the words 'genuinely penitent' as if holding them distastefully between thumb and forefinger, making clear that he was not so naïve as to share the opinion.

He continued, 'Penitence, however, whether genuine or otherwise, is not only belated but cannot mitigate your vicious, despicable attempt to thrust blame for your own malfeasance on to an innocent and unsuspecting person – a young woman – one, moreover, for whom you were responsible as a bank officer and who trusted you as her superior.

'On the basis of the evidence it is clear you would have persisted in that course, even to having your innocent victim accused, found guilty, and sentenced in your place. Fortunately, because of the vigilance of others, that did not occur. But it was not through any second thoughts or "penitence" of yours.'

From his seat in the body of the court, Nolan Wainwright had a partial view of Eastin's face which had suffused deep red.

Judge Underwood referred again to his papers, then looked up. His eyes, once more, impaled the prisoner.

'So far I have dealt with what I regard as the most contemptible part of your conduct. There is, additionally, the basic offence – your betrayal of trust as a bank officer, not merely once but on five occasions, widely separated. One such instance of dishonesty might be argued to be the result of reckless impulse. No such argument can be advanced for five carefully planned thefts, executed with perverted cleverness.

'A bank, as a commercial undertaking, is entitled to expect probity in those whom it selects – as you were selected – for exceptional trust. But a bank is more than a commercial institution. It is a place of public trust, and therefore the public is entitled to protection from those who abuse that trust – individuals such as you.'

The judge's gaze shifted to include the young defence counsel, waiting dutifully beside his client. Now the tone of voice from the bench became more brisk and formalized.

'Had this been a more ordinary case, and in view of the absence of a previous criminal record, I would have imposed probation as defence counsel eloquently urged last week. But this is no ordinary case. It is an exceptional one for the reasons I have stated. Therefore, Eastin, you will go to prison where you will have time to reflect on your own activities which brought you there.

'The sentence of the Court is that you be committed to the

155

custody of the Attorney General for a period of two years.'

At a nod from the court clerk, a jailer moved forward.

A brief conference took place, a few minutes after sentencing, in a small locked and guarded cubicle behind the courtroom, one of several reserved for prisoners and their legal counsel.

'The first thing to remember,' the young lawyer told Miles Eastin, 'is that a two-year prison term doesn't mean two years. You'll be eligible for parole after a third of the sentence is served. That's in less than a year.'

Miles Eastin, wrapped in misery and a sense of unreality, nodded dully.

'You can, of course, appeal the sentence, and you don't have to make a decision about that now. But I'll tell you frankly, I don't advise it. For one thing I don't believe you'd be released pending an appeal. For another, since you pleaded guilty, the grounds for appeal are limited. Also, by the time any appeal was heard, you might have served your sentence.'

'The ballgame's over. No appeal.'

'I'll be in touch with you anyway, in case you change your mind. And while I think of it, I'm sorry how things came out.'

Eastin acknowledged wryly, 'So am I.'

'It was your confession, of course, that did us in. Without that I don't believe the prosecution would have proved its case – at least the six-thousand-dollar cash theft, which weighed heaviest with the judge. I know, of course, why you signed that second statement – the FBI one; you thought the first was valid so another wouldn't make any difference. Well, it did. I'm afraid that security man, Wainwright, tricked you all the way.'

The prisoner nodded. 'Yes, I know that now.'

The lawyer looked at his watch. 'Well, I have to go. I've a heavy date tonight. You know how it is.'

A jailer let him out.

Next day Miles Eastin was transferred to a federal prison, out of state.

At First Mercantile American Bank, when news of Miles Eastin's sentencing was received among those who knew him, some felt regret, others held the view that the retribution was what he had deserved. One opinion was unanimous: no more would be heard of Eastin at the bank again.

Only time would prove how much in error that last assumption was.

part two

one

Like a bubble surfacing from underwater, the first hint of trouble appeared in mid-January. It was an item in a gossip column, 'Ear to the Ground', published in a city newspaper's Sunday edition.

The columnist wrote:

... Whispers around downtown predict major cutbacks soon at Forum East. 'Tis said the big-big rehab project has bankroll problems. Nowadays who hasn't? ...

Alex Vandervoort was unaware of the item until Monday morning when his secretary placed it, ringed in red, on his desk with other papers.

During Monday afternoon Edwina D'Orsey telephoned to enquire if Alex had read the rumour and if he knew of anything behind it. Edwina's concern was not surprising. Since the beginning of Forum East, her downtown branch bank had handled construction loans, many of the mortgages involved, and accompanying paperwork. By now the project represented an important segment of branch business.

'If there's something in the wind,' Edwina insisted, 'I want to be told.'

'So far as I know,' Alex reassured her, 'nothing's changed.'

Moments later he returned his hand to the telephone intending to check with Jerome Patterton, then changed his mind. Misinformation about Forum East was nothing new. The project had generated much publicity; inevitably some was inaccurate.

It was pointless, Alex decided, to bother the bank's new president with needless trivia, particularly when he wanted Patterton's support on a major issue – a large-scale expansion of FMA savings activity, now being planned for consideration by the board.

However, Alex was more concerned a few days later when a longer item appeared, this time in the regular news column of the daily *Times-Register*.

*   *   *

The report read:

Anxiety about the future of Forum East persists amid growing rumours that financial backing may shortly be reduced severely or withdrawn.

The Forum East project, which has as its long-term goal a total rehabilitation of the city's downtown core both business and residential, has been underwritten by a consortium of financial interests spearheaded by First Mercantile American Bank.

A spokesman for First Mercantile American today acknowledged the rumours but would make no comment except to say, 'An announcement will be forthcoming in due course.'

Under the Forum East plan, some inner city residential areas have already been modernized or rebuilt. A highrise, low-rental community development has been completed. Another is in progress.

A ten-year master plan includes programmes to improve schools, assist minority businesses, provide job training and employment as well as cultural opportunities and recreation. Major construction, begun two and a half years ago, has so far remained on schedule.

Alex read the morning news story at his apartment over breakfast. He was alone; Margot had been out of town on legal business for the past week.

On arrival at FMA Headquarters Tower he summoned Dick French. As vice-president of public relations, French, a burly, blunt-speaking ex-financial editor, ran his department knowledgeably.

'In the first place,' Alex demanded, 'who was the bank spokesman?'

'That was me,' French said. 'And I'll tell you right now I wasn't happy about that "statement in due course" crap. But Mr Patterton told me to use those words. He also insisted I shouldn't say more.'

'What more is there?'

'You tell me, Alex. Obviously something's going on and, good or bad, the sooner we put it on the line, the better.'

Alex curbed a rising anger. 'Is there a reason I wasn't consulted about any of this?'

The PR head appeared surprised. 'I thought you were. When I talked on the phone to Mr Patterton yesterday I know Roscoe was with him because I could hear them talking. I assumed you were in there, too.'

'Next time,' Alex said, 'don't assume anything.'

He dismissed French, then instructed his secretary to enquire if Jerome Patterton were free. He was informed that the president had not yet arrived at the bank, but was on his way, and Alex could see him at 11am. He grunted impatiently and went back to work on the savings expansion programme.

At eleven, Alex walked the few yards to the presidential suite – two corner rooms, each with a view of the city. Since the new president had taken over, the second room usually had the door closed and visitors were not invited in. Word had leaked out through secretaries that Patterton used it to practise putting on the rug.

Today, bright sunshine from a cloudless winter sky shone through the wall-wide windows on to Jerome Patterton's pink, near-hairless head. Seated behind a desk, he wore a light patterned suit, a switch from his usual tweeds. A newspaper in front of him was folded open to the news story which had brought Alex here.

On a sofa, in shadow, was Roscoe Heyward.

The three exchanged good mornings.

Patterton said, 'I asked Roscoe to stay because I'd a notion what the subject might be.' He touched the paper. 'You've seen this, of course.'

'I've seen it,' Alex said. 'I've also had Dick French in. He tells me that you and Roscoe discussed the press queries yesterday. So my first question is, why wasn't I informed? I'm as involved as anyone with Forum East.'

'You should have been informed, Alex.' Jerome Patterton seemed embarrassed. 'The truth is, I guess, we got a little rattled when the press calls showed there had been a leak.'

'A leak of what?'

It was Heyward who answered. 'Of a proposal I'll be bringing before the money policy committee next Monday. I'm suggesting a reduction of the bank's present commitment to Forum East by approximately fifty per cent.'

In view of the rumours which had surfaced, the confirmation was not surprising. What astounded Alex was the extent of the proposed incision.

He addressed Patterton. 'Jerome, do I understand that you are in favour of this incredible piece of folly?'

A flush suffused the president's face and egg-like head. 'It's neither true nor untrue. I've reserved judgement until Monday. What Roscoe has been doing here – yesterday and today – is some advance lobbying.'

'Right.' Heyward added blandly, 'An entirely legitimate tactic, Alex. And in case you object, let me remind you that on plenty of occasions you took your ideas to Ben in advance of money policy meetings.'

'If I did,' Alex said, 'they made a damn sight better sense than this one.'

'That, of course, is solely your opinion.'

'Not solely. Others share it.'

Heyward was unruffled. 'My own opinion is that we can put the bank's money to substantially better use.' He turned towards Patterton. 'Incidentally, Jerome, those rumours now circulating could be helpful to us if the proposal for a cutback is agreed to. At least the decision won't come as a sudden shock.'

'If you see it that way,' Alex said, 'maybe it was you who leaked the rumours.'

'I assure you it was not.'

'Then how do you explain them?'

Heyward shrugged. 'Coincidence, I suppose.'

Alex wondered: was it coincidence? Or had someone close to Roscoe Heyward floated a trial balloon on his behalf? Yes. It might well be Harold Austin, the Honourable Harold, who, as head of an advertising agency, would have plenty of contacts with the press. It seemed unlikely, though, that anyone would ever find out.

Jerome Patterton raised his hands. 'Both of you save any more arguments until Monday. We'll go over all of them then.'

*　　*　　*

'Let's not fool ourselves,' Alex Vandervoort insisted. 'The point we are deciding today is how much profit is reasonable and how much is excessive.'

Roscoe Heyward smiled. 'Frankly, Alex, I've never considered *any* profit excessive.'

'Nor have I,' Tom Straughan put in. 'I recognize, though, that making an exceptionally high profit is sometimes indiscreet and asking for trouble. It becomes known and criticized. At the end of the financial year we have to publish it.'

'Which is another reason,' Alex added, 'why we should strike a balance between achieving profit and giving service.'

'Profit is giving service to our shareholders,' Heyward said. 'That's the kind of service I put first.'

The bank's money policy committee was in session in an executive conference room. The committee, which had four members, met every other Monday morning with Roscoe Heyward as chairman. The other members were Alex and two senior vice-presidents – Straughan and Orville Young.

The committee's purpose was to decide the uses to which bank funds would be put. Major decisions were referred afterwards to the board of directors for confirmation, though the board rarely changed what the committee recommended.

Individual sums discussed here were seldom less than in the tens of millions.

The president of the bank sat in, ex officio, at the committee's more important meetings, voting only if it became necessary to break a tie. Jerome Patterton was here today, though so far he had not contributed to the discussion.

Being debated now was Roscoe Heyward's proposal for a drastic cut in Forum East financing.

Within the next few months, if Forum East was to continue as programmed, new construction loans and mortgage funds would be required. First Mercantile American's expected share of this financing was fifty million dollars. Heyward had proposed a reduction of that amount by half.

He had pointed out already, 'We will make clear to all concerned that we are not opting out of Forum East, nor do we intend to. The explanation we will give is simply that in light of

165

other commitments, we have adjusted the flow of funds. The project will not be halted. It will simply proceed more slowly than was planned.'

'If you look at it in terms of need,' Alex had protested, 'progress is already slower than it should be. Retarding it still further is the worst thing we can do in every way.'

'I am looking at it in terms of need,' Heyward said. 'The bank's need.'

The riposte was uncharacteristically flip, perhaps, Alex thought, because Heyward was confident that today's decision would go the way he wanted. Alex was sure that Tom Straughan would join him in opposing Heyward. Straughan was the bank's chief economist – young, studious, but with a broad spectrum of interests – whom Alex had personally promoted over the heads of others.

But Orville Young, treasurer of First Mercantile American, was Heyward's man and would undoubtedly vote with him.

In FMA, as in any major bank, the true lines of power were seldom reflected in organizational charts. Real authority flowed sideways or in detours, depending on loyalties of individuals to other individuals, so that those who chose not to join in power struggles were by-passed or marooned in backwaters.

The power struggle between Alex Vandervoort and Roscoe Heyward was already well known. Because of it, some FMA executives had chosen sides, pinning their hopes for advancement on the victory of one adversary or the other. The split was also evident in the line-up of the money policy committee.

Alex argued, 'Our profit last year was thirteen per cent. That's damned good for any business, as all of us know. This year the prospect's even better – a fifteen per cent return on investment maybe sixteen. But should we strain for more ?'

The treasurer, Orville Young, asked, 'Why not ?'

'I already answered that,' Straughan shot back. 'It's short-sighted.'

'Let's remind ourselves of one thing,' Alex urged. 'In banking it's not hard to make large profits, and any bank that doesn't is manned by simpletons. In plenty of ways the cards are stacked in our favour. We've opportunities, our own experience, and reasonable banking laws. The last is probably the most important. But the laws won't always be as reasonable – that is, if we go on abusing the situation and abdicating community responsibility.'

'I fail to see how staying in Forum East is abdicating,' Roscoe Heyward said. 'Even after the reduction I'm proposing, we'd still be committed substantially.'

'Substantially, my foot! It would be minimal, just as the social contribution of American banks has always been minimal. In financing of low-income housing alone the record of this bank and every other is dismal. Why fool ourselves ? For generations banking has ignored public problems. Even now we do the minimum we can get away with.'

The chief economist, Straughan, shuffling papers, consulted some handwritten notes. 'I intended to bring up the subject of home mortgages, Roscoe. Now Alex has, I'd like to point out that only twenty-five per cent of our savings deposits are currently in mortgage loans. That's low. We could increase it to fifty per cent of deposits without harming our liquidity position. I believe we should.'

'I'll second that,' Alex said. 'Our branch managers are pleading for mortgage money. The return on investment is fair. We know from experience the downside risk on mortgages is negligible.'

Orville Young objected, 'It ties up money for long term, money on which we can earn substantially higher rates elsewhere.'

Alex slammed the flat of his hand impatiently on the conference table. 'Once in a while we've a public obligation to accept lower rates. That's the point I'm making. It's why I object to weaselling out of Forum East.'

'There's one more reason,' Tom Straughan added. 'Alex touched on it – legislation. Already there are rumblings in Congress. A good many there would like to see a law similar to Mexico's – requiring a fixed percentage of bank deposits to be used for financing low-income housing.'

Heyward scoffed, 'We'd never let it happen. The banking lobby is the strongest in Washington.'

167

The chief economist shook his head. 'I wouldn't count on that.'

'Tom,' Roscoe Heyward said, 'I'll make a promise. A year from now we'll take a fresh look at mortgages; maybe we'll do what you advocate; maybe we'll re-open Forum East. But not this year. I want this to be a bumper profit year.' He glanced towards the bank president who had still not joined in the discussion. 'And so does Jerome.'

For the first time Alex perceived the shape of Heyward's strategy. A year of exceptional profit for the bank would make Jerome Patterton, as president, a hero to its shareholders and directors. All Patterton had was a one-year reign at the end of a so-so career, but he would go into retirement with glory and the sound of trumpets. And Patterton was human. Therefore it was understandable the idea would appeal to him.

The scenario afterwards was equally easy to guess. Jerome Patterton, grateful to Roscoe Heyward, would promote the idea of Heyward as his successor. And, because of the profitable year, Patterton would be in a strong position to make his wishes work.

It was a neatly ingenious sequence, devised by Heyward, which Alex would find hard to break.

'There's something else I haven't mentioned,' Heyward said. 'Not even to you, Jerome. It could have a bearing on our decision today.'

The others regarded him with fresh curiosity.

'I'm hopeful, in fact the probability is strong, that we shall shortly enjoy substantial business with Supranational Corporation. It's another reason I'm reluctant to commit funds elsewhere.'

'That's fantastic news,' Orville Young said.

Even Tom Straughan reacted with surprised approval.

Supranational – or SuNatCo, as identified by its familiar worldwide logo – was a multinational giant, the General Motors of global communications. As well, SuNatCo owned or controlled dozens of other companies, related and unrelated to its main purpose. Its prodigious influence with governments of all stripes, from democracies through dictatorships, was reportedly greater than that of any other business complex in history. Observers sometimes said that SuNatCo had more real power than most of the sovereign states in which it operated.

Until now, SuNatCo had confined its US banking activity to the big three – Bank of America, First National City, and Chase Manhattan. To be added to this exclusive trio would boost immeasurably the status of First Mercantile American.

'That's an exciting prospect, Roscoe,' Patterton said.

'I expect to have more details for our next money policy meeting,' Heyward added. 'It appears likely that Supranational will want us to open a substantial line of credit.'

It was Tom Straughan who reminded them, 'We still need a vote on Forum East.'

'So we do,' Heyward acknowledged. He was smiling confidently, pleased at the reaction to his announcement and certain of the way the Forum East decision would go.

Predictably, they divided two by two – Alex Vandervoort and Tom Straughan opposed to the cutback of funds, Roscoe Heyward and Orville Young in favour of it.

Heads swung to Jerome Patterton who had the decisive vote.

The bank president hesitated only briefly, then announced, 'Alex, on this one I'll go with Roscoe.'

two

'Sitting around here feeling sorry won't do one damn bit of good,' Margot declared. 'What we need is to rise off our collective asses and initiate some action.'

'Like dynamiting the goddam bank ?' someone asked.

'Nix on that! I've friends in there. Besides, blowing up banks isn't legal.'

'Who says we have to stay legal ?'

'I do,' Margot snapped. 'And if any smart cats think otherwise, you can find yourselves some other mouthpiece and another pad.'

Margot Bracken's law office, on a Thursday evening, was the scene of an executive committee meeting of the Forum East Tenants Association. The association was one of many groups in the inner city for which Margot was legal counsel and which used her office for meetings, a convenience for which she was occasionally paid, but mostly wasn't.

Fortunately her office was a modest affair – two rooms in what had once been a local grocer's shop and some of the ancient merchandise shelves now housed her law books. The remainder of the furnishings, mostly ill-assorted, comprised bits and pieces she had acquired cheaply.

Typical of the general neighbourhood, two other former shops, on either side, were abandoned and boarded up. Some day, with luck and enterprise, the rehabilitating tide of Forum East might lap this particular area. It hadn't yet.

But developments at Forum East had brought them here.

The day before yesterday, in a public announcement, First Mercantile American Bank had changed rumour into fact. Financing of future Forum East projects was to be cut in half, effective at once.

The bank's statement was couched in officialese with euphemistic phrases like 'temporary shortage of long-term funding' and 'periodic reconsideration will be given', but no one believed the last and everyone, inside and outside the bank, knew exactly what the statement meant – the axe.

The meeting now was to determine what, if anything, could be done.

The word 'tenants' in the association's name was a loose one. A large segment of members were Forum East tenants; many others were not, but hoped to be. As Deacon Euphrates, a towering steelworker who had spoken earlier, put it, 'There's plenty of us, expectin' to be in, who ain't gonna make it if the big bread doan' come through.'

Margot knew that Deacon, his wife and five children lived in a tiny, crowded walk-up, part of a rat-infested tenement that should have been torn down years ago. She had made several attempts to help them find other rental quarters, without success. A hope that Deacon Euphrates lived with was that he would move his family into one of the new Forum East housing units, but the Euphrates' name was only mid-way on a long waiting list and a slowdown in construction was likely to keep it there for a long time to come.

The FMA announcement had been a shock to Margot, too. Alex, she was sure, would have resisted any cutback proposal within the bank, but obviously he had been over-ruled. For that reason she had not discussed the subject with him yet. Also, the less Alex knew about some simmering plans of Margot's, the better for them both.

'The way I see the ball game,' Seth Orinda, another committee member, said, 'whatever we do, and legal or not, there's no way, but no way, we can squeeze that money out of those banks. That is, if they've their minds set on clamming up.'

Seth Orinda was a black high school teacher, already 'in' at Forum East. But he possessed a keen civic sense and cared greatly about the thousands of others still waiting hopefully on the outside. Margot relied a good deal on his stability and help.

'Don't be so sure, Seth,' she responded. 'Banks have soft underbellies. Stick a harpoon in a tender place and surprising things could happen.'

'What kind of harpoon?' Orinda asked. 'A parade? A sit-in? A demonstration?'

'No,' Margot said. 'Forget all that stuff. It's old hat. Nobody's impressed by conventional demonstrations any more. They're just a nuisance. They achieve nothing.'

She surveyed the group facing her in the crowded, cluttered, smoky office. They were a dozen or so, mixed blacks and whites, in assorted shapes, sizes, and demeanours. Some were perched precariously on rickety chairs and boxes, others squatted on the floor. 'Listen carefully, all of you. I said we need some action, and there *is* a kind of action which I believe will work.'

'Miss Bracken.' A small figure near the back of the room stood up. It was Juanita Núñez, whom Margot had greeted when she came in.

'Yes, Mrs Núñez?'

'I want to help. But you know, I think, that I work for the FMA bank. Perhaps I should not hear what you will tell the others . . .'

Margot said appreciatively, 'No, and I should have thought of that instead of embarrassing you.'

There was a general murmur of understanding. Amid it, Juanita made her way to the door.

'What you heard awready,' Deacon Euphrates said, 'that's a secret, ain't it ?'

As Juanita nodded, Margot said quickly, 'We can all trust Mrs Núñez. I hope her employers are as ethical as she is.'

When the meeting had settled down again, Margot faced the remaining members. Her stance was characteristic: hands on small waist, elbows aggressively out. A moment earlier she had pushed her long chestnut hair back – a gesture of habit before action, like the raising of a curtain. As she talked, interest heightened. A smile or two appeared. At one point Seth Orinda chuckled deeply. Near the end, Deacon Euphrates and others were grinning broadly.

'Man, oh man!' Deacon said.

'That's goddamn clever,' someone else put it.

Margot reminded them, 'To make the whole scheme work, we need a lot of people – at least a thousand to begin with, and more as time goes on.'

A fresh voice asked, 'How long we need 'em ?'

'We'll plan on a week. A banking week, that is – five days. If that doesn't work we should consider going longer and extending our scope of operations. Frankly, though, I don't believe it will be necessary. Another thing: everyone involved must be carefully briefed.'

'I'll help with that,' Seth Orinda volunteered.

There was an immediate chorus of, 'So will I.'

Deacon Euphrates's voice rose above others. 'I got time comin' to me. Goddamn, I'll use it; take a week off work, an' I can pull in others.'

'Good!' Margot said. She went on decisively, 'We'll need a master plan. I'll have that ready by tomorrow night. The rest of

172

you should begin recruiting right away. And remember, secrecy is important.'

Half an hour later the meeting broke up, the committee members far more cheerful and optimistic than when they had assembled.

At Margot's request, Seth Orinda stayed behind. She told him, 'Seth, in a special way I need your help.'

'You know I'll give it if I can, Miss Bracken.'

'When any action starts,' Margot said, 'I'm usually at the front of it. You know that.'

'I sure do.' The high school teacher beamed.

'This time I want to stay out of sight. Also, I don't want my name involved when newspapers, TV, and radio start their coverage. If that happened it could embarrass two special friends of mine – the ones I spoke about at the bank. I want to prevent that.'

Orinda nodded sagely. 'So far as I can see, no problem.'

'What I'm really asking,' Margot insisted, 'is that you and the others front this one for me. I'll be behind scenes, of course. And if there's need to, you can call me, though I hope you won't.'

'That's silly,' Seth Orinda said. 'How could we call you when none of us ever heard your name ?'

On Saturday evening, two days after the Forum East Tenants Association meeting, Margot and Alex were guests at a small dinner party given by friends, and afterwards went together to Margot's apartment. It was in a less fashionable part of the city than Alex's elegant suite, and was smaller, but Margot had furnished it pleasingly with period pieces she had collected at modest prices in the course of years. Alex loved to be there.

The apartment was greatly in contrast to Margot's law office.

'I missed you, Bracken,' Alex said. He had changed into pyjamas and a robe which he kept at Margot's and was relaxed in a Queen Anne wing chair, Margot curled on a rug before him, her head tilted back against his knees while he stroked her long hair gently. Occasionally his fingers strayed – gentle and sexually skilful, beginning to arouse her as he always did, and in the way she loved. Margot sighed with gratification. Soon they would go to bed. Yet, while mutual desire mounted, there was exquisite pleasure in self-imposed delay.

It was a week and a half since they had last been together, conflicting schedules having kept them apart.

'We'll make up for those lost days,' Margot said.

Alex was silent. Then, 'You know, I've been waiting all evening for you to fry me on a griddle about Forum East. Instead, you haven't said a word.'

Margot tilted her head farther back, looking at him upside down. She asked innocently, 'Why should I fry you, darling? The bank's money cutback wasn't your idea.' Her small brow furrowed. 'Or was it?'

'You know darn well it wasn't.'

'Of course I knew. Just as I was equally sure that you'd opposed it.'

'Yes, I opposed it.' He added ruefully, 'For all the good it did.'

'You tried your best. That's all anyone can ask.'

Alex regarded her suspiciously. 'None of this is like you.'

'Not like me in what way?'

'You're a fighter. It's one of the things I love about you. You don't give up. You won't accept defeat calmly.'

'Perhaps some defeats are total. In that case nothing can be done.'

Alex sat up straight. 'You're up to something, Bracken! I know it. Now tell me what it is.'

Margot considered, then said slowly, 'I'm not admitting anything. But even if what you just said is true, it could be there are certain things it's better you don't know. Something I'd never want to do, Alex, is embarrass you.'

He smiled affectionately. 'You *have* told me something after all. All right, if you don't want any probing, I won't do it. But I'll ask one assurance: that whatever you have in mind is legal.'

Momentarily, Margot's temper flared. 'I'm the lawyer around here. I'll decide what's legal and what isn't.'

'Even clever lady lawyers make mistakes.'

'Not this time.' She seemed about to argue further, then relented. Her voice softened. 'You know I always operate inside the law. Also you know why.'

'Yes, I do,' Alex said. Relaxed once more, he went back to stroking her hair.

She had confided in him once, after they knew each other well, about her reasoning, reached years before, the result of tragedy and loss.

At law school, where Margot was an honours student she had joined, like others at the time, in activism and protest. It was the period of increasing American involvement in Vietnam and bitter divisions in the nation. It was the beginning, too, of restlessness and change within the legal profession, a rebellion of youth against the law's elders and establishment, a time for a new breed of belligerent lawyer of whom Ralph Nader was the publicized, lauded symbol.

Earlier at college, and later at law school, Margot had shared her *avant-garde* views, her activism, and herself with a male fellow student – the only name Alex ever heard was Gregory – and Gregory and Margot cohabited, as was customary, too.

For several months there had been student-administration confrontations and one of the worst began over the official appearance on campus of US Army and Navy recruiters. A student body majority, including Gregory and Margot, wanted the recruiters ordered off. The school authorities took an opposite, strong view.

In protest, militant students occupied the Administration Building, barricading themselves in and others out. Gregory and Margot, caught up in the general fervour, were among them.

Negotiations began but failed, not least because the students presented 'non-negotiable demands'. After two days the administration summoned state police, later unwisely supplemented by the National Guard. An assault was launched upon the now beleaguered building. During the fighting, shots were fired and heads were cracked. By a miracle, the shots hit no one. But, by tragic misfortune, one of the cracked heads – Gregory's – suffered a brain haemorrhage, resulting in death a few hours later.

Eventually, because of public indignation, an inexperienced, young, and frightened policeman who had struck the mortal blow, was arraigned in court. Charges against him were dismissed.

Margot, though in deep grief and shock, was enough of an objective law student to understand the dismissal. Her law training helped her also, amid later calmness, to evaluate and codify her own convictions. It was a belated process which the pressures of excitement and emotion had prevented far too long.

None of Margot's political and social views were diminished, either then or since. But she had the honest perception to recognize that the student body faction had withheld from others those same freedoms of which they claimed to be defenders. They had also, in their zeal, transgressed the law, a system to which their scholarship was dedicated, and presumably their lives.

It was only one step further in reasoning, which Margot took, to acknowledge that no less would have been achieved, and probably far more, by staying within legal limits.

As she confided to Alex during the only time they ever talked about that portion of the past, it had become her guiding principle, in all her activism, ever since.

Still curled comfortingly close to him, she said, 'How are things at the bank?'

'Some days I feel like Sisyphus. Remember him?'

'Wasn't he the Greek who pushed a rock uphill? Every time he got near the top it rolled back down again.'

'That's the one. He should have been a bank executive trying to make changes. You know something about us bankers, Bracken?'

'Tell me.'

'We succeed despite our lack of foresight and imagination.'

'May I quote you?'

'If you do, I'll swear I never said it.' He mused. 'But between us privately, banking always reacts to social change, never anticipates it. All the problems which affect us now – environment, ecology, energy, minorities – have been with us a long time. What's happened in those areas to affect us could have been foreseen. We bankers could be leaders. Instead we're following, moving forward only when we have to, when we're pushed.'

'Why stay a banker then ?'

'Because it's important. What we do is worthwhile and whether we move forward voluntarily or not, we're professionals who are needed. The money system has become so huge, so complicated and sophisticated that only banks can handle it.'

'So your greatest need is a shove now and then. Right ?'

He looked at her intently, his curiosity reviving. 'You're planning *something* in that convoluted pixie mind of yours.'

'I admit nothing.'

'Whatever it is, I hope it doesn't involve pay toilets.'

'Oh God, no!'

At the year-old memory, both laughed aloud. It had been one of Margot's combat victories and created wide attention.

Her battle had been with the city's airport commission which, at the time, was paying its several hundred janitors and cleaners substantially lower wages than were normal in the area. The workers' union was corrupt, had a 'sweetheart contract' with the commission, and had done nothing to help. In desperation a group of airport employees sought help from Margot who was beginning to build a reputation in such matters.

A frontal approach by Margot to the commission produced merely a rebuff. She therefore decided that public attention must be gained and one way to obtain it was by ridiculing the airport and its rulers. In preparation, and working with several other sympathizers who had aided her before, she made an intelligence study of the big, busy airport during a heavy traffic night.

A factor noted by the study was that when evening flights, on which dinner and drinks had been served, disgorged their passengers, the bulk of the arrivals headed promptly for airport toilets, thus creating maximum demand for those facilities over a period of several hours.

The following Friday night, when incoming and departing air traffic was heaviest of all, several hundred volunteers, principally off-duty janitors and cleaners, arrived at the airport under Margot's direction. From then until they left much later, all were quiet, orderly, and law abiding.

The purpose was to occupy, continuously throughout the

evening, every public toilet in the airport. And they did. Margot and assistants had prepared a detailed plan and the volunteers went to assigned locations where they paid a dime and settled down, solaced by reading material, portable radios, and even food which many brought. Some of the women had their tapestry or knitting. It was the ultimate in legal sit-ins.

In the men's toilets, more volunteers formed lines in front of urinals, each dilatory line moving with stunning slowness. If a male not in the plot joined any lineup it took him an hour to reach the front. Few, if any, waited that long.

A floating contingent explained quietly to anyone who would listen what was happening, and why.

The airport became a shambles with hundreds of angry, anguished passengers complaining bitterly and heatedly to airlines who, in turn, assailed airport management. The latter found themselves frustrated and helpless to do anything. Other observers, not involved or in need, found the situation hilarious. No one was indifferent.

News media representatives, tipped off by Margot in advance were present in force. Reporters vied with each other to write stories which were carried nationwide by wire services, then repeated internationally and used by such differing journals as *Izvestia*, Johannesburg *Star*, and *The Times* of London. Next day, as a result, the entire world was laughing.

In most news reports the name Margot Bracken figured prominently. There were intimations that more 'sit-ins' would follow.

As Margot had calculated, ridicule is one of the stronger weapons in any arsenal. Over the week-end the airport commission conceded that discussions would be held on janitors' and cleaners' wages, which resulted in increases soon after. A further development was that the corrupt union was voted out, a more honest one replacing it.

Now Margot stirred, moving closer to Alex, then said softly, 'What kind of a mind was it that you said·I had ?'

'Convoluted pixie.'

'That's bad ? Or good ?'

'It's good for me. Refreshing. And most of the time I like the causes that you work for.'

'But not all the time?'

'No, not always.'

'Sometimes the things I do create antagonism. Lots of it. Suppose the antagonism was about something you didn't believe in, or disliked? Suppose our names were linked together at a time like that, when you wouldn't want to be associated with me?'

'I'd learn to live with it. Besides, I'm entitled to a private life, and so are you.'

'So is any woman,' Margot said. 'But I wonder sometimes if you really could live with it. That's if we were together all the time. I wouldn't change, you know; you have to understand that, Alex darling. I couldn't surrender independence, nor ever stop being myself and taking initiatives.'

He thought of Celia who had taken no initiatives, ever, and how he had wished she would. And he remembered, as always with remorse, what Celia had become. He had learned something from her though: that no man is whole unless the woman he loves is free, and knows the use of freedom, exploiting it in fulfilment of herself.

Alex dropped his hands to Margot's shoulders. Through a thin silk nightgown he could sense the fragrant warmth of her, feel the softness of her flesh. He said gently, 'It's the way you are that's the way I love and want you. If you changed, I'd hire some other lady lawyer and sue for breach of loving.'

His hands left her shoulders, moving slowly, caressingly lower. He heard her breathing quicken; a moment later she turned to him, urgent and gasping. 'What the hell are we waiting for?'

'God knows,' he said. 'Let's go to bed.'

three

The sight was so unusual that one of the branch's loan officers, Cliff Castleman, strolled over to the platform.

'Mrs D'Orsey, have you looked out of a window yet, by any chance ?'

'No,' Edwina said. She had been concentrating on the morning mail. 'Why should I ?'

It was 8.55am, Wednesday, at First Mercantile American's main downtown branch.

'Well,' Castleman said, 'I thought you might be interested. There's a line-up outside such as I've never seen ahead of opening time before.'

Edwina looked up. Several staff members were craning to look out of windows. There was a buzz of conversation among the employees generally, unusual this early in the day. She sensed an undercurrent of concern.

Leaving her desk, Edwina walked a few paces to one of the large plate-glass windows, part of the street frontage of the building. What she saw amazed her. A long queue of people, four or five abreast, extended from the main front door past the entire length of the building and out of sight beyond. It appeared as if all were waiting for the bank to open.

She stared incredulously. 'What on earth . . . ?'

'Someone went outside just now,' Castleman informed her. 'They say the line extends half-way across Rosselli Plaza and more people are joining it all the time.'

'Has anyone asked what they all want ?'

'One of the security guards did, I understand. The answer was, they've come to open accounts.'

'That's ridiculous! *All* of those people ? There must be three hundred I can see from here. We've never had that many new accounts in a single day.'

The loan officer shrugged. 'I'm simply passing on what I heard.'

Tottenhoe, the operations officer, joined them at the window, his face transmitting his normal grumpiness. 'I've notified Central Security,' he informed Edwina. 'They say they'll send more guards and Mr Wainwright's coming over. Also, they're advising the city police.'

Edwina commented, 'There's no outward sign of trouble. Those people all seem peaceful.'

It was a mixed group, she could see, about two thirds women, with a preponderance of blacks. Many of the women were accompanied by children. Among the men, some were in overalls, appearing as if they had left their jobs or were on the way to them. Others were in casual clothing, a few well dressed.

People in the line-up were talking to each other, some animatedly, but no one appeared antagonistic. A few, seeing themselves observed, smiled and nodded to the bank officials.

'Look at that!' Cliff Castleman pointed. A TV crew with camera had appeared. While Edwina and the others watched, it began filming.

'Peaceful or not,' the loan officer said, 'there has to be a motive behind all these people coming here at once.'

A flash of insight struck Edwina. 'It's Forum East,' she said. 'I'll bet it's Forum East.'

Several others whose desks were nearby had approached and were listening.

Tottenhoe said, 'We should delay opening until the extra guards get here.'

All eyes swung to a wall clock which showed a minute to nine.

'No,' Edwina instructed. She raised her voice so that others could hear. 'We'll open as usual, on time. Everyone go back to their work, please.'

Tottenhoe hurried away, Edwina returning to the platform and her desk.

From her vantage point she watched the main doors swing open and the first arrivals pour in. Those who had been at the head of the line paused momentarily on entry, looked around curiously, then quickly moved forward as others behind pressed in. Within moments the central public area of the big branch bank was filled with a chattering, noisy crowd. The building, relatively quiet less than a minute earlier, had become a babel.

Edwina saw a tall heavyset black man wave some dollar bills and declare loudly, 'Ah want to put ma money in th' bank.'

A security guard directed him, 'Over there for new accounts.'

The guard pointed to a desk where a clerk – a young girl – sat waiting. She appeared nervous. The big man walked towards her, smiled reassuringly, and sat down. Immediately a press of others moved into a ragged line behind him, waiting for their turns.

It seemed as if the report about everyone having come to open an account had been accurate after all.

Edwina could see the big man leaning back expansively, still holding his dollar bills. His voice cut across the noise of other conversations and she heard him proclaim, 'Ah'm in no hurry. There's some things ah'd like yo' to explain.'

Two other desks were quickly manned by other clerks. With equal speed, long wide lines of people formed in front of them.

Normally, three members of staff were ample to handle new account business, but obviously were inadequate now. Edwina could see Tottenhoe on the far side of the bank and called him on the intercom. She instructed, 'Use more desks for new accounts and take all the staff you can spare to man them.'

Even leaning close to the intercom, it was hard to hear above the noise.

Tottenhoe grumbled in reply, 'You realize we can't possibly process all these people today, and however many we do will tie us up completely.'

'I've an idea,' Edwina said, 'that's what someone has in mind. Just hurry the processing all you can.'

Yet she knew however much they hurried it would still take ten to fifteen minutes to open any single new account. It always did. The paperwork required that time.

First, an application form called for details of residence, employment, social security, and family matters. A specimen signature was obtained. Then proof of identity was needed. After that, the new accounts clerk would take all documents to an officer of the bank for approval and initialling. Finally, a savings passbook was made out or a temporary cheque book issued.

Therefore the most new accounts that any bank employee

could open in an hour were five, so the three clerks currently working might handle a total of ninety in one business day, *if* they kept going at top speed, which was unlikely.

Even tripling the present complement of clerks would permit very few more than two hundred and fifty accounts to be opened in a day, yet already, in the first few minutes of business, the bank was crammed with at least four hundred people, with still more flooding in, and the line outside, which Edwina rose to check, appeared as long as ever.

Still the noise within the bank increased. It had become an uproar.

A further problem was that the growing mass of arrivals in the central public area of the bank was preventing access to tellers' counters by other customers. Edwina could see a few of them outside, regarding the milling scene with consternation. While she watched, several gave up and walked away.

Inside the bank some of the newcomers were engaging tellers in conversation and the tellers, having nothing else to do because of the mêlée, chatted back.

Two assistant managers had gone to the central floor area and were trying to regulate the flood of people so as to clear some space at counters. They were having small success.

But still no hostility was evident. Everyone in the now jam-packed bank who was spoken to by members of the staff answered politely and with a smile. It seemed, Edwina thought, as if all who were here had been briefed to be on best behaviour.

She decided it was time for her own intervention.

Edwina left the platform and a railed-off staff area and, with difficulty, made her way through the milling crowd to the main front door. Signalling two security guards who elbowed their way towards her, she instructed, 'That's enough people in the bank. Hold everyone else outside, letting a few in as the others leave. Except, of course, allow our regular customers to enter as they arrive.'

The older of the two guards put his head close to Edwina's to make himself heard. 'That won't be so easy, Mrs D'Orsey. Some customers we'll recognize but a good many we won't. We get too many here each day to know 'em all.'

'Another thing,' the other guard put in, 'when anybody arrives, those outside are shouting, "Back of the line!" If we play favourites it could start a riot.'

Edwina assured him, 'There won't be any riot. Just do your best.'

Turning back, Edwina spoke to several of those waiting. The surrounding constant conversations made it difficult to be heard and she raised her voice. 'I'm the manager. Would some of you please tell me why you've all come here today?'

'We're opening accounts,' a woman with a child beside her said. She giggled. 'Nothing wrong with that, is there?'

'An' you guys put out them ads,' another voice injected. 'Ain't no amount too small to start one, is what they say.'

'That's true,' Edwina said, 'and the bank means it. But there has to be some reason why you all chose to come together.'

'You could say,' an elderly cadaverous man chimed in, 'we're all from Forum East.'

A younger voice added, 'Or want to be.'

'That still doesn't tell me . . .' Edwina began.

'Perhaps I can explain, ma'am.' A middle-aged, distinguished-looking black man was being shoved forward through the press of people.

'Please do.'

At the same moment Edwina was aware of a new figure beside her. Turning, she saw it was Nolan Wainwright. And at the main doorway several more security guards had arrived and were assisting the original two. She glanced interrogatively at the security chief who advised, 'Go ahead. You're doing okay.'

The man who had been thrust forward said, 'Good morning, ma'am. I didn't know there were lady bank managers.'

'Well, there are,' Edwina told him. 'And getting to be more of us all the time. I hope you believe in the equality of women, Mr . . . ?'

'Orinda. Seth Orinda, ma'am. And I sure do believe in that, and lots of other things besides.'

'Is it one of the other things that brings you here today?'

'In a way, you could say that.'

'Exactly what way?'

'I think you know we're all from Forum East.'

She acknowledged, 'I've been told that.'

'What we're doing might be called an act of hope.' The well-dressed spokesman mouthed his words carefully. They had been scripted and rehearsed. More people drew close, conversation stilling as they listened.

Orinda went on, 'This bank, so it says, doesn't have enough money to go on helping Forum East get built. Anyway, the bank has cut its lending cash in half and some of us think that other half will get chopped too, that's if someone doesn't beat a drum or take some action.'

Edwina said sharply, 'And taking action, I suppose, means bringing the business of this entire branch bank to a standstill.' As she spoke, she was aware of several new faces in the crowd and of open notebooks with racing pencils. She realized that reporters had arrived.

Obviously someone had alerted the press in advance, which explained the presence of the TV camera crew outside. Edwina wondered who had done it.

Seth Orinda looked pained. 'What we're doing, ma'am, is bringing all the money we poor folks can raise to help this bank through its time of trouble.'

'Yep,' another voice threw in, 'ain't that good neighbourin' for sure ?'

Nolan Wainwright snapped, 'That's nonsense! This bank is not in trouble.'

'If it ain't in trouble,' a woman asked, 'why'd it do what it done to Forum East ?'

'The bank's position was made perfectly clear in its announcement,' Edwina answered. 'It's a question of priorities. Furthermore, the bank has said it hopes to resume the full financing later.' Even to herself the words sounded hollow. Others evidently thought so too because a chorus of jeers erupted.

It was the first note of antagonism and ugliness. The distinguished-looking man, Seth Orinda, turned sharply, raising a hand in caution. The jeering ceased.

'Whichever way it looks to you folks here,' he asserted to Edwina, 'the fact is, we've all come to put some money in your bank. That's what I mean by an act of hope. We figure that when you see us all, and realize the way we feel, you'll maybe change your minds.'

'And if we don't ?'

'Then I reckon we'll go on finding more people and more bits of money. And we can do it. We've a lot more good souls coming here today, and tomorrow, and the day after. Then, by the week-end, word will have got around' – he swung towards the press reporters – 'so there'll be others, and not just from Forum East, who'll join with us next week. Just to open an account, of course. To help out this poor bank. Nothing else.'

More voices added cheerfully, 'Yeah man, a whole lot more people' . . . 'We ain't got much bread, but we sure got numbers' . . . 'Tell your friends to come an' support us.'

'Of course,' Orinda said, his expression innocent, 'some of the folks who are putting money in the bank today may have to come and take it out tomorrow, or the next day, or next week. Most haven't got so much that they can leave it in long. But then, soon as we can we'll be back to put it in again.' His eyes glittered mischievously. 'We aim to keep you busy.'

'Yes,' Edwina said, 'I understand your aim.'

One of the reporters, a slim blonde girl, asked, 'Mr Orinda, how much will all of you be depositing in the bank ?'

'Not much,' he told her cheerfully. 'Most have come with just five dollars. That's the smallest amount this bank will take. Isn't that right ?' He looked at Edwina who nodded.

Some banks, as Edwina and those listening were aware, required a minimum of fifty dollars to open a savings account, a hundred for checking. A few had no minimums at all. First Mercantile American – seeking to encourage small savers – compromised at five dollars.

Another thing – once an account was accepted, most of the original five dollars could be withdrawn, with any credit balance sufficient to keep the account open. Seth Orinda and others had clearly realized this and proposed to drown the downtown branch bank with in-and-out transactions. Edwina thought: they might well succeed.

Yet nothing illegal or provably obstructionist was being done.

Despite her responsibilities and annoyance of a few moments earlier, Edwina was tempted to laugh, though realized she mustn't. She glanced again at Nolan Wainwright who shrugged and said quietly, 'While there's no obvious disturbance there's nothing we can do except regulate the traffic.'

The bank security chief swung towards Orinda and said firmly, 'We'll expect all of you to help us keep this place orderly, inside and out. Our guards will give directions about how many people can come in at once, and where the waiting line should stay.'

The other nodded agreement. 'Naturally, sir, my friends and I will do everything possible to help. We don't want any disturbance either. But we shall expect you to be fair.'

'What's that mean?'

'Those of us in here,' Orinda declared, 'and those outside, are customers just like anybody else who comes to this bank. And while we're willing to wait our turn and be patient, we don't expect others to get specially favoured treatment or to be allowed in here ahead of us who've waited. What I mean is, anybody arriving – no matter who – must go to the back of the line.'

'We'll see about that.'

'So will we, sir. Because if you do it some other way, it'll be a clear case of discrimination. Then you'll hear us holler.'

The reporters, Edwina saw, were still making notes.

She eased her way through the press of people, to the three new account desks, already supplemented by two more, while a further two were being set up.

One of the auxiliary desks, Edwina noted, was occupied by Juanita Núñez. She caught Edwina's eyes, and they exchanged smiles. Edwina was suddenly reminded that the Núñez girl lived at Forum East. Had she known in advance of today's invasion? Then she reasoned: either way, it made no difference.

Two of the bank's junior officers were supervising the new account activity and it was clear that all other work today would fall seriously behind.

The heavyset black man, who had been among the earliest arrivals was getting up as Edwina arrived. The girl who had dealt with him, no longer nervous, said, 'This is Mr Euphrates. He just opened an account.'

'Deacon Euphrates. Least, that's what most call me.' Edwina was offered an enormous hand which she took.

'Welcome to First Mercantile American, Mr Euphrates.'

'Thank you, that's real nice. In fact, so nice that I think maybe after all I'll pop a little more bread in this here account.' He examined a handful of small change, selected a quarter and two dimes, then strolled over to a teller.

Edwina asked the new accounts clerk, 'What was the initial deposit ?'

'Five dollars.'

'Very well. Just try to keep going as fast as you can.'

'I'll do that, Mrs D'Orsey, but that one took a long time because he asked a lot of questions about withdrawals and interest rates. He had them written out on paper.'

'Did you get the paper ?'

'No.'

'Others will probably have the same thing. Try to get one and show it to me.'

It might provide a clue, Edwina thought, as to who had planned and executed this expert invasion. She did not believe that anyone she had spoken to so far was the key organizing figure.

Something else was emerging: the attempt to inundate the bank would not be limited to merely opening new accounts. Those who had already opened accounts were now forming lines at tellers' counters, paying in or withdrawing tiny amounts at a glacial pace, asking questions or engaging tellers in conversation.

So not only would regular customers have difficulty getting into the building but, once inside, they would be further impeded.

She told Nolan Wainwright about the written lists of questions and her instructions to the girl clerk.

The security chief approved. 'I'd like to see them, too.'

'Mr Wainwright,' a secretary called over, 'telephone.'

He took the call and Edwina heard him say, 'It *is* a demonstration, even if not in the legal sense. But it's peaceful and we could make trouble for ourselves by hasty decisions. The last thing we want is an ugly confrontation.'

It was comforting, Edwina reasoned, to have Wainwright's sane solidity available. As he replaced the phone a thought occurred to her. 'Someone mentioned calling the city police,' she said.

'They came when I first got here and I sent them away. They'll haul back fast if we need them. I hope we won't.' He motioned to the telephone, then in the direction of FMA Headquarters Tower. 'Word has got to the brass. They're pressing panic buttons over there.'

'One thing they could try is restoring funds to Forum East.'

For the first time since his arrival, a brief smile crossed Wainwright's face. 'I'd like to see that, too. But this isn't the way and, where the bank's money is on the line, outside pressure won't alter a thing.'

Edwina was about to say, 'I wonder,' then changed her mind, remaining silent.

While they watched, the crowd monopolizing the bank's central floor area remained as great; the uproar, if anything, a little louder than before.

Outside, the lengthening line stayed fixedly in place.

It was now 9.45.

four

Also at 9.45am, three blocks from First Mercantile American Headquarters Tower, Margot Bracken was operating a command post from an inconspicuously parked Volkswagen.

Margot had intended to remain remote from the execution of her pressure ploy, but in the end she hadn't been able to. Like a war horse which paws the ground at the scent of battle, her resolve had weakened then dissolved.

Margot's concern about embarrassing Alex or Edwina remained, however, and was the reason for her absence from the front line of action on Rosselli Plaza.

If she appeared she would be quickly identified by members of the press, whose presence Margot knew about since she had arranged advance tip-offs to newspapers, TV, and radio.

Therefore, messengers were discreetly bringing news of developments to her car and carrying instructions back.

Since Thursday night a sizeable feat of organization had been carried through.

On Friday, while Margot worked on the master plan, Seth, Deacon, and several committee members recruited block captains in and around Forum East. They described what was to be done only in general terms, but the response was overwhelming. Almost everyone wanted a piece of the action and knew others who could be counted on.

By late Sunday when lists were totalled, there were fifteen hundred names. More were coming in fast. According to Margot's plan it would be possible to maintain action for at least a week, longer if enthusiasm could be sustained.

Among the men with regular jobs who volunteered help, some like Deacon Euphrates had vacation time due which they declared they would use. Others simply said they would absent themselves as needed. Regrettably, many who volunteered were unemployed, their numbers swelled recently by a seasonal work shortage.

But women predominated, in part because of their greater availability in daytime, but also because – even more than with the men – Forum East had become a cherished, hopeful beacon in their lives.

Margot was aware of this, both from her advance staff work and this morning's reports.

The reports she was getting so far were highly satisfactory.

It had been Margot's insistence that at all times, and particularly during direct contacts with bank representatives, everyone in the Forum East contingent should be friendly, courteous, and ostensibly helpful. This was the reason for the phrase, 'Act of Hope,' which Margot coined, and the projected image that a group of interested individuals – though with limited means –

190

was coming to the 'help' of an FMA 'in trouble'.

She suspected, shrewdly, that any suggestion that First Mercantile American Bank was in trouble would touch a sensitive nerve.

And while there would be no concealment of the Forum East connection, at no point would outright threats be made, as – for example – that paralysis of the big bank would continue unless construction funds were reinstated. As Margot told Seth Orinda and the others, 'Let the bank come to that conclusion.'

At briefing sessions she had underlined the need to avoid any appearance of menace or intimidation. Those who attended the sessions made notes, then passed the instructions on.

Something else passed on were lists of questions to be asked by individuals while accounts were being opened. Margot had prepared those, too. There were hundreds of legitimate questions which anyone dealing with a bank could reasonably ask, though for the most part people didn't. Their ancillary effect would be to slow the bank to a near halt.

Seth Orinda would act as spokesman if an opportunity occurred. Margot's script needed little rehearsal. Orinda was a quick learner.

Deacon Euphrates had been assigned to be early in line and the first to open an account.

It was Deacon – no one knew whether Deacon was a given name or a title from one of the offbeat religions in the area – who headed the staff work in advising volunteers where to go and when. He had worked with an army of lieutenants, fanning out like radii of a spider web.

Initially, for Wednesday morning, it had been essential there should be a large attendance at the bank to create a strong impression. But some of the attendees must be relieved periodically. Others who had not yet appeared were to be held in reserve for later that day, or other days.

To accomplish all this, a patchwork communications system had been set up with heavy use of local call boxes, monitored by more helpers stationed on the streets. Already, allowing for weaknesses in a short-notice, improvised scheme, communication was functioning well.

All these and other reports were being funnelled to Margot in the back seat of her Volkswagen. Her information included the number of people in line, the length of time it was taking the bank to open each account, and the number of new account desks in operation. She had heard, too, about the jam-packed scene inside the bank; also the exchanges between Seth Orinda and bank officials.

Margot made a calculation, then instructed the latest messenger, a gangling youth now waiting in the car's front passenger seat, 'Tell Deacon not to call any more volunteers for the time being; it looks as if we've enough for the rest of today. Let some of those standing outside be relieved for a while, though not more than fifty at a time, and warn them to be back to collect their lunches. And about the lunches, caution everyone again there's to be no litter on Rosselli Plaza, and no food or drinks taken into the bank.'

The talk of lunch reminded Margot of money which, earlier in the week, had been a problem.

On Monday, reports filtering in through Deacon Euphrates made it clear that many of the willing volunteers lacked a spare five dollars – the minimum required to open an account at FMA. The Forum East Tenants Association had virtually no money. For a while it looked as if their scheme would founder.

Then Margot made a telephone call. It was to the union – the American Federation of Clerks, Cashiers & Office Workers – which now represented the airport janitors and cleaners whom she had aided a year ago.

Would the union help by lending money – enough to provide a five-dollar stake for each volunteer who could not afford it? Union leaders summoned a hasty meeting. The union said yes.

On Tuesday, employees from union headquarters helped Deacon Euphrates and Seth Orinda distribute the cash. All concerned knew that part of it would never be repaid and some of the five-dollar floats would be spent by Tuesday night, their original purpose forgotten or ignored. But most of the money, they believed, would be used as intended. Judging by this morning's showing, they were right.

It was the union which had offered to supply and pay for

lunches. The offer was accepted. Margot suspected a self-interest angle somewhere on the union's part but concluded it would not affect the Forum East objective, so was none of her business.

She continued to instruct the latest messenger. 'We must maintain a line-up until the bank closes at three o'clock.'

It was possible, she thought, that the news media might do some closing-time photography so a show of strength for the remainder of today was important.

Tomorrow's plans could be coordinated late tonight. Mostly, they would be a repetition of today's.

Fortunately the weather – a spell of mildness with mainly clear skies – was helping, and forecasts for the next few days seemed good.

'Keep on emphasizing,' Margot told another messenger a half hour later, 'that everyone must stay friendly, friendly, friendly. Even if the bank people get tough or impatient, the thing to do is smile back.'

At 11.45am Seth reported personally to Margot. He was grinning broadly and held out an early edition of the city's afternoon newspaper.

'Wow!' Margot spread the front page wide.

The activity at the bank commanded most of the available space. It was more, far more, attention than she had dared to hope for.

The main headline read:

BIG BANK IMMOBILIZED
BY FORUM EASTERS

And below:

First Merc American In Trouble ?
Many Come To 'Help'
With Small Deposits

Pictures and a two-column by-line story followed.
'Oh brother!' Margot breathed. 'How FMA will hate *that*!'

They did.

Shortly after mid-day a hastily called conference took place

on the thirty-sixth floor of First Mercantile American Headquarters Tower in the presidential suite.

Jerome Patterton and Roscoe Heyward were there, grim
faced. Alex Vandervoort joined them. He, too, was serious,
though as discussion progressed Alex seemed less involved than
the others, his expression mostly thoughtful, with once or twice
a flicker of amusement. The fourth attendee was Tom Straughan,
the bank's young and studious chief economist; the fifth, Dick
French, vice-president of public relations.

French, burly and scowling, strode in chewing an unlighted
cigar and carrying a bundle of afternoon newspapers which he
slapped down one by one in front of the others.

Jerome Patterton, seated behind his desk, spread out a paper.
When he read the words, 'First Merc American In Trouble ?'
he spluttered, 'That's a filthy lie! That paper should be sued.'

'There's nothing to sue about,' French said with his customary bluntness. 'The newspaper hasn't stated it as fact. It's put
as a question and in any case is quoting someone else. And the
original statement was not malicious.' He stood with a take-it-
or-leave-it attitude, hands behind his back, cigar projecting like
an accusatory torpedo.

Patterton flushed with anger.

'Of course it's malicious,' Roscoe Heyward snapped. He had
been standing, aloof, by a window and swung back towards the
other four. 'The entire exercise is malicious. Any fool can see
that.'

French sighed. 'All right, I'll spell it out. Whoever is behind
this is good at law *and* public relations. The exercise, as you call
it, is cleverly set up to be friendly and helpful to this bank.
Okay, we know it's neither. But you'll never prove that and I
suggest we stop wasting time with talk about trying to.'

He picked up one of the newspapers and spread the front page
open. 'One reason I earn my princely salary is because I'm an
expert about news and media. Right now my expertise tells me
that this same story – which is written and presented fairly, like
it or not – is spewing out through every news wire service in the
country *and will be used.* Why ? *Because it's a David and Goliath
piece which reeks of human interest.'*

Tom Straughan, seated beside Vandervoort, said quietly, 'I can confirm part of that. It *has* been on the Dow Jones news service and right afterwards our stock dropped one more point.'

'Another thing,' Dick French went on as though he had not been interrupted, 'we may as well brace ourselves now for the TV news tonight. There'll be plenty on local stations for sure, and my educated guess is we'll be on network, all three majors. Also, if any scripter can resist that "bank in trouble" phrase I'll swallow my picture tube.'

Heyward asked coldly, 'Have you finished ?'

'Not quite. I'd just like to say that if I'd blown this entire year's PR budget on one thing, *just one thing*, to try to make this bank look *bad*, I couldn't have improved on the damage you guys have done unaided.'

Dick French had a personal theory. It was that a good public relations man should go to work each day prepared to put his job on the line. If knowledge and experience required him to tell his superiors unpleasant facts they would prefer not to hear, and to be brutally frank while doing so, so be it. The frankness was part of PR too – a ploy to gain attention. To do less, or to court favour through silence or pussyfooting, would be to fail in his responsibilities.

Some days required more bluntness than usual. This was one.

Scowling, Roscoe Heyward asked, 'Do we know yet who the organizers are ?'

'Not specifically,' French said. 'I talked with Nolan who says he's working on that. Not that it makes much difference.'

'And if you're interested in the latest from the downtown branch,' Tom Straughan contributed, 'I went in through the tunnel just before coming here. The place is still packed with demonstrators. Almost no one can get in to do regular banking business.'

'They're not demonstrators,' Dick French corrected him. 'Let's get that clear, too, while we're about it. There's not a placard or a slogan among the lot, except maybe "Act of Hope". They're customers, and that's our problem.'

'All right,' Jerome Patterton said, 'since you know so much about it, what do you suggest ?'

195

The PR vice-president shrugged. 'You guys pulled the rug from under Forum East. You're the ones who could put it back.'

Roscoe Heyward's features tightened.

Patterton turned to Vandervoort. 'Alex?'

'You know my feelings,' Alex said; it was the first time he had spoken. 'I was against the cut in funds to begin with. I still am.'

Heyward said sarcastically, 'Then you're probably delighted about what's going on. And I suppose you'd give in gladly to those louts and their intimidation.'

'No, I'm not in the least delighted.' Alex's eyes flashed angrily. 'What I am is embarrassed and offended to see the bank in the position in which it's been placed. I believe what's happening could have been foreseen – that is, some response, some opposition. What matters most at the moment, though, is to set the situation right.'

Heyward sneered, 'So you *would* give in to intimidation. Just as I said.'

'Giving in or not giving in is immaterial,' Alex answered coldly. 'The real question is: Were we right or wrong in cutting off funds from Forum East? If we were wrong, we should have second thoughts, along with courage to admit our error.'

Jerome Patterton observed, 'Second thoughts or not, if we back down now we'll all look pretty foolish.'

'Jerome,' Alex said, 'In the first place, I don't believe so. In the second, does it matter?'

Dick French interposed, 'The financial end of this is none of my business. I know that. But I'll tell you one thing: If we decided now to change bank policy about Forum East, we'd look good, not bad.'

Roscoe Heyward said acidly to Alex, 'If courage is a factor here, I'd say that you are devoid of any. What you're doing is refusing to stand up to a mob.'

Alex shook his head impatiently. 'Stop sounding like a small-town sheriff, Roscoe. Sometimes, unwillingness to change a wrong decision is plain pigheadedness, nothing more. Besides, those people at the downtown branch are not a mob. Every report we've had has made that clear.'

Heyward said suspiciously, 'You seem to have a special affinity for them. Do you know something the rest of us don't ?'

'No.'

'Just the same, Alex,' Jerome Patterton ruminated, 'I don't like the idea of meekly giving in.'

Tom Straughan had been following both arguments. Now he said, 'I was opposed to cutting off Forum East funds, as everybody knows. But I don't like being pushed around by outsiders either.'

Alex sighed. 'If you all feel like that, we'd better accept that the downtown branch won't be much use to us for a while.'

'That rabble can't possibly keep up what they're doing,' Heyward declared. 'I predict that if we maintain our stand, refusing to be bluffed or stampeded, the entire exercise will fizzle out tomorrow.'

'And I,' Alex said, 'predict it will continue through next week.'

In the end, both predictions proved erroneous.

In the absence of any softening of attitude by the bank, inundation of the downtown branch by Forum East supporters continued through all of Thursday and Friday, until the close of business late Friday afternoon.

The big branch was almost helpless. And, as Dick French predicted, nationwide attention was focused on its plight.

Much of the attention was humorous. However, investors were less amused, and on the New York Stock Exchange on Friday, First Mercantile American Bank shares closed a further two and a half points lower.

Meanwhile, Margot Bracken, Seth Orinda, Deacon Euphrates, and others went on planning and recruiting.

On Monday morning the bank capitulated.

At a hastily called press conference at 10am, Dick French announced that full Forum East financing would be restored at once. On behalf of the bank, French expressed the goodnatured hope that the many from Forum East, and their friends, who had opened accounts at FMA over the past several days, would remain bank customers.

Behind the capitulation were several cogent reasons. One was:

prior to the downtown branch opening on Monday morning, the line-up outside the bank and on Rosselli Plaza was even larger than on previous days, so it became plain that the preceding week's performance would be repeated.

More disconcerting, a second long line-up appeared at another FMA branch bank, this in suburban Indian Hill. The development was not wholly unexpected. Extension of the Forum East activity to additional First Mercantile American branches had been forecast in Sunday's newspapers. When the line at Indian Hill began to form, an alarmed branch manager telephoned FMA Headquarters, asking for help.

But it was a final factor which clinched the outcome.

Over the week-end, the union which had loaned money to the Forum East Tenants Committee and provided free lunches for those in line – the American Federation of Clerks, Cashiers & Office Workers – publicly announced its involvement. They pledged additional support. A union spokesman castigated FMA as a 'selfish and gargantuan profit machine, geared to further enrich the wealthy at the expense of the have-nots'. A campaign to unionize the bank's employees, he added, would soon begin.

The union thus tilted the scale, not with a straw, but a bale of bricks.

Banks – all banks – feared, even hated, unions. Banking's leaders and executives eyed unions the way a snake might view a mongoose. What bankers foresaw if unions became entrenched was a lessening of banks' financial freedom. At times their fear was irrational, but it existed.

Though unions had tried often, few had made the slightest headway where bank employees were concerned. Time after time, bankers adroitly outwitted union organizers and intended to keep on doing so. If the Forum East situation afforded leverage to a union, *ipso facto*, the leverage must be removed. Jerome Patterton, in his office early and moving with unusual speed, made the final decision authorizing the restitution of funds to Forum East. At the same time he approved the bank's announcement which Dick French rushed to release.

Afterwards, to steady his nerves, Patterton cut off all communication and practised chip shots on the inner office rug.

Later the same morning, at a mainly informal session of the money policy committee, the reinstatement was recorded, though Roscoe Heyward grumbled, 'It's created a precedent and is a surrender we'll regret.'

Alex Vandervoort was silent.

When the FMA announcement was read to Forum East supporters at both branch banks, there was some cheering, after which the assembled groups quietly dispersed. Within half an hour, business at the two branches returned to normal.

The matter might have ended there except for an information leak which, viewed in retrospect, was perhaps inevitable. The lead resulted in a newspaper commentary two days later – an item in the same column, 'Ear to the Ground', which first brought the issue out into the open.

Were you wondering who was really behind those Forum Easters who this week brought the proud and mighty First Mercantile American Bank to heel? The Shadow knows. It's Civil Rights Lawyer-Feminist Margot Bracken – she of 'airport toilet sit-in' fame and other battles for the humble and stepped-on.

This time, despite the 'bank-in' being her idea, on which she laboured, Ms Bracken kept her activity tip-top secret. While others fronted, she stayed out of sight, avoiding the press, her normal allies. Are you wondering about that, too?

Stop wondering: Margot's great and good friend, most often seen with her around town, is Swinging Banker Alexander Vandervoort, exec veep of First Merc Am. If *you* were Margot and had that connection cooking, wouldn't *you* stay out of sight?

Only thing we're wondering: Did Alex know and approve the siege of his own home plate?

five

'Goddamit, Alex,' Margot said, 'I'm sorry!'

'The way it happened, so am I.'

'I could skin that louse of a columnist alive. The only good thing is that he didn't mention I'm related to Edwina.'

'Not many know that,' Alex said, 'even in the bank. Anyway, lovers make livelier news than cousins.'

It was close to midnight. They were in Alex's apartment, their first meeting since the siege of FMA's downtown branch began. The item in 'Ear to the Ground' had appeared the day before.

Margot had come in a few minutes ago after representing a client in night court – a well-to-do habitual drunk, whose habit of assaulting anyone in sight when he was boozed made him one of her few steady sources of income.

'The newspaper writer was doing his job, I suppose,' Alex said. 'And almost certainly your name would have come out anyway.'

She said contritely, 'I tried to make sure it didn't. Only a few people knew what I was doing, and I wanted it to stay like that.'

He shook his head. 'No way. Nolan Wainwright told me early this morning – these were his words – "the whole caper had Margot Bracken's handwriting on it". And Nolan had started to quiz people. He used to be a police detective, you know. Someone would have talked if the news item hadn't appeared first.'

'But they didn't have to use *your* name.'

'If you want the truth' – Alex smiled – 'I rather liked that "swinging banker" bit.'

But the smile was false and he sensed that Margot knew it. The real truth was that the column item had jolted and depressed him. He was still depressed tonight, though he had been pleased when Margot telephoned earlier to say that she was coming.

He asked, 'Have you talked to Edwina today ?'

'Yes, I phoned her. She didn't seem upset. I suppose we're used to each other. Besides, she's pleased that Forum East is back on the rails again – all of it. You must be glad about that, too.'

'You always knew my feelings on that subject. But it doesn't mean I approve your shady methods, Bracken.'

He had spoken more sharply than he intended. Margot reacted promptly. 'There was nothing shady in what I did, *or* my people. Which is more than I can say for your goddamn bank.'

He raised his hands defensively. 'Let's not quarrel. Not tonight.'

'Then don't say things like that.'

'All right, I won't.'

Their momentary anger disappeared.

Margot said thoughtfully, 'Tell me – when it all started, didn't you have *some* idea I was involved?'

'Yes. Partly because I know you very well. Also, I remembered you clammed up about Forum East when I expected you to tear me – and FMA – to shreds.'

'Did it make things difficult for you – while the bank-in was going on, I mean?'

He answered bluntly, 'Yes, it did. I wasn't sure whether to share what I'd guessed or to keep quiet. Since bringing in your name wouldn't have made any difference to what was happening, I kept quiet. As it turned out, it was the wrong decision.'

'So now some of the others believe you knew all the time.'

'Roscoe does. Maybe Jerome. I'm not sure about the rest.'

There was an uncertain silence before Margot asked, 'Do you care? Does it matter terribly?' For the first time in their relationship her voice was anxious. Concern clouded her face.

Alex shrugged, then decided to reassure her. 'Not really, I guess. Don't worry. I'll survive.'

But it did matter. It mattered very much at FMA, despite what he had just said, and the incident had been doubly unfortunate at this time.

Alex was sure that most of the bank's directors would have seen the newspaper item which included his name and the pertinent question: *Did Alex know and approve the siege of his own home plate?* And if there were a few who hadn't seen it, Roscoe Heyward would make certain that they did.

Heyward had made his attitude plain.

This morning, Alex had gone directly to Jerome Patterton when the bank president arrived at 10am. But Heyward, whose office was nearer, had got there first.

'Come in, Alex,' Patterton had said. 'We might just as well have a threesome as two meetings of deuces.'

'Before we talk, Jerome,' Alex told him, 'I want to be the first to bring up a subject. You've seen this?' He put a clipping of the previous day's 'Ear to the Ground' on the desk between them.

Without waiting, Heyward said unpleasantly, 'Do you imagine there's anyone in the bank who hasn't?'

Patterton sighed. 'Yes, Alex, I've seen it. I've also had a dozen people direct my attention to it, and no doubt there'll be others.'

Alex said firmly, 'Then you're entitled to know that what was printed is mischief-making and nothing more. You have my word that I knew absolutely nothing in advance about what happened at the downtown branch, and no more than the rest of us while it was going on.'

'A good many people,' Roscoe Heyward commented, 'might consider that with your connections' – he put sardonic emphasis on the word *connections* – 'such ignorance would be unlikely.'

'Any explanations I'm making,' Alex snapped, 'are directed at Jerome.'

Heyward declined to be put off. 'When the bank's reputation is demeaned in public, all of us are concerned. As to your so-called explanation, do you seriously expect anyone to believe that through Wednesday, Thursday, Friday, over a week-end and into Monday, you had no idea, no idea at all, your girl friend was involved?'

Patterton said, 'Yes, Alex; how about that?'

Alex felt his face flush red. He felt resentful, as he had several times since yesterday, that Margot had placed him in this absurd position.

As calmly as he could, he told Patterton of his guess last week that Margot might be involved, his decision that nothing would be gained by discussing the possibility with others. Alex explained that he still had not seen Margot since more than a week ago.

'Nolan Wainwright had the same idea,' Alex added. 'He told me earlier this morning. But Nolan kept quiet, too, because for both of us it was no more than an impression, a hunch, until the news item appeared.'

'Someone will believe you, Alex,' Roscoe Heyward said. His tone and expression declared: *I don't.*

'Now, now, Roscoe!' Patterton remonstrated mildly. 'All right, Alex, I accept your explanation. Though I trust you'll use your influence with Miss Bracken to see that in future she directs her artillery elsewhere.'

Heyward added, 'Or better still, not at all.'

Ignoring the last remark, Alex told the bank president with a tight, grim smile, 'You can count on that.'

'Thank you.'

Alex was certain he had heard Patterton's last word on the subject and that their relationship could revert to normal, at least on the surface. As to what went on beneath the surface, he was less sure. Probably in the minds of Patterton and others – including some members of the board – Alex's loyalty would, from now on, have an asterisk of doubt beside it. If not that, there could be reservations about Alex's discretion in the company he kept.

Either way, those doubts and reservations would be in the directors' minds near the end of this year, as Jerome Patterton's retirement neared, and the board reopened the subject of the bank presidency. And while directors were big men in some ways, in others, as Alex knew, they could be petty and prejudiced.

Why? Why did it all have to happen *now*?

His dark mood deepened while Margot regarded him, her eyes questioning, her expression still anxious and uncertain.

She said more seriously than before, 'I've caused you trouble. Quite a lot, I think. So let's both stop pretending that I didn't.'

He was about to reassure her again, then changed his mind,

knowing this was a time for honesty between them.

'Another thing that has to be said,' Margot went on, 'is we talked about this, knowing it might happen, wondering whether we could remain the kind of people we are – independent – yet stay together.'

'Yes,' he told her, 'I remember.'

'The only thing is,' she said wryly, 'I didn't expect it all to come to a head so soon.'

He reached for her, as he had done so often before but she moved away from him and shook her head. 'No, let's settle this.'

Without warning, he realized, and without either of them intending it, their relationship had reached a crisis.

'It will happen again, Alex. Let's not fool ourselves it won't. Oh, not with the bank, but with other related things. And I want to be sure we can handle it whenever it does, and not just for one time only, hoping it will be the last.'

He knew that what she had said was true. Margot's life was one of confrontations; there would be many more. And while some would be remote from his own interests, others would not.

It was equally true, as Margot had pointed out, that they had spoken of this before – just a week and a half ago. But then the discussion had been in abstract, the choice less clear, not sharply defined as events of the past week had made it.

'One thing you and I could do,' Margot said, 'is call it quits now, while we've had fun, while we're still ahead. No hard feelings either side; just a sensible conclusion. If we did that, stopped seeing each other and being seen together, word would travel quickly. It always does. And while it wouldn't wipe out what happened at the bank, it could make things easier for you there.'

That, too, was true, Alex knew. He had a swift temptation to accept the offer, to exorcize – cleanly and swiftly – a complication from his life, a complication likely to become greater, not less, as years went by. Again he wondered: why did so many problems, pressures, come together – Celia worsening; Ben Rosselli's death; the struggle at the bank; the undeserved harassment today. And now Margot and a choice. Why?

The question reminded him of something which happened

years before when he once visited the Canadian city of Vancouver. A young woman had jumped to her death from a 24th floor hotel room and, before jumping, scrawled in lipstick on the window glass, *Why, oh why?* Alex had never known her, or even learned later what were her problems which she believed beyond solution. But he had been staying on the same floor of the hotel and a talkative assistant manager had shown him the sad, lipsticked window. The memory always stayed with him.

Why, oh why, do we make choices that we do? Or why does life make them? Why had he married Celia? Why had she become insane? Why did he still hold back from the catharsis of divorce? Why did Margot need to be an activist? Why would he consider losing Margot now? How much did he want to be president of FMA?

Not that much!

He made a forceful, self-controlled decision and thrust his gloom away. *The hell with it all!* Not for FMA, nor boards of directors, or personal ambition, would he surrender, *ever,* his private freedom of action and independence. Or give up Margot.

'The most important thing is,' he told her, 'do *you* want it to be the way you said just now – a "sensible conclusion"?'

Margot spoke through tears. 'Of course not.'

'Then I don't either, Bracken. Or am I ever likely to. So let's be glad this happened, that we've proved something, and that neither of us has to prove it any more.'

This time, when he put out his arms, she did not hold back.

six

'Roscoe, my boy,' the Honourable Harold Austin said on the telephone, sounding pleased with himself. 'I've been talking with Big George. He's invited you and me to play golf in the Bahamas next Friday.'

Roscoe Heyward pursed his lips doubtfully. He was at home, in the study of his Shaker Heights house, on a Saturday afternoon in March. Before taking the phone call he had been examining a portfolio of financial statements, with other papers spread on the floor around his leather armchair.

'I'm not certain I can get away that soon or go that far,' he told the Honourable Harold. 'Couldn't we try for a conference in New York?'

'Sure we could try. Except we'd be stupid, because Big George prefers Nassau; and because Big George likes doing business on a golf course – *our* kind of business that he attends to personally.'

It was unnecessary for either of them to identify 'Big George'. For that matter, few others in industry, banking, or public life would have needed to.

G. G. Quartermain, board chairman and chief executive of Supranational Corporation – SuNatCo – was a bravura bull of a man who possessed more power than many heads of state and exercised it like a king. His interests and influence extended world-wide, like those of the corporation whose destiny he directed. Inside SuNatCo and out he was variously admired, hated, courted, lionized, and feared.

His strength lay in his record. Eight years earlier – on the basis of some previous financial wizardry – G. G. Quartermain had been summoned to the rescue of Supranational, then ailing and debt-ridden. Between then and now he had restored the company's fortune, enlarged it to a spectacular conglomerate, thrice split its shares and quadrupled its dividend. Shareholders, whom Big George had made wealthy, adored him; they also allowed him all the freedom of action he desired. True, a few Cassandras argued he had built an empire of cardboard. But financial statements of SuNatCo and its many subsidiaries – which Roscoe Heyward had been studying when the Honourable Harold telephoned – resoundingly contradicted them.

Heyward had met the SuNatCo chairman twice: once briefly in a crowd, the second occasion in a Washington, DC hotel suite with Harold Austin.

The Washington meeting came about when the Honourable

Harold reported to Quartermain on the subject of a mission he had carried out for Supranational. Heyward had no idea what the assignment was – the other two had completed the main part of their conversation when he joined them – except that in some way it involved government.

The Austin Agency handled national advertising for Hepple-white Distillers, a large SuNatCo subsidiary, although the Honourable Harold's personal relationship with G. G. Quartermain appeared to extend beyond this.

Whatever the report was, it appeared to have put Big George in a jovial humour. On being introduced to Heyward, he observed, 'Harold tells me he's a director of your little bank and you'd both like a spoonful of our gravy. Well, sometime soon we'll see about it.'

The Supranational chieftain had then clapped Heyward across the shoulder and talked of other things.

It was his Washington conversation with G. G. Quartermain which prompted Heyward in mid-January – two months ago – to inform the FMA money policy committee that doing business with SuNatCo was a probability. Later, he realized he had been premature. Now it seemed the prospect was revived.

'Well,' Heyward conceded on the telephone, 'perhaps I could get away next Thursday for a day or two.'

'That's more like it,' he heard the Honourable Harold say. 'Whatever you might have planned can't be more important to the bank than this. And, oh yes, one thing I haven't mentioned – Big George is sending his personal aeroplane for us.'

Heyward brightened. 'Is he now? Is it big enough for a fast trip?'

'It's a 707. I thought that would please you.' Harold Austin chuckled. 'So we'll fly from here Thursday at noon, have all of Friday in the Bahamas, and be back on Saturday. By the way, how do the new SuNatCo statements look?'

'I've been studying them.' Heyward glanced at the mess of financial data spread around his chair. 'The patient appears healthy; very healthy indeed.'

'If you say so,' Austin said, 'that's good enough for me.'

As he replaced the telephone, Heyward permitted himself a

slight, sly smile. The impending trip, its purpose, and the fact of travelling to the Bahamas by private plane, would make a pleasant item to drop casually in conversation next week. Also, if anything came of it, it would enhance his own status with the board – something he never lost sight of nowadays, remembering the interim nature of Jerome Patterton's appointment as FMA president.

He was pleased, too, about the scheduled return by air next Saturday. It meant he would not have to miss an appearance in his church – St Athanasius's – where he was a lay reader and delivered the lesson, clearly and solemnly, every Sunday.

The thought reminded him of tomorrow's reading which he had planned to go over in advance, as he usually did. Now he lifted a heavy family Bible from a bookshelf and turned to a page already flagged. The page was in *Proverbs* where tomorrow's reading included a verse which was a Heyward favourite: *Righteousness exalteth a nation: but sin is a reproach to any people.*

To Roscoe Heyward, the Bahamas excursion was an education.

He was not unfamiliar with high living. Like most senior bankers, Heyward had mingled socially with customers and others who used money freely, even aggressively, in achieving princely comforts and amusements. Almost always, he envied their financial freedom.

But G. G. Quartermain outdid them all.

The 707 jet, identified by a large *Q* on fuselage and tail, landed at the city's international airport precisely as scheduled, to the minute. It taxied to a private terminal where the Honourable Harold and Heyward left the limousine which had brought them from downtown and were whisked aboard, entering at the rear.

In a foyer like a miniature hotel lobby, a quartet greeted them – a middle-aged man, greying and with the mix of authority and deference which stamped him a major-domo, and three young women.

'Welcome aboard, gentlemen,' the major-domo said. Heyward nodded, but scarely noticed the man, his attention being distracted by the women – breathtakingly beautiful girls in their twenties – who were smiling agreeably. It occurred to Roscoe Heyward that the Quartermain organization must have assembled the most comely stewardesses from TWA, United, and American, then skimmed off these three, like cream from richest milk. One girl was honey-blonde, another a striking brunette, the third a long-haired redhead. They were long-legged, willowy, healthily suntanned. The tans contrasted against their stylish but abbreviated pale beige uniforms.

The major-domo's uniform was of the same smart material as the girls'. All four had an embroidered *Q* on the left breast pocket.

'Good afternoon, Mr Heyward,' the redhead said. Her voice, pleasantly modulated, had a soft, almost seductive quality. She went on, 'I'm Avril. If you'll come this way, I'll show you to your room.'

As Heyward followed her, surprised at the reference to a 'room', the Honourable Harold was being greeted by the blonde.

The elegant Avril preceded Heyward down a corridor extending part way along the aircraft on one side. Several doors opened from it.

Over her shoulder, she announced, 'Mr Quartermain is having a sauna and massage. He'll join you later in the lounge.'

'A sauna? Aboard *here*?'

'Oh, yes. There's one directly behind the flight deck. A steam room, too. Mr Quartermain likes either a sauna or a Russian bath wherever he is, and he has his own masseur always with him.' Avril flashed a dazzling smile. 'If you'd like a bath and massage there'll be plenty of time on the flight. I'll be glad to attend to it.'

'No, thank you.'

The girl stopped at a doorway. 'This is your room, Mr Heyward.' As she spoke, the aircraft moved forward, beginning to taxi. At the unexpected movement, Heyward stumbled.

'Oops!' Avril put out her arm, steadying him, and for a moment they were close. He was conscious of long slim fingers, bronze-orange polished nails, a light firm touch and a waft of perfume.

She kept her hand on his arm. 'I'd better strap you in for take-off. The captain always goes quickly. Mr Quartermain doesn't like lingering at airports.'

He had a quick impression of a small, sumptuous parlour into which the girl led him, then he was seated on a softly comfortable settee while the fingers he had already become aware of deftly fastened a strap around his waist. Even through the strap he could feel the fingers moving. The sensation was not disagreeable.

'There!' The aircraft was taxiing fast now. Avril said, 'If you don't mind, I'll stay until we're airborne.'

She sat beside him on the settee and fastened a strap herself.

'No,' Roscoe Heyward said. He felt absurdly dazed. 'I don't mind at all.'

Looking around, he took in more details. The parlour or cabin, such as he had seen on no aircraft before, had been designed to make efficient but luxurious use of space. Three of the walls were panelled in teak, with carved Q motifs embellished in gold leaf. The fourth wall was almost entirely mirror, ingeniously making the compartment seem larger than it was. Recessed into the wall on his left was a compactly organized office bureau, including a telephone console and glass-shielded teleprinter. Nearby a small bar was stocked with an array of miniature bottles. Built into the mirror wall, which faced Heyward and Avril, was a TV screen with duplicate sets of controls, reachable from either side of the settee. A folding door behind was presumably to a bathroom.

'Would you like to watch our take-off?' Avril asked. Without waiting for an answer, she touched the TV controls nearest her and a picture, clear and in colour, sprang to life. Obviously a camera was in the aircraft nose and, on the screen, they could see a taxiway leading to a wide runway, the latter coming fully into view as the 707 swung on to it. With no time wasted, the aircraft moved forward, simultaneously the runway began to rush beneath them, then the remainder of it tilted downwards as the big jet angled up and they were airborne. Roscoe Heyward had a sense of soaring, not merely because of the TV image. With only sky and clouds ahead, Avril snapped it off.

'The regular TV channels are there if you need them,' she informed him, then motioned to the teleprinter. 'Over there you can get the Dow Jones, AP, UPI, or Telex. Just phone the flight deck and they'll feed in whichever you say.'

Heyward observed cautiously, 'All this is a little beyond my normal experience.'

'I know. It has that effect on people sometimes, though it's surprising how quickly everyone adapts.' Again the direct look and dazzling smile. 'We have four of these private cabins and each one converts to a bedroom quite easily. You just push some buttons. I'll show you if you like.'

He shook his head. 'It seems unnecessary now.'

'Whatever you wish, Mr Heyward.'

She released her seat belt and stood up. 'If you want Mr Austin, he's in the cabin immediately behind. Up forward is the main lounge you're invited to when you're ready. Then there's a dining-room, offices, and beyond that Mr Quartermain's private apartment.'

'Thank you for the geography.' Heyward removed his rimless glasses and took out a handkerchief to wipe them.

'Oh, please let me do that!' Gently but firmly Avril took the glasses from his hand, produced a square of silk and polished them. Then she replaced the glasses on his face, her fingers travelling lightly behind his ears in doing so. Heyward had a feeling he should protest, but didn't.

'My job on this trip, Mr Heyward, is to take care of you exclusively and make sure you have everything you want.'

Was it imagination, he wondered, or had the girl placed subtle emphasis on the word 'everything'? He reminded himself sharply that he hoped not. If she had, the implication would be shocking.

'Two other things,' Avril said. Gorgeous and slender, she had moved to the doorway, preparing to leave. 'If you want me for anything at all, please press button number seven on the telephone.'

Heyward answered gruffly, 'Thank you, young lady, but I doubt if I'll do that.'

She seemed unperturbed. 'And the other thing: on the way

to the Bahamas we'll be landing in Washington briefly. The Vice-President is joining us there.'

'A vice-president from Supranational?'

Her eyes were mocking. 'No, silly. The Vice-President of the United States.'

Some fifteen minutes later, Big George Quartermain demanded of Roscoe Heyward, 'For Chrissakes! Whatinhellzat you're drinking? Mother's milk?'

'It's lemonade.' Heyward held up his glass, inspecting the insipid liquid. 'I rather enjoy it.'

The Supranational chairman shrugged his massive shoulders. 'Every addict to his own poison. Girls taking care of you both?'

'No complaints from this quarter,' the Honourable Harold Austin offered with a chuckle. Like the others, he was reclining comfortably in the 707's splendidly appointed main lounge with the blonde, who had revealed her name as Rhetta, curled on the rug at his feet.

Avril said sweetly, 'We're trying our best.' She was standing behind Heyward's chair and let a hand travel lightly across his back. He felt her fingers touch the base of his neck, linger momentarily, then move on.

Moments earlier, G. G. Quartermain had come into the lounge, resplendent in a crimson towel robe with white piping, the inevitable Q embroidered largely. Like a Roman senator, he was attended by acolytes – a hard-faced, silent man in gym whites, presumably the masseur, and still another hostess in trim beige uniform, her features delicately Japanese. The masseur and the girl supervised Big George's entry into a broad, throne-like chair, clearly reserved for him. Then a third figure – the original major-domo – as if by magic produced a chilled martini and eased it into G. G. Quartermain's awaiting hand.

Even more than on previous occasions they had met, Heyward decided, the name 'Big George' seemed apposite in every way. Physically their host was a mountain of man – at least six and a half feet in height, his chest, arms and torso like a village blacksmith's. His head was half the size again of most other men's and his facial features matched – prominent, large eyes, swift-moving and darkly shrewd, the mouth wide-lipped and strong, as accustomed to issuing commands as a Marine drill sergeant's, though on larger issues. Equally clearly, surface joviality could be banished instantly by powerful displeasure.

Yet he stopped short of coarseness, nor was there any sign of overweight or flab. Through the enfolding towel robe, muscles bulged. Heyward observed, too, that Big George's face betrayed no fat layers, his massive chin no jowls. His belly appeared flat and taut.

As to other bigness, his corporate reach and appetite were reported daily in the business press. And his living style aboard this twelve-million-dollar aeroplane was unabashedly royal.

The masseur and major-domo quietly disappeared. Replacing them, like one more character emerging on stage, was a chef – a pale, worried pencil of a man, immaculate in kitchen whites with a high chef's hat which brushed the cabin ceiling. Heyward wondered just how big the on-board staff was. Later, he learned it totalled sixteen.

The chef stood stiffly beside Big George's chair, proffering an outsize black leather folder embossed with a golden *Q*. Big George ignored him.

'That trouble at your bank.' Quartermain addressed Roscoe Heyward. 'Demonstrations. All the rest. Is everything settled? Are you solid?'

'We were always solid,' Heyward answered. 'That was never in question.'

'The market didn't think so.'

'Since when was the stock market an accurate barometer of anything?'

Big George smiled fleetingly, then swung to the petite Japanese hostess. 'Moonbeam, get me the latest quote on FMA.'

'Yes, Misto Q,' the girl said. She went out by a forward door.

Big George nodded in the direction she had gone. 'Still can't get that tongue of hers around Quartermain. Always calls me "Misto Q".' He grinned at the others. 'Manages nicely elsewhere, though.'

Roscoe Heyward said quickly, 'The reports you heard about our bank concerned a trifling incident, magnified beyond importance. It happened also at a time of management transition.'

'But you people didn't stand firm,' Big George insisted. 'You let outside agitators have their way. You went soft and surrendered.'

'Yes, we did. And I'll be frank to say I didn't like the decision. In fact, I opposed it.'

'Stand up to 'em! Always clobber the bastards one way or another! Never back down!' The Supranational chairman drained his martini and the major-domo appeared from nowhere, removed the original glass and placed a fresh one in Big George's hand. The drink's perfect chill was apparent from its outside frosting.

The chef was still standing, waiting. Quartermain continued to ignore him.

He rumbled reminiscently, 'Had a sub-assembly manufacturing plant near Denver. Lots of labour trouble. Wage demands beyond all reason. Early this year, union called a strike, the last of many. I told our people – the subsidiary which ran it – warn the sons of bitches we'll close the plant down. Nobody believed us. So we made studies, planned arrangements. Shipped tools and dies to one of our other companies. They took up the manufacturing slack. At Denver we closed. Suddenly no plant, no jobs, no payroll. Now, the lot of 'em – employees, union, Denver city, state government, you name it – are down on their knees pleading with us to reopen.' He considered his martini, then said magnanimously, 'Well, we may. Doing other manufacturing, and on our terms. But we didn't back down.'

'Good for you, George!' the Honourable Harold said. 'We need more people to take that kind of stand. The problem at our bank, though, has been somewhat different. In some ways we're still in an interim situation which began, as you know, with Ben Rosselli's death. But by spring next year a good many of us on the board hope to see Roscoe here firmly at the helm.'

'Glad to hear it. Don't like dealing with people not at the top. Those I do business with must be able to decide, then make decisions stick.'

'I assure you, George,' Heyward said, 'that any decisions you and I arrive at will be adhered to by the bank.'

In an adroit way, Heyward realized, their host had manoeuvred Harold Austin and himself into the stance of supplicants – a reversal of a banker's usual role. But the fact was, any loan to Supranational would be worry-free, as well as prestigious for FMA. Equally important, it would be a precursor of other new industrial accounts since Supranational Corporation was a pacesetter whose example others followed.

Big George snapped abruptly at the chef. 'Well, what is it ?'

The figure in white was galvanized to action. He thrust forward the black leather folder he had been holding since his entry. 'The luncheon menu, monsieur. For your approval.'

Big George made no attempt to take the folder but scanned its contents held before him. He stabbed with a finger. 'Change that Waldorf salad to a Caesar.'

'Oui, monsieur.'

'And dessert. Not Glacé Martinique. A Soufflé Grand Marnier.'

'Certainly, monsieur.'

A nod of dismissal. Then, as the chef turned away, Big George glared. 'And when I order a steak, how do I like it ?'

'Monsieur' – the chef gestured imploringly with his free hand – 'I 'ave already apologize twice for the unfortunate last night.'

'Never mind that. The question was: *how do I like it ?*'

With a Gallic shrug, repeating a lesson learned, the chef intoned, 'On the slightly well-done side of medium-rare.'

'Just remember that.'

The chef asked despairingly, "Ow can I forget, monsieur ?' Crestfallen, he went out.

'Something else that's important,' Big George informed his guests, 'is not to let people get away with things. I pay that frog a fortune to know *exactly* how I like my food. He slipped last night – not much, but enough to ream him out so next time he'll remember. What's the quote ?' Moonbeam had returned with a slip of paper.

She read out in accented English, 'FMA trading now at forty-five and three-quarters.'

215

'There we are,' Roscoe Heyward said, 'we're up another point.'

'But still not as high as before Rosselli bit the bullet,' Big George said. He grinned. 'Though when word gets out that you're helping finance Supranational, your stock'll soar.'

It could happen, Heyward thought. In the tangled world of finance and stock prices, inexplicable things occurred. That someone would lend money to someone else might not seem to mean much – yet the market would respond.

More importantly, though, Big George had now declared positively that some kind of business *was* to be transacted between First Mercantile American Bank and SuNatCo. No doubt they would thrash out details through the next two days. He felt his excitement rising.

Above their heads a chime sounded softly. Outside, the jet thrum changed to lower tempo.

'Washington, ho!' Avril said. She and the other girls began fastening the men to their seats with heavy belts and light fingers.

The time on the ground in Washington was even briefer than at the previous stop. With a 14-carat VIP passenger, it seemed, top priorities for landing, taxiing, and take-off were axiomatic.

Thus, in less than twenty minutes they had returned to cruising altitude en route to the Bahamas.

The Vice-President was installed, with the brunette, Krista, taking care of him, an arrangement which he patently approved.

Secret Service men, guarding the Vice-President, had been accommodated somewhere at the rear.

Soon after, Big George Quartermain, now attired in a striking cream silk one-piece suit, jovially led the way forward from the lounge into the airliner's dining-room – a richly decorated apartment, predominantly silver and royal blue. There, the four men, seated at a carved oak table beneath a crystal chandelier, and with Moonbeam, Avril, Rhetta, and Krista hovering deliciously behind, lunched in a style and on cuisine which any of the world's great restaurants would have found it hard to equal.

Roscoe Heyward, while relishing the meal, did not share in

the several wines or a thirty-year-old Cognac brandy at the end. But he did observe that the heavy, gold-rimmed brandy goblets omitted the traditional decorative *N* of Napoleon in favour of a *Q*.

seven

Warm sunshine from an unbroken azure sky shone on the lush green fairway of the long par-5 fifth hole at the Bahamas' Fordly Cay Club golf course. The course and its adjoining luxury club were among the half-dozen most exclusive in the world.

Beyond the green, a white sand beach, palm-fringed, deserted, extended like a strip of Paradise into the distance. At the edge of the beach a pellucid turquoise sea lapped gently in tiny wavelets. Half a mile out from shore a line of breakers creamed on coral reefs.

Nearer to hand, beside the fairway, an exotic crazy-quilt of flowers – hibiscus, bougainvillaea, poinsettia, frangipani – competed in belief-defying colours. The fresh, clear air, moved agreeably by a zephyr breeze, held a scent of jasmine.

'I imagine,' the Vice-President of the United States observed, 'that this is as close to heaven as any politician gets.'

'My idea of heaven,' the Honourable Harold Austin told him, 'would not include slicing.' He grimaced and swung his four iron viciously. 'There must be some way to get better at this game.'

The four were playing a best-ball match – Big George and Roscoe Heyward against Harold Austin and the Vice-President.

'What you should do, Harold,' the Vice-President, Byron Stonebridge, said, 'is get back into Congress, then work your way to the job I have. Once there, you'd have nothing else to do but golf; you could take all the time you wanted to improve your game. It's an accepted historical fact that almost every Vice-

217

President in the past half century left office a better golfer than when he entered it.'

As if to confirm his words, moments later he lofted his third shot – a beautiful eight iron – straight at the pin.

Stonebridge, lean and lithe, his movements fluid, was playing a spectacular game today. He had begun life as a farmer's son, working long hours on a family smallholding, and across the years had kept his body sinewy. Now his homely plainsman's features beamed as his ball dropped, then rolled to within a foot of the hole.

'Not bad,' Big George acknowledged as his caddy-car drew even. 'Washington not keeping you too busy, eh, By ?'

'Oh, I suppose I shouldn't complain. I ran an inventory of Administration paper clips last month. And there's been a news leak from the White House – it seems there's a chance I'll sharpen pencils over there quite soon.'

The others chuckled dutifully. It was no secret that Stonebridge, ex-State governor, ex-Minority Leader in the Senate, was fretful and restless in his present role. Before the election which had thrust him there, his running mate, the presidential candidate, declared that *his* Vice-President would – in a new post-Watergate era – play a meaningful, busy part in government. As always after inauguration, the promise stayed unfulfilled.

Heyward and Quartermain chipped on to the green, then waited with Stonebridge as the Honourable Harold, who had been playing erratically, shanked, laughed, flubbed, laughed, and finally chipped on.

The four men made a diverse foursome. G. G. Quartermain, towering above the others, was expensively immaculate in tartan slacks, a Lacoste cardigan, and navy suède Foot-Joys. He wore a red golf cap, its badge proclaiming the coveted status of a member of Fordly Cay Club.

The Vice-President portrayed stylish neatness – double knit slacks, a mildly colourful shirt, his golfing footwear an ambivalent black and white. In dramatic contrast was Harold Austin, the most flamboyant dresser and a study in shocking pink and lavender. Roscoe Heyward was efficiently practical in dark grey slacks, a white, short-sleeved 'dress' shirt and soft black shoes. Even on a golf course he looked like a banker.

Their progress since the first tee had been something of a cavalcade. Big George and Heyward shared one electric caddy-car; Stonebridge and the Honourable Harold occupied another. Six more electric cars had been requisitioned by the Vice-President's Secret Service escort and now surrounded them – on both sides and fore and aft – like a destroyer squadron.

'If you had free choice, By,' Roscoe Heyward said, 'free choice to set some government priorities, what would they be ?'

Yesterday, Heyward had addressed Stonebridge formally as 'Mr Vice-President,' but was quickly assured, 'Forget the formality; I get weary of it. You'll find I answer best to "By".' Heyward, who cherished first name friendships with important people, was delighted.

Stonebridge answered, 'If I had my choice I'd concentrate on economics – restoring fiscal sanity, some balanced national book-keeping.'

G. G. Quartermain, who had overheard, remarked, 'A brave few tried it, By. They failed. And you're too late.'

'It's late, George, but not *too* late.'

'I'll debate that with you.' Big George squatted, considering the line of his putt. 'After nine. Right now the priority is sinking this.'

Since the game started, Quartermain had been quieter than the others, and intense. He had his handicap down to three and always played to win. Winning or turning in a sub-par score pleased him (so he said) as much as acquiring a new company for Supranational.

Heyward was playing with consistent competence, his performance neither flashily spectacular nor anything to be ashamed of.

As all four walked from their caddy-cars at the sixth tee, Big George cautioned: 'Keep your banker's eye on the scores of those two, Roscoe. To a politician and an advertising man, accuracy's not a natural habit.'

'My exalted status requires that I win,' the Vice-President said. 'By any means.'

'Oh, I have the scores.' Roscoe Heyward tapped his forehead. 'They're all in here. On 1, George and By had fours, Harold a six, and I had a bogey. We all had pars on 2 except for By with that incredible birdie. Of course, Harold and I had net birds there, too. Everyone held par on 3 except Harold; he had another six. The fourth hole was our good one, fours for George and me (and I had a stroke there), a five for By, a seven for Harold. And, of course, this last hole was a real disaster for Harold but then his partner comes through with another bird. So as far as the match is concerned, right now we're even.'

Byron Stonebridge stared at him. 'That's uncanny! I'll be damned.'

'You have me wrong for that first hole,' the Honourable Harold said. 'I had a five, not a six.'

Heyward said firmly, 'Not so, Harold. Remember, you drove into that palm grove, punched out, hit your fairway wood short of the green, chipped long and two-putted.'

'He's right,' Stonebridge confirmed. 'I remember.'

'Goddamit, Roscoe,' Harold Austin grumbled, 'whose friend are you?'

'Mine, by God!' Big George exclaimed. He draped a friendly arm over Heyward's shoulders. 'I'm beginning to like you, Roscoe, especially your handicap!' As Heyward glowed, Big George lowered his voice to a confidential level. 'Was everything satisfactory last night?'

'Perfectly satisfactory, thank you. I enjoyed the journey, the evening, and I slept extremely well.'

He had not slept well at first. In the course of the previous evening at G. G. Quartermain's Bahamas mansion it had become evident that Avril, the slim and lovely redhead was available to Roscoe Heyward on any terms he chose. That was made plain both by innuendo from the others and Avril's increasing nearness as the day, then night, progressed. She lost no opportunity to lean towards Heyward so that sometimes her soft hair brushed his face, or to make physical contact with him on the slightest pretext. And while he did not encourage her, neither did he object.

Equally clear was that the gorgeous Krista was available to

Byron Stonebridge and the glamorous blonde Rhetta to Harold Austin.

The exquisitely beautiful Japanese girl, Moonbeam, was seldom more than a few feet away from G. G. Quartermain.

The Quartermain ménage, one of a half dozen owned by the Supranational chairman in various countries, was on Prospero Ridge, high above Nassau city and with a panoramic view of land and sea. The house was in landscaped grounds behind high stone walls. Heyward's room on the second floor, to which Avril escorted him on arrival, commanded the view. It also afforded a glimpse, through trees, of the house of a near-neighbour – the prime minister, his privacy protected by patrolling Royal Bahamas Police.

In late afternoon they had drinks beside a colonnaded swimming pool. Dinner followed, served on a terrace out of doors, by candlelight. This time the girls, who had shed their uniforms and were superbly gowned, joined the men at table. Hovering white-gloved waiters served while two strolling players added music. Companionship and conversation flowed.

After dinner, while Vice-President Stonebridge and Krista elected to stay on at the house, the others entered a trio of Rolls-Royces – cars which had met them at Nassau Airport earlier – and were driven to the Paradise Island gambling casino. There Big George played heavily and appeared to win. Austin participated mildly, Roscoe Heyward not at all. Heyward disapproved of gambling but was interested in Avril's description of the finer points of chemin de fer, roulette, and blackjack, which were new to him. Because of the hum of other conversations, Avril kept her face close to Heyward's while she talked and, as on the aeroplane earlier, he found the sensation not unpleasing.

But then, with disconcerting suddenness, his body began taking greater cognizance of Avril so that ideas and inclinations which he knew to be reprehensible were increasingly hard to banish. He sensed Avril's amused awareness of his struggle, which failed to help. Finally, at his bedroom door to which she escorted him at 2am, it was with the greatest effort of will – particularly when she showed a willingness to linger – that he did not invite her in.

Before Avril left for wherever her own room was, she swirled her red hair and told him, smiling, 'There's an intercom beside the bed. If there's *anything* you want, press button number seven and I'll come.' This time there was no doubt of what 'anything' meant. And the number seven, it seemed, was a code for Avril wherever she might be.

Inexplicably his voice had thickened and his tongue seemed over-sized as he informed her, 'Thank you, no. Good night.'

Even then his inner conflict was not over. Undressing, his thoughts returned to Avril and he saw to his chagrin that his body was undermining his will's resolve. It had been a long time since, unbidden, it had happened.

It was then that he had fallen on his knees and prayed to God to protect him from sin and relieve him of temptation. And after a while, it seemed, the prayer was answered. His body drooped with tiredness. Later still, he slept.

Now, as they drove down the sixth fairway, Big George volunteered, 'Look, fella, tonight if you like I'll send Moonbeam to you. A man wouldn't believe the tricks that little lotus blossom knows.'

Heyward's face flushed. He decided to be firm. 'George, I'm enjoying your company and I'd like to have your friendship. But I must tell you that in certain areas our ideas differ.'

The big man's features stiffened. 'In just what areas?'

'I imagine, moral ones.'

Big George considered, his face a mask. Then suddenly he guffawed. 'Morals – what are they?' He stopped the caddy-car as the Honourable Harold prepared to hit from a fairway bunker on their left. 'Okay, Roscoe, cut it your way. Just tell me if you change your mind.'

Despite the firmness of his resolution, over the next two hours Heyward found his imagination turning to the fragile and seductive Japanese girl.

At the end of nine holes, at the course refreshment counter, Big George resumed his fifth hole argument with Byron Stonebridge.

'The US government and other governments,' Big George

declared, 'are being run by those who don't, or won't understand economic principles. It's a reason – the only reason – we have runaway inflation. It's why the world's money system is breaking down. It's why everything moneywise can only get worse.'

'I'll go part way with you on that,' Stonebridge told him. 'The way Congress is spending money, you'd think the supply is inexhaustible. We've supposedly sane people in the House and Senate who believe that for every dollar coming in you can safely put out four or five.'

Big George said impatiently, 'Every businessman knows that. Known it for a generation. The question is not if, but when, will the American economy collapse?'

'I'm not convinced it has to. We could still avert it.'

'Could, but won't. Socialism – which is spending money you don't have and never will – is too deep-rooted. So there comes a point when government runs out of credit. Fools think it can't happen. But it will.'

The Vice-President sighed. 'In public I'd deny the truth of that. Here, among us privately, I can't.'

'The sequence which is coming,' Big George said, 'is easy to predict. It'll be much the way things went in Chile. A good many think that Chile was different and remote. It wasn't. It was a small-scale model of the USA – and Canada and Britain.'

The Honourable Harold ventured thoughtfully, 'I agree with your point about sequence. First a democracy – solid, world-acknowledged, and effective. Then socialism, mild at first but soon increasing. Money spent wildly until nothing's left. After that, financial ruin, anarchy, dictatorship.'

'No matter how much in a hole we get,' Byron Stonebridge said, 'I'll not believe we'd go that far.'

'We wouldn't need to,' Big George told him. 'Not if some of us with intelligence and power think ahead, and plan. When financial collapse comes, in the US we've two strong arms to stop us short of anarchy. One is big business. By that I mean a cartel of multi-national companies like mine, and big banks like yours and others, Roscoe – which could run the country financially, exerting fiscal discipline. *We* would be solvent because of

223

world-wide operation; we'd have put our own resources where inflation didn't swallow them. The other strong arm is the military and police. In partnership with big business, they'd keep order.'

The Vice-President said dryly, 'In other words, a police state. You might encounter opposition.'

Big George shrugged. 'Some maybe; not much. People will accept the inevitable. Especially when democracy, so-called, has split apart, the money system shattered, individual purchasing power nil. Besides that, Americans don't believe in democratic institutions any more. You politicians undermined them.'

Roscoe Heyward had kept silent, listening. Now he said, 'What you foresee, George, is an extension of the present military-industrial complex into an elitist government.'

'Exactly! And industrial-military – I prefer it that way – is becoming stronger as American economics weaken. And we've organization. It's loose, but tightening fast.'

'Eisenhower was first to recognize the military-industrial structure,' Heyward said.

'And warn against it,' Byron Stonebridge added.

'Hell, yes!' Big George agreed. 'And more fool him! Ike, of all people, should have seen the possibilities for strength. Don't you?'

The Vice-President sipped his Planter's Punch. 'This is off the record. But yes, I do.'

'I'll say this,' Big George assured him, *'you're* one who should be joining *us.'*

The Honourable Harold asked, 'How much time, George, do you believe we have?'

'My own experts tell me eight to nine years. By then, collapse of the money system is inevitable.'

'What appeals to me as a banker,' Roscoe Heyward said, 'is the idea of discipline at last in money and government'.

G. G. Quartermain signed the bar chit and stood up. 'And you'll see it. That I promise you.'

They drove to the tenth tee.

Big George called over to the Vice-President, 'By, you've been playing 'way over your head and it's your honour. Tee it

224

up and let's see some *disciplined* and *economic* golf. You're only one-up and there are nine tough holes to go.'

Big George and Roscoe Heyward waited on the caddy-car path while Harold Austin looked over his lie on the fourteenth hole; after general searching, a Secret Service man had located his ball beneath a hibiscus bush. Big George had relaxed since he and Heyward had taken two holes and were now one-up. As they sat in the caddy-car, the subject which Heyward had been hoping for was raised. It happened with surprising casualness.

'So your bank would like some Supranational business.'

'The thought had occurred to us.' Heyward tried to match the other's casualness.

'I'm extending Supranational's foreign communications holdings by buying control of small, key telephone and broadcast companies. Some owned by governments, others private. We do it quietly, paying off local politicians where we have to; that way we avoid nationalistic fuss. Supranational provides advanced technology, efficient service, which small countries can't afford, and standardization for global linkage. There's good profitability for ourselves. In three more years we'll control, through subsidiaries, forty-five per cent of communications linkages, worldwide. No one else comes close. It's important to America; it'll be vital in the kind of industrial-military liaison we were talking about.'

'Yes,' Heyward agreed, 'I can see the significance of that.'

'From your bank I'd want a credit line of fifty million dollars. Of course, at prime.'

'Naturally, whatever we arranged would be at prime.' Heyward had known that any loan to Supranational would be at the bank's best interest rate. In banking it was axiomatic that the richest customers paid least for borrowed money; highest interest rates were for the poor. 'What we would have to review,' he pointed out, 'is our bank's legal limitation under Federal law.'

'Legal limit, hell! There are ways around that, methods used every day. You know it as well as I do.'

'Yes, I'm aware that there are ways and means.'

What both men were speaking of, and fully understood, was a

225

US banking regulation forbidding any bank to loan more than ten per cent of its capital and paid-in surplus to a single debtor. The purpose was to guard against bank failure and protect depositors from loss. In the case of First Mercantile American, a fifty-million-dollar loan to Supranational would substantially exceed that limit.

'The way to beat the regulation,' Big George said, 'is for you to split the loan among our subsidiary companies. Then we'll reallocate it as and where we need.'

Roscoe Heyward mused, 'It could be done that way.' He was aware that the proposal violated the spirit of the law while remaining technically within it. But he also knew that what Big George had said was true: Such methods were in everyday use by the biggest, most prestigious banks.

Yet even with that problem handled, the size of the proposed commitment staggered him. He had envisaged twenty or twenty-five million as a starting point, with the sum increasing perhaps as relationships between Supranational and the bank developed.

As if reading his mind, Big George said flatly, 'I never deal in small amounts. If fifty million is bigger than you people can handle, let's forget the whole thing. I'll give it to Chase.'

The elusive, important business which Heyward had come here hoping to capture seemed suddenly to be slipping away.

He said emphatically, 'No, no. It's not too large.'

Mentally he reviewed other FMA commitments. No one knew them better. Yes, fifty million to SuNatCo *could* be managed. It would necessitate turning off taps within the bank – cutting back drastically on smaller loans and mortgages, but this could be handled. A large single loan to a client like Supranational would be immensely more profitable than a host of small loans, costly to process and collect.

'I intend to recommend the line of credit strongly to our board,' Heyward said decisively, 'and I'm certain they'll agree.'

His golfing partner acknowledged curtly, 'Good.'

'Of course, it would strengthen my position if I could inform our directors that we would have some bank representation on the Supranational board.'

Big George drove the golf car up to his ball, which he studied

226

before replying. 'That might be arranged. If it was, I'd expect your trust department to invest heavily in our stock. It's time some fresh buying pushed the price up.'

With growing confidence, Heyward said, 'The subject could be explored, along with other matters. Obviously Supranational will have an active account with us now, and there's the question of a compensating balance . . .'

They were, Heyward knew, going through a banker-client ritualistic dance. What it symbolized was a fact of banking-corporate life: *you scratch my back, I'll scratch yours.*

G. G. Quartermain, jerking an iron from his alligator bag, said irritably, 'Don't bother me with details. My financial man, Inchbeck, will be here today. He'll fly back with us tomorrow. You two can get together then.'

Plainly, the brief business session was concluded.

By this time the Honourable Harold's erratic game seemed to have affected his partner. 'You're psyching me,' Byron Stonebridge complained at one point. At another: 'Dammit, Harold that slice of yours is contagious as smallpox. Anyone you play with should be vaccinated.' And for whatever reason, the Vice-President's swing shots and poise began to go awry for costly strokes.

Since Austin did not improve, even with the chiding, by the seventeenth hole, Big George and short-but-straight Roscoe remained one up in the lead. This suited G. G. Quartermain and he crunched his tee shot on eighteen about two hundred and seventy yards, straight down the middle, then proceeded to birdie the hole, giving his side the match.

Big George was jovial at his victory and clasped Byron Stonebridge around the shoulders. 'I guess that makes my credit balance in Washington even better than before.'

'Depends on what you want,' the Vice-President said. He added pointedly, 'and how discreet you are.'

Over drinks in the men's locker room, the Honourable Harold and Stonebridge each paid G. G. Quartermain a hundred dollars – a bet they had agreed on before the game began. Heyward had demurred from betting, so was not included in the payoff.

It was Big George who said magnanimously, 'I like the way

you played, partner.' He appealed to the others. 'I think Roscoe ought to get some recognition. Don't you two ?'

As they nodded, Big George slapped his knee. 'I got it! A seat on the Supranational board. Howzat for a prize ?'

Heyward smiled. 'I'm sure you're joking.'

Momentarily, the smile left the SuNatCo chairman's face. 'About Supranational I never joke.'

It was then Heyward realized that this was Big George's way of implementing their earlier conversation. If he agreed, of course, it would mean accepting the other obligations . . .

His hesitation lasted seconds only. 'If you do mean it, I'll be delighted to accept.'

'It will be announced next week.'

The offer was so swift and staggering that Heyward still had difficulty believing. He had expected that someone else from among the directors of First Mercantile American Bank would be invited to join the board of Supranational. To be chosen himself, and personally by G. G. Quartermain, was an accolade of accolades. The SuNatCo board, as composed now, read like a blue ribboned Who's Who of business and finance.

As if reading his mind, Big George chuckled. 'Among other things, you can keep an eye on your bank's money.'

Heyward saw Honourable Harold glance his way questioningly. As Heyward gave a small slight nod, his fellow FMA director beamed.

eight

The second evening at G. G. Quartermain's Bahamas mansion held a subtly different quality from the first. It was as if all eight of them – the men and girls – shared a relaxed intimacy, lacking the night before. Roscoe Heyward, aware of the contrast, suspected he knew the reason for it.

Intuition told him that Rhetta had spent the previous night with Harold Austin, Krista with Byron Stonebridge. He hoped the two men did not believe the same was true of himself and Avril. He was sure that his host did not; his remarks of this morning indicated it, probably because Big George was kept informed about what went on, or didn't, within this house.

Meanwhile, the evening gathering – again around the pool and on the terrace at dinnertime – was delectable for its own sake. Roscoe Heyward allowed himself to be an untautened, cheerful part of it.

He was enjoying, quite frankly, the continued attentions of Avril who showed no sign of resenting his rejection of her last night. Since he had proven to himself that he could resist her ultimate temptations, he saw no reason to deny himself Avril's pleasant companionship now. Two other reasons for his euphoric state were the pledge of Supranational business for First Mercantile American Bank and the unexpected, dazzling trophy of a seat for himself on the SuNatCo board. He had no doubt whatever that both would enhance his own prestige importantly at FMA. Already his succession to the bank's presidency seemed nearer.

Earlier, he had had a short meeting with the Supranational comptroller, Stanley Inchbeck, who had arrived as Big George said. Inchbeck was a balding, bustling New Yorker and he and Heyward arranged to work out details of the SuNatCo loan on the flight northwards tomorrow. Apart from his meeting with Heyward, Inchbeck had been closeted through most of the afternoon with G. G. Quartermain. Although he was apparently staying somewhere in the house, Inchbeck did not appear for drinks or dinner.

Something else Roscoe Heyward had noticed earlier, from the window of his second-floor room, was G. G. Quartermain and Byron Stonebridge strolling in the grounds for almost an hour in the early evening, deep in conversation. They were too far from the house for anything they said to be overheard but Big George appeared to be talking persuasively, with the Vice-President interrupting occasionally with what probably were questions. Heyward remembered this morning's remark on the golf course about 'a credit balance in Washington', then wondered which of Supranational's many interests were being discussed. He decided he would never know.

Now, after dinner, in the cool, sweet-scented darkness out of doors, Big George was once more the genial host. Cupping his hands around a _Q_ emblazoned brandy glass, he announced, 'No excursions tonight. We'll keep the party here.'

The major-domo, waiters, and musicians had discreetly slipped away.

Rhetta and Avril, who were drinking champagne, chorused, 'A party here!'

By Stonebridge raised his voice to match the girls'. 'What kind of party ?'

'A swinging party!' Krista declared, then corrected herself, her speech slurred slightly from dinner wine and champagne. 'No, a swimming party! I want to swim.'

Stonebridge challenged her, 'What's stopping you ?'

'Nothing, By, darling! Absolutely nothing!' In a series of swift movements, Krista set down her champagne glass, kicked off her shoes, unfastened straps on her dress and wiggled. The long green dress she had been wearing cascaded to her feet. Beneath it was a slip. She pulled that over her head and tossed it away. She had been wearing nothing else.

Naked, smiling, her exquisitely proportioned body with high firm breasts and jet black hair making her like a Maillol sculpture in motion, Krista walked with dignity from the terrace, down steps to the lighted swimming pool, and dived in. She swam the length of the pool, turned and called to the others, 'It's glorious! Come in!'

'By God!' Stonebridge said, 'I reckon I will.' He tossed off his sports shirt, slacks and shoes, and naked as Krista, though less alluring, padded over and dived.

Moonbeam, with a small high giggle, and Rhetta were already taking off their clothes.

'Hold on!' Harold Austin called. 'This sport's coming, too.'

Roscoe Heyward, who had watched Krista with a mixture of shock and fascination, found Avril close beside him. 'Rossie, sweetie, undo my zipper.' She presented him her back.

Uncertainly, he tried to reach the zipper from his chair.

'Stand up, you old silly,' Avril said. As he did, with her head half turned she leaned against him, her warmth and fragrance overpowering.

'Have you done it yet?'

He was having difficulty concentrating. 'No, it seems to be...'

Adroitly, Avril reached behind her. 'Here, let me.' Finishing what he had begun, she tugged the zipper down. With a shrug of her shoulders, her dress fell away.

She swirled her red hair in the gesture he had come to know.

'Well, what are you waiting for? Undo my bra.'

His hands were trembling, his eyes riveted on her, as he did as he was told. The bra dropped. His hands did not.

With a minimal, graceful movement, Avril pivoted. She leaned forward and kissed him fully on the lips. His hands, remaining where they were, touched the forward thrusting nipples of her breasts. Involuntarily, it seemed, his fingers curled and tightened. Electric, sensual waves shot through him.

'Um,' Avril purred. 'That's nice. Coming swimming?'

He shook his head.

'See you later, then.' She turned, walking away like a Grecian goddess in her nudity, and joined the other five cavorting in the pool.

G. G. Quartermain had remained seated, his chair pushed back from the dinner table. He sipped his brandy, eyeing Heyward shrewdly. 'I'm not much for swimming either. Though once in a while, if he's sure he's among friends, it's good for a man to let himself go.'

'I suppose I should concede that. And I certainly do feel among friends.' Heyward sank down into his chair again; removing his glasses, he began to polish them. He had control of himself now. The instant of mad weakness was behind him. He went on, 'The problem is, of course: one occasionally goes slightly further than intended. However, if one maintains overall control, that's really the important thing.'

Big George yawned.

While they talked, the others, by this time out of the water, were towelling themselves and slipping on robes from a pile beside the pool.

Two hours or so later, as she had the night before, Avril escorted Roscoe Heyward to his bedroom doorway. At first, downstairs, he had decided to insist that she not accompany him, then changed his mind, confident of his reasserted strength of will and positive now he would not succumb to wild, erotic impulses. He even felt assured enough to say cheerfully, 'Good night, young lady. And, yes, before you tell me, I know your intercom number is seven, but I assure you there is nothing that I'll need.'

Avril had looked at him with an enigmatic half smile, then turned away. He immediately closed and locked the bedroom door, afterwards humming softly to himself as he prepared for bed.

But, in bed, sleep eluded him.

He lay awake for nearly an hour, the bed-clothes thrown back, the bedding soft beneath him. Through an open window he could hear a drowsy hum of insects and, distantly, the sound of breakers on the shore.

Despite his best intentions, the focus of his thoughts was Avril.

Avril . . . as he had seen and touched her . . . breathtakingly beauteous, naked and desirable. Instinctively he moved his fingers, reliving the sensation of those full, firm breasts, their nipples extended, as he had cupped them in his hands.

And all the while his body . . . striving, burgeoning . . . made mock of his intended righteousness.

He tried to move his thoughts away – to banking affairs, to the Supranational loan, to the directorship which G. G. Quartermain had promised. But thoughts of Avril returned, stronger than ever, impossible to eclipse. He remembered her legs, her thighs, her lips, her soft smile, her warmth and perfume . . . her availability.

He got up and began pacing, seeking to redirect his energy elsewhere. It would not be redirected.

Stopping at the window, he observed that a bright three-quarter moon had risen. It bathed the garden, beaches, and the sea in white ethereal light. Watching, a long-forgotten phrase returned to him: *The night was made for loving . . . by the moon.*

He paced again, then returned to the window, standing there, erect.

Twice he made a move towards the bedside table with its intercom. Twice, resolve and sternness turned him back.

The third time he did not turn back. Grasping the instrument in his hand, he groaned – a mixture of anguish, self-reproach, heady excitement, heavenly anticipation.

Decisively and firmly, he pressed button number seven.

nine

Nothing in Miles Eastin's experience or imagination, before entering Drummonburg Penitentiary, had prepared him for the merciless, degrading hell of prison.

It was now six months since his exposure as an embezzler, and four months since his trial and sentencing.

In rare moments, when his objectivity prevailed over physical misery and mental anguish, Miles Eastin reasoned that if society had sought to impose savage, barbaric vengeance on someone like himself, it had succeeded far beyond the knowing of any who had not endured, themselves, the brutish purgatory of prison. And if the object of such punishment, he further reasoned, was to push a human being out of his humanity, and make of him an animal of lowest instincts, then the prison system was the way to do it.

What prison did not do, and never would – Miles Eastin told himself – was make a man a better member of society than when he entered it. Given any time at all, prison could only degrade and worsen him; could only increase his hatred of 'the system' which had sent him there; could only reduce the possibility of his becoming, ever, a useful, law-abiding citizen. And the longer his sentence, the less likelihood there was of any moral salvage.

Thus, most of all, it was time which eroded and eventually destroyed any potential for reform which a prisoner might have when he arrived.

Even if an individual hung on to some shards of moral values, like a drowning swimmer to a lifebelt, it was because of forces within himself, and not because of prison but despite it.

Miles was striving to hang on, straining to retain some semblance of the best of what he had been before, trying not to become totally brutalized, entirely unfeeling, utterly despairing, savagely embittered. It was so easy to slip into a garment of all four, a hair shirt which a man would wear for ever. Most prisoners did. They were those either brutalized before they came here and made worse since, or others whom time in prison had worn down; time and the cold-hearted inhumanity of a world outside, indifferent to which horrors were perpetrated or decencies neglected – all in society's name – behind these walls.

In Miles's favour, and in his mind while he clung on, was one dominant possibility. He had been sentenced to two years. It made him eligible for parole in four more months.

The contingency that he might not receive parole was one he did not dare consider. The implications were too awful. He did not believe he could go through two years of prison and fail to emerge totally, irreparably, debased in brain and body.

Hold on ! he told himself each day and in the nights. *Hold on* for the hope, the deliverance, of parole!

At first, after arrest and detention while awaiting trial, he had thought that being locked into a cage would send him mad. He remembered reading once that freedom, until lost, was seldom valued. And it was true that no one realized how much their physical freedom of movement meant – even going from one room to another or briefly out of doors – until such choices were denied them totally.

Just the same, compared with conditions in the penitentiary, the pre-trial period was a luxury.

The cage of Drummonburg in which he was confined was a six-by-eight foot cell, part of a four-tiered, X-shaped cell house.

234

When the prison was built more than half a century ago, each cell was intended for one person; today, because of prison overpopulation, most cells, including Miles's, housed four. On most days prisoners were locked into the tiny spaces for eighteen hours out of twenty-four.

Soon after Miles had come here, and because of trouble elsewhere in the prison, they had remained locked in – 'lock-in, feed-in', the authorities called it – for seventeen whole days and nights. After the first week, the desperate cries of twelve hundred near-demented men made one more agony piled upon the others.

The cell to which Miles Eastin was allotted had four bunks clamped to walls, one sink and a single, seatless toilet which all four inmates shared. Because water pressure through ancient, corroded pipes was poor, water supply – cold only – to the sink was usually a trickle; occasionally it stopped entirely. For the same reason, the toilet often wouldn't flush. It was bad enough to be confined in the same close quarters where four men defecated with a total lack of privacy, but staying with the stench long after, while waiting for sufficient water to remove it, was a disgusting, stomach-heaving horror.

Toilet paper and soap, even when used sparingly, were never enough.

A brief shower was allowed once weekly; in between showers, bodies grew rancid, adding to close quarters misery.

It was in the showers, during his second week in prison, that Miles was gang raped. Bad as other experiences were, this had been the worst.

He had become aware, soon after his arrival, that other prisoners were attracted to him sexually. His good looks and youthfulness, he soon found out, were to be a liability. Marching to meals or at exercise in the yard, the more aggressive homosexuals managed to crowd around and rub against him. Some reached out to fondle him; others, from a distance, pursed their lips and blew him kisses. The first he squirmed away from, the second he ignored, but as both became more difficult his nervousness, then fear, increased. It became plain that inmates not involved would never help him. He sensed that guards who

235

looked his way knew what was happening. They merely seemed amused.

Though the inmate population was predominantly black, the approaches came equally from blacks and whites.

He was in the shower house, a single-storey corrugated structure to which prisoners were marched in groups of fifty, escorted by guards. The prisoners undressed, leaving their clothing in wire baskets, then trooped naked and shivering through the unheated building. They stood under shower heads, waiting for a guard to turn on the water.

The shower-room guard was high above them on a platform, and control of the showers and water temperature was under the guard's whim. If the prisoners were slow in moving, or seemed noisy, the guard could send down an icy blast of water, raising screams of rage and protest while prisoners jumped around like wild men, trying to escape. Because of the shower-house design, they couldn't. Or sometimes the guard would maliciously bring the hot water close to scalding, to the same effect.

On a morning when a group of fifty which included Miles was emerging from the showers, and another fifty, already undressed, were waiting to go in, Miles felt himself surrounded closely by several bodies. Suddenly his arms were gripped tightly by half a dozen hands and he was being hustled forward. A voice behind him urged, 'Move your ass, pretty boy. We ain't got long.' Several others laughed.

Miles looked up towards the elevated platform. Seeking to draw the guard's attention, he shouted, 'Sir! sir!'

The guard, who was picking his nose and looking elsewhere, appeared not to hear.

A fist slammed hard into Miles's ribs. A voice behind him snarled, 'Shaddup!'

He cried out again from pain and fear and either the same fist or another thudded home once more. The breath went out of him A fiery hurt shot through his side. His arms were being twisted savagely. Whimpering now, his feet barely touching the floor, he was hustled along.

The guard still took no notice. Afterwards, Miles guessed the man had been tipped off in advance and bribed. Since guards were abysmally underpaid, bribery in the prison was a way of life.

Near the exit from the showers, where others were beginning to dress, was a narrow open doorway. Still surrounded, Miles was shoved through. He was conscious of black and white bodies. Behind them, the door slammed shut.

The room inside was small and used for storage. Brooms, mops, cleaning materials were in screened and padlocked cupboards. Near the room's centre was a trestle table. Miles was slammed face downwards on it; his mouth and nose hit the wooden surface hard. He felt teeth loosen. His eyes filled with tears. His nose began to bleed.

While his feet stayed on the floor, his legs were roughly pulled apart. He fought desperately, despairingly, trying to move. The many hands restrained him.

'Hold still, pretty boy.' Miles heard grunting and felt a thrust. A second later he screamed in pain, disgust, and horror. Whoever was holding his head seized it by the hair, raised and slammed it down. 'Shaddup!'

Now pain, in waves, was everywhere.

'Ain't she lovely?' The voice seemed in the distance, echoing and dreamlike.

The penetration ended. Before his body could know relief, another began. Despite himself, knowing the consequences, he screamed again. Once more his head was banged.

During the next few minutes and the monstrous repetition, Miles's mind began to drift, his awareness waned. As strength left him, his struggles lessened. But the physical agony intensified – a searing of membrane, the fiery abrasion of a thousand sensory nerve ends.

Consciousness must have left him totally, then returned. From outside he heard a guard's whistle being blown. It was a signal to hurry with the dressing and assemble in the yard. He was aware of restraining hands withdrawn. Behind him a door opened. The others in the room were running out.

Bleeding, bruised, and barely conscious, Miles staggered out. The merest movement of his body caused him suffering.

'Hey, you!' the guard bawled from the platform. 'Move ass, you goddamn pansy!'

Groping, only half aware of what he was doing, Miles took the wire basket with his clothes and began to pull them on. Most of the others in his group of fifty were already outside in the yard. Another fifty men who had been under the showers were ready to transfer to the dressing area.

The guard shouted fiercely for the second time, 'Shithead! I said move!'

Stepping into his rough drill prison pants, Miles stumbled and would have fallen, but for an arm which reached out, holding him.

'Take it easy, kid,' a deep voice said. 'Here, I'll help.' The first hand continued to hold him steady while a second aided in putting the pants on.

The guard's whistle blasted shrilly. 'Nigger, you hear me! You an' that pansy get the hell outside, or be on report.'

'Yassir, yassir, big boss. Right away, now. Let's go, kid.'

Miles was aware, hazily, that the man beside him was huge and black. Later, he would learn the other's name was Karl and that he was serving a life sentence for murder. Miles would wonder, too, if Karl had been among the gang which raped him. He suspected that he was, but never asked, and never knew for sure.

What Miles did discover was that the black giant, despite his size and uncouthness, had a gentleness of manner and a sensitive consideration almost feminine.

From the shower house, supported by Karl, Miles walked unsteadily outdoors.

There were some smirks from other prisoners but on the faces of most Miles read contempt. A wizened old-timer spat disgustedly and turned away.

Miles made it through the remainder of the day – back to his cell, later to the mess hall where he couldn't eat the slop he usually forced down from hunger, and finally to his cell again, with help along the way from Karl. His other three cell companions ignored him as if he were a leper. Racked by pain and misery he slept, tossed, woke, lay fitfully awake for hours suffer-

238

ing the fetid air, slept briefly, woke again. With daybreak, and the clangour of cell doors opening, came renewed fear: when would it happen again? He suspected soon.

In the yard during 'exercise' – two hours during which most of the prison population stood around aimlessly – Karl sought him out.

'How y' feel, kid?'

Miles shook his head dejectedly. 'Awful.' He added, 'Thanks for what you did.' He was aware that the big black had saved him from being on report, as the shower-room guard had threatened. That would have meant punishment – probably time in the hole – and an adverse mark on his record for parole.

'It's okay, kid. One thing, though, you gotta figure. One time, like yesterday, ain't gonna satisfy them guys. They like dogs now, with you a bitch in heat. They'll be after you again.'

'What can I do?' The confirmation of Miles's fears made his voice quaver and his body tremble. The other watched him shrewdly.

'What you need, kid, is a protector. Some stud t' look out for you. How'd you like me for yours?'

'Why should you do that?'

'You start bein' my reg'lar boy friend, I take care o' you. Them others know you 'n me's steady, they ain't gonna lay no hard on you. They know they do, there's me to reckon with.' Karl curled one hand into a fist; it was the size of a small ham.

Though he already knew the answer, Miles asked, 'What would *you* want?'

'Your sweet white ass, baby.' The big man closed his eyes and went on dreamily. 'Your body just for me. Any time I need it. I'll take care of where.'

Miles Eastin wanted to be sick.

'How 'bout it, baby? Waddya say?'

As he had so many times already, Miles thought despairingly: *whatever was done before, does anyone deserve this?*

Yet he was here. And had learned that prison was a jungle – debased and savage, lacking justice – where a man was stripped of human rights the day he came. He said bitterly, 'Do I have a choice?'

'Put it that way, no I guess you ain't.' A pause, then impatiently, 'Well, we on?'

Miles said miserably, 'I suppose so.'

Looking pleased, Karl draped an arm proprietorially around the other's shoulders. Miles, shrivelling inside, willed himself not to draw away.

'We gotta git you moved some, baby. To my tier. Maybe my pad.' Karl's cell was in a lower tier than Miles's, in an opposite wing of the X-shaped cell house. The big man licked his lips. 'Yeah, man.' The hand on Miles was already wandering.

Karl asked, 'You got bread?'

'No.' Miles knew that if he had had money it could have eased his way already. Prisoners with financial resources on the outside, and who used them, suffered less than prisoners with none.

'Ain't got none neither,' Karl confided. 'Guess I'll hafta figure sumpum.'

Miles nodded dully. Already, he realized, he had begun to accept the ignominious 'girl friend' role. But he knew, too, the way things worked here, that while the arrangement with Karl lasted he was safe. There would be no further gang rape.

The belief proved correct.

There were no more attacks, or attempted fondlings, or kisses blown. Karl had a reputation for knowing how to use his mighty fists. It was rumoured that a year ago he had used a shiv to kill a fellow prisoner who angered him, though officially the murder was unsolved.

Miles also was transferred, not only to Karl's tier, but to his cell. Obviously the transfer was a result of money changing hands. Miles asked Karl how he had managed it.

The big black chuckled. 'Them guys in Mafia Row put up the bread. Over there they like you, baby.'

'Like *me*?'

In common with other prisoners, Miles was aware of Mafia Row, otherwise known as the Italian Colony. It was a segment of cells housing the big wheels of organized crime whose outside contacts and influence made them respected and feared even, some said, by the prison governor. Inside Drummonburg their privileges were legendary.

Such privileges included key prison jobs, extra freedom of movement, and superior food, the latter either smuggled in by guards or pilfered from the general ration system. The Mafia Row inhabitants, Miles had heard, frequently enjoyed steaks and other delicacies, cooked on forbidden grills in workshop hideaways. They also managed extra comforts in their cells – among them, television and sun lamps. But Miles himself had had no contact with Mafia Row, nor been aware that anyone in it knew of his existence.

'They say you're a stand-up guy,' Karl told him.

Part of the mystery was resolved a few days later when a weasel-faced, pot-bellied prisoner named LaRocca sidled alongside Miles in the prison yard. LaRocca, while not part of Mafia Row, was known to be on its fringes and acted as a courier.

He nodded to Karl, acknowledging the big black's proprietorial interest, then told Miles, 'Gotta message f' ya from Russian Ominsky.'

Miles was startled and uneasy. Igor (the Russian) Ominsky was the loan shark to whom he had owed – and still owed – several thousand dollars. He realized, too, there must also be enormous accrued interest on the debt.

Six months ago it was Ominsky's threats which prompted Miles's six-thousand-dollar cash theft from the bank, following which his earlier thefts had been exposed.

'Ominsky knows ya kept ya trap shut,' LaRocca said. 'He likes the way ya did, 'n figures ya for a stand-up guy.'

It was true that during interrogation prior to his trial, Miles had not divulged the names, either of his bookmaker or the loan shark, both of whom he feared at the time of his arrest. There had seemed nothing to be gained by doing so, perhaps much to lose. In any event he had not been pressed hard on the point either by the bank security chief, Wainwright, or the FBI.

'Because ya buttoned up,' LaRocca now informed him, 'Ominsky says to tell ya he stopped the clock while you're inside.'

What that meant, Miles knew, was the interest on what he owed was no longer accumulating during his time in prison. He had learned enough of loan sharks to know the concession was a large one. The message also explained how Mafia Row, with its outside connections, knew of Miles's existence.

'Tell Mr Ominsky thanks,' Miles said. He had no idea, though, how he would repay the capital sum when he left prison, or even earn enough to live on.

LaRocca acknowledged, 'Someone'll be in touch before ya get sprung. Maybe we can work a deal.' With a nod which included Karl he slipped away.

In the weeks which followed, Miles saw more of the weasel-faced LaRocca who several times sought out his company, along with Karl's, in the prison yard. Something which appeared to fascinate LaRocca and other prisoners was Miles's knowledge about the history of money. In a way, what had once been an interest and hobby achieved for Miles the kind of respect which prison inmates have for those whose background and crimes are cerebral, as opposed to the merely violent. Under the system a mugger is at the bottom of the prison social scale, an embezzler or con artist near the top.

What intrigued LaRocca, in particular, was Miles's description of massive counterfeiting, by governments, of other countries' money. 'Those have always been the biggest counterfeit jobs of all,' Miles told an interested audience of half a dozen one day.

He described how the British government sanctioned forgery of great quantities of French assignats in an attempt to undermine the French Revolution. This, despite the fact that the same crime by individuals was punishable by hanging, a penalty which continued in Britain until 1821. The American Revolution began with official forgery of British banknotes. But the greatest counterfeit venture of all, Miles reported, was during World War Two when Germany forged £140 million in British money and unknown amounts of US dollars, all of highest quality. The British also printed German money and so, rumour said, did most of the other Allies.

'Wouncha know it!' LaRocca declared. 'Them's the kinda bastards put us in here. Betcha they're doing some o' the same right now.'

LaRocca was appreciative of the cachet which attached to himself as a result of Miles's knowledge. He also made it clear that he was relaying some of the information to Mafia Row.

'Me and my people'll take care of ya outside,' he announced one day, amplifying his earlier promise. Miles already knew that his own release from prison and LaRocca's could occur about the same time.

Talking money was a form of mental suspension for Miles, pushing away, however briefly, the horror of the present. He supposed, too, he should feel relief about the stopping of the loan clock. Yet neither talking nor thinking of other things was sufficient to exclude, except momentarily, his general wretchedness and self-disgust. Because of it he began to consider suicide.

The self-loathing focused on his relationship with Karl. The big man had declared he wanted, '*Your sweet white ass, baby. Your body just for me. Any time I need it.*' Since their agreement, he had made the promise come true with an appetite which seemed insatiable.

At the beginning Miles tried to anaesthetize his mind, telling himself that what was happening was preferable to gang rape, which – because of Karl's instinctive gentleness – it was. Yet disgust and consciousness remained.

But what had developed since was worse.

Even in his own mind Miles found it hard to accept, but the fact was: he was beginning to *enjoy* what was occurring between himself and Karl. Furthermore, Miles was regarding his protector with new feelings . . . Affection? *Yes* . . . Love? *No !* He *dared* not, for the moment, go that far.

The realizations shattered him. Yet he followed new suggestions which Karl made, even when these caused Miles's homosexual role to become more positive.

After each occasion questions haunted him. Was he a man any longer? He knew he had been before, but now could not be sure. Had he become perverted totally? Was this a way it happened? Could there ever be a turnabout, a reversion to normalcy later, cancelling out the tasting, savouring, here and now? If not, was life worth living? He doubted it.

It was then that despair enveloped him and that suicide seemed logical – a panacea, an ending, a release. Though difficult in

243

the crowded prison, it could be done – by hanging. Five times since Miles's arrival there had been cries of 'hang-up!' – usually in the night – when guards would rush like storm troopers, cursing, pulling levers to unlock tiers, 'cracking' a cell open, racing to cut down a would-be suicide before he died. On three of the five occasions, cheered on by prisoners' raucous cries and laughter, they were too late. Immediately after, because suicides were an embarrassment to the prison, night guard patrols were increased, but the effort seldom lasted.

Miles knew how it was done. You soaked a length of sheet or blanket so it wouldn't tear – urinating on it would be quieter – then secured it to an overhead beam which could be reached from a top bunk. It would have to be done silently while others in the cell were sleeping...

In the end one thing, and one thing only, stopped him. No other factor swayed Miles's decision to hang on.

He wanted, when his time in prison was done, to tell Juanita Núñez he was sorry.

Miles Eastin's penitence at his time of sentencing had been genuine. He had felt remorse at having stolen from First Mercantile American Bank where he had been treated honourably, and had given dishonour in return. In retrospect he wondered how he could have stifled his conscience as he did.

Sometimes, when he thought about it now, it seemed as if a fever had possessed him. The betting, socializing, sporting events, living beyond his means, the insanity of borrowing from a loan shark, and the stealing, appeared in hindsight like crazily mismated parts of a distemper. He had lost touch with reality and, as with a fever in advanced stages, his mind had been distorted until decency and moral values disappeared.

How else, he had asked himself a thousand times, could he have stooped so despicably, have been guilty of such vileness, as to cast blame for his own offence on Juanita Núñez?

At the trial, so great had been his shame, he could not bear to look Juanita's way.

Now, six months later, Miles's concern about the bank was less. He had wronged FMA but in prison would have paid his debt in full. *By God, he had paid!*

But not even Drummonburg in all its awfulness made up for what he owed Juanita. Nothing ever would. It was why he must seek her out and beg forgiveness.

Thus, since he needed life to do it, he endured.

ten

'This is First Mercantile American Bank,' the FMA money trader snapped crisply into the telephone; he had it cradled expertly between his shoulder and left ear so his hands were free. 'I want six million dollars overnight. What's your rate ?'

From the California West Coast the voice of a money trader in the giant Bank of America drawled, 'Thirteen and five eighths.'

'That's high,' the FMA man said.

'Tough titty.'

The FMA trader hesitated, trying to outguess the other, wondering which way the rate would go. From habit he filtered out the persistent drone of voices around him in First Mercantile American's Money Trading Centre – a sensitive, security-guarded nerve core in FMA Headquarters Tower, which few of the bank's customers knew about and only a privileged handful ever saw. But it was in centres like this that much of a big bank's profit was made – or could be lost.

Reserve requirements made it necessary for a bank to hold specific amounts of cash against possible demand, but no bank wanted too much idle money or too little. Bank money traders kept amounts in balance.

'Hold, please,' the FMA trader said to San Francisco. He pressed a 'hold' button on his phone console, then another button near it.

A new voice announced, 'Manufacturers Hanover Trust, New York.'

'I need six million overnight. What's your rate ?'

'Thirteen and three-quarters.'

On the East Coast the rate was rising.

'Thanks, no thanks.' The FMA trader broke the connection with New York and released the 'hold' button where San Francisco was waiting. He said, 'I guess I'll take it.'

'Six million sold to you at thirteen and five eighths,' Bank of America said.

'Right.'

The trade had taken twenty seconds. It was one of thousands daily between rival banks in a contest of nerve and wits, with stakes in seven figures. Bank money traders were invariably young men in their thirties – bright and ambitious, quick-minded, unflustered under pressure. Yet, since a record of success in trading could advance a young man's career and mistakes blight it, tension was constant so that three years on a money-trading desk was considered a maximum. After that, the strain began to show.

At this moment, in San Francisco and at First Mercantile American Bank the latest transaction was being recorded, fed to a computer, then transmitted to the Federal Reserve System. At the 'Fed', for the next twenty-four hours, reserves of Bank of America would be debited by six million dollars, the reserves of FMA credited with the same amount. FMA would pay Bank of America for the use of its money for that time.

All over the country similar transactions between other banks were taking place.

It was a Wednesday, in mid-April.

Alex Vandervoort, visiting the Money Trading Centre, a part of his domain within the bank, nodded a greeting to the trader who was seated on an elevated platform surrounded by assistants, the latter funnelling information and completing paper work. The young man, already immersed in another trade, returned the greeting with a wave and cheerful smile.

Elsewhere in the room – the size of an auditorium and with similarities to the control centre of a busy airport – were other traders in securities and bonds, flanked by aides, accountants, secretaries. All were engaged in deploying the bank's money – lending, borrowing, investing, selling, reinvesting.

Beyond the traders, a half-dozen financial supervisors worked at larger, plusher desks.

Traders and supervisors alike faced a huge board, running the trading centre's length and giving quotations, interest rates and other information. The remote-controlled figures on the board changed constantly.

A bond trader at a desk not far from where Alex was standing rose to his feet and announced loudly, 'Ford and United Auto Workers just announced a two-year contract.' Several other traders reached for telephones. Important industrial and political news, because of its instant effect on securities prices, was always shared this way by the first in the room to hear of it.

Seconds later, a green light above the information board winked off and was replaced by flashing amber. It was a signal to traders not to commit themselves because new quotations, presumably resulting from the auto industry settlement, were coming in. A flashing red light, used rarely, was a warning for more cataclysmic change.

Yet the money-trading desk, whose operation Alex had been watching, remained a pivot point.

Federal regulations required banks to have seventeen and a half per cent of their demand deposits available in liquid cash. Penalties for non-compliance were severe. Yet it was equally poor banking to leave large sums uninvested, even for a day.

Therefore banks maintained a continual tally of all money moving in and out. A central cashier's department kept a finger on the flow like a physician on a pulse. If deposits within a banking system such as First Mercantile American's were heavier than anticipated, the bank – through its money trader – promptly loaned surplus funds to other banks who might be short of their reserve requirements. Conversely, if customer withdrawals were unusually heavy, FMA would borrow.

A bank's position changed from hour to hour, so that a bank which was a lender in the morning could be a borrower at midday and a lender again before the close of business. This way, a large bank might trade more than a billion dollars in a day.

Two other things could be said – and often were – about the system. First, banks were usually faster in pursuing earnings for themselves than for their clients. Second, banks did far, far better in the way of profit for themselves than they achieved for outsiders who entrusted money to them.

Alex Vandervoort's presence in the Money Trading Centre had been partly to keep in touch with money flow, which he often did, and partly to discuss bank developments in recent weeks which had distressed him.

He was with Tom Straughan, a senior vice-president and fellow member of FMA's money policy committee. Straughan's office was immediately outside. He had walked into the Money Trading Centre with Alex. It was young Straughan who, back in January, had opposed a cutback of Forum East funds but now welcomed the proposed loan to Supranational Corporation.

They were discussing Supranational now.

'You're worrying too much, Alex,' Tom Straughan insisted. 'Besides being a nil-risk situation, SuNatCo will be good for us. I'm convinced of it.'

Alex said impatiently, 'There's no such thing as nil-risk. Even so, I'm less concerned about Supranational than I am about the taps we'll have to turn off elsewhere.'

Both men knew which taps, within First Mercantile American, Alex was referring to. A memorandum of proposals, drafted by Roscoe Heyward and approved by the bank's president, Jerome Patterton, had been circulated to members of the money policy committee a few days earlier. To make possible the fifty million dollar Supranational line of credit, it was proposed to cut back drastically on small loans, home mortgages and municipal bond financing.

'If the loan goes through and we make those cutbacks,' Tom Straughan argued, 'they'll be only temporary. In three months maybe less, our funding can revert to what it was before.'

'You may believe that, Tom. I don't.'

Alex was dispirited before he came here. His conversation with young Straughan now depressed him further.

The Heyward-Patterton proposals ran counter, not only to Alex's beliefs, but also his financial instincts. It was wrong, he believed, to channel the bank's funds so substantially into one industrial loan at the expense of public service, even though the industrial financing would be far more profitable. But even from a solely business viewpoint, the extent of the bank's commitment to Supranational – through SuNatCo subsidiaries – made him uneasy.

On the last point, he realized, he was a minority of one. Everyone else in the bank's top management was delighted with the new Supranational connection and Roscoe Heyward had been congratulated effusively for achieving it. Yet Alex's uneasiness persisted, though he was unable to say why. Certainly Supranational seemed to be sound financially; its balance sheets showed the giant conglomerate radiating fiscal health. And in prestige, SuNatCo rated alongside companies like General Motors, IBM, Exxon, Du Pont, and US Steel.

Perhaps, Alex thought, his doubts and depression stemmed from his own declining influence within the bank. And it *was* declining. That had become evident in recent weeks.

In contrast, Roscoe Heyward's star was high in the ascendant. He had the ear and confidence of Patterton, a confidence expanded by the dazzling success of Heyward's two-day sojourn in the Bahamas with G. G. Quartermain. Alex's own reservations about that success were, he knew, regarded as sour grapes.

Alex sensed, too, that he had lost his personal influence with Straughan and others who formerly considered themselves on the Vandervoort bandwagon.

'You have to admit,' Straughan was saying, 'that the Supranational deal is sweet. You've heard that Roscoe made them agree to a compensating balance of ten per cent?'

A compensating balance was an arrangement, arrived at after tough bargaining between banks and borrowers. A bank insisted that a predetermined portion of any loan be kept on deposit in current account, where it earned no interest for the depositor yet was available to the bank for its own use and investment. Thus a borrower failed to have full use of all of his loan, making the real rate of interest substantially higher than the apparent rate. In the case of Supranational, as Tom Straughan had pointed out, five million dollars would remain in new SuNatCo checking accounts – very much to FMA's advantage.

'I presume,' Alex said tautly, 'you're aware of the other side of the cosy deal.'

Tom Straughan appeared uncomfortable. 'Well, I've been advised there was an understanding. I'm not sure we should call it "the other side".'

'Dammit, that's what it is! We both know that SuNatCo insisted, and Roscoe agreed, our trust department would invest heavily in Supranational common stock.'

'If they did, there's nothing down on paper.'

'Of course not. No one would be that foolish.' Alex eyed the younger man. 'You've access to the figures. How much *have* we bought so far?'

Straughan hesitated, then walked to the desk of one of the Trading Centre supervisors. He returned with a pencilled note on a slip of paper.

'As of today, ninety-seven thousand shares.' Straughan added, 'The latest quote was at fifty-two.'

Alex said dourly, 'There'll be a rubbing of hands at Supranational. Our buying has already pushed up their price five dollars a share.' He calculated mentally. 'So in the past week we've bulldozed nearly five million dollars of trust clients' money into Supranational. Why?'

'It's an excellent investment.' Straughan tried a light touch. 'We'll make capital gains for all those widows and orphans and educational foundations whose money we take care of.'

'Or erode it – while abusing our trust. What do we know about SuNatCo, Tom – any of us – that we didn't two weeks ago? Why, until this week, has the trust department never bought a single Supranational share?'

The younger man was silent, then said defensively, 'I suppose Roscoe feels that now he'll be on the board he can watch the company more closely.'

'I'm disappointed in you, Tom. You never used to be dishonest with yourself, especially when you know the real reasons as well as I do.' As Straughan flushed, Alex persisted, 'Have you any idea what kind of scandal would blow up if SEC stumbled on to this? There's conflict of interest; abuse of lending limitation law; the use of trust funds to influence the bank's own business; and I've not the least doubt there's agreement to vote the Supranational stock with management at the next SuNatCo annual meeting.'

Straughan said sharply, 'If it's so, it wouldn't be the first time – even here.'

'Unfortunately that's true. But it doesn't make this smell any sweeter.'

The question of trust department ethics was an old one. Supposedly, banks maintained an internal barrier – sometimes called a Chinese Wall – between their own commercial interests and trust investments. In fact, they didn't.

When a bank had billions of dollars in clients' trust funds to invest, it was inevitable that the 'clout' this gave should be employed commercially. Companies in which a bank invested heavily were expected to respond with reciprocal banking business. Often, too, they were pressured into having a bank director on their board. If they did neither, other investments would speedily replace their own in trust portfolios, with their stock nudged downward as the result of a bank sell-off.

As well, brokerage houses which handled the huge volume of trust department buying and selling were expected to maintain large bank balances themselves. They usually did. If not, the coveted brokerage business went elsewhere.

Despite banks' public relations propaganda, the interests of trust department clients, including proverbial widows and orphans, often rated second to a bank's own interests. It was one reason why trust department results were generally so poor.

Thus, Alex knew, the Supranational-FMA situation was not unique. Just the same, the knowledge did not make him like it any more.

'Alex,' Tom Straughan volunteered, 'I may as well tell you that at the money committee tomorrow I intend to support the Supranational loan.'

'I'm sorry to hear that.'

But the news was not unexpected. And Alex wondered how much longer it would be before he would stand so alone and isolated that his position in the bank would be untenable. It could happen soon.

After tomorrow's money policy committee meeting, where the proposals concerning Supranational were certain to be approved by a majority, the full board of directors would meet next Wednesday with Supranational on its agenda too. At both meetings, Alex was sure, his would be a lone, dissenting voice.

He surveyed, once more, the ever-busy Money Trading Centre, dedicated to wealth and profit, unchanged in principle from the ancient money temples of Babylon and Greece. Not, he thought, that money, commerce, and profit were in themselves unworthy. Alex was dedicated to all three, though not blindly, and with reservations involving moral scruples, the reasonable distribution of wealth, and banking ethics. Yet, when exceptional profit was in prospect, as all history showed, those with such reservations were shouted down or swept aside.

Facing the powerhouse forces of big money and big business – exemplified now by Supranational and a majority in FMA – what could one individual, alone in opposition, hope to do ?

Little, Alex Vandervoort concluded dismally. Maybe nothing.

eleven

The meeting of the Board of Directors of First Mercantile American Bank, in the third week of April, was memorable on several counts.

Two major items of bank policy were the subject of intense discussion – one, the Supranational line of credit, the other a proposed expanding of the bank's savings activity and the opening of many new suburban branches.

Even before proceedings began, the meeting's tone was evident. Heyward, unusually jovial and relaxed, and wearing a smart new light grey suit, was on hand early. He greeted other directors at the boardroom door as they arrived. From the cordial responses it was clear that most members of the board had not only heard of the Supranational agreement through the financial grapevine but were heartily in favour of it.

'Congratulations, Roscoe,' Philip Johannsen, president of MidContinent Rubber, said, 'you've really moved this bank into the big league. More power to you, fella!'

A beaming Heyward acknowledged, 'I appreciate your support, Phil. I'd like you to know I've other targets in mind.'

'You'll hit them, never fear.'

A beetle-browed director from upstate, Floyd LeBerre, board chairman of General Cable and Switchgear Corporation, came in. In the past LeBerre had never been especially cordial to Heyward, but now he shook the other's hand warmly. 'Delighted to hear you're going on the Supranational board, Roscoe.' The General Cable chairman lowered his voice. 'My switchgear sales division is putting in some bids for SuNatCo business. Sometime soon I'd like to talk about them.'

'Let's make it next week,' Heyward said agreeably. 'You can be sure I'll help all I can.'

LeBerre moved on, his expression pleased.

Harold Austin, who had heard the exchange, winked knowingly. 'Our little trip paid off. You're riding high.'

Today, the Honourable Harold looked more than ever the ageing playboy: a colourful plaid jacket, brown bell-bottom trousers, his gaily patterned shirt sporting a cerulean blue bow tie. The white flowing hair was newly trimmed and styled.

'Harold,' Heyward said, 'if there's anything at all I can do in return . . .'

'There will be,' the Honourable Harold assured him, then strolled to his seat at the boardroom table.

Even Leonard L. Kingswood, the energetic chairman of Northam Steel and Alex Vandervoort's most fervent supporter on the board, had a good word as he passed by. 'Hear you corralled Supranational, Roscoe. That's first-class business.'

Other directors were equally complimentary.

Among the last arrivals were Jerome Patterton and Alex Vandervoort. The bank president, his white-fringed, bald head gleaming, and looking as usual like a gentleman farmer, went at once to the head of the long, elliptical boardroom table. Alex, carrying a file folder of papers, took his regular seat mid-way on the left-hand side.

Patterton gavelled for attention and speedily disposed of several routine matters. Then he announced, 'The first main item of business is : *Loans submitted for board approval.*'

Around the table a flurry of turning pages signalled the opening of FMA's traditional blue, confidential loan folders, prepared for directors' use.

'As usual, gentlemen, you have in front of you details of management's proposals. What's of special interest today, as most of you know already, is our new account with Supranational Corporation. Personally, I'm delighted with the terms negotiated and strongly recommend approval. I'll leave it to Roscoe, who's responsible for bringing this new, important business to the bank, to fill in background and answer any questions.'

'Thank you, Jerome.' Roscoe Heyward eased on his rimless glasses which he had been polishing out of habit and leaned forward in his chair. When he spoke his manner seemed less austere than usual, his voice pleasant and assured.

'Gentlemen, in embarking on any large loan commitment, it is prudent to seek assurance of the borrower's financial soundness, even when that borrower has a triple-A credit rating, as Supranational does. In appendix "B" of your blue folders' – around the table there was again a riffling of pages – 'you will find a summary I have personally prepared of assets and projected profits of the SuNatCo group, including all subsidiaries. This is based on audited financial statements plus additional data supplied at my request by Supranational's comptroller, Mr Stanley Inchbeck. As you can see, the figures are excellent. Our risk is minimal.'

'I don't know Inchbeck's reputation,' a director interjected; he was Wallace Sperrie, owner of a scientific instrument company. 'But I know yours, Roscoe, and if you approve these figures then they're quadruple-A for me.'

Several others chimed in their assent.

Alex Vandervoort doodled with a pencil on a pad in front of him.

254

'Thank you, Wally, and gentlemen.' Heyward permitted himself a slight smile. 'I'm hopeful your confidence will extend to the concomitant action I have recommended.'

Although the recommendations were listed in the blue folder, he described them anyway – the fifty-million-dollar line of credit to be granted in full to Supranational and subsidiaries immediately, with financial cutbacks in other areas of the bank to become effective at the same time. The cutbacks, Heyward assured the listening directors, would be restored 'as soon as possible and wise', though he preferred not to specify when. He concluded, 'I recommend this package to the board and I promise that, in light of it, our own profit figures will look very good indeed.'

As Heyward leaned back in his chair, Jerome Patterton announced, 'The meeting is open for questions and discussion.'

'Frankly,' Wallace Sperrie said, 'I see no need for either. Everything's clear. I think we're witnesses to a masterstroke of business for the bank and I propose approval.'

Several voices together called out, 'Second!'

'Proposed and seconded,' Jerome Patterton intoned. 'Are we ready to vote?' He obviously hoped so. His gavel was poised.

'No,' Alex Vandervoort said quietly. He pushed his pencil and doodling away. 'Nor do I think anyone else should vote without a great deal more discussion.'

Patterton sighed. He set the gavel down. Alex had already warned him, as a courtesy, of his intentions, but Patterton had hoped that Alex, sensing the near-unanimous mood of the board, would change his mind.

'I genuinely regret,' Alex Vandervoort was saying now, 'to find myself before the board in conflict with my fellow officers, Jerome and Roscoe. But I cannot, as a matter of duty and conscience, conceal my anxiety about this loan and my opposition to it.'

'What's the trouble? Doesn't your girl friend like Supranational?' The barbed question came from Forrest Richardson, a long-time FMA director; he was brusque-mannered, had a reputation as a martinet, and was a crown prince of meatpacking.

Alex flushed with anger. No doubt directors remembered the

public linking of his name with Margot's 'bank-in' campaign three months earlier; just the same, he was not prepared to have his personal life dissected here. But he withheld a strong retort and answered, 'Miss Bracken and I rarely discuss banking nowadays. I assure you we haven't this.'

Another director asked, 'Just what is it you don't like about the deal, Alex ?'

'Everything.'

Around the table there was a restless stirring and exclamations of annoyed surprise. Faces which had turned towards Alex betrayed a lack of friendliness.

Jerome Patterton advised curtly, 'You'd better lay the whole thing out.'

'Yes, I will.' Alex reached into the file folder he had brought and extracted a single page of notes.

'To begin with, I object to the *extent* of the commitment to a single account. And not only is it an ill-advised concentration of risk, in my opinion it is fraudulent under Section 23A of the Federal Reserve Act.'

Roscoe Heyward leaped to his feet. 'I object to that word "fraudulent".'

'Objecting doesn't change the truth,' Alex said calmly.

'It is not the truth! We have made plain that the full commitment is not to Supranational Corporation itself, but to its subsidiaries. They are Hepplewhite Distillers, Greenapastures Land, Atlas Jet Leasing, Caribbean Finance, and International Bakeries.' Heyward snatched up a blue folder. 'The allocations are spelled out specifically in here.'

'All those companies are controlled subsidiaries of Supranational.'

'But also long-established, viable companies in their own right.'

'Then why, today and all other times, have we been speaking solely of Supranational ?'

'For simplicity and convenience.' Heyward glowered.

'You know as well as I do,' Alex insisted, 'that once the bank's money is in *any* of those subsidiaries, G. G. Quartermain can, and will, move it around any way he chooses.'

'Now *hold everything!*' The interruption came from Harold Austin who had leaned forward, slapping a hand on the table for attention. 'Big George Quartermain is a good friend of mine. I won't sit quietly hearing an accusation of bad faith.'

'There was no accusation of bad faith,' Alex responded. 'What I'm talking about is a fact of conglomerate life. Large sums of money are transferred frequently between Supranational subsidiaries; their balance sheets show it. And what that confirms is – we'll be lending to a single entity.'

'Well,' Austin said; he turned from Alex, addressing other members of the board, 'I'll simply repeat that I know Quartermain well, and Supranational too. As most of you here are aware, I was responsible for the Bahamas meeting between Roscoe and Big George where this line of credit was arranged. In view of everything, I say it's an exceptionally good deal for the bank.'

There was a momentary silence which Philip Johannsen broke.

'Could it be, Alex,' the MidContinent Rubber president inquired, 'that you're just a little sore because Roscoe, and not you, was invited to that Bahamas golf game?'

'No. The point I'm making has nothing to do with personalities.'

Someone else said sceptically, 'It sure doesn't look that way.'

'Gentlemen, gentlemen!' Jerome Patterton rapped sharply with his gavel.

Alex had expected something of this kind. Keeping his cool, he persisted, 'I repeat, the loan is too big a commitment to one borrower. Furthermore, pretending it isn't to a single borrower is an artful attempt to circumvent the law, and all of us in this room know it.' He threw a challenging glance around the table.

'I don't know it,' Roscoe Heyward said, 'and I say your interpretation is biased and in error.'

By now it was obvious this had become an extraordinary occasion. Board meetings normally were either rubber-stamp affairs or, in event of mild disagreement, directors exchanged polite, gentlemanly comments. Angry, acerbic argument was virtually unknown.

For the first time Leonard L. Kingswood spoke. His voice was conciliatory. 'Alex, I'll admit there's some substance to what

257

you say, but the fact is, what's being suggested here is done all the time between big banks and large corporations.'

Intervention by the Northam Steel chairman was significant. At last December's board meeting Kingswood had been a leader in urging Alex's appointment as chief executive officer of FMA. Now he went on, 'Frankly, if there's anything to be guilty of with that kind of financing, my own company has been guilty of it too.'

Regretfully, knowing it was costing him a friend, Alex shook his head. 'I'm sorry, Len. I still don't believe that it's right, any more than I think we should leave ourselves open to a conflict-of-interest charge by Roscoe going on the Supranational board.'

Leonard Kingswood's mouth tightened. He said nothing more.

But Philip Johannsen did. He told Alex sourly, 'If, after that last remark, you expect us to believe there is nothing personal here, you're crazy.'

Roscoe Heyward tried, but failed, to conceal a smile.

Alex's face was set grimly. He wondered if this was the last FMA board meeting he would attend, though whether it was or wasn't he would complete what he had begun. Ignoring Johannsen's remark, he declared, 'As bankers we just don't learn. From all sides – Congress, consumers, our own customers, the press – we're accused of perpetuating conflict of interest through interlocking directorates. If we're honest with ourselves, most accusations are on target. Everyone here knows how the big oil companies liaise with each other by working closely on bank boards, and that's only one example. Yet we continue and continue with this same kind of inbreeding: *you be on my board, I'll be on yours.* When Roscoe is a director of Supranational, whose interests will be put first? Supranational's? Or First Mercantile American's? And on our board here will he favour SuNatCo over other companies because of his directorship over there? The shareholders of both companies are entitled to answers to those questions; so are legislators and the public. What's more, if we don't provide some convincing answers soon, if we don't cease being as high-handed as we are, all of banking will be faced with tough, restrictive laws. And we'll deserve them.'

'If you followed through logically on all that,' Forrest Richardson objected, 'half the members of this board could be accused of conflict of interest.'

'Precisely. And the time is close when the bank will have to face that situation and amend it.'

Richardson growled, 'There may be other opinions on that score.' His own meat-packing company, as they all knew, was a large borrower from FMA and Forrest Richardson had participated in board meetings where loans to his company were approved.

Disregarding the growing hostility, Alex ploughed on. 'Other aspects of the Supranational loan disturb me equally. To make the money available we're to cut back mortgage lending and small loans. In these two areas alone the bank will be defective in its public service.'

Jerome Patterton said huffily, 'It's been clearly stated that those cutbacks are temporary.'

'Yes,' Alex acknowledged. 'Except no one will say just how temporary, or what happens to the business and goodwill the bank will lose while the ban is on. And then there's the third area of cutback which we haven't touched on yet – municipal bonds.' Opening his file folder, he consulted a second sheet of notes. 'In the next six weeks, eleven issues of county and school district bonds within the state will be up for bid. If our bank fails to participate, at least half those bonds are certain to remain unsold.' Alex's voice sharpened. 'Is it the board's intention to dispense, *so quickly after Ben Rosselli's death*, with a tradition spanning three Rosselli generations ?'

For the first time since the meeting began directors exchanged uneasy glances. A policy established long ago by the bank's founder, Giovanni Rosselli, had First Mercantile American Bank taking the lead in underwriting and selling bond issues of small municipalities in the state. Without such aid from the state's largest bank, such bond issues – never large, important, or well known – might go unmarketed, leaving financial needs of their communities unmet. The tradition had been faithfully adhered to by Giovanni's son, Lorenzo, and grandson Ben. The business was not especially profitable, though neither did it represent a loss. But it was a significant public service and also returned to small communities some of the money their own people deposited in FMA.

'Jerome,' Leonard Kingswood suggested, 'maybe you should take another look at that situation.'

There were murmurs of assent.

Roscoe Heyward made a swift assessment. 'Jerome . . . if I may.'

The bank president nodded.

'In view of what seems a sentiment of the board,' Heyward offered smoothly, 'I'm certain we can make a fresh appraisal and perhaps restore a portion of municipal bond funding without impeding any of the Supranational arrangements. May I suggest that the board, having made its feeling clear, leaves details to the discretion of Jerome and myself.' Notably, he did not include Alex.

Nods and voices signified agreement.

Alex objected, 'That's not a full commitment, nor does it do anything to restore home mortgages and small loans.'

The other board members were pointedly silent.

'I believe we've heard all viewpoints,' Jerome Patterton suggested. 'Perhaps we can now vote on the proposal as a whole.'

'No,' Alex said, 'there's still one other matter.'

Patterton and Heyward exchanged glances of half-amused resignation.

'I've already pointed to a conflict of interest,' Alex stated sombrely. 'Now I warn the board of an even larger one. Since negotiation of the Supranational loan, and up to yesterday afternoon, our own trust department has bought' – he consulted his notes – 'one hundred and twenty-three thousand Supranational shares. In that time, and almost certainly because of the substantial buying with our trust clients' money, the SuNatCo share price has risen seven and a half points which I'm sure was intended and agreed to as a condition . . .'

He was drowned out by protesting voices – Roscoe Heyward's, Jerome Patterton's, and those of other directors.

Heyward was on his feet again, eyes blazing. 'That's a deliberate distortion!'

Alex slammed back, 'The purchasing is no distortion.'

'But your interpretation *is*. SuNatCo is an excellent investment for our trust accounts.'

'What makes it *suddenly* so good?'

Patterton protested heatedly, 'Alex, specific transactions of the trust department are not a matter for discussion here.'

Philip Johannsen snapped, 'I agree with that.'

Harold Austin and several others called out loudly, 'So do I!'

'Whether they are or aren't,' Alex persisted, 'I warn you all that what is happening may be in contravention of the Glass-Steagall Act of 1933, and that directors can be held responsible...'

A half dozen more voices erupted angrily at once. Alex knew he had touched a sensitive nerve. While board members were undoubtedly aware that the kind of duplicity he had described went on, they preferred not to know of it specifically. Knowledge implied involvement and responsibility. They wanted neither.

Well, Alex thought, like it or not, they knew now. Above the other voices he continued firmly, 'I advise the board that if it ratifies the Supranational loan with all its ramifications, we'll regret it.' He leaned back in his chair. 'That's all.'

As Jerome Patterton pounded with his gavel, the hubbub quietened.

Patterton, paler than before, announced, 'If there is no further discussion we will record a vote.'

Moments later the Supranational proposals were approved, with Alex Vandervoort the sole dissenter.

twelve

A coolness towards Vandervoort was evident when the directors resumed their meeting after lunch. Normally a two-hour morning session disposed of all board business. Today, however, extra time had been allotted.

Aware of the board's antagonism, Alex had suggested to Jerome Patterton during lunch that his presentation be deferred until next month's meeting. But Patterton told him curtly, 'Nothing doing. If the directors are in a surly mood, you made them that way and you can damn well take your chances.'

It was an extraordinarily strong statement for the mild-mannered Patterton, but illustrated the tide of disfavour now running against Alex. It also convinced him that the next hour or so would be an exercise in futility. His proposals seemed certain to be rejected out of perversity, if for no other reason.

As directors settled down, Philip Johannsen set the mood by pointedly consulting his watch. 'I've already had to cancel one appointment this afternoon,' the MidContinent Rubber chief grumbled, 'and I've other things to do, so let's keep it short.' Several others nodded agreement.

'I'll be as brief as possible, gentlemen,' Alex promised when Jerome Patterton had introduced him formally. 'My intention is to make four points.' He ticked them off on his fingers as he spoke.

'One, our bank is losing important, profitable business by failing to make the most of opportunities for savings growth. Two, an expansion of savings deposits will improve the bank's stability. Third, the longer we delay, the harder it will be to catch up with our many competitors. Fourth, there is scope for leadership – which we and other banks should exercise – in a return to habits of personal, corporate, and national thrift neglected far too long.'

He described methods by which First Mercantile American could gain an edge over competitors – a higher savings interest rate, to the top legal limit; more attractive terms for one-to-five-year certificates of deposit; checking facilities for savings depositors as far as banking law allowed; gifts for those opening new accounts; a massive advertising campaign embodying the savings programme and the nine new branches.

For his presentation Alex had left his usual seat to stand at the head of the boardroom table. Patterton had moved his own chair to one side. Alex had brought in, also, the bank's chief economist, Tom Straughan, who had prepared charts displayed on easels for the board to view.

Roscoe Heyward had eased forward in his seat and was listening, his face expressionless.

As Alex paused, Floyd LeBerre interjected, 'I have one observation right away.'

Patterton, his habit of politeness back in place, inquired, 'Do you want to take questions as we go, Alex, or leave them to the end?'

'I'll take Floyd's now.'

'This isn't a question,' the General Cable chairman said unsmilingly. 'It's a matter of record. I'm against a major savings expansion because if we do it we'll be ripping our own gut. Right now we've big deposits from correspondent banks . . .'

'Eighteen million dollars from the savings and loan institutions,' Alex said. He had expected LeBerre's objection, and it was valid. Few banks existed alone; most had financial ties with others and First Mercantile American was no exception. Several local savings and loan institutions maintained large deposits with FMA and fear that these sums would be withdrawn had deterred other proposed savings activity in the past.

Alex stated, 'I've taken that into account.'

LeBerre was unsatisfied. 'Have you taken into account that if we compete intensively with our own customers we'll lose every bit of that business?'

'Some of it. I don't believe all. In any case, new business we'll generate should far exceed what's lost.'

'So you say.'

Alex insisted, 'I see it as an acceptable risk.'

Leonard Kingswood said quietly, 'You were against any risk with Supranational, Alex.'

'I'm not against risks. This is a far smaller risk. The two have no relation.'

Faces around the table mirrored scepticism.

LeBerre said, 'I'd like to hear Roscoe's view.'

Two others echoed, 'Yes, let's hear Roscoe.'

Heads turned to Heyward who had been studying his folded

263

hands. He said blandly, 'One doesn't like to torpedo a colleague.'

'Why not ?' someone asked. 'It's what he tried to do to you.'

Heyward smiled faintly. 'I prefer to rise above that.' His face went serious. 'I do, however, agree with Floyd. Intensive savings activity on our part would lose us important correspondent business. I do not believe any theoretical potential gain is worth it.' He pointed to one of Straughan's charts indicating the geography of proposed new branches. 'Board members will observe that five of the suggested branches would be in locations close to savings and loan associations who are large depositors with FMA. We can be sure that that will not escape their attention either.'

'Those locations,' Alex said, 'have been carefully chosen as a result of population studies. They're where the *people* are. Sure the S&Ls got there first; in many ways they've been more far-sighted than banks like ours. But it doesn't mean we should stay away for ever.'

Heyward shrugged. 'I've already given my opinion. I'll say one thing, though – I dislike the entire idea of store-front branches.'

Alex snapped, 'They'll be money shops – the branch banks of the future.' Everything, he realized, was coming out contrary to the way he had intended. The subject of the branches themselves he had planned to get to later. Well, he supposed it made no difference now.

'From their description,' Floyd LeBerre said – he was reading an information sheet Tom Straughan had circulated – 'those branches sound like laundromats.'

Heyward, also reading, shook his head. 'Not in keeping with our style. No dignity.'

'We'd do better to shed some dignity and add more business,' Alex declared. 'Yes, store-front banks resemble laundromats; just the same, they're the kind of branch banks which are coming in. I'll make a prediction to the board: neither we nor our competitors can go on affording the gilded sepulchres we have as branch banks now. The cost of land and construction make it senseless. In ten years, half – at least – of our present branch banks will have ceased to exist as we know them. We'll retain a few key ones. The rest will be in less expensive premises, totally automated, with machine tellers, TV monitors to answer queries, and all linked to a computer centre. In planning new branches – including the nine I'm advocating here – it's that transition we should be anticipating.'

'Alex is right about automation,' Leonard Kingswood said. 'Most of us see it in our own businesses, moving in faster than we ever expected.'

'What's equally important,' Alex asserted, 'is that we've a chance to jump ahead profitably – that is, if we do it dramatically, with flair and fanfare. The advertising and promotion campaign would be massive, saturation coverage. Gentlemen, look at the figures. First, our present savings deposits – substantially lower than they should be . . .'

He moved on, aided by the charts and an occasional amplification by Tom Straughan. Alex knew that the figures and proposals, which he and Straughan had toiled over, were solid and logical. Yet he sensed flat opposition from some board members, a lack of interest by others. Lower down the table a director put a hand over his mouth, stifling a yawn.

Obviously he had lost. The savings and branch expansion plan would be rejected – and would be, in effect, a vote of 'no confidence' in him as well. As he had earlier, Alex wondered how long his own tenure with FMA could continue. There seemed little future for him, nor could he see himself as a participant in a Heyward-dominated regime.

He decided not to waste more time. 'Okay, I'll leave it there, gentlemen. Unless there are further questions.'

He had not expected any. Least of all did he anticipate support from the source from which suddenly, amazingly, it came.

'Alex,' Harold Austin said with a smile and friendly tone, 'I'd like to say thank you. Frankly, I'm impressed. I hadn't expected to be, but your presentation was convincing. What's more, I like the idea of those new branch banks.'

A few seats away Heyward looked startled, then glared at Austin. The Honourable Harold ignored him and appealed to others at the table. 'I think we should look at this with an open mind, putting aside our disagreements of this morning.'

265

Leonard Kingswood nodded, as did several others. Still more directors shed post-lunch drowsiness, their attention returning. Not for nothing was Austin the FMA board member with longest service. His influence was pervasive. He also was adept at swinging others to his points of view.

'Near the beginning of your remarks, Alex,' he said, 'you spoke of a return to personal thrift, and leadership which banks like ours might give.'

'Yes, I did.'

'Could you expand that thought ?'

Alex hesistated. 'I suppose so.'

Should he ? Alex weighed choices. He was no longer surprised at the interjection. He knew exactly why Austin had switched sides.

Advertising. Earlier, when Alex had suggested a 'massive advertising campaign' with 'saturation coverage', he had seen Austin's head come up, his interest clearly quicken. From that point it was not hard to see inside that head. The Austin Advertising Agency, by reason of the Honourable Harold's directorship and influence at FMA, had a monopoly of the bank's advertising business. A campaign such as Alex envisaged would bring substantial profit to the Austin Agency.

Austin's action was conflict of interest in its grossest form – the same conflict of interest which Alex had attacked this morning over Roscoe Heyward's appointment to the board of Supranational. Alex had asked then: *Whose interests would Roscoe put first ? Supranational's or those of First Mercantile American shareholders ?* Now, a parallel question should be asked of Austin.

The answer was obvious. Austin was looking out for his own interests; FMA came second. Never mind that Alex believed in the plan. The support – for selfish reasons – was unethical, an abuse of trust.

Should Alex say so ? If he did, it would touch off an uproar even greater than this morning's, and he would lose again. Directors clung together like lodge brothers. Furthermore, such a confrontation would end, for sure, Alex's own effectiveness at FMA. So was it worth it ? Was it necessary ? Did his duties require him to be keeper of the board's conscience ? Alex wasn't sure. Meanwhile the directors were watching him and waiting.

'Yes,' he said, 'I did refer – as Harold has reminded me – to thrift and a need for leadership.' Alex glanced at notes which, a few minutes ago, he had decided to discard.

'It is often said,' he told the listening directors, 'that government, industry, and commerce of all kinds are founded upon credit. Without credit, without borrowing, without loans – small, medium, and massive – business would disintegrate and civilization wither. Bankers know this best.

'Yet, increasingly, there are those who believe that borrowing and deficit financing have gone mad, and have eclipsed all reason. Especially is this true of governments. The United States government has amassed an appalling mountain range of debt, far beyond our ability ever to repay. Other governments are in as bad, or worse, condition. This is the real reason for inflation and the undermining of currencies at home and internationally.

'To a remarkable extent,' Alex continued, 'overwhelming government debt is matched by gargantuan corporate debt. And, at a lower financial level, millions of people – individuals following examples nationally set – have assumed debt burdens which they cannot pay. Total US indebtedness is two-and-a-half *trillion* dollars. National consumer debt is now approaching two hundred billion dollars. In the past six years more than a million Americans have gone bankrupt.

'Somewhere along the way – nationally, corporately, individually – we have lost the ancient verity of thrift and husbandry, of balancing what we spend against what we earn, and of keeping what we owe within honest limitations.'

Suddenly the mood of the board had become sober. Responding to it, Alex said quietly, 'I wish I could say there is a trend away from what I have described. I am not convinced there is. But trends begin with resolute action somewhere. Why not here ?

'In the nature of our times, savings deposits – more than any other type of monetary activity – represent financial prudence. Nationally and individually we need more prudence. A way to achieve it is through enormous increases in savings.

'There *can* be tremendous increases – if we commit ourselves, and if we work. And while personal savings alone will not re-

store fiscal sanity everywhere, it is at least one major move towards that end.

'This is why there is an opportunity for leadership and also
why – here and now – I believe this bank should exercise it.'

Alex sat down. Seconds later he realized he had said nothing
about his doubts concerning Austin's intervention.

Leonard Kingswood broke the brief, ensuing silence. 'Sense
and truth don't always make palatable listening. But I think we
all just heard some.'

Philip Johannsen grunted, then said grudgingly, 'I'll buy part
of that.'

'I buy it all,' the Honourable Harold said. 'In my opinion the
board should approve the savings and branch expansion plan as
presented. I intend to vote for it. I urge the rest of you to do the
same.'

This time Roscoe Heyward did not display his outrage,
though his face was tightly set. Alex figured that Heyward, too,
had guessed Harold Austin's motivation.

For another fifteen minutes discussion swirled until Jerome
Patterton rapped with his gavel and called for a vote. By an
overwhelming majority Alex Vandervoort's proposals were approved. Floyd LeBerre and Roscoe Heyward were the only dis-
senters.

On his way out of the boardroom Alex was aware that the
earlier hostility had not vanished. Some directors made it plain
that they still resented his strong stance of this morning on
Supranational. But the latest, unexpected outcome had made
him more buoyant, less pessimistic about his continuing role at
FMA.

Harold Austin intercepted him. 'Alex, when will you move on
the savings plan ?'

'Immediately.' Not wishing to seem ungracious, he added,
'Thank you for your support.'

Austin nodded. 'What I'd like to do now is come in with two
or three of my agency people to discuss the campaign.'

'Very well. Next week.'

So Austin had confirmed – without delay or embarrassment –
what Alex had deduced. Though to be fair, Alex thought, the

Austin Advertising Agency did good work and could be selected to handle the savings campaign on merit.

But he was rationalizing and knew it. By keeping silent a few minutes ago he had sacrificed principle to achieve an end. He wondered what Margot would think of his defection.

The Honourable Harold said affably, 'Then I'll be seeing you.'

Roscoe Heyward, leaving the boardroom just ahead of Alex, was accosted by a uniformed bank messenger who handed him a sealed envelope. Heyward ripped it open and took out a folded message slip. Reading it, he brightened visibly, glanced at his watch, and smiled. Alex wondered why.

thirteen

The note was a simple one. Typed by Roscoe's trusted senior secretary, Dora Callaghan, it informed him that Miss Deveraux had telephoned, leaving word she was in town and would like him to call as soon as possible. The note supplied a phone number and extension.

Heyward recognized the number: the Columbia Hilton Hotel. Miss Deveraux was Avril.

They had met twice since the trip to the Bahamas a month and a half ago. Both times it had been at the Columbia Hilton. And on each occasion, as well as during that night in Nassau when he had pressed button number seven to bring Avril to his room, she had taken him to a kind of paradise, a place of sexual ecstasy such as he had never dreamed existed. Avril knew incredible things to do to a man which – during that original night – had at first shocked and then delighted him. Later, her skill aroused wave after wave of sensual pleasure until he had cried out in sheer joy, using words which he did not know he knew. Afterwards Avril had been gentle, caressing, loving, and patient, until, to his surprise and exultation, he was aroused once more.

It was then he began to realize, with an awareness which had heightened since, how much of life's passion and glory – the mutual exploring, uplifting, sharing, giving, and receiving – he and Beatrice had never known.

For Roscoe and Beatrice his discovery had come too late, though perhaps for Beatrice it was a discovery she never would have wanted. But there was time still for Roscoe and Avril; on the occasions since Nassau they had proved it. He glanced at his watch, smiling – the smile which Vandervoort had seen.

He'd go to Avril as soon as possible, of course. It would mean rearranging his schedule for this afternoon and evening, but no matter. Even now, the thought of seeing her once more excited him, so that his body was stirring and reacting like a youth's.

On a few occasions since the affair with Avril began, conscience had troubled him. During recent Sundays in church, the text he had read aloud before going to the Bahamas came back to haunt him: *Righteousness exalteth a nation: but sin is a reproach to any people.* At such moments he consoled himself with the words of Christ in the Gospel of St John: *He that is without sin among you, let him first cast a stone . . .* And: *Ye judge after the flesh; I judge no man.* Heyward even permitted himself to reflect – with a levity which not long ago would have appalled him – that the Bible, like statistics, could be used to prove anything.

In any case, debate was immaterial. The intoxication of Avril was stronger than any stab of conscience.

Walking from the boardroom to his office suite on the same floor, he reflected, glowing: A session with Avril would consummate a triumphal day, with his Supranational proposals approved and his professional prestige at a zenith with the board. He had, of course, been disappointed at this afternoon's outcome and downright angry at what he saw as Harold Austin's betrayal, though he had deduced at once the selfish reasoning behind it. However, Heyward had little fear that Vandervoort's ideas would produce much real success. The plus-effect on bank profits this year of his own Supranational arrangements would be far, far greater.

Which reminded him – he must make a decision about the

additional half million dollars requested by Big George Quartermain as a further loan to Q-Investments.

Roscoe Heyward frowned slightly. He supposed in the whole matter of Q-Investments there was some mild irregularity, though in view of the bank's commitment to Supranational, and vice versa, it didn't seem too serious.

He had raised the matter in a confidential memo to Jerome Patterton a month or so ago.

G. G. Quartermain of Supranational phoned me twice yesterday from New York about a personal project of his called Q-Investments. This is a small private group of which Quartermain (Big George) is the principal, and our own director, Harold Austin, is a member. The group has already bought large blocks of common stock of various Supranational enterprises at advantageous terms. More purchases are planned.

What Big George wants from us is a loan to Q-Investments of $1½ million – at the same low rate as the Supranational loan, though without any requirement of a compensating balance. He points out that the SuNatCo compensating balance will be ample to offset this personal loan – which is true, though of course there is no cross guarantee.

I might mention that Harold Austin also telephoned me to urge that the loan be made.

The Honourable Harold, in fact, had bluntly reminded Heyward of a *quid pro quo* – a debt for Austin's strong support at the time of Ben Rosselli's death. It was a support which Heyward would continue to need when Patterton – the interim Pope – retired in eight months' time.

The memo to Patterton continued:

Frankly, the interest rate on this proposed loan is too low, and waiving a compensating balance would be a large concession. But in view of the Supranational business which Big George has given us, I think we would be wise to go along.

I recommend the loan. Do you agree?

Jerome Patterton had sent the memo back with a laconic pencilled *Yes* against the final question. Knowing Patterton, Heyward doubted if he had given the whole thing more than a cursory glance.

Heyward had seen no reason why Alex Vandervoort need be involved, nor was the loan large enough to require approval by the money policy committee. Therefore, a few days later, Roscoe Heyward had initialled approval himself, which he had authority to do.

What he did *not* have authority for – and had reported to no one – was a personal transaction between himself and G. G. Quartermain.

During their second telephone conversation about Q-Investments, Big George – calling from a SuNatCo offshoot in Chicago – had said, 'Been talking to Harold Austin about you, Roscoe. We both think it's time you got involved in our investment group. Like to have you with us. So what I've done is allot two thousand shares which we'll regard as fully paid for. They're nominee certificates endorsed in blank – more discreet that way. I'll have 'em put in the mail.'

Heyward had demurred. 'Thank you, George, but I don't believe I should accept.'

'For Chrissakes, why not ?'

'It would be unethical.'

Big George had guffawed. 'This is the real world, Roscoe. Same kind of thing happens between clients and bankers all the time. You know it. I know it.'

Yes, Heyward knew it happened, though not 'all the time', as Big George claimed, and Heyward had never let it happen to himself.

Before he could answer, Quartermain persisted, 'Listen, fella, don't be a damn fool. If it makes you feel better we'll say the shares are in return for your investment advice.'

But Heyward knew he had given no investment advice, either then or subsequently.

A day or two later, the Q-Investments share certificates arrived by registered airmail, in an envelope with elaborate seals, and marked STRICTLY PERSONAL AND CONFIDENTIAL. Even Dora Callaghan hadn't opened that one.

At home that evening, studying the Q-Investments financial

272

statement which Big George had also supplied, Heyward realized his two thousand shares had a net asset value of twenty thousand dollars. Later, if Q-Investments prospered or went public, their worth would be much greater.

At that point he had every intention of returning the shares to G. G. Quartermain; then, reassessing his own precarious finances – no better than they had been several months ago – he hesitated. Finally he yielded to temptation and later that week put the certificates in his safe deposit box at FMA's main downtown branch. It was not, Heyward rationalized, as if he had deprived the bank of money. He hadn't. In fact, because of Supranational, the reverse was true. So if Big George chose to make a friendly gift, why be churlish and refuse it?

But his acceptance still worried him a little, especially since Big George had telephoned at the end of last week – this time from Amsterdam – seeking an additional half million dollars for Q-Investments.

'There's a unique chance for our Q group to pick up a block of stock over here in Guilderland that's certain to be high flying. Can't say too much on an open line, Roscoe, so trust me.'

'I do, of course, George,' Heyward had said, 'but the bank will need details.'

'You'll get 'em – by courier tomorrow.' To which Big George had added pointedly, 'Don't forget you're one of us now.'

Briefly, Heyward had a second uneasy feeling: G. G. Quartermain might be paying more attention to his private investments than to management of Supranational. But the next day's news had reassured him. *The Wall Street Journal* and other papers carried prominent stories about a major, Quartermain-engineered industrial takeover by SuNatCo in Europe. It was a commercial *coup d'état* which sent Supranational shares soaring on the New York and London markets and made FMA's loan to the corporate giant seem even sounder.

As Heyward entered his outer office, Mrs Callaghan offered him her usual matronly smile. 'The other messages are on your desk, sir.'

He nodded, but inside pushed the pile aside. He hesitated over papers which had been prepared, but were not yet approved, concerning the additional Q-Investments loan. Then he dismissed that too, and, using a phone which was a direct outside line, dialled the number of paradise.

'Rossie, sweetie,' Avril whispered as the tip of her tongue explored his ear, 'you're hurrying too much. *Wait!* Lie still! *Still! Hold back!*' She stroked his naked shoulder, then his spine, her fingernails hovering, sharp but gossamer light.

Heyward moaned – a mixture of savoured, sweetest pleasure, pain, and postponed fulfilment – as he obeyed.

She whispered again, 'It'll be worth waiting, I promise.'

He knew it would be. It always was. He wondered again how someone so young and beautiful could have learned so much, be so emancipated ... uninhibited ... gloriously wise.

'*Not yet,* Rossie! Darling, *not yet! There! That's good.* Be patient!'

Her hands, skilled and knowing, went on exploring. He let his mind and body float, knowing from experience it was best to do everything ... exactly as ... she said.

'Oh, *that's good,* Rossie. Isn't it lovely?'

He breathed, 'Yes. *Yes!*'

'Soon, Rossie. *Very soon.*'

Beside him, over the bed's two pillows, close together, Avril's red hair tumbled. Her kisses had devoured him. The ambrosial, heady fragrance of her filled his nostrils. Her marvellous, willowy, willing body was beneath him. This, his senses shouted, was the *best* of life, of earth and heaven, here and now.

The only bittersweet sadness was that he had waited so many years to find it.

Again Avril's lips searched for his and found them.

She urged him, '*Now,* Rossie! *Now,* sweetie! *Now!*'

The bedroom, as Heyward had observed when he arrived, was standard Hilton – clean, efficiently comfortable, and a characterless box. A compact sitting-room of the same genre was outside; on this occasion, as on the others, Avril had taken a suite.

They had been here since late afternoon. After the lovemaking they had dozed, awakened, made love again – though not

274

with entire success – then slept for an hour more. Now both were dressing. Heyward's watch showed eight o'clock.

He was exhausted, physically drained. More than anything else he wanted to go home and go to bed – alone. He wondered how soon he could decently slip away.

Avril had been outside in the sitting-room, telephoning. When she returned, she said: 'I ordered dinner for us, sweetie. It'll be up soon.'

'That's wonderful, my dear.'

Avril had put on a filmy slip and tights. No bra. She began brushing her long hair which had become disordered. He sat on the bed watching her, despite his tiredness aware that every movement she made was lithe and sensuous. Compared with Beatrice, whom he was used to seeing daily, Avril was so *young*. Suddenly he felt depressingly old.

They went into the sitting-room where Avril said, 'Let's open the champagne.'

It was on a sideboard in an ice bucket. Heyward had noticed it earlier. By this time most of the ice had melted but the bottle was still cold. He fumbled inexpertly with wire and cork.

'Don't try to move the cork,' Avril told him. 'Tilt the bottle to forty-five degrees, then hold the cork and twist the bottle.'

It worked easily. She knew *so much*.

Taking the bottle from him, Avril poured into two glasses. He shook his head. 'You know I don't drink, my dear.'

'It'll make you feel younger.' She held out a glass. As he surrendered and took it, he wondered if she had read his mind.

Two refills later, when their room service meal arrived, he *did* feel younger.

When the waiter had gone, Heyward said, 'You should have let me pay for that.' A few minutes earlier he had brought out his wallet but Avril waved it away and signed the bill.

'Why, Rossie ?'

'Because you must allow me to give you back some of your expenses – the hotel bills, the cost of flying here from New York.' He had learned that Avril had an apartment in Greenwich Village. 'It's too much for you to spend yourself.'

She looked at him curiously, then gave a silvery laugh. 'You didn't think *I* was paying for all this?' She gestured around the suite. 'Using *my* money? Rossie, baby, you have to be crazy!'

'Then who *is* paying?'

'Supranational of course, you old silly! Everything's charged to them – this suite, the meal, my air fare, my time.' She crossed to his chair and kissed him; her lips were full and moist. 'Just don't worry about it!'

He sat still, crushed and silent, absorbing the impact of what had just been said. The mellowing potency of the champagne still coursed through his body, yet his mind was sharp.

'*My time*.' That hurt most of all. Until now he had assumed the reason Avril telephoned him after the Bahamas, suggesting that they meet, was because she liked him and had enjoyed – as much as he did – what happened between them.

How *could* he have been so naïve? *Of course* the entire exercise had been arranged by Quartermain and was at Supranational's expense. Shouldn't commonsense have told him? Or had he shielded himself by not enquiring sooner because he hadn't wanted to know? Something else: if Avril were being paid for 'my time', what did that make her? A whore? If so, what then was Roscoe Heyward? He closed his eyes. *St Luke 18:13*, he thought: *God be merciful to me a sinner*.

There was one thing he could do, of course. Immediately. That was find out how much had been expended until now, and afterwards send his personal cheque for that amount to Supranational. He began calculating, then realized he had no idea of the cost of Avril. Instinct told him it would not be small.

In any case he doubted the wisdom of such a move. His comptroller's mind reasoned: how would Supranational show the payment on its books? Even more to the point, he didn't have that much money to spare. And besides, what would happen when he wanted Avril again? He knew, already, that he would.

The telephone rang, filling the small sitting-room with sound. Avril answered it, spoke briefly, then announced, 'It's for you.'

'For *me*?'

As he took the receiver, the voice boomed, 'Hi there, Roscoe!'

Heyward asked sharply, 'Where are you, George?'

'Washington. What's the difference? Got some real good

276

news about SuNatCo. Quarterly earnings statement. You'll read about it in tomorrow's papers.'

'You called me here to tell me that?'

'Interrupted you, did I?'

'No.'

Big George chuckled. 'Just a friendly phone call, fella. Checking that all arrangements were okay.'

If he wanted to protest, Heyward realized, this was the moment. But protest what? The generous availability of Avril? Or his own acute embarrassment?

The booming telephone voice cut through his dilemma. 'That Q-Investments credit okayed yet?'

'Not quite.'

'Taking your time, aren't you?'

'Not really. There are formalities.'

'Let's move 'em, or I'll have to give some other bank that business, and maybe shift some of Supranational's over, too.'

The threat was clear. It did not surprise Heyward because pressures and concessions were a normal part of banking.

'I'll do my best, George.'

A grunt. 'Avril still there?'

'Yes.'

'Lemme talk to her.'

Heyward passed the phone to Avril. She listened briefly, said, 'Yes, I will,' smiled, and hung up.

She went into the bedroom where he heard a suitcase snap open and a moment later she emerged with a large manila envelope. 'Georgie said I was to give you this.'

It was the same kind of envelope, and with similar seals, as the one which had contained the Q-Investments share certificates.

'Georgie told me to say it's a reminder of our good time in Nassau.'

More share certificates? He doubted it. He considered refusing to accept, but curiosity was strong.

Avril said, 'You're not to open it here. Wait till you're away.'

He seized the opportunity and checked his watch. 'I shall have to go anyway, my dear.'

'Me, too. I'm flying back to New York tonight.'

They said goodbye in the suite. There could have been an awkwardness at parting. Because of Avril's practised *savoir-faire* there wasn't.

She draped her arms around him and they held each other closely while she whispered, 'You're a sugarplum, Rossie. We'll see each other soon.'

Notwithstanding what he had learned, or his present tiredness, his passion for her hadn't changed. And whatever the cost of 'my time', he thought, one thing was sure: Avril delivered value in return.

Roscoe Heyward took a taxi from the hotel to First Mercantile American Headquarters Tower. In the main floor foyer of the bank building he left word that in fifteen minutes he would require a car and driver to take him home. Then he took a lift to the thirty-sixth floor and walked through silent corridors, past deserted desks, to his office suite.

At his desk he opened the sealed envelope which Avril had given him. In a second package inside, interleaved with tissue, were a dozen enlarged photographs.

That second night in the Bahamas, when the girls and men had bathed naked in Big George's pool, the photographer had remained discreetly invisible. Perhaps he employed a telephoto lens, possibly was screened from view by shrubbery in the lush garden. He had certainly used a fast film because there had been no betraying flash. It scarcely mattered. He – or she – had been there just the same.

The photos showed Krista, Rhetta, Moonbeam, Avril, and Harold Austin undressing and unclothed. Roscoe Heyward appeared with the naked girls around him, his face a study in fascination. There was a view of Heyward unfastening Avril's dress and bra; another of her kissing him, his fingers curled around her breasts. Whether by accident or design, only the back of Vice-President Stonebridge could be seen.

Technically and artistically the quality of all photographs was high and obviously the photographer had been no amateur. But then, Heyward thought, G. G. Quartermain was accustomed to paying for the best.

Notably, in none of the photographs did Big George appear.

The photos appalled Heyward by their existence. And why had they been sent? Were they some kind of threat? Or a heavy-handed joke? Where were the negatives and other copies? He was beginning to realize that Quartermain was a complex, capricious, perhaps even dangerous, man.

On the other hand, despite the shock, Heyward found himself fascinated. As he studied the photographs, unconsciously he moistened his lips with his tongue. His first impulse had been to destroy them. Now he couldn't do it.

He was startled to find he had been at his desk for nearly half an hour.

Obviously he couldn't take the photos home. What then? Carefully repacking them, he locked the envelope in a desk drawer where he kept several personal, private files.

Out of habit, he checked another drawer where Mrs Callaghan was apt to leave current papers when she cleared his desk at night. On top of the pile inside were those concerning the additional Q-Investments loan. He reasoned: why delay? Why vacillate? Was there really any need to consult Patterton a second time? The loan was sound, as were G. G. Quartermain and Supranational. Removing the papers, Heyward scribbled an *approved* and added his initials.

A few minutes later he came down to the foyer. His driver was waiting, the limousine outside.

fourteen

Only rarely, nowadays, did Nolan Wainwright have occasion to visit the city morgue. The last time, he recalled, was three years before when he identified the body of a bank guard killed in a robbery shoot-out. When Wainwright was a police detective, visiting morgues and viewing the victims of violent crime was a necessary and frequent part of his job. But even then he had never grown used to it. A morgue, any morgue, with its aura of death and charnel house smell, depressed him and sometimes turned his stomach. It did now.

The sergeant of city detectives, who had met him by arrangement, walked stolidly beside Wainwright down a gloomy passageway, their footsteps echoing sharply off the ancient, cracked tile floor. The morgue attendant preceding them, who looked as if he would soon be a customer here himself, was wearing rubber-soled shoes and shambled ahead silently.

The detective, whose name was Timberwell, was young, overweight, had unkempt hair and needed a shave. Many things had changed, Nolan Wainwright ruminated, in the twelve years since he had been a city police lieutenant.

Timberwell said, 'If the dead guy *is* your man, when was the last time you saw him?'

'Seven weeks ago. Beginning of March.'

'Where?'

'A little bar across town. The Easy Over.'

'I know the place. Did you hear from him after that?'

'No.'

'Any idea where he lived?'

Wainwright shook his head. 'He didn't want me to know. So I played it his way.'

Nolan Wainwright hadn't been sure of the man's name either. He had been given one, but almost certainly it was false. As a matter of fairness he hadn't tried to discover the real one. All he knew was that 'Vic' was an ex-con who needed money and was prepared to be an undercover informer.

Last October, on Wainwright's urging, Alex Vandervoort had authorized him to employ an informer to seek out the source of counterfeit Keycharge bank credit cards, then appearing in disquieting numbers. Wainwright put out feelers, using contacts in the inner city, and later, through more intermediaries, a meeting between himself and Vic had been arranged and a deal agreed on. That was in December. The security chief remembered it well because Miles Eastin's trial had taken place the same week.

There were two other encounters between Vic and Wainwright in the months which followed, each in a different out-of-the-way bar, and on all three occasions Wainwright had handed over money, gambling on receiving value for it later. Their communications scheme was one-sided. Vic could telephone him, setting up a meeting at a place of Vic's choosing, though Wainwright had no means of contact in return. But he saw the reasoning behind the arrangement and accepted it;

Wainwright hadn't liked Vic, but then had not expected to. The ex-con was shifty, evasive, with the perpetually drippy nose and other outward signs of a narcotics user. He exhibited contempt for everything, including Wainwright; his lip was permanently curled. But at their third meeting, in March, it seemed as if he might have stumbled on a lead.

He reported a rumour: a big supply of bogus twenty-dollar bills of high quality was ready to be spread out through distributors and passers. According to still more scuttlebutt, somewhere back in the shadows – behind the distributors – was a high-powered, competent organization into other lines of action, including credit cards. This last information was vague, and Wainwright suspected Vic might have made it up to please him. On the other hand he might not.

More specifically, Vic claimed he had been promised a small piece of the action with the counterfeit money. He figured that if he got it and became trusted, he could work his way deeper into the organization. One or two details which, in Wainwright's opinion, Vic would not have had the knowledge or wit to invent, convinced the bank security chief that the main thrust of the information was authentic. The proposed plan also made sense.

Wainwright had always assumed that whoever was producing the fraudulent Keycharge bank cards was likely to be involved with other forms of counterfeiting. He had told Alex Vandervoort so last October. One thing he knew for certain: it would be highly dangerous to try to penetrate the organization and an informer – if discovered – was dead. He had felt obliged to warn Vic of this and was rewarded for his trouble by a sneer.

After that meeting, Wainwright had not heard from Vic again.

Yesterday a small news item in the *Times-Register*, about a body found floating in the river, caught his attention.

'I should warn you,' Detective Sergeant Timberwell said, 'that what's left of this guy isn't pretty. The medics figure he was in the water for a week. Also, there's a lot of traffic on that river and it looks as if some boat propeller cut him up.'

Still trailing the elderly attendant, they entered a brightly lit long, low-ceilinged room. The air was chill. It smelled of disinfectant. Occupying one wall, facing them, was what looked like a giant filing cabinet with stainless steel drawers, each identified by a number. A hum of refrigeration equipment came from behind the cabinet.

The attendant peered shortsightedly at a clipboard he was carrying, then went to a drawer mid-way down the room. He pulled and the drawer slid out silently on nylon bearings. Inside was the lumpy shape of a body, covered by a paper sheet.

'These are the remains you wanted, officers,' the old man said. As casually as if uncovering cucumbers, he folded back the sheet.

Wainwright wished he hadn't come. He felt sick.

Once, the body they were looking at had had a face. It didn't have any more. Immersion, putrefaction and something else – probably a boat propeller, as Timberwell said – had left flesh layers exposed and lacerated. From the mess, white bones protruded.

They studied the corpse in silence, then the detective asked, 'You see anything you can identify?'

'Yes,' Wainwright said. He had been peering at the side of the face where what remained of the hairline met the neck. The apple-shaped red scar – undoubtedly a birthmark – was still clearly visible. Wainwright's trained eye had observed it on each of the three occasions that he and Vic had met. Though the lips that had sneered so frequently were gone, without doubt the body was that of his undercover agent. He told Timberwell, who nodded.

'We identified him ourselves from fingerprints. They weren't the clearest, but good enough.' The detective took out a notebook and opened it. 'His real name, if you'll believe it, was

Clarence Hugo Levinson. He had several other names he used, and a long record, mostly petty stuff.'

'The news report said he died of stab wounds, not drowning.'

'It's what the autopsy showed. Before that he was tortured.'

'How do you know?'

'His balls were crushed. The pathologist's report said they must have been put in some kind of vice which was tightened until they burst. You want to see?'

Without waiting to be told, the attendant pulled back the remainder of the paper sheet.

Despite shrinkage of the genitals during immersion, autopsy had exposed enough to show the truth of Timberwell's statement. Wainwright gulped. 'Oh, Christ!' He motioned to the old man. 'Cover him up.'

Then he urged Timberwell, 'Let's get out of here.'

Over strong black coffee in a tiny restaurant a half block from the morgue, Detective Sergeant Timberwell soliloquized, 'Poor bastard! Whatever he'd done, no one deserves that.' He produced a cigarette, lit it, and offered the pack. Wainwright shook his head.

'I guess I know how you're feeling.' Timberwell said. 'You get hardened to some things. But there sure are others that make you think.'

'Yes.' Wainwright was remembering his own responsibility for what happened to Clarence Hugo Levinson, alias Vic.

'I'll need a statement from you, Mr Wainwright. Summarizing those things you told me about your arrangement with the deceased. If it's all the same to you, I'd like to go to the precinct house and take it after we're finished here.'

'All right.'

The policeman blew a smoke ring and sipped his coffee. 'What's the score about counterfeit credit cards – right now?'

'More and more are being used. Some days it's like an epidemic. It's costing banks like ours a lot of money.'

Timberwell said sceptically, 'You mean it's costing the public money. Banks like yours pass those losses on. It's why your top management people don't care as much as they should.'

'I can't argue with you there.' Wainwright remembered his own lost arguments about bigger budgets to fight bank-related crime.

'Is the quality of the cards good?'

'Excellent.'

The detective ruminated. 'That's exactly what the Secret Service tell us about the phoney money that's circulating in the city. There's a lot of it. I guess you know.'

'Yes, I do.'

'So maybe that dead guy was right in figuring both things came from the same source.'

Neither man spoke, then the detective said abruptly. 'There's something I should warn you about. Maybe you've thought of it already.'

Wainwright waited.

'When he was tortured, whoever did it made him talk. You saw him. There's no way he wouldn't have. So you can figure he sang about everything, including the deal he had with you.'

'Yes, I'd thought of it.'

Timberwell nodded. 'I don't think you're in any danger yourself, but as far as the people who killed Levinson are concerned, you're poison. If anyone *they* deal with as much as breathes the same air as you, and they find out, he's dead – nastily.'

Wainwright was about to speak when the other silenced him.

'Listen, I'm not saying you shouldn't send some other guy underground. That's your business and I don't want to know about it – at least, not now. But I'll say this: if you do, be super-careful and stay away from him yourself. You owe him that much.'

'Thanks for the warning,' Wainwright said. He was still thinking about the body of Vic as he had seen it with the covering removed. 'I doubt very much if there'll be anyone else.'

part three

one

Though it continued to be difficult on her $98 weekly bank tel-
ler's wage ($83 take-home after deductions), somehow Juanita
managed, week by week, to support herself and Estela and to
pay the fees for Estela's nursery school. Juanita had even – by
August – slightly reduced the debt to the finance company
which her husband, Carlos, had burdened her with before abandoning her. The finance firm had obligingly rewritten the contract, making the monthly instalments smaller, though they now
stretched on – with heavier interest payments – three years into
the future.

At the bank, while Juanita had been treated considerately
after the false accusations against her last October, and staff
members had gone out of their way to be cordial, she had established no close friendships. Intimacy did not come easily to her.
She had a natural wariness of people, partly inbred, partly conditioned by experience. The centre of her life, the apogee to
which each working day progressed, were the evening hours
which she and Estela spent together.

They were together now.

In the kitchen of their tiny but comfortable Forum East apartment, Juanita was preparing dinner, assisted – and at times hin-
dered – by the three-year-old. They had both been rolling and
shaping Bisquick baking mix, Juanita to provide a top for the
meat pie, Estela manipulating a purloined piece of the dough
with her tiny fingers as imagination prompted.

'Mommy! Look, I made a magic castle!'

They laughed together. '¡ Qué lindo, mi cielo !' Juanita said
affectionately. 'We will put the castle in the oven with the pie.
Then both will become magic.'

For the pie Juanita had used stewing beef, mixing in onions,
a potato, fresh carrots, and a tin of peas. The vegetables made
up in volume for the small quantity of meat, which was all
Juanita could afford. But she was an instinctively inventive cook
and the pie would be tasty and nutritious.

287

It had been in the oven for twenty minutes, with another ten to go, and Juanita was reading to Estela from a Spanish translation of Hans Andersen, when a knock sounded on the apartment door. Juanita stopped reading, listening uncertainly. Visitors at any time were rare; it was especially unusual for anyone to call this late. After a few moments the knock was repeated. With some nervousness, motioning Estela to remain where she was, Juanita got up and went slowly to the door.

Her apartment was on a floor by itself at the top of what had once been a single dwelling, but which long ago was divided into separately rented living quarters. The Forum East developers retained the divisions in the building, while modernizing and repairing. But redevelopment alone did not amend the fact that Forum East generally was in an area notorious for a high crime rate, especially muggings and break-ins. Thus, although the apartment complexes were fully populated, at night most occupants locked and bolted themselves in. There was a stout outer door, useful for protection, on the main floor of Juanita's building, except that other tenants often left it open.

Immediately outside Juanita's apartment was a narrow landing at the head of a flight of stairs. With her ear pressed against the door, she called out, 'Who is there?' There was no answer, but once more the knock – soft but insistent – was repeated.

She made certain that the inside protective chain was in place, then unlocked the door and opened it a few inches – all the chain allowed.

At first, because of dim lighting, she could see nothing, then a face came into view and a voice asked, 'Juanita, may I talk to you? I have to – please! Will you let me come in?'

She was startled. Miles Eastin. But neither the voice nor the face were those of the Eastin she had known. Instead, the figure which she could see better now was pale and emaciated, his speech unsure and pleading.

She stalled for time to think. 'I thought you were in prison.'

'I got out. Today.' He corrected himself. 'I was released on parole.'

'Why have you come here?'

'I remembered where you lived.'

288

She shook her head, keeping the door chain fastened. 'It was not what I asked. Why come to *me* ?'

'Because all I've thought about for months, all through that time inside, was seeing you, talking to you, explaining . . .'

'There is nothing to explain.'

'But there *is*! Juanita, I'm begging you. Don't turn me away! Please!'

From behind her, Estela's bright voice asked, 'Mommy, who is it ?'

'Juanita,' Miles Eastin said, 'there's nothing to be frightened about – for you or your little girl. I've nothing with me except this.' He held up a small battered suitcase. 'It's just the things they gave me back when I came out.'

'Well . . .' Juanita wavered. Despite her misgivings, her curiosity was strong. Why *did* Miles want to see her ? Wondering if she would regret it, she closed the door slightly and released the chain.

'Thank you.' He came in tentatively, as if even now he feared Juanita might change her mind.

'Hullo,' Estela said, 'are you my mommy's friend ?'

For a moment Eastin seemed disconcerted, then he answered, 'I wasn't always. I wish I had been.'

The small, dark-haired child regarded him. 'What's your name ?'

'Miles.'

Estela giggled. 'You're a thin man.'

'Yes, I know.'

Now that he was fully in view, Juanita was even more startled by the change in Miles. In the eight months since she had seen him, he had lost so much weight that his cheeks were sunken, his neck and body scrawny. His crumpled suit hung loosely, as if tailored for someone twice his size. He looked tired and weak. 'May I sit down ?'

'Yes.' Juanita motioned to a wicker chair, though she continued to stand, facing him. She said, illogically accusing. 'You did not eat well in prison.'

He shook his head, for the first time smiling slightly. 'It isn't exactly gourmet living. I suppose it shows.'

'*Sí, me di cuenta*. It shows.'

Estela asked, 'Have you come for dinner ? It's a pie Mommy made.'

He hesitated. 'No.'

Juanita said sharply, 'Did you eat today ?'

'This morning. I had something at the bus station.' The aroma of the almost-cooked pie was wafting from the kitchen. Instinctively Miles turned his head.

'Then you will join us.' She began setting another place at the small table where she and Estela took their meals. The action came naturally. In any Puerto Rican home – even the poorest – tradition demanded that whatever food was available be shared.

As they ate, Estela chattered, and Miles responded to her questions ; some of the earlier tension began visibly to leave him. Several times he looked around at the simply furnished but pleasant apartment. Juanita had a flair for homemaking. She loved to sew and decorate. In the modest living-room was an old, used sofa bed she had slip-covered with a cotton material, brightly patterned in white, red, and yellow. The wicker chair which Miles had sat in earlier was one of two she had bought cheaply and repainted in Chinese red. For the windows she had created simple, inexpensive curtains of bright yellow bark cloth. A primitive painting and some travel posters adorned the walls.

Juanita listened to the other two but said little, within herself still doubtful and suspicious. Why had Miles really come ? Would he cause her as much trouble as he had before ? Experience warned her that he might. Yet at the moment he seemed harmless – certainly weak physically, a little frightened, possibly defeated. Juanita had the practical wisdom to recognize those symptoms.

What she did *not* feel was antagonism. Though Miles had tried to have her blamed for the theft of money he himself had stolen, time had made his treachery remote. Even originally, when he was exposed, her principal feeling had been relief, not hate. Now, all Juanita wanted for herself and Estela was to be left alone.

Miles Eastin sighed as he pushed away his plate. He had left nothing on it. 'Thank you. That was the best meal in quite some time.'

Juanita asked, 'What are you going to do ?'

'I don't know. Tomorrow I'll start looking for a job.' He took a deep breath and seemed about to say something else, but she motioned him to wait.

'*Estelita, vamos, amorcito.* Bedtime!'

Soon after, washed, her hair brushed, and wearing tiny pink pyjamas, Estela came to say good night. Large liquid eyes regarded Miles gravely. 'My daddy went away. Are you going away ?'

'Yes, very soon.'

'That's what I thought.' She put up her face to be kissed.

When she had tucked in Estela, Juanita came out of the apartment's single bedroom, closing the door behind her. She sat down facing Miles, hands folded in her lap. 'So. You may talk.'

He hesitated, moistening his lips. Now that the moment had arrived he seemed irresolute, bereft of words. Then he said, 'All this time since I was ... put away ... I've been wanting to say I'm sorry. Sorry for everything I did, but mostly for what I did to you. I'm ashamed. In one way I don't know how it happened. In another I think I do.'

Juanita shrugged. 'What happened is gone. Does it matter now ?'

'It matters to me. Please, Juanita – let me tell you the rest, the way it was.'

Then, like a gusher uncapped, words flooded out. He spoke of his awakened conscience, and remorse, of last year's insanity of gambling and debts, and how they had possessed him like a fever which distorted moral values and perception. Looking back, he told Juanita, it seemed as if someone else had inhabited his mind and body. He proclaimed his guilt at stealing from the bank. But worst of all, he avowed, was what he had done to her, or tried to. His shame about that, he declared emotionally, had haunted him through every day in prison and would never leave him.

When Miles began speaking, Juanita's strongest instinct was suspicion. As he continued, not all of it left her; life had fooled and short-changed her too often to permit total belief in anything. Yet her judgement inclined her to accept what Miles had said as genuine, and a sense of pity overwhelmed her.

She found herself comparing Miles with Carlos, her absentee husband. Carlos had been weak; so had Miles. Yet, in a way, Miles's willingness to return and face her penitently argued a strength and manhood which Carlos never had.

Suddenly she saw the humour in it all: the men in her life – for one reason or another – were flawed and unimpressive. They were also losers, like herself. She almost laughed, then decided not to because Miles would never understand.

He said earnestly, 'Juanita, I want to ask you something. Will you forgive me?'

She looked at him.

'And if you do, will you say it to me?'

The silent laughter died; tears filled her eyes. That she could understand. She had been born a Catholic, and though nowadays she rarely bothered with church, she knew the solace of confession and absolution. She rose to her feet.

'Miles,' Juanita said. 'Stand up. Look at me.'

He obeyed her, and she said gently, '*Has sufrido bastante.* Yes, I forgive you.'

The muscles of his face twisted and worked. Then she held him as he wept.

When Miles had composed himself, and they were seated again, Juanita spoke practically. 'Where will you spend the night?'

'I'm not sure. I'll find somewhere.'

She considered, then told him, 'You may stay here if you wish.' As she saw his surprise, she added quickly, 'You can sleep in this room for tonight only. I will be in the bedroom with Estela. Our door will be locked.' She wanted no misunderstandings.

'If you really don't mind,' he said, 'I'd like to do that. And you'll have nothing to worry about.'

He did not tell her the real reason she had no cause to worry: that there were other problems within himself – psychological and sexual – which he had not yet faced. All that Miles knew, so

292

far, was that because of repeated homosexual acts between himself and Karl, his protector in prison, his desire for women had evaporated. He wondered if he would be a man – in any sexual way – again.

Shortly after, as tiredness overcame them both, Juanita went to join Estela.

In the morning, through the closed bedroom door, she heard Miles stirring early. A half hour later, when she emerged from the bedroom, he had left.

A note was propped up on the living-room table.

Juanita—
With all my heart, thank you!
Miles

While she prepared breakfast for herself and Estela, she was surprised to find herself regretting he had gone.

two

In the four and a half months since approval of his savings and branch bank expansion plan by FMA's board of directors, Alex Vandervoort had moved swiftly. Planning and progress sessions between the bank's own staff and outside consultants and contractors had been held almost daily. Work continued during week-ends, and holidays, spurred on by Alex's insistence that the programme be operating before the end of summer and in high gear by mid-autumn.

The savings reorganization was easiest to accomplish in the time. Most of what Alex wanted done – including launching four new types of savings accounts, with increased interest rates and geared to varying needs – had been the subject of earlier studies at his behest. It was merely necessary to translate these into reality. Some fresh ground to be covered involved a strong programme of advertising to attract new depositors and this – conflict of interest or not – the Austin Agency produced with speed and competence. The theme of the savings campaign was:

WE'LL PAY YOU TO BE THRIFTY
AT FIRST MERCANTILE AMERICAN

Now, in early August, double-page spreads in newspapers proclaimed the virtues of savings à la FMA. They also showed locations of eighty bank branches in the state where gifts, coffee, and 'friendly financial counselling' were available to anyone opening a new account. The value of a gift depended on the size of an initial deposit, along with agreement not to disturb it for a stated time. Spot announcements on TV and radio hammered home a parallel campaign.

As to the nine new branches – 'our money shops', as Alex called them – two were opened in the last week of July, three more in the first few days of August, and the remaining four would be in business before September. Since all were in rented premises, which involved conversion rather than construction, speed had been possible here, too.

It was the money shops – a name that caught on quickly – which attracted most attention to begin with. They also produced far greater publicity than either Alex Vandervoort, the bank's PR department, or the Austin Advertising Agency had foreseen. And the spokesman for it all – soaring to prominence like an ascending comet – was Alex.

He had not intended it to be that way. It simply happened.

A reporter from the morning *Times-Register*, assigned to cover the new branch openings, dipped into that newspaper's morgue in search of background and discovered Alex's tenuous connection with the previous February's pro-Forum East 'bank-in'. Discussion with the features editor hatched the notion that Alex would make good copy for an expanded story. This proved true.

When you think of modern bankers [the reporter later wrote] don't think of solemn, cautious functionaries in traditional double-breasted, dark blue suits, pursing their lips and saying 'no'. Think, instead, of Alexander Vandervoort.

Mr Vandervoort, who's an executive veep at our own First Mercantile American Bank, to begin with doesn't look like a banker. His suits are from the fashion section of *Esquire*, his mannerisms *à la* Johnny Carson, and when it comes to loans, especially small loans, he's conditioned – with rare exceptions – to pronouncing 'yes'. But he also believes in thrift and says most of us aren't being as wise about money as our parents and grand-parents.

Another thing about Alexander Vandervoort is that he's a leader in modern bank technology, some of which arrived in our city's suburbs just this week.

The new look in banking is embodied in branch banks not having the appearance of banks at all – which seems appropriate because Mr Vandervoort (who doesn't look like a banker, as we said) is the local driving force behind them.

This reporter went along with Alexander Vandervoort this week for a glimpse of what he calls 'consumer banking of the future that's here right now'.

The bank's public relations chief, Dick French, had set up the arrangements. The reporter was a middle-aged, floppy blonde called Jill Peacock, no Pulitzer journalist, but the story interested her and she was friendly.

Alex and Ms Peacock stood together in one of the new branch banks, located in a suburban shopping precinct. It was about equal in size to a family drugstore, brightly lighted, and pleas-antly designed. The principal furnishings were two stainless-steel Docutel automatic tellers, which customers operated them-selves, and a closed-circuit television console in a booth. The auto-tellers, Alex explained, were linked directly to computers at FMA Headquarters.

'Nowadays,' he went on, 'the public is conditioned to expect service, which is why there's a demand for banks to stay open longer, and at more convenient hours. Money shops like this one will be open twenty-four hours a day, seven days a week.'

'With staff here all that time?' Ms Peacock asked.

'No. In daytime we'll have a clerk on hand to handle queries. The rest of the time there'll be no one except customers.'

'Aren't you afraid of robberies ?'

Alex smiled. 'The auto-teller machines are built like fortresses, with every alarm system known to man. And TV scanners – one in each money shop – are monitored at a control centre downtown. Our immediate problem isn't security – it's getting our customers to adapt to new ideas.'

'It looks,' Ms Peacock said, 'as if some have adapted already.'

Though it was early – 9.30am – the small bank already had a dozen people in it and others were arriving. Most were women.

'Studies we've made,' Alex volunteered, 'show that women accept merchandising changes faster, which is probably why department stores have always been so innovative. Men are slower, but eventually women persuade them.'

Short lines had formed in front of the automatic tellers, but there was virtually no delay. Transactions were completed quickly after each customer had inserted a plastic identifying card and pressed a simple selection of buttons. Some were depositing cash or cheques, others withdrawing money. One or two had come to pay bills – either for their bank card account or electricity and other public services. Whatever the purpose, the machine swallowed paper and cash or spat them out at lightning speed.

Ms Peacock pointed to the auto-tellers. 'Have people learned to use these faster or slower than you expected ?'

'Much, much faster. It's an effort to persuade people to try the machines the first time. But once they have, they become fascinated, and love them.'

'You always hear that humans prefer dealing with other humans, rather than machines. Why should banking be different ?'

'Those studies I mentioned tell us it's because of privacy.'

There really *is* privacy [Jill Peacock acknowledged in her bylined, Sunday edition feature story], and not just with those Frankenstein-monster tellers.

Sitting alone in a booth in the same money shop, facing a combination TV camera and screen, I opened an account and then negotiated a loan.

Other times I've borrowed money from a bank I felt embarrassed. This time I didn't because the face in front of me on the screen was impersonal. The owner of it – a disembodied male whose name I didn't know – was miles away.

'Seventeen miles, to be exact,' Alex had said. 'The bank officer you were talking with is in a control room of our downtown Headquarters Tower. From there he, and others, can contact any branch bank equipped with closed-circuit TV.'

Ms Peacock considered. 'How fast, really, is banking changing?'

'Technologically, we're developing more swiftly than aerospace. What you're seeing here is the most important development since introduction of the checking account and, within ten years or less, most banking will be done this way.'

'Will there still be *some* human tellers?'

'For a while, but the breed will disappear quickly. Quite soon, the notion of having an individual count out cash by hand, then pass it over a counter will be antediluvian – as outmoded as the old-fashioned grocer who used to weigh out sugar, peas and butter, then put them into paper bags himself.'

'It's all rather sad,' Ms Peacock said.

'Progress often is.'

Afterwards I asked a dozen people at random how they liked the new money shops. Without exception they were enthusiastic.

Judging by the large numbers using them, the view is widespread and their popularity, Mr Vandervoort told me, is helping a current savings drive . . .

Whether the money shops were helping the savings drive, or vice versa, was never entirely clear. What did become clear was that FMA's most optimistic savings targets were being reached and exceeded with phenomenal speed. It seemed – as Alex expressed it to Margot Bracken – as if the public mood and First Mercantile American's timing had uncannily coincided.

'Stop preening yourself and drink your orange juice,' Margot told him. Sunday morning in Margot's apartment was a pleasure. Still in pyjamas and a robe, he had been reading, for the first time, Jill Peacock's feature story in the *Sunday Times-Register* while Margot prepared a breakfast of Eggs Benedict.

Alex was still glowing while they ate. Margot read the *Times-Register* story herself and conceded, 'It's not a bad piece.' She leaned over and kissed him. 'I'm glad for you.'

'It's better publicity than the last you got me, Bracken.'

She said cheerfully, 'Can never tell how it'll go. The press giveth and the press taketh away. Tomorrow you and your bank may be attacked.'

He sighed. 'You're so often right.'

But this time she was wrong.

A condensed version of the original news feature was syndicated and used by papers in forty other cities. AP, observing the wide, general interest, did its own report for the national wire; so did UPI. *The Wall Street Journal* dispatched a staff reporter and several days later featured First Mercantile American Bank and Alex Vandervoort in a front-page review of automated banking. An NBC affiliate sent a TV crew to interview Alex at a money shop and the videotaped result was aired on the network's NBC Nightly News.

With each burst of publicity the savings campaign gained fresh momentum and money shop business boomed.

Unhurriedly, from its lofty eminence, *The New York Times* brooded and took note. Then, in mid-August, its Sunday Business and Finance section proclaimed: *A Banking Radical We May Hear More About.*

The New York Times interview with Alex consisted of questions and answers. It began with automation, then moved to broader terrain.

Question What's mostly wrong with banking nowadays?

Vandervoort We bankers have had things our own way too long. We're so preoccupied with our own welfare, we give too little thought to the interests of our customers.

Question Can you quote an example?

Vandervoort Yes. Customers of banks – particularly individuals – ought to receive much more money in interest than they do.

Question In what way?

Vandervoort In several ways – in their savings accounts; also

298

with certificates of deposit; and we should be paying interest on demand deposits – that is, checking accounts.

Question Let's take savings first. Surely there's a federal law that places a ceiling on savings interest rates at commercial banks.

Vandervoort Yes, and the purpose of it is to protect savings and loan banks. Incidentally, there's another law which prevents savings and loan banks from letting their customers use cheques. That's to protect commercial banks. What ought to happen is that laws should stop protecting banks and protect people instead.

Question By 'protecting people' you mean letting those with savings enjoy the maximum interest rate and other services which any bank will give?

Vandervoort Yes, I do.

Question You mentioned certificates of deposit.

Vandervoort The US Federal Reserve has prohibited large banks, like the one I work for, advertising long-term certificates of deposit at high interest rates. These kinds of CDs are especially good for anyone looking ahead to retirement and wanting to defer income tax until later, low income, years. The Fed hands out phoney excuses for this ban. But the real reason is to protect small banks against big ones, the big banks being more efficient and able to give better deals. As usual, it's the public which is last to be considered and individuals who lose out.

Question Let's be clear about this. You're suggesting that our central bank – the Federal Reserve – cares more about small banks than the general populace?

Vandervoort Damn right.

Question Let's move on to demand deposits – checking accounts. Some bankers are on record as saying they would like to pay interest on checking accounts, but federal law prohibits it.

Vandervoort Next time a banker tells you that, ask him when our powerful banking lobby in Washington last did anything about getting the law changed. If there's ever been an effort in that direction, I've not heard of it.

Question You're suggesting, then, that most bankers really don't want that law changed?

Vandervoort I'm not suggesting it. I know it. The law preventing payment of interest on checking accounts is very convenient if you happened to own a bank. It was introduced in 1933, right after the Depression, with the object of strengthening banks because so many had failed in the previous few years.

Question And that was more than forty years ago.

Vandervoort Exactly. The need for such a law has long passed. Let me tell you something. Right at this moment, if all the checking account balances in this country were added together, they'd total more than $200 billion. You can bet your life the banks are earning interest on this money, but the depositors – the bank's customers – aren't getting a cent.

Question Since you yourself are a banker, and your own bank profits from the law we are talking about, why do you advocate change?

Vandervoort For one thing, I believe in fairness. For another, banking doesn't need all those crutches in the way of protective laws. In my opinion we can do better – by that I mean render improved public service and be more profitable – without them.

Question Haven't there been recommendations in Washington about some of those changes you've spoken of?

Vandervoort Yes. The Hunt Commission report of 1971, and proposed legislation resulting from it, which would benefit consumers. But the whole deal is stalled in Congress, with special interests – including our own banking lobby – holding up progress.

Question Do you anticipate antagonism from other bankers because of your frankness here?

Vandervoort I really hadn't thought about it.

Question Apart from banking, do you have any overall view on the current economic scene?

Vandervoort Yes, but an overall view should not be limited to economics.

Question Please state your view – and don't limit it.

Vandervoort Our greatest problem, and our big shortcoming as a nation, is that almost everything nowadays is geared *against* the individual and in favour of the big institutions – big corporations, big business, big unions, big banking, big government. So not only does an individual have trouble getting ahead and staying there, he often has difficulty merely in surviving. And whenever bad things happen – inflation, devaluation, depression, shortages, higher taxes, even wars – it isn't the big institutions which get hurt, at least not much; it's the individual, all the time.

Question Do you see historical parallels to this?

Vandervoort I do indeed. It may seem strange to say this, but the closest one, I think, is France immediately before the Revolution. At that time, despite unrest and a bad economy, everyone assumed there'd be business as usual. Instead, the mob – composed of individuals who rebelled – overthrew the tyrants who oppressed them. I'm not suggesting our conditions now are precisely the same, but in many ways we're remarkably close to tyranny, once more, against the individual. And telling people who can't feed their families because of inflation that 'You never had it so good' is uncomfortably like 'Let them eat cake'. So I say, if we want to preserve our so-called way of life and individual freedom which we claim to value, we'd better start thinking and acting about the interests of individuals again.

Question And in your own case, you'd begin by making banks serve individuals more.

Vandervoort Yes.

'Darling, it's magnificent! I'm proud of you, and I love you more than ever,' Margot assured Alex when she read an advance copy a day before the interview was published. 'It's the most honest thing I've ever read. But other bankers will hate you. They'll want your balls for breakfast.'

'Some will,' Alex said. 'Others won't.'

But now that he had seen the questions and replies in print, and despite the wave of success on which he had been riding, he was slightly worried himself.

three

'What saved you from being crucified, Alex', Lewis D'Orsey declaimed, 'was that it happened to be *The New York Times*. If you'd said what you did for any other paper in the country, your bank's directors would have disowned you and cast you out like a pariah. But not with the *Times*. It clothed you in respectability, though never ask me why.'

'Lewis, dear,' Edwina D'Orsey said, 'could you interrupt your speech to pour more wine?'

'I'm not making a speech.' Her husband rose from the dinner table and reached for a second decanter of Clos de Vougeot '62. Tonight Lewis looked as puny and as underfed as ever. He continued, 'I'm talking calmly and lucidly about *The New York Times* which, in my opinion, is an effete pinko rag, its unwarranted prestige a monument to American imbecility.'

'It has a bigger circulation than your newsletter,' Margot Bracken said. 'Is that a reason you don't like it?'

She and Alex Vandervoort were guests of Lewis and Edwina in the D'Orseys' elegant Cayman Manor penthouse. At the table, in soft candlelight, linen, crystal, and polished silver gleamed. Along one side of the spacious dining-room a wide, deep window framed the shimmering lights of the city far below. Through the lights a sinuous blackness marked the river's course.

It was a week since the controversial interview with Alex had appeared in print.

Lewis picked at a *médaillon* of beef and answered Margot disdainfully. 'My twice-a-month newsletter represents high quality and superior intellect. Most daily newspapers, including the *Times*, are vulgar quantity.'

'Stop sparring, you two!' Edwina turned to Alex. 'At least a dozen people who came into the downtown branch this week told me they'd read what you said and admired your outspokenness. What was the reaction in the Tower?'

'Mixed.'

'I'll bet I know someone who didn't approve.'

'You're right.' Alex chuckled. 'Roscoe did not lead the cheering section.'

Heyward's attitude had recently become even icier than before. Alex suspected that Heyward was resentful, not only of the attention Alex was receiving, but also because of successes with the savings drive and money shops, both of which Roscoe Heyward had opposed.

Another downbeat prediction of Heyward and his supporters on the board had concerned the eighteen million dollars in deposits from savings and loan institutions. Though the S&L's managements had huffed and puffed, they had not withdrawn their deposits from First Mercantile American. Nor, it now seemed, did they intend to.

'Apart from Roscoe and any others,' Edwina said, 'I hear you've a big following these days among the staff.'

'Maybe I'm a swiftly passing fad. Like streaking.'

'Or an addiction,' Margot said. 'I've found you habit-forming.'

He smiled. It had been heartening over the past week to receive congratulations from people whom Alex respected, like Tom Straughan, Orville Young, Dick French, and Edwina, and from others, including junior executives he had not previously known by name. Several directors had telephoned with words of praise. 'You're doing the bank's image a power of good,' Leonard L. Kingswood had called to say. And Alex's progress through the FMA Tower had, at times, been near-triumphant, with clerks and secretaries greeting him and smiling warmly.

' 'Talking of your staff, Alex,' Lewis D'Orsey said, 'reminds me you've something missing over in that Headquarters Tower of yours – Edwina. It's time she moved higher. While she doesn't, you people are losing out.'

'Really, Lewis, how *could* you?' Even in the candlelight it could be seen that Edwina had flushed deep red. She protested, 'This is a social occasion. Even if it weren't, that kind of remark is quite improper. Alex, I apologize.'

Lewis, unperturbed, regarded his wife over his half-moon glasses. 'You may apologize, my dear. I won't. I'm aware of your ability and value; who's closer to it? Furthermore, it's my custom to draw attention to anything outstanding which I see.'

'Well, three cheers for you, Lewis!' Margot said. 'Alex, how about it? When does my esteemed cousin move over to the Tower?'

Edwina was becoming angry. 'Stop it, please! You're embarrassing me acutely.'

'No one need be embarrassed.' Alex sipped his wine appreciatively. 'Um! '62 was a fine year for Burgundy. Every bit as good as '61, don't you think?'

'Yes,' his host acknowledged. 'Fortunately I put down plenty of both.'

'We're all four of us friends,' Alex said, 'so we can speak frankly, knowing it's in confidence. I don't mind telling you I've already been thinking about a promotion for Edwina and I've a particular job in mind. How soon I can swing that, and some other changes, depends on what happens in the next few months, as Edwina is well aware.'

'Yes,' she said, 'I am.' Edwina knew, too, that her personal allegiance to Alex was well known within the bank. Since Ben Rosselli's death, and even before, she realized that Alex's promotion to the presidency would almost certainly advance her own career. But if Roscoe Heyward succeeded instead, it was unlikely she would go any higher at First Mercantile American.

'Something else I'd like to see,' Alex said, 'is Edwina on the board of directors.'

Margot brightened. 'Now you're talking! That would be an onward-up for women's lib.'

'No!' Edwina reacted sharply. 'Don't equate me with women's lib – ever! Anything I've achieved has been on my own, competing honestly with men. Women's lib – its catchwords, asking for favouritism and preference *because* you're a woman – has set sex equality back, not forward.'

'That's nonsense!' Margot seemed shocked. 'You can say that now because you've been unusual and lucky.'

'There was no luck,' Edwina said. 'I've worked.'

'*No* luck?'

'Well, not much.'

Margot argued. 'There has to have been luck involved because

304

you're a woman. For as long as anybody can remember, banking's been an exclusive men's club – yet without the slightest reason.'

'Hasn't experience been a reason ?' Alex asked.

'No. Experience is a smokescreen, blown up by men, to keep women out. There's nothing masculine about banking. All it requires is brains – which women have, sometimes more abundantly than men. And everything else is either on paper, in the head, or in talk, so the only physical labour is hoisting money in and out of armoured cars, which women guards could undoubtedly do, too.'

'I won't dispute any of that,' Edwina said. 'Except you're out of date. The male exclusivity has already been broken – by people like me – and is being penetrated more and more. Who needs women's libbers ? I don't.'

'You haven't penetrated all that far,' Margot shot back. 'Otherwise you'd be in the Headquarters Tower already, and not just talking about it, as we are tonight.'

Lewis D'Orsey chortled. '*Touché*, my dear.'

'Others in banking need women's lib,' Margot concluded, 'and will for a long time.'

Alex leaned back – as always, enjoying an argument when Margot was involved. 'Whatever else might be said about our dinners together,' he observed, 'they're never dull.'

Lewis nodded agreement. 'Let me say – as the one who started all this – I'm glad about your intentions for Edwina.'

'All right,' his wife said firmly, 'and I thank you too, Alex. But that's enough. Let's leave it there.'

They did.

Margot told them about a legal class action she had brought against a department store which had been systematically cheating charge-account customers. The printed totals on monthly bills, Margot explained, were always a few dollars larger than they should have been. If anyone complained, the difference was explained away as an error, but hardly anyone did. 'When people see a machine printed total they assume it has to be right. What they forget, or don't know, is that machines can be programmed to *include* an error. In this case, one was.' Margot added that the store had profited by tens of thousands of dollars, as she intended to prove in court.

'We don't programme errors at the bank,' Edwina said, 'but they happen, machines or not. It's why I urge people to check their statements.'

In her department store investigation, Margot told the others, she had been helped by a private detective named Vernon Jax. He had been diligent and resourceful. She was strong in her praise of him.

'I know of him,' Lewis D'Orsey said. 'He's done investigative work for the SEC* – something I put them on to once. A good man.'

As they left the dining-room, Lewis said to Alex, 'Let's get liberated. How about joining me for a cigar and cognac? We'll go to my study. Edwina doesn't like cigar smoke.'

Excusing themselves, the men went one floor down – the D'Orseys' penthouse occupied two levels – to Lewis's sanctum sanctorum. Inside, Alex looked around curiously.

The room was spacious, with bookcases on two sides and, on another, racks for magazines and newspapers. The shelves and racks were overflowing. There were three desks, one with an electric typewriter, and all with papers, books, and files piled high. 'When one desk becomes impossible to work at,' Lewis explained, 'I simply move to the next.'

An open door revealed what, in daytime, was a secretary's office and file room. Stepping inside, Lewis returned with two brandy goblets and a bottle of Courvoisier from which he poured.

'I've often wondered,' Alex mused, 'about the background of a successful financial newsletter.'

'I can only speak personally for mine, which is regarded by competent judges as the best there is.' Lewis gave Alex a cognac, then motioned to an open box of cigars. 'Help yourself – they're Macanudos, none better. Also tax deductible.'

'How do you manage that?'

Lewis chuckled. 'Take a look at the band around each cigar. At trifling cost I have the original band removed and a special

*Securities and Exchange Commission.

one put on which reads *The D'Orsey Newsletter*. That's advertising – a business expense, so every time I smoke a cigar I've the satisfaction of knowing it's on Uncle Sam.'

Without comment, Alex took a cigar which he sniffed appreciatively. He had long since ceased to make moral judgements about tax loopholes. Congress made them the law of the land, and who could blame an individual for using them ?

'Answering your question,' Lewis said, 'I make no secret of the purpose of *The D'Orsey Newsletter*.' He lit Alex's cigar, then his own, and inhaled luxuriously. 'It's to help the élite get richer – or, at worst, keep what they have.'

'So I've noticed.'

Each newsletter, as Alex was aware, contained moneymaking advice – securities to buy or sell, currencies to switch into or out of, commodities to deal in, foreign stock markets to favour or avoid, tax loopholes for the wealthy and freewheeling, how to deal through Swiss accounts, political background likely to affect money, impending disasters which those with inside knowledge could turn to profit. The list was always long, the tone of the newsletter authoritative and absolute. There was seldom any hedging.

'Unfortunately,' Lewis added, 'there are lots of phonies and charlatans in the financial newsletter business, which do the serious, honest letters harm. Some so-called newsletters are skims of newspapers, and therefore valueless; others tout stocks and take payoffs from brokers and promoters, though in the end that kind of chicanery shows. There are maybe half a dozen worthwhile newsletters, with mine at the apex.'

In anyone else, Alex thought, the continual ego-thumping would be offensive. Somehow, with Lewis, it wasn't, perhaps because he had the track record to sustain it. And as to Lewis's extreme right-wing politics, Alex found he could screen them out, leaving a clear financial distillate – like tea passed through a strainer.

'I believe you're one of my subscribers,' Lewis said.

'Yes – through the bank.'

'Here's a copy of my new issue. Take it, even though you'll get yours in the mail on Monday.'

'Thank you.' Alex accepted the pale blue lithographed sheet – four quarto-size pages when folded, and unimpressive in appearance. The original had been closely typewritten, then photographed and reduced. But what the newsletter lacked in visual style, it made up in monetary value. It was Lewis's boast that those who followed his advice could increase whatever capital they had by a quarter to a half in any given year, and in some years double or triple it.

'What's your secret?' Alex said. 'How is it you're so often right?'

'I've a mind like a computer with thirty years of input.' Lewis puffed at his cigar, then tapped his forehead with a bony finger. 'Every morsel of financial knowledge that I've ever learned is stored in there. I also can relate one item to another, and the future to the past. In addition I've something a computer hasn't – instinctive genius.'

'Why bother with a newsletter then? Why not just make a fortune for yourself?'

'No satisfaction in it. No competition. Besides,' Lewis grinned, 'I'm not doing badly.'

'As I recall, your subscription rate . . .'

'Is three hundred dollars a year for the newsletter. Two thousand dollars an hour for personal consultations.'

'I've sometimes wondered how many subscribers you have.'

'So do others. It's a secret I guard carefully.'

'Sorry. I didn't mean to pry.'

'No reason not to. In your place, I'd be curious.'

Tonight, Alex thought, Lewis seemed more relaxed than at any time before.

'Maybe I'll share that secret with you,' Lewis said. 'Any man likes to boast a little. I've more than five thousand newsletter subscribers.'

Alex did mental arithmetic and whistled softly. It meant an annual income of more than a million and a half dollars.

'As well as that,' Lewis confided, 'I publish a book each year and do about twenty consultations every month. The fees and book royalties cover all my costs, so the newsletter is entirely profit.'

'That's amazing!' And yet, Alex reflected, perhaps it really wasn't. Anyone who heeded Lewis's counsel could recoup their outlay hundreds of times over. Besides which, both the newsletter subscription and consultation fee were tax deductible.

'Is there any one piece of over-all guidance,' Alex asked, 'that you'd give to people with money to invest or save ?'

'Absolutely, yes! – take care of it yourself.'

'Supposing it's someone who doesn't know . . .'

'Then find out. Learning isn't all that hard, and looking after your own money can be fun. Listen to advice, of course, though be sceptical and wary, and selective about which advice you take. After a while you'll learn whom to trust, and not. Read widely, including newsletters like mine. But never give anyone else the right to make decisions for you. Especially that means stockbrokers, who represent the fastest way to lose what you already have, and bank trust departments.'

'You don't like trust departments ?'

'Dammit, Alex, you know perfectly well the record of yours and other banks is awful. Big trust accounts get individual service – of a sort. Medium and small ones are either in a general pot or are handled by low-salaried incompetents who can't tell a bull market from bearshit.'

Alex grimaced, but didn't protest. He knew too well that – with a few honourable exceptions – what Lewis had said was true.

Sipping their cognac in the smoke-filled room, both men were silent. Alex turned the pages of the latest *Newsletter*, skimming its contents which he would read in detail later. As usual, some material was technical.

Chartwise we appear to be off on the 3rd leg of the bear market. The 200 day moving average has been broken in all 3 Dow-Jones averages which are in perfect downside synchronization. The advance-decline line is crashing.

More simple was:
Recommended mix of currencies:

Swiss Francs	40%	Canadian Dollars	10%
Dutch Guilders	25%	Austrian Schillings	5%
Deutsche Marks	20%	US Dollars	0%

Also, Lewis advised his readers, they should continue to hold 40% of total assets in gold bullion, gold coins and gold mining shares.

A regular column listed international securities to trade or hold. Alex's eyes ran down the 'buy' and 'hold' lists, then the 'sell'. He stopped sharply at: '*Supranational* – sell immediately at market.'

'Lewis, this Supranational item – why sell Supranational? And "immediately at market"? You've had it for years as a "long-term hold".'

His host considered before answering. 'I'm uneasy about SuNatCo. I'm getting too many fragments of negative information from unrelated sources. Some rumours about big losses which haven't been reported. Also stories of sharp accounting practices among subsidiaries. An unconfirmed story out of Washington that Big George Quartermain is shopping for a Lockheed-type subsidy. What it amounts to is – maybe – maybe not . . . shoal waters ahead. As a precaution, I prefer my people out.'

'But everything you've said is rumour and shadow. You can hear it about any company. Where's the substance?'

'There is none. My "sell" recommendation is on instinct. There are times I act on it. This is one.' Lewis D'Orsey placed his cigar stub in an ashtray and put down his empty glass. 'Shall we rejoin the ladies?'

'Yes,' Alex said, and followed Lewis. But his mind was still on Supranational.

four

'I wouldn't have believed,' Nolan Wainwright said harshly, 'that you'd have the nerve to come here.'

'I didn't think I would either.' Miles Eastin's voice betrayed his nervousness. 'I thought of coming yesterday, then decided I just couldn't. Today I hung around outside for half an hour, getting up courage to come in.'

'You may call it courage. I call it gall. Now you're here, what do you want?'

The two men faced each other, both standing, in Nolan Wainwright's private office. They were sharply in contrast: the stern, black, handsome bank vice-president of security, and Eastin, the ex-convict – shrunken, pale, unsure, a long way from the bright and affable assistant operations manager who had worked at FMA less than a year ago.

Their surroundings at this moment were spartan, compared with most other departments in the bank. Here were plain painted walls and grey metal furniture, including Wainwright's desk. The floor was carpeted, but thinly and economically. The bank lavished money and artistry on revenue-producing areas. Security was not among them.

'Well,' Wainwright repeated, 'what do you want?'

'I came to see if you'll help me.'

'Why should I?'

The younger man hesitated before answering, then said, still nervously, 'I know you tricked me with that first confession. The night I was arrested. My lawyer said it was illegal, it could never have been used in court. You knew that. But you let me go on thinking it was a legit confession, so I signed that second one for the FBI, not knowing there was any difference . . .'

Wainwright's eyes narrowed suspiciously. 'Before I answer that, I want to know something. Are you carrying a recording device?'

'No.'

'Why should I believe you?'

Miles shrugged, then held his hands above his head in the way he had learned from law-enforcement friskings and in prison.

For a moment it seemed as if Wainwright would refuse to search him, then quickly and professionally he patted down the other man. Miles lowered his arms.

'I'm an old fox,' Wainwright said. 'Guys like you think they can get smart and catch someone out, then start a legal suit. So you got to be a jailhouse lawyer?'

'No. All I found out about was the confession.'

'All right, you've brought it up, so I'll tell you about that. Sure I knew it might not hold water legally. Sure I tricked you. And something else: in the same circumstances, I'd do the same again. You were guilty, weren't you? You were about to send the Núñez girl to jail. What difference do the niceties make?'

'I only thought . . .'

'I know what you thought. You thought you'd come back here, and my conscience would be bleeding, and I'd be a push-over for some scheme you have or whatever else you want. Well, it isn't and I'm not.'

Miles Eastin mumbled, 'I had no scheme. I'm sorry I came.'

'What *do* you want?'

There was a pause while they appraised each other. Then Miles said, 'A job.'

'Here? You must be mad.'

'Why? I'd be the most honest employee the bank ever had.'

'Until somebody put pressure on you to steal again.'

'It wouldn't happen!' Briefly, a flash of Miles Eastin's former spirit surfaced. 'Can't you, can't anybody, believe I've learned something? Learned about what happens when you steal. Learned never, ever, to do the same again. Don't you think there's not a temptation in the world I wouldn't resist now, rather than take a chance of going back to prison?'

Wainwright said gruffly, 'What I believe or disbelieve is immaterial. The bank has policies. One is not to employ anyone with a criminal record. Even if I wanted to, I couldn't change that.'

'But you could try. There are jobs, even here, where a criminal record would make no difference, where there's *no way* to be dishonest. Couldn't I get some kind of work like that?'

'No.' Then curiosity intruded. 'Why are you so keen to come back, anyway?'

'Because I can't get any kind of work, not *anything*, not a look-in, not a chance, anywhere else.' Miles's voice faltered. 'And because I'm hungry.'

'You're what?'

'Mr Wainwright, it's been three weeks since I came out on parole. I've been out of money for more than a week. I haven't eaten in three days. I guess I'm desperate.' The voice which had faltered, cracked and broke. 'Coming here ... having to see you, guessing what you'd say ... it was the last ...'

While Wainwright listened, some of the hardness left his face. Now he motioned to a chair across the room. 'Sit down.'

He went outside and gave his secretary five dollars. 'Go to the cafeteria,' he instructed. 'Get two roast beef sandwiches and a pint of milk.'

When he returned, Miles Eastin was still sitting where he had been told, his body slumped, his expression listless.

'Has your parole officer helped?'

Miles said bitterly, 'He has a case load – so he told me – of a hundred and seventy-five parolees. He has to see everybody once a month, and what can he do for one? There are no jobs. All he gives is warnings.'

From experience, Wainwright knew what the warnings would be: not to associate with other criminals whom Eastin might have met in prison; not to frequent known haunts of criminals. To do either, and be officially observed, would ensure a prompt return to prison. But in practice the rules were as unrealistic as they were archaic. A prisoner without financial means had the dice loaded against him so that association with others like himself was frequently his only method of survival. It was also a reason why the rate of recidivism among ex-convicts was so high.

Wainwright asked, 'You've really looked for work?'

'Everywhere I could think of. And I haven't been fussy either.'

The closest Miles had been to a job in three weeks of searching had been as a kitchen helper in a third-rate, crowded Italian restaurant. The job was vacant and the proprietor, a sad whippet of a man, had been inclined to hire him. But when Miles revealed his prison record, as he knew he had to, he had seen the other glance at the cash register nearby. Even then the restaurateur had hesitated but his wife, a female drill sergeant, ruled, 'No! We can't afford to take a chance.' Pleading with them both had done no good.

Elsewhere, his parolee status had eliminated possibilities even faster.

'If I could do something for you, maybe I would.' Wainwright's tone had softened since the beginning of the interview. 'But I can't. There's nothing here. Believe me.'

Miles nodded glumly. 'I guess I knew anyway.'

'So what will you try next?'

Before there was time to answer, the secretary returned, handing Wainwright a paper bag and change. When the girl had gone, he took out the milk and sandwiches and set them down as Eastin watched, moistening his lips.

'You can eat those here if you like.'

Miles moved quickly, removing the wrapping from the first sandwich with plucking fingers. Any doubts about the truth of his statement that he was hungry were banished as Wainwright observed the food devoured silently, with speed. And while the security chief watched, an idea began to form.

At the end, Miles emptied the last of the milk from a paper cup and wiped his lips. Of the sandwiches, not a crumb remained.

'You didn't answer my question,' Wainwright said. 'What will you try next?'

Perceptibly Eastin hesitated, then said flatly, 'I don't know.'

'I think you do know. And I think you're lying – for the first time since you came in.'

Miles Eastin shrugged. 'Does it matter any more?'

'My guess is this,' Wainwright said; he ignored the question. 'Until now you've stayed away from the people you knew in prison. But because you gained nothing here you've decided to go to them. You'll take a chance on being seen, and your parole.'

'What the hell other kind of chance is there? And if you know so much, why ask?'

'So you *do* have those contacts.'

'If I say yes,' Eastin said contemptuously, 'the first thing you'll do when I've gone is telephone the parole board.'

'No.' Wainwright shook his head. 'Whatever we decide, I promise you I won't do that.'

'What do you mean: "Whatever we decide"?'

314

'There might just be something we could work out. If you were willing to run some risks. Big ones.'

'What kind of risks?'

'Leave that for now. If we need to, we'll come back to it. Tell me first about the people you got to know inside and those you can make contact with now.' Sensing continued wariness, Wainwright added, 'I give you my word I won't take advantage – without your agreement – of anything you tell me.'

'How do I know this isn't a trick – the way you tricked me once before?'

'You don't. You'll take a chance on trusting me. Either that, or walk out of here and don't come back.'

Miles sat silent, thinking, occasionally moistening his lips in the nervous gesture he had exhibited earlier. Then abruptly, without outward sign of a decision, he began to talk.

He revealed the approach first made to him in Drummonburg Penitentiary by the emissary from Mafia Row. The message relayed to Miles Eastin, he told Wainwright, had originated with the outside loan shark, Igor (the Russian) Ominsky, and was to the effect that he, Eastin, was a 'stand-up guy' because he had not disclosed the identity of the shark or the bookmaker at the time of his arrest or afterwards. As a concession, interest on Eastin's loan would be waived during his time in prison. 'Mafia Row's messenger boy said that Ominsky stopped the clock while I was inside.'

'But you're not inside now,' Wainwright pointed out. 'So the clock is running again.'

Miles looked worried. 'Yes, I know.' He had realized that, and tried not to think about it while he searched for work. He had also stayed away from the location he had been told of where he could make contact with the loan shark Ominsky and others. It was the Double-Seven Health Club near the city's centre, and the information had been passed to him a few days before leaving prison. He repeated it now under Wainwright's probing.

'Figures. I don't know the Double-Seven,' the bank security chief mused, 'but I've heard of it. It has the reputation of being a mob hangout.'

The other thing Miles had been told at Drummonburg was

that there would be ways for him, through contacts he would make, to earn money to live and begin paying off his debt. He had not needed a diagram to know that such 'ways' would be outside the law. That knowledge, and his dread of a return to prison, had kept him resolutely removed from the Double-Seven. So far.

'My hunch was right then. You would have gone there from here.'

'Oh, God, Mr Wainwright, I didn't want to! I still don't.'

'Maybe, between us, you can cut it both ways.'

'How?'

'You've heard of an undercover agent?'

Miles Eastin looked surprised before admitting, 'Yes.'

'Then listen carefully.'

Wainwright began talking.

Four months earlier, when the bank security chief viewed the drowned and mutilated body of his informer, Vic, he had doubted if he would send anyone undercover again. At that moment, shocked and with a sense of personal guilt, he had meant what he said and had done nothing since to recruit a replacement. But this opportunity – Eastin's desperation and ready-made connections – was too promising to be ignored.

Equally to the point: more and more counterfeit Keycharge credit cards were appearing, in what seemed a deluge, while their source remained unknown. Conventional methods of locating the producers and distributors had failed, as Wainwright knew; also hampering investigation was the fact that credit card counterfeiting, under federal law, was not a criminal offence. Fraud had to be proven; intention to defraud was not enough. For all these reasons, law-enforcement agencies were more interested in other forms of counterfeiting, so their concern with credit cards was only incidental. Banks – to the chagrin of professionals like Nolan Wainwright – had made no serious effort to get this situation changed.

Most of this, the bank security chief explained at length to Miles Eastin. He also unfolded a basically simple plan. Miles would go to the Double-Seven Health Club, making such contacts as he could. He would try to ingratiate himself, and would also take whatever opportunities occurred to earn some money.

'Doing that will mean a risk two ways, and you'll have to realize it,' Wainwright said. 'If you do something criminal and get caught, you'll be arrested, tried, and no one else can help you. The other risk is, even if you don't get caught and the parole board hears rumours, that'll put you back in prison just as surely.'

However, Wainwright continued, if neither mischance happened, Miles should try to widen his contacts, listening hard and accumulating information. At first, he should be wary of appearing curious. 'You'd take it easy,' Wainwright cautioned. 'Don't hurry, be patient. Let word get around; let people come to you.'

Only after Miles was accepted, would he work harder at learning more. At that time he could begin discreet enquiries about fake credit cards, exhibiting an interest for himself and seeking to move closer to wherever they were traded. 'There's always somebody,' Wainwright advised, 'who knows somebody else, who knows some other guy who has a rumble of some action. That's the way you'd weasel in.'

Periodically, Wainwright said, Eastin would report to him. Though never directly.

The mention of reporting was a reminder to Wainwright of his obligation to explain about Vic. He did so bluntly, omitting no details. As he spoke, he saw Miles Eastin go pale and remembered the night in Eastin's apartment, the time of the confrontation and exposure, when the younger man's instinctive fear of physical violence showed so clearly.

'Whatever happens,' Wainwright said sternly, 'I don't want you to say or think, later on, that I didn't warn you of the dangers.' He paused, considering. 'Now, about money.'

If Miles agreed to go undercover on the bank's behalf, the security chief stated, he would guarantee a payment of five hundred dollars a month until – one way or another – the assignment ended. The money would be paid through an intermediary.

'Would I be employed by the bank?'

'Absolutely no.'

The answer was unequivocal, emphatic, final. Wainwright elaborated: involvement of the bank officially would be nil. If Miles Eastin agreed to assume the role suggested, he would be entirely on his own. If he ran into trouble and tried to implicate First Mercantile American, he would be disowned and disbelieved. 'Since you were convicted and went to jail,' Wainwright declared, 'we never even heard of you.'

Miles grimaced. 'It's one-sided.'

'Damn right! But remember this: you came here. I didn't come to you. So what's your answer – yes or no ?'

'If you were me, which would it be ?'

'I'm not you, nor likely to be. But I'll tell you how I see it. The way things are, you don't have many choices.'

For a moment the old Miles Eastin humour and good nature flashed. 'Heads I lose; tails I lose. I guess I hit the loser's jackpot. Let me ask one thing more.'

'What ?'·

'If it all works out, if I get – if *you* get – the evidence you need, afterwards will you help me find a job at FMA ?'

'I can't promise that. I already said I didn't write the rules.'

'But you've influence to bend them.'

Wainwright considered before answering. He thought: if it came to it, he could go to Alex Vandervoort and present a case on behalf of Eastin. Success would be worth it. He said aloud, 'I'll try. But that's *all* I promise.'

'You're a hard man,' Miles Eastin said. 'All right, I'll do it.'

They discussed an intermediary.

'After today,' Wainwright warned, 'you and I won't meet again directly. It's too dangerous; either one of us may be watched. What we need is someone who can be a conduit for messages – both ways – and money; someone whom we both trust totally,'

Miles said slowly, 'There's Juanita Núñez. *If* she'd do it.'

Wainwright looked incredulous. 'The teller who you . . .'

'Yes. But she forgave me.' There was a mixture of elation and excitement in his voice. 'I went to see her and Heaven bless her, she forgave me!'

'I'll be damned.'

'*You* ask her,' Miles Eastin said. 'There's not a single reason why she should agree. But I think . . . just think, she might.'

five

How sound was Lewis D'Orsey's instinct about Supranational Corporation ? How sound was Supranational ? That worry continued to vex Alex Vandervoort.

It was on Saturday night that Alex and Lewis had talked about SuNatCo. Over what remained of the week-end, Alex pondered *The D'Orsey Newsletter* recommendation to sell Supranational shares at whatever the market would pay and Lewis's doubts about the conglomerate's solidity.

The entire subject was exceedingly important, even vital, to the bank. Yet it could be a delicate situation in which, Alex realized, he would need to move cautiously.

For one thing, Supranational was now a major client and any client would be righteously indignant if its own bankers circulated adverse rumours about it, particularly if false. And Alex had no illusions: once he began asking questions widely, word of them, and their source, would travel fast.

But were the rumours false ? Certainly – as Lewis D'Orsey had admitted – they were insubstantial. But then so had the original rumours been about such spectacular business failures as Penn Central, Equity Funding, Franklin National Bank, Security National Bank, American Bank & Trust, US National Bank of San Diego, others. There was also Lockheed, which hadn't failed, but came close to it, being bailed out by a US government handout. Alex remembered with disquieting clarity Lewis D'Orsey's reference to SuNatCo's chairman, Quartermain, shopping in Washington for a Lockheed-type loan – except that Lewis used the word 'subsidy', which wasn't far from truth.

It was possible, of course, that Supranational was merely suffering a temporary cash shortage, which sometimes happened to the soundest of companies. Alex hoped that that – or something less – was true. However, as an officer of FMA he could not afford to sit back and hope. Fifty million dollars of bank money had been funnelled into SuNatCo; also, using funds which it was the bank's job to safeguard, the trust department had invested heavily in Supranational shares, a fact which still made Alex shiver when he thought about it.

He decided the first thing he should do, in fairness, was inform Roscoe Heyward.

On Monday morning he walked from his office, down the carpeted thirty-sixth-floor corridor, to Heyward's. Alex took with him the latest issue of *The D'Orsey Newsletter* which Lewis had given him on Saturday night.

Heyward was not there. With a friendly nod to the senior secretary, Mrs Callaghan, Alex strolled in and put the newsletter directly on Heyward's desk. He had already ringed the item about Supranational and clipped on a note which read:

Roscoe—
I thought you should see this.
A.

Then Alex returned to his own office.

Half an hour later, Heyward stormed in, his face flushed. He tossed down the newsletter. 'Did you put this disgusting insult-to-intelligence on my desk?'

Alex pointed to his own handwritten note. 'It rather looks like it.'

'Then do me the favour of not sending me any more drivel written by that conceited ignoramus.'

'Oh, come on! Sure, Lewis D'Orsey is conceited, and I dislike part of what he writes, just as you obviously do. But he isn't an ignoramus, and some of his viewpoints are at least worth hearing.'

'You may think so. Others don't. I suggest you read this.' Heyward slapped an opened magazine on top of the newsletter.

Alex looked down, surprised at the other's vehemence. 'I *have* read it.'

The magazine was *Forbes*, the two-page article in question a slashing attack on Lewis D'Orsey. Alex had found the piece long on spite, short on fact. But it underscored what he already knew – that attacks on *The D'Orsey Newsletter* by the financial establishment press were frequent. Alex pointed out, '*The Wall Street Journal* had something similar a year ago.'

'Then I'm amazed you don't accept the fact that D'Orsey has absolutely no training or qualifications as an investment adviser. In a way, I'm sorry his wife works for us.'

Alex said sharply, 'Edwina and Lewis D'Orsey make a point of keeping their occupations entirely separate, as I'm sure you know. As to qualifications, I'll remind you that plenty of degree-loaded experts haven't done well in financial forecasting. Quite frequently, Lewis D'Orsey has.'

'Not where Supranational is concerned.'

'Do you still think SuNatCo is sound?'

Alex asked the last question quietly, not from antagonism, but seeking information. But its effect on Roscoe Heyward seemed near-explosive. Heyward glared through his rimless glasses; his face suffused an even deeper red. 'I'm sure that nothing would delight you more than to see a setback for SuNatCo, and thereby me.'

'No, that isn't . . .'

'Let me finish!' Heyward's facial muscles twitched as anger poured out. 'I've observed more than enough of your petty conniving and doubt-casting, like passing around this garbage' – he motioned to *The D'Orsey Newsletter* – 'and now I'm telling you to cease and desist. Supranational was, and is, a sound, progressive company with high earnings and good management. Getting the SuNatCo account – much as you may be jealous about it personally – was my achievement; it's my business. Now I'm warning you: stay out of it!'

Heyward wheeled and stalked out.

For several minutes Alex Vandervoort sat silently thoughtful, weighing what had just occurred. The outburst had amazed him. In the two and a half years that he had known and worked with Roscoe Heyward, the two of them had suffered disagreements and occasionally revealed their mutual dislike. But never before had Heyward lost control as he had this morning.

Alex thought he knew why. Underneath the bluster, Roscoe Heyward was worried. The more Alex thought about it, the more he was convinced.

Earlier, Alex had been worried himself – about Supranational. Now the question posed itself: was Heyward worrying about SuNatCo, too ? If so, what next ?

As he pondered, memory stirred. A fragment from a recent conversation. Alex pressed an intercom button and told his secretary, 'See if you can locate Miss Bracken.'

It took fifteen minutes before Margot's voice said brightly, 'This had better be good. You got me out of court.'

'Trust me, Bracken.' He wasted no time. 'In your department store class action – the one you talked about on Saturday night – you told us you used a private investigator.'

'Yes, Vernon Jax.'

'I think Lewis knew him, or of him.'

'That's right.'

'And Lewis said he was a good man who'd done work for the SEC.'

'I heard that, too. Probably it's because Vernon has a degree in economics.'

Alex added the information to notes he had already made. 'Is Jax discreet ? Trustworthy ?'

'Totally.'

'Where do I find him ?'

'I'll find him. Tell me where and when you want him.'

'In my office, Bracken. Today – without fail.'

Alex studied the untidy, balding, nondescript man seated opposite him in his office conference area. It was mid-afternoon.

Jax, Alex guessed, was in his early fifties. He looked like a small-town grocer, not too prosperous. His shoes were scuffed and there was a food stain on his jacket. Alex had already learned that Jax had been a staff investigator for the IRS before going into business for himself.

'I'm told you also have a degree in economics,' Alex said.

The other shrugged deprecatingly. 'Night school. You know how it is. Time on your hands.' His voice tailed off, leaving the explanation incomplete.

'How about accounting? Do you have much knowledge there?'

'Some. Studying for CPA exams right now.'

'Night school, I suppose.' Alex was beginning to catch on.

'Yep.' A pale ghost of a smile.

'Mr Jax,' Alex began.

'Most folks just call me Vernon.'

'Vernon. I'm considering having you undertake an enquiry. It will require absolute discretion and speed is essential. You've heard of Supranational Corporation?'

'Sure.'

'I want a financial investigation of that company. But it will have to be – I'm afraid there's no other word for it – an outside snooping job.'

Jax smiled again. 'Mr Vandervoort' – this time his tone was crisper – 'that's precisely the business I'm in.'

It would require a month, they agreed, though an interim report would be made to Alex if it seemed warranted. Complete confidentiality concerning the bank's investigative role would be preserved. Nothing illegal would be done. The investigator's fee was to be fifteen thousand plus reasonable expenses, half the fee payable immediately, the balance after a final report. Alex would arrange payment from FMA operating funds. He realized he might have to justify the expense later, but would worry about it when the time came.

Late in the afternoon, when Jax had gone, Margot phoned.

'Did you hire him?'

'Yes.'

'Were you impressed?'

Alex decided he would play the game. 'Not really.'

Margot laughed softly. 'You will be. You'll see.'

But Alex hoped he wouldn't. He hoped fervently that Lewis D'Orsey's instincts were wrong, that Vernon Jax would discover nothing, and that adverse rumours about Supranational would prove rumours – nothing more.

That night, Alex paid one of his periodic visits to Celia at the Remedial Centre. He had come to dread the visits even more; he always came away deeply depressed, but continued them out of a sense of duty. Or was it guilt? He was never sure.

As usual, he was escorted by a nurse to Celia's private room in the institution. When the nurse had gone, Alex sat talking, chatting in an inane, one-sided conversation about whatever things occurred to him, though Celia gave no sign of hearing, or even an awareness of his presence. Once, on an earlier occasion, he spoke gibberish just to see if her blankness of expression changed. It hadn't. Afterwards he felt ashamed and hadn't done it since.

Even so, he had formed the habit during these sessions with Celia, of prattling on, scarcely listening to himself, while half his mind was wandering elsewhere. Tonight, among other things, he said, 'People have all kinds of problems nowadays, Celia; problems which no one ever thought of a few years ago. Along with every clever thing mankind discovers or invents, come dozens of questions and decisions we never had to face before. Take electric can openers. If you have one – and I do in my apartment – there's a problem of where to plug it, when to use it, how to clean it, what to do when it goes wrong; all problems nobody would have if there weren't electric can openers and, after all, who needs them? Speaking of problems, I have several at this moment – personal and at the bank. A big one came up today. In some ways you may be better off in here ...'

Alex checked himself, realizing he was talking, if not gibberish then rubbish. No one was better off here, in this tragic twilight quarterlife.

Yet nothing else was left for Celia; in the past few months that fact had become even clearer than before. As recently as a year ago there had been traces of her former girlish, fragile beauty. Now they were gone. Her once-glorious fair hair was dull and sparse. Her skin had a greyish texture; in places eruptions showed where she had scratched herself.

Where once her curled-up foetal position had been occasional, now she adopted it most of the time. And though Celia was ten years younger than Alex, she appeared hag-like and twenty years older.

It was nearly five years since Celia had entered the Remedial Centre. In the meantime she had become totally institutionalized, and was likely to remain so.

Watching his wife, and continuing to talk, Alex felt compassion and sadness, but no sense of attachment or affection any more. Perhaps he ought to experience some of those emotions but, being honest with himself, he no longer found it possible. Yet he was tied to Celia, he recognized, by bonds he would never sever until one or the other of them died.

He remembered his conversation with Dr McCartney, head of the Remedial Centre, almost eleven months ago, the day after Ben Rosselli so dramatically announced his impending death. Answering Alex's question about the effect on Celia of a divorce and Alex's remarriage, the psychiatrist had said: *It might drive her over the brink into a totally demented state.*

And, later, Margot had declared: *What I won't have on my conscience, or yours, is shoving what's left of Celia's sanity into a bottomless pit.*

Tonight, Alex wondered if Celia's sanity was in some bottomless pit already. But even if true, it didn't change his reluctance to set in motion the final, ruthless machinery of divorce.

Nor had he gone to live permanently with Margot Bracken, or she with him. Margot remained agreeable to either arrangement, though Alex still wanted marriage – which obviously he couldn't have without divorcing Celia. Lately, though, he had sensed Margot's impatience at the lack of a decision.

How strange that he, accustomed at First Mercantile American to taking large decisions swiftly in stride, should wrestle with indecision in his private life!

The essence of the problem, Alex realized, was his old ambivalence about his personal guilt. Could he, years ago, by greater effort, love, and understanding, have saved his young, nervous, insecure bride from what she had become? If he had been more a devoted husband, less a devoted banker, he still suspected that he might.

325

It was why he came here, why he continued doing the little that he could.

When it was time to leave Celia, he rose and went towards her intending to kiss her forehead as he did whenever she allowed him. But tonight she shrank away, curling her body even tighter, her eyes alert with sudden fear. He sighed and abandoned the attempt.

'Good night, Celia,' Alex said.

There was no answer and he went out, leaving his wife to whatever lonely world she now inhabited.

Next morning Alex sent for Nolan Wainwright. He told the security chief that the investigator's fee to be paid to Vernon Jax would be remitted through Wainwright's department. Alex would authorize the expense. Alex didn't state, and Wainwright didn't ask, the specific nature of Jax's investigation. For the moment, Alex decided, the fewer people who knew the target, the better.

Nolan Wainwright had a reciprocal report for Alex. It concerned his arrangement that Miles Eastin would be an undercover agent for the bank. Alex's reaction was immediate.

'No. I don't want that man ever again on our payroll.'

'He won't be on the payroll,' Wainwright argued. 'I've explained to him that as far as the bank is concerned, he has no status. Any money he'll receive will be in cash, with nothing to show where it came from.'

'That's hairsplitting, Nolan. One way or the other he'd be employed by us, and that I can't agree to.'

'If you don't agree,' Wainwright objected, 'You'll be tying my hands, not letting me do my job.'

'Doing your job doesn't require you to hire a convicted thief.'

'Ever hear of using one to catch one?'

'Then use one who didn't personally defraud this bank.'

They argued back and forth, at moments heatedly. In the end, Alex reluctantly conceded. Afterwards he asked, 'Does Eastin realize how much of a risk he's taking?'

'He knows.'

'You told him about the dead man?' Alex had learned about Vic, from Wainwright, several months ago.

'Yes.'

'I still don't like the idea – any of it.'

'You'll like it even less if Keycharge fraud losses keep increasing, as they are.'

Alex sighed. 'All right. It's your department and you're entitled to run it your way, which is why I've given in. But I'll impress one thing on you: if you've reason to believe Eastin is in immediate danger, then pull him out at once.'

'I intended that.'

Wainwright was glad that he had won, though it had been a tougher argument than he expected. However, it seemed unwise right now to mention anything else – for example, his hope of enlisting Juanita Núñez as an intermediary. After all, he rationalized, the principle was established, so why bother Alex with details?

six

Juanita Núñez was torn between suspicion and curiosity. Suspicion because she disliked and distrusted the bank's vice-president of Security, Nolan Wainwright. Curiosity because she wondered why he wanted to see her, apparently in secrecy.

There was nothing for her to be concerned about personally, Wainwright had assured Juanita on the telephone yesterday when he called her at the main downtown branch. He would merely like the two of them, he said, to have a confidential talk. 'It's a question of whether you'd be willing to help someone else.'

'Like you?'

'Not exactly.'

'Then who?'

'I'd prefer to tell you privately.'

From his voice, Juanita sensed that Wainwright was trying to be friendly. But she parried the friendliness, still remembering his unfeeling harshness when she had been under suspicion of theft. Not even his subsequent apology had wiped out that memory. She doubted if anything ever would.

Just the same, he was a senior officer of FMA and she a junior employee. 'Well,' Juanita said, 'I'm here, and last time I looked the tunnel was open.' She assumed that either Wainwright would walk over from the Headquarters Tower or she would be told to report there. However, he surprised her.

'It would be best if we didn't meet in the bank, Mrs Núñez. When I've explained, you'll understand why. Suppose I pick you up in my car from your home this evening, and we talk while we drive.'

'I can't do that.' She was more wary than ever.

'You mean, not tonight?'

'Yes.'

'How about tomorrow?'

Juanita was stalling, trying to decide. 'I'll have to let you know.'

'All right, call me tomorrow. As early as you can. And meanwhile, please don't tell anyone else we had this conversation.' Wainwright hung up.

Now it *was* tomorrow – Tuesday in the third week of September. At mid-morning, Juanita knew that if she failed to call Wainwright soon, he would call her.

She was still uneasy. Sometimes, she thought, she had a nose for trouble and scented it now. Earlier Juanita had considered asking the advice of Mrs D'Orsey whom she could see, on the other side of the bank, at the manager's desk on the platform. But she hesitated, remembering Wainwright's cautionary words about not telling anyone else. That, as much as anything, had piqued her curiosity.

Today Juanita was working on new accounts. Beside her was a phone. She stared at it, picked it up, and dialled the internal number of Security. Moments later, Nolan Wainwright's deep voice asked, 'Can you make it tonight?'

Curiosity won out. 'Yes, but not for long.' She explained that she would leave Estela alone for half an hour; no more.

'That will be long enough. What time and where?'

Dusk was settling in when Nolan Wainwright's Mustang II nosed to the kerb outside the Forum East apartment building where Juanita Núñez lived. Moments later she emerged through the main floor entranceway, closing it carefully behind her. Wainwright reached over from behind the wheel to open the nearside door and she climbed in.

He helped fasten her seat belt, then said, 'Thank you for coming.'

'Half an hour,' Juanita reminded him. 'That's all.' She made no attempt to be friendly and was already nervous about leaving Estela alone.

The bank security chief nodded as he eased the car away from the kerb and into traffic. They drove two blocks in silence, then made a left turn on to a busier, divided road, lined with brightly lighted shops and cafés. Still driving, Wainwright said, 'I hear young Eastin came to see you.'

She responded sharply, 'How did you know?'

'He told me. He also said that you've forgiven him.'

'If he said it, then you know.'

'Juanita – may I call you that?'

'It is my name. I suppose so.'

Wainwright sighed. 'Juanita, I already told you I'm sorry about the way things went between us once before. If you still hold that against me, I don't blame you.'

She thawed slightly. '*Bueno*, you had better tell me what it is you want.'

'I want to know if you'd be willing to help Eastin'

'So he is the one.'

'Yes.'

'Why should I? Isn't forgiving him enough?'

'If you ask my opinion – more than enough. But he was the one who said you might . . .'

She interrupted. 'What kind of help?'

'Before I tell you, I'd like your promise that what we say tonight will go no further than the two of us.'

She shrugged. 'There is no one to tell. But you have the promise.'

'Eastin is going to do some investigative work. It's for the bank, though unofficial. If he succeeds it may help him get rehabilitated, which is what he wants.' Wainwright paused while he manoeuvred the car around a slow-moving tractor-trailer. He continued, 'The work is risky. It would be riskier still if Eastin reported directly to me. What the two of us need is someone to carry messages both ways – an intermediary.'

'And you decided it should be me?'

'No one's decided. It's a question of whether you'd be willing. If you were, it would help Eastin help himself.'

'And is Miles the only one this would help?'

'No,' Wainwright admitted. 'It would help me; also the bank.'

'Somehow that is what I thought.'

They had left the bright lights now and were crossing the river by a bridge; in the gathering darkness the water gleamed blackly far below. The road surface was metallic and the car wheels hummed. At the end of the bridge was the entrance to an interstate highway. Wainwright turned on to it.

'The investigation you speak of,' Juanita prompted. 'Tell me more about it.' Her voice was low, expressionless.

'All right.' He described how Miles Eastin would operate under cover, using his contacts made in prison, and the kind of evidence Miles would search for. There was no point, Wainwright decided, in holding anything back because what he didn't tell Juanita now she would find out later. So he added the information about the murder of Vic, though omitting the more unpleasant details. 'I'm not saying the same will happen to Eastin,' he concluded. 'I'll do everything possible to make sure it won't. But I mention it so you know the risk he's running, and he understands it, too. If you were to help him, as I said, it would keep him safer.'

'And who will keep *me* safe?'

'For you there'd be virtually no risk. The only contact you'd have would be with Eastin and with me. No one else would know, and you wouldn't be compromised. We'd make sure of that.'

'If you are so sure, why are we meeting this way now?'

'Simply a precaution. To make certain we're not seen together and can't be overheard.'

Juanita waited, then she asked, 'And that is all? There is nothing more to tell me?'

Wainwright said, 'I guess that's it.'

They were on the highway now and he held the car at a steady 45, staying in the right-hand lane while other vehicles speeded past. On the opposite side of the divided highway three lines of headlights streamed towards them, passing in a blur. Soon he would turn off at an exit and return the way they had come. Meanwhile, Juanita sat silently beside him, her eyes directed straight ahead.

He wondered what she was thinking and what her answer would be. He hoped it would be yes. As on earlier occasions he found this petite, elfin girl-woman provocative and sexually attractive. Her perversity was part of it; so was the smell of her – a bodily feminine presence in the small closed car. There had been few women in Nolan Wainwright's life since his divorce, and at any other time he might have tried his luck. But what he wanted from Juanita now was too important to take a chance with self-indulgence.

He was about to break the silence when Juanita turned to face him. Even in the semi-darkness he could see her eyes were blazing.

'You must be *mad, mad, mad!*' Her voice rose heatedly. 'Do you think I am a little fool? *¡Una boba! ¡Una tonta!* No risk for me, you say! Of course there is a risk, and I take all of it. And for what? For the glory of Mr Security Wainwright and his bank.'

'Now wait . . .'

She brushed aside the interruption, storming on, her anger spilling out like lava. 'Am I such an easy target? Does being alone or Puerto Rican qualify me for all the abuses of this world? Do you not care *who* you use, or how? *Take me home!* What kind of *pendejada* is this anyway?'

'Hold it!' Wainwright said; the reaction had astonished him. 'What's *pendejada* ?'

'Idiocy! *Pendejada* that you would throw a man's life away for your selfish credit cards. *Pendejada* that Miles would agree to do it.'

'He came to me asking for help. I didn't go to him.'

'You call *that* help ?'

'He'll be paid for what he does. He wanted that, too. And it was he who suggested you.'

'Then what is wrong with him that he cannot ask me himself ? Has Miles lost his tongue ? Or is he ashamed, and hiding behind your skirts ?'

'Okay, okay,' Wainwright protested. 'I get the message. I'll take you home.' An exit was close ahead; he turned on to it, crossed an overpass and headed back towards the city.

Juanita sat fuming.

At first, she had tried to consider calmly what Wainwright was suggesting. But while he had talked, and she had listened, doubts and questions besieged her, then afterwards, as she considered each, her anger and emotion grew, and finally exploded. Coupled with her outburst was a fresh hate and disgust for the man beside her. All the old painful feelings of her earlier experience with him now returned and were augmented. And she was angry, not only for herself, but about the use which Wainwright and the bank proposed to make of Miles.

At the same time Juanita was incensed *at* Miles. Why had he not approached her himself, directly ? Was he not man enough ? She remembered that less than three weeks ago she had admired his courage in coming to her, facing her penitently, and asking forgiveness. But his actions now, the method of working on her through someone else, seemed more in keeping with his earlier deceit when he had blamed her for his own malfeasance. Suddenly her thinking veered. Was she being harsh, unjust ? Looking inside herself, Juanita asked: wasn't part of her frustration at this moment a disappointment that Miles had not returned after the encounter in her apartment ? And wasn't there – exacerbating that disappointment here and now – a resentment that Miles, whom she liked despite everything, was being represented to her by Nolan Wainwright, whom she didn't?

Her anger, never long sustained, diminished. Uncertainty replaced it. She asked Wainwright, 'So what will you do now?'

'Whatever I decide, I'm certainly not likely to confide in you.' His tone was curt, the attempt at friendliness gone.

With sudden alarm, Juanita wondered if she had been needlessly belligerent. She *could* have turned down the request without the insults. Would Wainwright find some way to retaliate within the bank? Had she put her job in jeopardy? – the job she depended on to support Estela. Juanita's anxiety increased. She had a sense, after all, of being trapped.

And something else, she thought: if she were honest – which she tried to be – she regretted that because of her decision she would see no more of Miles.

The car had slowed. They were near the turn-off which would take them back across the river bridge.

Surprising herself, Juanita said in a flat, small voice, 'Very well, I will do it.'

'You'll what?'

'I will be – whatever it was – an . . .'

'Intermediary.' Wainwright glanced sideways at her. 'You're sure?'

'*Sí, estoy segura.* I am sure.'

For the second time tonight he sighed. 'You're a strange one.'

'I am a woman.'

'Yes,' he said, and some of the friendliness was back. 'I'd noticed.'

A block and a half from Forum East, Wainwright stopped the car, leaving the motor running. He removed two envelopes from an inside jacket pocket – one fat, the other smaller – and handed the first to Juanita.

'That's money for Eastin. Keep it until he gets in touch with you.' The envelope, Wainwright explained, contained four hundred and fifty dollars in cash – the agreed monthly payment, less a fifty-dollar advance which Wainwright had given Miles last week.

'Later this week,' he added, 'Eastin will phone me and I'll announce a code word we've already arranged. Your name will not be mentioned. But he'll know that he's to contact you, which he'll do soon after.'

Juanita nodded, concentrating, storing the information away.

'After that phone call, Eastin and I won't contact each other directly again. Our messages, both ways, will go through you. It would be best if you didn't write them down, but carry them in your head. I happen to know your memory is good.'

Wainwright smiled as he said it, and abruptly Juanita laughed. How ironic that her remarkable memory, which was once a cause of her troubles with the bank and Nolan Wainwright, should be relied on by him now!

'By the way,' he said, 'I'll need to know your home phone number. I couldn't find it listed.'

'That is because I do not have a telephone. It costs too much.'

'Just the same, you'll need one. Eastin may want to call you; so might I. If you'll have a phone installed immediately, I'll see that the bank reimburses you.'

'I will try. But I have heard from others that phones are slow to be put in at Forum East.'

'Then let me arrange it. I'll call the phone company tomorrow. I guarantee fast action.'

'Very well.'

Now Wainwright opened the second, smaller envelope. 'When you give Eastin the money, also give him this.'

'This' was a Keycharge bank credit card, made out in the name of H. E. LYNCOLP. On the rear of the card a space for signature was blank.

'Have Eastin sign the card, in that name, in his normal handwriting. Tell him the name is a fake, though if he looks at the initials and the last letter, he'll see they spell H-E-L-P. That's what the card is for.'

The bank security chief said that the Keycharge computer had been programmed so that if this card was presented anywhere, a purchase of up to a hundred dollars would be approved, but simultaneously an automatic alert would be raised within the bank. This would notify Wainwright that Eastin needed help, and where he was.

'He can use the card if he's on to something hot and wants support, or if he knows he's in danger. Depending on what's happened up to then, I'll decide what to do. Tell him to buy something worth more than fifty dollars; that way the store will be certain to phone in for confirmation. After that phone call, he should dawdle as much as he can, to give me time to move.'

Wainwright added, 'He may never need the card. But if he does, it's a signal no one else will know about.'

At Wainwright's request, Juanita repeated his instructions almost word for word. He looked at her admiringly. 'You're pretty bright.'

'¿ De qué me vale, muerta ?'

'What does that mean ?'

She hesitated, then translated, 'What good will it do me if I'm dead ?'

'Stop worrying!' Reaching across the car he gently touched her folded hands. 'I promise it'll all work out.'

At that moment his confidence was infectious. But later, back in her apartment with Estela sleeping, Juanita's instinct about impending trouble persistently returned.

seven

The Double-Seven Health Club smelled of boiler steam, stale urine, body odour, and booze. After a while, though, to anyone inside, the various effluvia merged into a single pungency, curiously acceptable, so that fresh air which occasionally blew in seemed alien.

The club was a boxlike, four-storey brown brick building in a decaying, dead-end street on the fringes of downtown. Its façade was scarred by a half century of wear, neglect, and – more recently – graffiti. At the building's peak was an unadorned stub of flagpole which no one remembered seeing whole. The main entrance consisted of a single, solid, unmarked door abutting directly on a sidewalk notable for cracks, overturned rubbish bins, and innumerable dog turds. A paint-flaking lobby just inside was supposed to be guarded by a punch-drunk bruiser who let members in and churlishly kept strangers out, but he was sometimes missing, which was why Miles Eastin wandered in unchallenged.

It was shortly before noon, midweek, and a dissonance of raised voices drifted back from somewhere in the rear. Miles walked towards the sound, down a main-floor corridor, none too clean and hung with yellowed prizefight pictures. At the end was an open door to a semi-darkened bar from where the voices came. Miles went in.

At first he could scarcely see in the dimness and moved uncertainly so that a hurrying waiter with a tray of drinks cannoned into him. The waiter swore, somehow managed to keep the glasses upright, and moved on. Two men perched on bar-stools turned their heads. One said, 'Thisa private club, buster. If you aina member – out!'

The other complained, "S 'at lazy bum Pedro goofin' off. Some doorman! Hey, who are ya? Wadda ya want?'

Miles told him, 'I was looking for Jules LaRocca.'

'Look someplace else,' the first man ordered. 'No wunna that name here.'

'Hey, Milesy baby!' A squat pot-bellied figure bustled forward through the gloom. The familiar weasel face came into focus. It was LaRocca who in Drummonburg Penitentiary had been an emissary from Mafia Row, and later attached himself to Miles and his protector Karl. Karl was still inside, and likely to remain there. Jules LaRocca had been released on parole shortly before Miles Eastin.

'Hi, Jules,' Miles acknowledged.

'Come over. Meet some guys.' LaRocca seized Miles's arm in pudgy fingers. 'Frenna mine,' he told the two men on barstools who turned their backs indifferently.

'Listen,' Miles said, 'I won't come over. I'm out of bread. I can't buy.' He slipped easily into the argot he had learned in prison.

'Forget it. Hava coupla beers on me.' As they passed between tables, LaRocca asked, 'Whereya bin?'

'Looking for work. I'm all beat, Jules. I need some help. Before I got out you said you'd give it to me.'

'Sure, sure.' They stopped at a table where two other men were seated. One was skinny with a mournful, pockmarked face; the other had long blond hair, cowboy boots, and wore dark glasses. LaRocca pulled up an extra chair. 'Thissa my buddy, Milesy.'

The man with dark glasses grunted. The other said, 'The guy knows about dough?'

'That's him.' LaRocca shouted across the room for beer, then urged the man who had spoken first to, 'Ask him sumpum.'

'Like what?'

'Like about money, asshole,' dark glasses said. He considered. 'Where'da first dollar get started?'

'That's easy,' Miles told him. 'Lots of people think America invented the dollar. Well, we didn't. It came from Bohemia in Germany, only first it was called a *thaler*, which other Europeans couldn't pronounce, so they corrupted it to dollar and it stayed that way. One of the first references to it is in *Macbeth* – "ten thousand dollars to our general use".'

'Mac who?'

'Macshit,' LaRocca said. 'You wanna printed programme?' He told the other two proudly, 'See what I mean? This kid knows it all.'

'Not quite,' Miles said, 'or I'd know how to make some money at this moment.'

Two beers were slapped in front of him. LaRocca fished out cash which he gave the waiter.

'Before ya make dough,' LaRocca said to Miles, 'ya gotta pay Ominsky.' He leaned across confidingly, ignoring the other two. 'The Russian knows ya outta the can. Bin askin' for ya.'

The mention of the loan shark, to whom he still owed at least three thousand dollars, left Miles sweating. There was another debt, too – roughly the same amount– to the bookie he had dealt with, but the chance of paying either seemed remote at this moment. Yet he had known that coming here, making himself visible, would reopen the old accounts and that savage reprisals would follow if he failed to pay.

He asked LaRocca, 'How can I pay any of what I owe if I can't get work?'

The pot-bellied man shook his head. 'First off, ya gotta see the Russian.'

'Where?' Miles knew that Ominsky had no office but operated wherever business took him.

LaRocca motioned to the beer. 'Drink up, then you 'n me go look.'

'Look at it from my point of view,' the elegantly dressed man said, continuing his lunch. His diamond ringed hands moved deftly above his plate. 'We had a business arrangement, you and me, which both of us agreed to. I kept my part. You've not kept yours. I ask you, where does that leave me?'

'Look,' Miles pleaded, 'you know what happened, and I appreciate your stopping the clock the way you did. But I can't pay now. I want to, but I can't. Please give me time.'

Igor (the Russian) Ominsky shook his expensively barbered head; manicured fingers touched a pink clean-shaven cheek. He was vain about his appearance, and lived and dressed well, as he could afford to.

'Time,' he said softly, 'is money. You've had too much of both already.'

On the opposite side of the booth, in the restaurant where LaRocca had brought him, Miles had the feeling of being a mouse before a cobra. There was no food on his side of the table, not even a glass of water, which he could have used because his lips were dry and fear gnawed at his stomach. If he could have gone to Nolan Wainwright now and cancelled their arrangement, which had exposed him in this way, Miles would have done it instantly. As it was, he sat sweating, watching, while Ominsky continued his meal of Sole Bonne Femme. Jules La-Rocca had strolled discreetly away to the restaurant's bar.

The reason for Miles's fear was simple. He could guess the size of Ominsky's business and knew the absoluteness of his power.

Once, Miles had watched a TV special on which an authority on American crime, Ralph Salerno, was asked the question: If you had to live illegally, what kind of criminal would you be? The expert's answer instantly: a loan shark. What Miles knew, from his contacts in prison and before, confirmed this view.

A loan shark like Russian Ominsky was a banker harvesting a staggering profit with minimal risk, dealing in loans large and small, unhampered by regulations. His customers came to him; he seldom sought them out, or needed to. He rented no expensive premises and did his business in a car, a bar – or at lunch, as now. His record keeping was the simplest, usually in code, and his transactions – largely in cash – were untraceable. His losses from bad debts were minor. He paid no federal, state, or city taxes. Yet interest rates – or 'vig' – he charged were normally 100 per cent p.a., and often higher.

At any given time, Miles guessed, Ominsky would have at least two million dollars 'on the street'. Some of it would be the loan shark's own money, the rest invested with him by bosses of organized crime for whom he made a handsome profit, taking a commission for himself. It was normal for an initial $100,000 invested in loan-sharking to be pyramided, within five years, to $1.5 million – a 1,400 per cent capital gain. No other business in the world could equal it.

Nor were a loan shark's clients always small-time. With surprising frequency, big names and reputable businesses borrowed from loan sharks when other credit sources were exhausted. Sometimes, in lieu of repayment, a loan shark would become a partner – or owner – of another business. Like a sea shark, his bite was large.

The loan shark's main expenses were for enforcement, and he kept those minimal, knowing that broken limbs and hospitalized bodies produced little, if any, money; and knowing, too, his strongest collection aide was fear.

Yet the fear needed a basis in reality; therefore when a borrower defaulted, punishment by hired goons was swift and savage.

As to risks a loan shark ran, these were slight compared with other forms of crime. Few loan sharks were ever prosecuted, fewer still convicted. Lack of evidence was the reason. A loan shark's customers were closemouthed, partly from fear, some from shame that they needed his services at all. And those who were physically beaten never lodged complaints, knowing that if they did there would be more of the same to come.

Thus, Miles sat, apprehensive, while Ominsky finished his sole.

Unexpectedly, the loan shark said, 'Can you keep a set of books?'

'Book-keeping? Why, yes; when I worked for the bank . . .'

He was waved to silence; cold, hard eyes appraised him. 'Maybe I can use you. I need a book-keeper at the Double-Seven.'

'The Health Club?' It was news to Miles that Ominsky owned or managed it. He added, 'I was there today, before . . .'

The other cut him off. 'When I'm talking, stay quiet and listen; just answer questions when you're asked. LaRocca says you want to work. If I give you work, everything you earn goes to me to pay your loan and vig. In other words, I *own* you. I want that understood.'

'Yes, Mr Ominsky.' Relief flooded Miles. He was to be given time after all. The how and why were unimportant.

'You'll get your meals, a room,' Russian Ominsky said, 'and one thing I'll warn you – keep your fingers out of the till. If I ever find you didn't, you'll wish you'd stolen from the bank again, not me.'

Miles shivered instinctively, less for concern about stealing – which he had no intention of doing – than his awareness of what Ominsky would do if he ever learned a Judas had come into his camp.

'Jules will take you and get you set up. You'll be told what else to do. That's all.' Ominsky dismissed Miles with a gesture and nodded to LaRocca who had been watching from the bar. While Miles waited near the restaurant's outer door, the other two conferred, the loan shark issuing instructions and LaRocca nodding.

Jules LaRocca rejoined Miles. 'You gotta swell break, kid. Let's move ass.'

As they left, Ominksy began to eat dessert while another waiting figure slipped into the seat facing him.

*   *   *

The room at the Double-Seven was on the building's top floor and little more than a shabbily furnished cubicle. Miles didn't mind. It represented a frail beginning, a chance to reshape his life and regain something of what he had lost, though he knew it would take time, grave risk, and enterprise. For the moment, he tried not to think too much about his dual role, concentrating instead on making himself useful and becoming accepted, as Nolan Wainwright had cautioned him to do.

He learned the geography of the club first. Most of the main floor – apart from the bar he had been in originally – was taken up by a gymnasium and handball courts. On the second floor were steam rooms and massage parlours. The third comprised offices; also several other rooms which he learned the use of later. The fourth floor, smaller than the others, contained a few more cubicles like Miles's where club members occasionally slept overnight.

Miles slipped easily into the book-keeper's work. He was good at the job, catching up on a backlog and improving postings which had been done sloppily before. He made suggestions to the club manager for making other record keeping more efficient, though was careful not to seek credit for the changes.

The manager, an ex-fight promoter named Nathanson, to whom office work did not come easily, was grateful. He was even more appreciative when Miles offered to do extra chores around the club, such as reorganizing stores and inventory procedures. Nathanson, in return, allowed Miles use of the handball courts during some of his free time, which provided an extra chance of meeting members.

The club's all-male membership, as far as Miles could see, was divided broadly into two groups. One comprised those who seriously used the club's facilities, including the steam baths and massage parlours. These people came and went individually, few of them appearing to know each other, and Miles guessed they were salaried workers or minor business executives who belonged to the Double-Seven simply to keep fit. He suspected, too, that the first group provided a conveniently legitimate front for the second, which usually didn't use the athletic facilities, except the steam baths on occasion.

Those in this second group congregated mainly in the bar or the upstairs rooms on the third floor. They were present in greatest numbers late at night, when the exercise-seeking members seldom used the club. It became evident to Miles that this second element was what Nolan Wainwright had in mind when he described the Double-Seven as a 'mob hangout'.

Something else Miles Eastin learned quickly was that the upstairs rooms were used for illegal, high stakes card and dice games. By the time he had worked a week, some of the night regulars had come to know Miles, and were relaxed about him, being assured by Jules LaRocca that he was 'okay, a stand-up guy'.

Shortly after, and pursuing his policy of being useful, Miles began helping out when drinks and sandwiches had to be carried to the third floor. The first time he did, one of a half-dozen burly men standing outside the gaming rooms, who were obviously guards, took the tray from him and carried it in. But next night, and on subsequent ones, he was allowed into the rooms where gambling was taking place. Miles also obliged by buying cigarettes downstairs and bringing them up for anyone who needed them, including the guards.

He knew he was becoming liked.

One reason was his general willingness. Another was that some of his old cheerfulness and good nature were returning, despite the problems and dangers of being where he was. And a third was that Jules LaRocca, who seemed to flit around the fringes of everything, had become Miles's sponsor, even though LaRocca made Miles feel, at times, like a vaudeville performer.

It was Miles Eastin's knowledge about money and its history which fascinated – it seemed endlessly – LaRocca and his cronies. A favourite item was the saga of counterfeit money printed by governments, which Miles had first described in prison. In his early weeks at the club he repeated it, under LaRocca's prodding, at least a dozen times. It always produced nods of belief, along with comments about 'stinkin' hypocrites' and 'goddamn gumment crooks'.

To supplement his fund of stories, Miles went one day to the apartment block where he had lived before imprisonment, and retrieved his reference books. Most of his other few possessions had long since been sold to pay arrears of rent, but the caretaker had kept the books and let Miles have them. Once, Miles had owned a coin and banknote collection, then sold it when he was heavily in debt. Some day, he hoped, he might become a collector again, though the prospect seemed far away.

Able to dip into his books, which he kept in the fourth-floor cubicle, Miles talked to LaRocca and the others about some of the stranger forms of money. The heaviest currency ever, he told them, was the agronite stone discs used on the Pacific island of Yap up to the outbreak of World War II. Most of the discs, he explained, were one foot wide, but one denomination had a width of twelve feet and, when used for purchasing, was transported on a pole. 'Waddabout change?' someone asked amid laughter, and Miles assured them it was given – in smaller stone discs.

In contrast, he reported, the lightest-weight money was scarce types of feathers, used in the New Hebrides. Also, for centuries salt circulated as money, especially in Ethiopia, and the Romans used it to pay their workers, hence the word 'salary' which evolved from 'salt'. And in Borneo, as recently as the nineteenth century, Miles told the others, human skulls were legal tender.

But invariably, before such sessions ended, the talk swung back to counterfeiting.

After one such occasion, a hulking driver-bodyguard who hung around the club while his boss played cards upstairs, took Miles aside.

'Hey, kid, you talk big about counterfeit. Take a looka this.' He held out a clean, crisp twenty-dollar bill.

Miles accepted the banknote and studied it. The experience was not new to him. When he worked at First Mercantile American Bank, suspected bogus bills were usually brought to him because of his specialist knowledge.

The big man was grinning. 'Pretty good, huh?'

'If this is a fake,' Miles said, 'it's the best I've ever seen.'

343

'Wanna buy a few ?' From an inner pocket the bodyguard produced nine more twenties. 'Gimme forty bucks in real stuff, kid, that whole two hunnert's yours.'

It was about the going rate, Miles knew, for high-grade queer. He observed, too, that the other bills were just as good as the first.

About to refuse the offer, he hesitated. He had no intention of passing any fake money, but realized it was something he could send to Wainwright.

'Hold it!' he told the burly man, and went upstairs to his room where he had squirrelled away slightly more than forty dollars. Some of it had been left over from Wainwright's original fifty-dollar stake; the rest was from tips Miles had been given around the gaming rooms. He took the money, mostly in small bills, and exchanged it downstairs for the counterfeit two hundred. Later that night he hid the counterfeit money in his room.

The next day, Jules LaRocca, grinning, told him, 'Hear ya didda stroka business.' Miles was at his book-keeper's desk in the third floor offices.

'A little,' he admitted.

LaRocca moved his pot belly closer and lowered his voice. 'Ya wanna piece more action ?'

Miles said cautiously, 'It depends what kind.'

'Like makin' a trip to Louisville. Movin' summa the stuff you bought last night.'

Miles felt his stomach tighten, knowing that if he agreed and were caught, it would not only put him back in prison, but for much longer than before. Yet if he didn't take risks, how could he continue learning, and gaining the confidence of others here ?

'All it is, is drivin' a car from here to there. You get paid two C notes.'

'What happens if I'm stopped ? I'm on parole and not allowed a driver's licence.'

'A licence ain't no problem if you gotta photo – front view, head 'n shoulders.'

'I haven't, but I could get one.'

'Do it fast.'

During his lunch break, Miles walked to a downtown bus station and obtained a photograph from an automatic machine. He gave it to LaRocca the same afternoon.

Two days later, again while Miles was working, a hand silently placed a small rectangle of paper on the ledger in front of him. With amazement he saw it was a state driver's licence, embodying the photo he had supplied.

When he turned, LaRocca stood behind him, grinning. 'Better service unna Licence Bureau, eh ?'

Miles said incredulously, 'You mean it's a forgery ?'

'Can ya tella difference ?'

'No, I can't.' He peered at the licence which appeared to be identical with an official one. 'How did you get it ?'

'Never mind.'

'No,' Miles said, 'I'd really like to know. You know how interested I am in things like this.'

LaRocca's face clouded; for the first time his eyes revealed suspicion. 'Why ya wanna know ?'

'Just interest. The way I told you.' Miles hoped a sudden nervousness didn't show.

'Some questions ain't smart. A guy asks too many, people start wondering. He might get hurt. He might get hurt bad.'

Miles stayed silent, LaRocca watching. Then, it seemed, the moment of suspicion passed.

'It'll be tomorrow night,' Jules LaRocca informed him. 'You'll be told wotta do, and when.'

Next day, in the early evening, the instructions were delivered – again by the perennial messenger, LaRocca, who handed Miles a set of car keys, a parking receipt from a city lot, and a one-way airline ticket. Miles was to pick up the car – a maroon Chevrolet Impala – drive it off the lot, then continue through the night to Louisville. On arrival he would go to Louisville airport and park the car there, leaving the airport parking ticket and keys under the front seat. Before leaving the car he was to wipe it carefully to remove his own fingerprints. Then he would take an early-morning flight back.

The worst minutes for Miles were early on, when he had

located the car and was driving it from the city parking lot. He wondered tensely: had the Chevrolet been under surveillance by police? Perhaps whoever parked the car was suspect, and was followed here. If so, now was the moment the law was most likely to close in. Miles knew there had to be a high risk; otherwise someone like himself would not have been sought as courier. And although he had no actual knowledge, he presumed the counterfeit money – probably a lot of it – was in the boot.

But nothing happened, though it was not until he had left the parking lot well behind and was near the city limits that he began to relax.

Once or twice on the highway, when he encountered state police patrol cars, his heart beat faster, but no one stopped him, and he reached Louisville shortly before dawn after an uneventful journey.

Only one thing happened which was not in the plan. Thirty miles or so from Louisville, Miles pulled off the highway and, in darkness, aided by a flashlight, opened the car's boot. It contained two heavy suitcases, both securely locked. Briefly he considered forcing one of the locks, then commonsense told him he would jeopardize himself by doing so. After that he closed the boot, copied down the Impala's licence number, and continued on.

He found the Louisville airport without difficulty and after observing the rest of his instructions, boarded a flight back and was at the Double-Seven Health Club shortly before 10am. No questions were asked about his absence.

Through the remainder of the day Miles was weary from the lack of sleep, though he managed to keep working. In the afternoon LaRocca arrived, beaming and smoking a fat cigar.

'Ya whacked off a clean job, Milesy. Nobody's pissed off. Everybody pleased.'

'That's good,' Miles said. 'When do I get paid the two hundred dollars?'

'Y' awready did. Ominsky took it. Goes towards what ya owe him.'

Miles sighed. He supposed he should have expected something of the kind, though it seemed ironic to have risked so

346

much, solely for the loan shark's benefit. He asked LaRocca, 'How did Ominsky know?'

'Ain't much he don't.'

'A minute ago you said everybody was pleased, Who's "everybody"? If I do a job like yesterday's, I like to know who I'm working for.'

'Like I told ya, there's some things it ain't smart to know or ask.'

'I suppose so.' Obviously he would learn nothing more and he forced a smile for LaRocca's benefit, though today Miles's cheerfulness was gone and depression had replaced it. The overnight trip had been a strain and, despite the horrendous chances he had taken, he realized how little he had really learned.

Some forty-eight hours later, still weary and disheartened, he communicated his misgivings to Juanita.

eight

Miles Eastin and Juanita had met on two earlier occasions during the month he had been working at the Double-Seven Health Club.

The first time – a few days after Juanita's evening ride with Nolan Wainwright and her agreement to act as intermediary – had been an awkward, uncertain encounter for them both. Although a telephone had been installed promptly in Juanita's apartment, as Wainwright promised, Miles had not known about it and came unannounced, at night, having travelled there by bus. After a cautious inspection through the partially opened apartment door, Juanita had taken off the safety chain and let him in.

'Hullo,' Estela said. The small, dark child – a miniature Juanita – looked up from a colouring book, her large, liquid eyes regarding Miles. 'You're the thin man who came before. You're fatter now.'

'I know,' Miles said. 'I've been eating magic giant food.'

Estela giggled, but Juanita was frowning. He told her apologetically, 'There was no way to warn you I was coming. But Mr Wainwright said you'd be expecting me.'

'That hypocrite!'

'You don't like him?'

'I hate him.'

'He isn't my idea of Santa Claus,' Miles said. 'But I don't hate him either. I guess he has a job to do.'

'Then let *him* do it. Not make use of others.'

'If you feel so strongly, why did you agree . . . ?'

Juanita snapped, 'Do you think I have not asked myself? *Maldito sea el día que lo conocí.* Making the promise that I did was an instant's foolishness, to be regretted.'

'There's no need to regret it. Nothing says you can't back down.' Miles's voice was gentle. 'I'll explain to Wainwright.' He made a move towards the door.

Juanita flared at him, 'And what of you? Where will you pass your messages?' She shook her head in exasperation. 'Were you insane when you agreed to such stupidity?'

'No,' Miles said. 'I saw it as a chance; in a way the only chance, but there's no reason it should involve you. When I suggested that it might, I hadn't thought it through. I'm sorry.'

'Mommy,' Estela said, 'why are you so angry?'

Juanita reached down and hugged her daughter. '*No te preocupes, mi cielo.* I am angry at life, little one. At what people do to each other.' She told Miles abruptly, 'Sit, sit!'

'You're sure?'

'Sure of what? That you should sit down? No, I am not even sure of that. *But do it!*'

He obeyed her.

'I like your temper, Juanita.' Miles smiled, and for a moment, she thought, he looked the way he used to at the bank. He went on, 'I like that and other things about you. If you want the truth, the reason I suggested this arrangement was that it would mean I'd have to see you.'

'Well, now you have.' Juanita shrugged. 'And I suppose you will again. So make your secret agent's report and I will give it to Mr Spider Wainwright, spinning webs.'

'My report is that there isn't any report. At least, not yet.' Miles told her about the Double-Seven Health Club, the way it looked and smelled, and saw her nose wrinkle in distaste. He described, too, his encounter with Jules LaRocca, then the meeting with the loan shark, Russian Ominsky, and Miles's employment as the health club book-keeper. At that point, when Miles had worked at the Double-Seven only a few days, that was all he knew. 'But I'm in,' he assured Juanita. 'That was what Mr Wainwright wanted.'

'Sometimes it is easy to get in,' she said. 'As with a lobster trap, getting out is harder.'

Estela had listened gravely. Now she asked Miles, 'Will you come again?'

'I don't know.' He glanced enquiringly at Juanita who surveyed them both, then sighed.

'Yes, *amorcito*,' she told Estela. 'Yes, he will come.'

Juanita went into the bedroom and returned with the two envelopes Nolan Wainwright had given her. She handed them to Miles. 'These are for you.'

The larger envelope contained money, the other the Keycharge credit card in the fictitious name of H. E. LYNCOLP. She explained the purpose of the card – a signal for help.

Miles pocketed the plastic credit card but replaced the money in the first envelope and gave it back to Juanita. 'You take this. If I'm seen with it, someone might become suspicious. Use it for yourself and Estela. I owe it to you.'

Juanita hesitated. Then, her voice softer than before, she said, 'I will keep it for you.'

Next day, at First Mercantile American Bank, Juanita had called Wainwright on an internal telephone and made her report. She was careful not to identify by name either herself, Miles, or the Double-Seven Health Club. Wainwright listened, thanked her, and that was all.

The second encounter between Juanita and Miles occurred a

week and a half later, on Saturday afternoon. This time Miles had telephoned in advance and when he arrived both Juanita and Estela seemed pleased to see him. They were about to go shopping and he joined them, the three browsing through an open-air market where Juanita bought Polish sausage and cabbage. She told him, 'It is for our dinner. Will you stay?'

He assured her he would, adding that he need not return to the health club until late that night, or even the following morning.

While they walked, Estela said suddenly to Miles, 'I like you.' She slipped her tiny hand into his and kept it there. Juanita, when she noticed, smiled.

Through dinner there was an easy camaraderie. Then Estela went to bed, kissing Miles good night, and when he and Juanita were alone he recited his report for Nolan Wainwright. They were seated, side by side, on the sofa bed. Turning to him when he had finished, she said, 'If you wish, you may stay here tonight.'

'Last time I did, you slept in there.' He motioned to the bedroom.

'This time I will be here. Estela sleeps soundly. We shall not be disturbed.'

He reached for Juanita and she came to him eagerly. Her lips, slightly parted, were warm, moist, and sensual, as if a foretaste of still sweeter things to come. Her tongue danced and delighted him. Holding her, he could hear her breathing quicken and felt the small, slim girl-woman body quiver with pent-up passion, responding fiercely to his own. As they drew closer and his hands began exploring, Juanita sighed deeply, savouring the waves of pleasure now, anticipating her ecstasy ahead. It had been a long time since any man had taken her. She made clear she was excited, urgent, waiting. Impatiently they opened the sofa bed.

What followed next was a disaster. Miles had wanted Juanita with his mind and – he believed – his body. But when the moment came in which a man must prove himself, his body failed to function as it should. Despairingly, he strained, concentrated, closed his eyes and wished, but nothing changed. What should have been a young man's ardent, rigid sword was flaccid, ineffectual. Juanita tried to soothe and aid him. 'Stop worrying, Miles darling, and be patient. Let me help, and it will happen.'

They tried, and tried again. In the end, it was no use. Miles lay back, ashamed and close to tears. He knew, unhappily, that behind his impotence was the awareness of his homosexuality in prison. He had believed, and hoped, it would not inhibit him with a woman, but it had. Miles concluded miserably: now he knew for sure what he had feared. He was no longer a man.

At last, weary, unhappy, unfulfilled, they slept.

In the night Miles awoke, tossed restlessly for a while, and then got up. Juanita heard him and switched on a light beside the sofa bed. She asked, 'What is it now?'

'I was thinking,' he said. 'And couldn't sleep.'

'Thinking of what?'

It was then he told her – sitting upright, his head turned partially away so as not to meet Juanita's eyes; told her the totality of his experience in prison, beginning with the gang rape; then his 'boy friend' relationship with Karl as a means of self-protection; the sharing of the big black man's cell; the homosexuality continuing, and Miles beginning to enjoy it. He spoke of his ambivalent feelings about Karl, whose kindness and gentleness Miles still remembered with . . . affection? . . . love? Even now he wasn't sure.

It was at that point Juanita stopped him. 'No more! I have heard enough. It makes me sick.'

He asked her, 'How do you think I feel?'

'*No quiero saber*. I neither know nor care.' All the horror and disgust she felt was in her voice.

As soon as it was light, he dressed and left.

Two weeks later. Again a Saturday afternoon – the best time, Miles had discovered, for him to slip away unnoticed from the health club. He was still tired from his nerve-straining trip to Louisville the night before last, and dispirited at his lack of progress.

He had worried, too, about whether he should go to Juanita again; wondered if she would want to see him. But then he decided that at least one more visit was necessary, and when he came she was matter-of-fact and businesslike, as if what had happened on the last occasion had been put behind her.

She listened to his report, then he told her of his doubts. 'I'm just not finding out anything important. Okay, so I deal with Jules LaRocca and the guy who sold me those counterfeit twenties, but both are small fry. Also, when I ask LaRocca questions – such as where the fake driver's licence came from – he clams up tight and gets suspicious. I've no more idea now than when I started of any bigger people in the rackets, or what goes on beyond the Double-Seven.'

'You cannot find out everything in a month,' Juanita said.

'Perhaps there isn't anything to be found – at least, not what Wainwright wants.'

'Perhaps not. But if so, it is not your fault. Besides, it is possible you have discovered more than you know. There is the forged money you have given me, the licence number of the car you drove . . .'

'Which was probably stolen.'

'Let Mr Sherlock Holmes Wainwright find that out.' A thought struck Juanita. 'What about your airline ticket? The one they gave you to come back?'

'I used it.'

'There is always a copy that you keep.'

'Maybe I . . .' Miles felt in his jacket pocket; he had worn the same suit when he went to Louisville. The airline envelope was there, the ticket counterfoil inside.

Juanita took both. 'Perhaps it will tell somebody something. And I will get your forty dollars back that you paid for the bad money.'

'You're taking good care of me.'

'¿ Por qué no ? It appears someone must.'

Estela, who had been visiting a friend in a nearby apartment, came in. 'Hullo,' she said, 'are you going to stay again ?'

'Not today,' he told her. 'I'll be leaving soon.'

Juanita asked sharply, 'Why do you need to ?'

'No reason. I just thought . . .'

'Then you will have dinner here. Estela will like it.'

'Oh, good,' Estela said. She asked Miles, 'Will you read me a story?'

When he said he would, she brought a book and perched herself happily on his knee.

After dinner, before Estela said good night and went to bed, he read to her again.

'You are a kind person, Miles,' Juanita said as she emerged from the bedroom, closing the door behind her. While she had been helping Estela into bed, he had risen to go, but she motioned to him, 'No, stay. There is something I wish to say.'

As before, they sat beside each other on the living-room sofa. Juanita spoke slowly, choosing her words.

'Last time, after you had gone, I regretted the harsh things I thought and said while you were here. One should not judge too much, yet that is what I did. I know that in prison you suffered. I have not been there, but perhaps can guess how bad it was, and how can anyone know – unless they themselves were there – what they might do? As to the man you spoke of, Karl, if he was kind when so much else was cruel, that is what should matter most.'

Juanita stopped, considered, then went on, 'For a woman, it is hard to understand how men could love each other in the way you said, and do to each other what you did. Yet I know there are women who love each other in that way, as well as men, and perhaps when all is said, love like that is better than none, better than to hate. So wipe out, please, the hurtful words I spoke, and go on remembering your Karl, admitting to yourself you loved him.' She raised her eyes and looked at Miles directly. 'You did love him, didn't you?'

'Yes,' he said; his voice was low. 'I loved him.'

Juanita nodded. 'Then it is better said. Perhaps now you will love other men. I do not know. I do not understand these things – only that love is better, wherever it is found.'

'Thank you, Juanita.' Miles saw that she was crying and found his own face wet with tears.

They stayed silent a long time listening to the Saturday evening hum of traffic and voices from the street outside. Then both began to talk – as friends, closer than they had ever been before. They talked on, forgetting time, and where they were; talked far into the night, about themselves, their experiences, lessons learned, their once-held dreams, their present hopes, objectives they might yet attain. They talked until drowsiness eclipsed their voices. Then, still beside each other, holding hands, they drifted into sleep.

Miles awoke first. His body was uncomfortable and cramped . . . but there was something else which filled him with excitement.

Gently he awakened Juanita, guiding her from the sofa to the rug in front of it where he placed cushions for their pillows. Tenderly and lovingly he undressed her, then himself, and after that he kissed, embraced and confidently mounted her, thrusting himself strongly forward, gloriously inward, while Juanita seized and clasped him, and cried aloud with joy.

'I love you, Miles! *Cariño mío*, I love you!'

Then he knew that, through her, he had found his manhood once again.

nine

'I'll ask you two questions,' Alex Vandervoort said. He spoke less crisply than usual; his mind was preoccupied and somewhat dazed by what he had just read. 'First, how in God's name did you get all this information? Second, how reliable is it?'

'If you don't mind,' Vernon Jax acknowledged, 'I'll answer those in reverse order.'

They were in Alex's office suite in FMA Headquarters Tower, in the late afternoon. It was quiet outside. Most of the staff from the 36th floor had already gone home.

The private investigator whom, a month ago, Alex had retained to make an independent study of Supranational Corporation – an 'outside snooping job', as they agreed – had stayed quietly seated, reading an afternoon newspaper, while Alex studied the seventy-page report, including an appendix of photocopied documents, which Jax had brought in personally.

Today, Vernon Jax was, if anything, more unimpressive in appearance than the last time. The shiny blue suit he was wearing might have been donated to the Salvation Army – and rejected. His socks drooped around his ankles, above shoes even less cared for than before. What hair remained on his balding head stuck out untidily like well-used Brillo pads. Just the same, it was equally clear that what Jax lacked in sartorial style he made up in espionage skill.

'About reliability,' he said. 'If you're asking me whether the facts I've listed could be used, in their present form, as evidence in court, the answer's no. But I'm satisfied the information's all authentic, and I haven't included anything which wasn't checked with at least two good sources, in some cases three. Another thing, my reputation for getting at the truth is my most important business asset. It's a good reputation. I intend to keep it that way.

'Now then, how do I do it? Well, people I work for usually ask me that, and I suppose you're entitled to an explanation, even though I'll be holding some things back which come under the heading of "trade secrets" and "protecting sources".

'I worked for the US Treasury Department for twenty years, most of it as an IRS investigator, and I've kept my contacts green, not only there but in a lot of other places. Not many know it, Mr Vandervoort, but a way investigators work is by trading confidential information, and in my business you never know when you'll need someone else or they'll need you. You help another man this week, sooner or later he'll come through for you. That way, too, you build up debts and credits, and the pay-offs – in tip-offs and intelligence – go both ways. So what I'm selling when you hire me is not just my financial savvy, which I like to think is pretty fair, but a web of contacts. Some of them might surprise you.'

'I've had all the surprises I need today,' Alex said. He touched the report in front of him.

'Anyway,' Jax said, 'that's how I got a lot of what's in there.

355

The rest was drudgery, patience, and knowing which rocks to look under.'

'I see.'

'There's one other thing I'd like to clear up, Mr Vandervoort, and I guess you'd call it personal pride. I've watched you look me over both times we've met, and you haven't much cared for what you've seen. Well, that's the way I prefer people to see me because a man who's nondescript and down-at-the-heel isn't as likely to be noticed or taken seriously by those he's trying to investigate. It works another way, too, because people I talk to don't think I'm important and they aren't on guard. If I looked anything like you, they would be. So that's the reason, but I'll also tell you this: the day you invite me to your daughter's wedding I'll be as well turned out as any other guest.'

'If I should ever have a daughter,' Alex said, 'I'll bear that in mind.'

When Jax had gone, he studied the shocking report again. It was, he thought, fraught with the gravest implications for First Mercantile American Bank. The mighty edifice of Supranational Corporation – SuNatCo – was crumbling and about to topple.

Lewis D'Orsey, Alex recalled, had spoken of rumours about 'big losses which haven't been reported . . . sharp accounting practices among subsidiaries . . . Big George Quartermain shopping for a Lockheed-type subsidy.' Vernon Jax had confirmed them all and discovered much, much more.

It was too late to do anything today, Alex decided. He had overnight to consider how the information should be used.

ten

Jerome Patterton's normally ruddy face suffused an even deeper red. He protested, 'Dammit! – what you're asking is ridiculous.'

'I'm not asking.' Alex Vandervoort's voice was tight with anger which had simmered since last night. 'I'm telling you – *do it!*'

'Asking, telling – what's the difference? You want me to take an arbitrary action without substantial reason.'

'I'll give you plenty of reasons later. Strong ones. Right now there isn't time.'

They were in the FMA president's suite where Alex had been waiting when Patterton arrived this morning.

'The New York stock market has already been open fifty minutes,' Alex warned. 'We've lost that much time, we're losing more. Because you're the only one who can give an order to the trust department to sell every share of Supranational we're holding.'

'I won't!' Patterton's voice rose. 'Besides, what the devil is this? Who do you think you are, storming in here, giving orders . . .'

Alex glanced over his shoulder. The office door was open. He walked to close it, then returned.

'I'll tell you who I am, Jerome. I'm the guy who warned you, and warned the board, against in-depth involvement with Su-NatCo. I fought against trust department buying of the shares, but no one – including you – would listen. Now Supranational is caving in.' Alex leaned across the desk and slammed a fist down hard. His face, eyes blazing, was close to Patterton's. 'Don't you understand? Supranational can bring this bank down with it.'

Patterton was shaken. He sat down heavily behind the desk. 'But *is* SuNatCo in real trouble? Are you *sure*?'

'If I weren't, do you think I'd be here, behaving this way? Don't you understand I'm giving you a chance to salvage something out of what will be catastrophic anyway?' Alex pointed to his wrist watch. 'It's now an *hour* since the market opening. Jerome, get on a phone and give that order!'

Muscles around the bank president's face twitched nervously. Never strong or decisive, he reacted to situations rather than created them. Strong influence often swayed him, as Alex's was doing now.

'For God's sake, Alex, for your sake, I hope you know what

you're doing.' Patterton reached for one of two telephones beside his desk, hesitated, then picked it up.

'Get me Mitchell in Trust . . . No, I'll wait . . . Mitch? This is Jerome. Listen carefully. I want you to give a sell order immediately on all the Supranational stock we hold . . . Yes, *sell*. Every share.' Patterton listened, then said impatiently, 'Yes, I know what it'll do to the market, and I know the price is down already. I saw yesterday's quote. We'll take a loss. But still sell . . . Yes, I do know it's irregular.' His eyes sought Alex's as if for reassurance. The hand holding the telephone trembled as he said, 'There's no time to hold meetings. So do it! Don't waste . . .' Patterton grimaced, listening. 'Yes, I accept responsibility.'

When he had hung up the telephone, Patterton poured and drank a glass of water. He told Alex, 'You heard what I said. The stock is already down. Our selling will depress it more. We'll be taking a big beating.'

'You're wrong,' Alex corrected him. 'Our trust clients – people who trusted *us* – will take the beating. And it would be bigger still if we'd waited. Even now we're not out of the woods. A week from now the SEC may disallow those sales.'

'Disallow? Why?'

'They may rule we had insider knowledge which we should have reported, and which would have halted trading in the stock.'

'What kind of knowledge?'

'That Supranational is about to be bankrupt.'

'Jesus!' Patterton got up from his desk and took a turn away. He muttered to himself, 'SuNatCo! Jesus Christ, SuNatCo!' Swinging back on Alex, he demanded, 'What about our loan? *Fifty million*.'

'I checked. Almost the full extent of the credit has been drawn.'

'The compensating balance?'

'Is down to less than a million.'

There was a silence in which Patterton sighed deeply. He was suddenly calm. 'You said you had strong reasons. You obviously know something. You'd better tell me what.'

'It might be simpler if you read this.' Alex laid the Jax report on the president's desk.

'I'll read it later,' Patterton said. 'Right now, *you* tell me what it is and what's in it.'

Alex explained the rumours about Supranational which Lewis D'Orsey had passed on, and Alex's decision to employ an investigator – Vernon Jax.

'What Jax has reported, in total hangs together,' Alex declared. 'Last night and this morning I've been phoning around, confirming some of his separate statements. All of them check out. The fact is, a good deal of what's been learned could have been discovered by anyone through patient digging – except that no one did it or, until now, put the pieces together. On top of that, Jax has obtained confidential information, including documents, I presume by . . .'

Patterton interrupted peevishly, 'Okay, okay. Never mind all that. Tell me what the meat is.'

'I'll give you it in five words: Supranational is out of money. For the past three years the corporation has had enormous losses and survived on prestige and credit. There's been tremendous borrowing to pay off debts; borrowing again to repay *those* debts; then borrowing still more, and so on. What they've lacked is real cash money.'

Patterton protested, 'But SuNatCo has reported excellent earnings, year after year, and never missed a dividend.'

'It now appears the past few dividends have been paid from borrowings. The rest is fancy accounting. We all know how it can be done. Plenty of the biggest, most reputable companies use the same methods.'

The bank president weighed the statement, then said gloomily, 'There used to be a time when an accountant's endorsement on a financial statement spelled integrity. Not any more.'

'In here' – Alex touched the report on the desk between them – 'are examples of what we're talking about. Among the worst is Greenapastures Land Development. That's a SuNatCo subsidiary.'

'I know, I know.'

'Then you may also know that Greenapastures has big land holdings in Texas, Arizona, Canada. Most of the land tracts are remote, maybe a generation from development. What Greenapastures has been doing is making sales to speculators, accepting small down payments with hedged agreements, and pushing payment of the full price away into the future. On two deals, final payments totalling eighty million dollars are due forty years from now – well into the twenty-first century. Those payments may never be made. Yet on Greenapastures and Supranational balance sheets, that eighty million is shown as current earnings. Those are just two deals. There are more, only smaller, utilizing the same kind of Chinese accounting. Also, what's happened in one SuNatCo subsidiary has been repeated in others.'

Alex paused, then added, 'What all of it has done, of course, is make everything look great on paper and push up – unrealistically – the market price of Supranational shares.'

'Somebody's made a fortune,' Patterton said sourly. 'Unfortunately it wasn't us. Do we have any idea of the extent of SuNatCo borrowing?'

'Yes. It seems that Jax managed to get a look at some tax records which show interest deductions. His estimate of short-term indebtedness, including subsidiaries, is a billion dollars. Of that, five hundred million appears to be bank loans. The rest is mainly ninety-day commercial paper, which they've rolled over.'

Commercial paper, as both men knew, were IOUs bearing interest but backed only by a borrower's reputation. 'Rolling over' was issuing still more IOUs to repay the earlier ones, plus interest.

'But they're close to the limit of borrowing,' Alex said. 'Or so Jax believes. One of the things I confirmed myself is that buyers of commercial paper are beginning to be wary.'

Patterton mused, 'It's the way Penn Central fell apart. Everybody believed the railroad was blue chip – the safest stock to buy and hold, along with IBM and General Motors. Suddenly, one day, Penn Central was in receivership, wiped out, done.'

'Add a few more big names since then,' Alex reminded him.

The same thought was in both their minds: after Supranational would First Mercantile American Bank be added to the list?

Patterton's ruddy face had gone pale. He appealed to Alex, 'Where do we stand ?' No pretence of leadership now. The bank president was leaning heavily on the younger man.

'A lot depends on how much longer Supranational stays afloat. If they can hang on for several months, our sales of their stock today might be ignored, and the breach of the Federal Reserve Act with the loan may not be investigated closely. If the breakup happens quickly, we're in serious trouble – with the SEC for not revealing what we know, with the Comptroller of Currency over abuse of trust, and, over the loan, with the Fed Reserve. Then, I need hardly remind you, we're facing an outright loss of fifty million dollars, and you know what that will do to this year's earnings statement, so there'll be angry shareholders howling for someone's head. On top of that there could be lawsuits against directors.'

'*Jesus !*' Patterton repeated. 'Jesus H. Christ!' He took out a handkerchief and mopped his face and egg-like dome.

Alex went on relentlessly, 'There's something else we'll have to consider – publicity. If Supranational goes under there will be investigations. But even before that the press will be on to the story and do probing of their own. Some of the financial reporters are pretty good at it. When the questioning starts, it's unlikely our bank will escape attention, and the extent of our losses will become known and publicized. That kind of news can make depositors uneasy. It could cause heavy withdrawals.'

'You mean a run on the bank! That's unthinkable.'

'No, it isn't. It's happened elsewhere – remember Franklin in New York. If you're a depositor, the only thing you care about is whether your money's safe. If you think it might not be, you take it out – fast.'

Patterton drank more water, then slumped into his chair. If possible, he looked even paler than before.

'What I suggest,' Alex said, 'is that you call the money policy committee together immediately and we concentrate, during the next few days, on attaining maximum liquidity. That way, we'll be prepared if there's a sudden drain on cash.'

Patterton nodded. 'All right.'

'Apart from that there's not much else to. do but pray.' For the first time since coming in, Alex smiled. 'Maybe we should get Roscoe working on that.'

'*Roscoe !*' Patterton said, as if suddenly reminded. '*He* studied the Supranational figures, recommended the loan, assured us everything was great.'

'Roscoe wasn't alone,' Alex pointed out. 'You and the board supported him. And plenty of others studied the figures and drew the same conclusion.'

'You didn't.'

'I was uneasy; suspicious, maybe. But I had no idea SuNatCo was in the mess it is.'

Patterton picked up the telephone he had used earlier. 'Ask Mr Heyward to come in.' A pause, then Patterton snapped, 'I don't care if *God* is with him. I need him now.' He slammed down the instrument and mopped his face again.

The office door opened softly and Heyward came in. He said, 'Good morning, Jerome,' and nodded to Alex coolly.

Patterton growled, 'Close the door.'

Looking surprised, Heyward did. 'They said it was urgent. If it isn't, I'd like to . . .'

'Tell him about Supranational, Alex,' Patterton said.

Heyward's face froze.

Quietly, matter-of-factly, Alex repeated the substance of the Jax report. His anger of last night and this morning – anger at shortsighted foolishness and greed which had brought the bank to the edge of disaster – had left him now. He felt only sorrow that so much was about to be lost, and so much effort wasted. He remembered with regret how other worthwhile projects had been cut back so that money could be channelled to the Supranational loan. At least, he thought, Ben Rosselli, by death, had been spared this moment.

Roscoe Heyward surprised him. Alex had expected antagonism, perhaps bluster. There was none. Instead, Heyward listened quietly, interjecting a question here and there, but made no other comments. Alex suspected that what he was saying amplified other information Heyward had received himself, or guessed at.

There was a silence when Alex was done.

362

Patterton, who had recovered some of his aplomb, said, 'We'll have a meeting of the money policy committee this afternoon to discuss liquidity. Meanwhile, Roscoe, get in touch with Supranational to see what, if anything, we can salvage of our loan.'

'It's a demand loan,' Heyward said. 'We can call it any time.'

'Then do it now. Do it verbally today and follow up in writing. There isn't much hope SuNatCo will have fifty million dollars cash on hand; not even a sound company keeps that kind of money in the till. But they may have something, though I'm not hopeful. Either way, we'll go through the motions.'

'I'll call Quartermain at once,' Heyward said. 'May I take that report?'

Patterton glanced at Alex.

'I've no objection,' Alex said, 'but I'd suggest we don't make copies. And the fewer people who know of this, the better.'

Heyward nodded agreement. He seemed restless, anxious to get away.

eleven

Alex Vandervoort had been partly right in supposing Roscoe Heyward to have some information of his own. Rumours had reached Heyward that Supranational was having problems and he had learned, in the past few days, that some of SuNatCo's commercial paper was meeting resistance from investors. Heyward had also attended a Supranational board meeting – his first – and sensed that information supplied to directors was less than complete and frank. But, as a 'new boy', he had withheld questions, intending to begin probing later. Subsequent to the meeting he had observed a decline in Supranational's share price and decided, only yesterday, to advise the bank's trust department to 'lighten up' its holdings as a precaution. Unfortunately – when Patterton summoned him this morning – he had still not put the intention into effect. Yet nothing Heyward had heard or guessed suggested the situation was as urgent or as bad as the report, produced by Vandervoort, portrayed it.

Yet having heard the gist of the report, Heyward did not dispute it. Grim and jolting as it was, instinct told him that – as Vandervoort put it – everything hung together.

It was the reason Heyward had stayed mostly silent while with the other two, knowing – at this stage – there was little to be said. But his mind had been active, with alarm signals flashing while he weighed ideas, eventualities, and possible escape routes for himself. There were several actions which needed to be taken quickly, though first he would complete his personal knowledge by studying the Jax report. Back in his office, Heyward hurried through some remaining business with a visitor, then settled down to read.

He soon realized that Alex Vandervoort had been accurate in summarizing the report's highlights and the documentary evidence. What Vandervoort had not mentioned were some details of Big George Quartermain's lobbying in Washington for a government-guaranteed loan to keep Supranational solvent. Appeals for such a loan had been made to members of Congress, and at the Department of Commerce and the White House. At one point, it was stated, Quartermain took Vice-President Byron Stonebridge on a trip to the Bahamas with the objective of enlisting the Vice-President's support for the loan idea. Later, Stonebridge discussed the possibility at Cabinet level, but the consensus was against it.

Heyward thought bitterly: now he knew what Big George and the Vice-President were discussing the night they had walked, deep in conversation, in the garden of the Bahamas house. And while, in the end, the Washington political machine made one of its wiser decisions in rejecting a loan to Supranational, First Mercantile American Bank – on Roscoe's urging – had bestowed one eagerly. Big George had proved himself the maestro of the soft sell. Heyward could hear him saying, even now: *If fifty million is bigger than you people can handle, let's forget the whole thing. I'll give it to Chase.* It was an ancient, con man's ploy and Heyward – the shrewd, experienced banker – had fallen for it.

One thing, at least, was to the good. In the reference to the Vice-President's journey to the Bahamas, details were sketchy and obviously little was known about the trip. Nor, to Heyward's great relief, did the report refer to Q-Investments.

Heyward wondered if Jerome Patterton had remembered the additional loan, totalling two million dollars, committed by FMA to Q-Investments, the private speculators' group headed by Big George. Probably not. Nor did Alex Vandervoort have any knowledge of it, though he was bound to find out soon. What was more important, though, was to ensure that Heyward's own acceptance of 'bonus' Q-Investments shares should never be discovered. He wished fervently he had returned them to G. G. Quartermain, as he had at first intended. Well, it was too late for that now, but what he could do was remove the share certificates from his safe deposit box and shred them. That would be safest. Fortunately, they were nominee certificates, not registered in his name.

For the moment, Heyward realized, he was ignoring the competitiveness between himself and Alex Vandervoort, concentrating instead on survival. He had no illusions about what the collapse of Supranational would do to his own standing in the bank and with the board. He would be a pariah – the focus of everybody's blame. But perhaps, even now, with quick action and some luck, it was not too late for a recovery. If the loan money was regained, he might become a hero.

The first order of business was to get in touch with Supranational. He instructed his secretary, Mrs Callaghan, to get G. G. Quartermain on the telephone.

Several minutes later she reported, 'Mr Quartermain is out of the country. His office is vague about where he is. They won't give any other information.'

It was an inauspicious start and Heyward snapped, 'Then get Inchbeck.' He had had several conversations with Stanley Inchbeck, Supranational's comptroller, since they first met in the Bahamas.

Inchbeck's voice, with its nasal New York accent, came briskly on the line. 'Roscoe, what can I do?'

'I've been trying to locate George. Your people don't seem to...'

'He's in Costa Rica.'

'I'd like to speak to him. Is there a number I can call?'

'No. He left instructions he doesn't want calls.'

'This is urgent.'

'Then tell me.'

'Very well. We're calling our loan. I'm advising you now, and formal written notice will follow in tonight's mail.'

There was a silence. Inchbeck said, 'You can't be serious.'

'I'm entirely serious.'

'But *why*?'

'I think you can guess. I also believe you wouldn't want me to go into reasons on the telephone.'

Inchbeck was silent – in itself significant. Then he protested, 'Your bank is being ridiculous and unreasonable. Only last week Big George told me he was willing to let you people increase the loan by fifty per cent.'

The audacity astounded Heyward, until he realized audacity had paid off – for Supranational – once before. It wouldn't now.

'If the loan were repaid promptly,' Heyward said, 'any information that we have here would remain confidential. I'd guarantee that.'

What it came down to, he thought, was whether Big George, Inchbeck, and any others who knew the truth about SuNatCo, were willing to buy time. If so, FMA might steal an advantage over other creditors.

'Fifty million dollars!' Inchbeck said. 'We don't keep that much cash on hand.'

'Our bank would agree to a series of payments, providing they followed each other quickly.' The real question was, of course: where would SuNatCo find fifty million in its present cash-starved condition? Heyward found himself sweating – a combination of nervousness, suspense, and hope.

'I'll talk to Big George,' Inchbeck said. 'But he isn't going to like this.'

'When you talk to him, tell him I'd like to discuss, also, our loan to Q-Investments.

Heyward wasn't sure but, as he hung up, he thought he heard Inchbeck groan.

In the silence of his office, Roscoe Heyward leaned backwards in the upholstered swivel chair, letting the tenseness drain out of him. What had occurred in the past hour had come as a stunning shock. Now, as reaction set in, he felt dejected and alone. He wished he could get away from everything for a while. If he had the choice, he knew whose company he would welcome. Avril's. But he had not heard from her since their last meeting, which was over a month ago. In the past, she had always called him. He had never called her.

On impulse, he opened a pocket address book he always carried and looked for a telephone number he remembered pencilling in. It was Avril's in New York. Using a direct outside line, he dialled it.

He heard ringing, then Avril's soft and pleasing voice. 'Hello.' His heart leaped at the sound of her.

'Hi, Rossie,' she said when he identified himself.

'It's been a while since you and I met, my dear. I've been wondering when I'd hear from you.'

He was aware of hesitation. 'But Rossie, sweetie, you aren't on the list any more.'

'What list ?'

Once more, uncertainty. 'Maybe I shouldn't have said that.'

'No, please tell me. This is between the two of us.'

'Well, it's a very confidential list which Supranational puts out, about who can be entertained at their expense.'

He had the sudden sense of a cord around him being tightened. 'Who gets the list ?'

'I don't know. I know us girls do. I'm not sure who else.'

He stopped, thinking nervously, and reasoned: what was done, was done. He supposed he should be glad he was not on any such list now, though found himself wondering – with a twinge of jealousy – who was. In any case, he hoped that back copies were carefully destroyed. Aloud he asked, 'Does that mean you can't come here to meet me any more ?'

'Not exactly. But if I did, you'd have to pay yourself, Rossie.'

'How much would that be ?' As he asked, he wondered if it were really himself speaking.

'There'd be my air fare from New York,' Avril said matter-

367

of-factly. 'Then the cost at the hotel. And for me – two hundred dollars.'

Heyward remembered wondering once before how much Supranational had paid out on his behalf. Now he knew. Holding the telephone away, he wrestled within his mind: commonsense against desire; conscience against the knowledge of what it was like to be alone with Avril. The money was also more than he could afford. But he wanted her. Very much indeed.

He moved the telephone back. 'How soon could you be here ?'

'Tuesday of next week.'

'Not before ?'

'Afraid not, sweetie.'

He knew he was being a fool; that between now and Tuesday he would be standing in line behind other men whose priorities, for whatever reason, were greater than his own. But he couldn't help himself, and told her, 'Very well. Tuesday.'

They arranged that she would go to the Columbia Hilton and phone him from there.

Heyward began savouring the sweetness to come.

He reminded himself of one other thing he had to do – destroy his Q-Investments share certificates.

From the thirty-sixth floor he used the express lift to descend to the main foyer, then walked through the tunnel to the adjoining downtown branch. It took minutes only to gain access to his personal safe deposit box and remove the four certificates, each for five hundred shares. He carried them back upstairs, where he would feed them into a shredding machine personally.

But back in his office he had second thoughts. Last time he checked, the shares were worth twenty thousand dollars. Was he being hasty ? After all, if necessary he could destroy the certificates at a moment's notice.

Changing his mind, he locked them in a desk drawer with other private papers.

twelve

The big break came when Miles Eastin was least expecting it.

Only two days earlier, frustrated and depressed, convinced that his servitude at the Double-Seven Health Club would produce no results other than enmeshing him deeper in criminality, the renewed shadow of prison loomed terrifyingly over him. Miles had communicated his depression to Juanita and, though tempered briefly by their lovemaking, the basic mood remained.

On Saturday he had met Juanita. Late Monday evening at the Double-Seven, Nate Nathanson, the club manager, sent for Miles who had been helping out as usual by carrying drinks and sandwiches to the card and dice players on the third floor.

When Miles entered the manager's office, two others were there with Nathanson. One was the loan shark, Russian Ominsky. The second was a husky, thick-featured man whom Miles had seen at the club several times before and had heard referred to as Tony Bear Marino. The 'Bear' seemed appropriate. Marino had a heavy, powerful body, loose movements and a suggestion of underlying savagery. That Tony Bear carried authority was evident, and he was deferred to by others. Each time he arrived at the Double-Seven it was in a Cadillac limousine, accompanied by a driver and a companion, both clearly bodyguards.

Nathanson seemed nervous when he spoke. 'Miles, I've been telling Mr Marino and Mr Ominsky how useful you've been here. They want you to do a service for . . .'

Ominsky said curtly to the manager, 'Wait outside.'

'Yes, sir.' Nathanson left quickly.

'There's an old guy in a car outside,' Ominsky said to Miles. 'Get help from Mr Marino's men. Carry him in, but keep him out of sight. Take him up to one of the rooms near yours and make sure he stays there. Don't leave him longer than you have to, and when you do go away, lock him in. I'm holding you responsible he doesn't leave here.'

Miles asked uneasily, 'Am I supposed to keep him here by force?'

'You won't need force.'

'The old man knows the score. He won't make trouble,' Tony Bear said. For someone of his bulk, his voice was surprisingly falsetto. 'Just remember he's important to us, so treat him okay. But don't let him have booze. He'll ask for it. Don't give him *any*. Understand?'

'I think so,' Miles said. 'Do you mean he's unconscious now?'

'He's dead drunk,' Ominsky answered. 'He's been on a bender for a week. Your job is to take care of him and dry him out. While he's here—for three, four days—your other work can wait.' He added, 'Do it right, you get another credit.'

'I'll do my best,' Miles told him. 'Does the old man have a name? I'll have to call him something.'

The other two glanced at each other. Ominsky said, 'Danny. That's all you need to know.'

A few minutes later, outside the Double-Seven, Tony Bear Marino's driver-bodyguard spat in disgust on the sidewalk and complained, 'For Chrissakes! The old fart stinks like a shithouse.'

He, the second bodyguard, and Miles Eastin were looking at an inert figure on the rear seat of a Dodge sedan, parked at the kerb. The car's nearside rear door was open.

'I'll try to clean him up,' Miles said. His own face wrinkled at the overpowering stench of vomit. 'But we'll need to get him inside first.'

The second bodyguard urged, 'Goddamn! Let's get it over with.'

Together they reached in and lifted. In the poorly lighted street, all that could be distinguished of their burden was a tangle of grey hair, pasty hollow cheeks stubbled with beard, closed eyes and an open, slack mouth revealing toothless gums. The clothes the unconscious man was wearing were stained and torn.

'You reckon he's dead?' the second bodyguard asked as they lifted the figure from the car.

Precisely at that moment, probably induced by movement, a stream of vomit emerged from the open mouth and cascaded over Miles.

The driver-bodyguard, who had been untouched, chuckled. 'He ain't dead. Not yet.' Then, as Miles retched, 'Better you 'n me, kid.'

They carried the recumbent figure into the club, then, using a back staircase, up to the fourth floor. Miles had brought a room key and unlocked a door. It was to a cubicle like his own in which the sole furnishings were a single bed, a chest of drawers, two chairs, a washbasin and some shelving. Panelling around the cubicle stopped a foot short of the ceiling, leaving the top open. Miles glanced inside, then told the other two, 'Hold it.' While they waited he ran downstairs and got a rubber sheet from the gymnasium. Returning, he spread it on the bed. They dumped the old man on it.

'He's all yours, Milesy,' the driver-bodyguard said. 'Let's get outta here before I puke.'

Stifling his distaste, Miles undressed the old man, then, while he was still on the rubber sheet, still comatose, washed and sponged him. When that was done, and with some lifting and shoving, Miles removed the rubber sheet and got the now cleaner, less evil-smelling figure into bed. During the process the old man moaned, and once his stomach heaved, though this time producing only a trickle of spittle which Miles wiped away. When Miles had covered him with a sheet and blanket the old man seemed to rest more easily.

Earlier, as he removed the clothing, Miles had allowed it to fall to the cubicle floor. Now he gathered it up and began putting it in two plastic bags for cleaning and laundering tomorrow. While doing so, he emptied all the pockets. One coat pocket yielded a set of false teeth. Others held miscellaneous items – a comb, a pair of thick-lensed glasses, a gold pen and pencil set, several keys on a ring and – in an inside pocket – three Key-charge credit cards and a wallet tightly packed with money.

Miles took the false teeth, rinsed them, and placed them beside the bed in a glass of water. The spectacles he also put close by. Then he examined the bank credit cards and wallet.

The credit cards were made out to Fred W. Riordan, R. K. Bennett, Alfred Shaw. Each card was signed on the back but, despite the name differences, the handwriting in each case was the same. Miles turned the cards over again, checking the commencement and expiration dates which showed that all three were current. As far as he could tell, they were genuine.

He turned his attention to the wallet. Under a plastic window was a state driver's licence. The plastic was yellowed and hard to see through, so Miles took the licence out, discovered that beneath it was a second licence, beneath that a third. The names on the licences corresponded to those on the credit cards, but the head and shoulders photographs on all three licences were identical. He peered closer. Allowing for differences when the photograph was taken, it was undoubtedly of the old man on the bed.

Miles removed the money from the wallet to count it. He would ask Nate Nathanson to put the credit cards and wallet in the club safe, but should know how much he was handing over. The sum was unexpectedly large – five hundred and twelve dollars, about half in new twenty-dollar notes. The twenties stopped him. Miles looked at several of them carefully, feeling the texture of the paper with his fingertips. Then he glanced at the man on the bed who appeared to be sleeping deeply. Quietly, Miles left the room and crossed the fourth-floor corridor to his own. He returned moments later with a pocket magnifier through which he viewed the twenty-dollar notes again. His intuition was right. They *were* counterfeit, though of the same high quality as those he had bought, here in the Double-Seven, a week ago.

He reasoned: the money, or rather half of it, was counterfeit. So, obviously, were the three drivers' licences and it seemed probable that they were from the same source as Miles's own fake licence, given him last week by Jules LaRocca. Therefore, wasn't it likely that the credit cards were also counterfeit? Perhaps, after all, he was close to the source of the false Keycharge cards which Nolan Wainwright wanted to locate so badly. Miles's excitement rose, along with a nervousness which set his heart pounding.

He needed a record of the new information. On a paper towel he copied down details from the credit cards and drivers'

372

licences, occasionally checking to be sure the figure in the bed was not stirring.

Soon after, Miles turned out the light, locked the door from outside and took the wallet and credit cards downstairs.

He slept fitfully that night, with his door ajar, aware of his responsibility for the inmate of the cubicle across the hall. Miles spent time, too, speculating on the role and identity of the old man whom he began to think of as Danny. What was Danny's relationship to Ominsky and Tony Bear Marino? Why had they brought him here? Tony Bear had declared: *he's important to us.* Why?

Miles awoke with daylight and checked his watch: 6.45. He got up, washed quickly, shaved and dressed. There were no sounds from across the corridor. He walked over, inserted the key quietly, and looked in. Danny had changed position in the night but was still asleep, snoring gently. Miles gathered the plastic bags of clothing, relocked the door, and went downstairs.

He was back twenty minutes later with a breakfast tray of strong coffee, toast, and scrambled eggs.

'Danny!' Miles shook the old man's shoulder. 'Danny, wake up!'

There was no response. Miles tried again. At length two eyes opened warily, inspected him, then hastily closed tight. 'Go 'way,' the old man mumbled. 'Go 'way. I ain't ready for hell yet.'

'I'm not the devil,' Miles said. 'I'm a friend. Tony Bear and Russian Ominsky told me to take care of you.'

Rheumy eyes reopened. 'Them sons-o'-Sodom found me, eh? Figures, I guess. They usually do.' The old man's face creased in pain. 'Oh, Jesus! My suffering head!'

'I brought some coffee. Let's see if it will help.' Miles put an arm around Danny's shoulders, assisting him to sit upright, then carried the coffee over. The old man sipped and grimaced.

He seemed suddenly alert. 'Listen, son. What'll set me straight is a hair of the dog. Now you take some money ...' He looked around him.

'Your money's okay,' Miles said. 'It's in the club safe. I took it down last night.'

373

'This the Double-Seven?'

'Yes.'

'Brought me here once before. Well, now you know I can pay, son, just you nip down to the bar . . .'

Miles said firmly, 'There won't be any nipping. For either of us.'

'I'll make it worthwhile.' The old eyes gleamed with cunning. 'Say forty dollars for a fifth. Howzat?'

'Sorry, Danny. I had orders.' Miles weighed what he would say next, then took the plunge. 'Besides, if I used those twenties of yours, I could get arrested.'

It was as if he had fired a gun. Danny shot upright, alarm and suspicion on his face. 'Who said you could . . .' He stopped with a moan and grimace, putting a hand to his head in pain.

'Someone had to count the money. So I did it.'

The old man said weakly, 'Those are good twenties.'

'Sure are,' Miles agreed. 'Some of the best I've seen. Almost as good as the US Bureau of Engraving.'

Danny raised his eyes. Interest competed with suspicion. 'How come you know so much?'

'Before I went to prison I worked for a bank.'

A silence. Then the old man asked, 'What were you in the can for?'

'Embezzlement. I'm on parole now.'

Danny visibly relaxed. 'I guess you're okay. Or you wouldn't be working for Tony Bear and the Russian.'

'That's right,' Miles said. 'I'm okay. The next thing is to get you the same way. Right now we're going to the steam room.'

'It ain't steam I need. It's a short snort. Just one, son,' Danny pleaded. 'I swear that's all. You wouldn't deny an old man that small favour.'

'We'll sweat some out you already drank. Then you can lick your fingers.'

The old man groaned, 'Heartless! Heartless!'

In a way it was like taking care of a child. Overcoming token protest, Miles wrapped Danny in a robe and shepherded him downstairs, then escorted him naked through successive steam rooms, towelled him, and finally eased him on to a masseur's table where Miles himself gave a creditable pummelling and rub-down. This early, the gym and steam rooms were deserted and few of the club staff had arrived. No one else was in sight when Miles escorted the old man back upstairs.

Miles remade the bed with clean sheets, and Danny, by now quietened and obedient, climbed in. Almost at once he was asleep, though unlike last night, he appeared tranquil, even angelic. Strangely, without really knowing him, Miles already liked the old man. Carefully, while he slept, Miles put a towel under his head and shaved him.

In late morning, while reading in his room across the hall, Miles drifted off to sleep.

'Hey, Milesy! Baby, stir ass!' The rasping voice was Jules LaRocca's.

Startled, Miles jerked awake to see the familiar pot-bellied figure standing in the doorway. Miles's hand reached out, seeking the key of the cubicle across the hall. Reassuringly, it was where he had left it.

'Gotsum threads for the old lush,' LaRocca said. He was carrying a fibreboard suitcase. 'Ominsky said ta deliver 'em ta ya.'

LaRocca, the ubiquitous messenger.

'Okay.' Miles stretched, and went to a sink where he splashed cold water on his face. Then, followed by LaRocca, he opened the door across the hall. As the two came in, Danny eased up gingerly in bed. Though still drawn and pale, he appeared better than at any time since his arrival. He had put his teeth in and had his glasses on.

'Ya useless old bum!' LaRocca said. 'Ya always givin' everybody a lotta trouble.'

Danny sat up straighter, regarding his accuser with distaste. 'I'm far from useless. As you and others know. As for the sauce, every man has his little weakness.' He motioned to the suitcase. 'If you brought my clothes, do what you were sent for and hang them up.'

Unperturbed, LaRocca grinned. 'Sounds like ya bouncin' back, ya old fart. Guess Milesy done a job.'

'Jules,' Miles said, 'Will you stay here while I go down and get a sunlamp? I think it'll do Danny good.'

'Sure.'

'I'd like to speak to you first.' Miles motioned with his head and LaRocca followed him outside.

Keeping his voice low, Miles asked, 'Jules, what's this all about? Who is he?'

'Just an old geezer. Once in a while he slips away, goes on a bender. Then somebody hasta find him, dry the old barfly out.'

'Why? And where does he slip away from?'

LaRocca stopped, his eyes suspicious, as they had been a week ago. 'Ya askin' questions again, kid. Whadid Tony Bear and Ominsky tell ya?'

'Nothing, except the old man's name is Danny.'

'If 'n they wanna tell ya more, they'll tell ya. Not me.'

When LaRocca had gone, Miles set up a sunlamp in the cubicle and sat Danny under it for half an hour. Through the remainder of the day, the old man lay quietly awake or dozed. In the early evening Miles brought dinner from downstairs, most of which Danny ate – his first full meal since arrival twenty-four hours ago.

Next morning – Wednesday – Miles repeated the steam room and sunlamp treatments and later the two of them played chess. The old man had a quick, astute mind and they were evenly matched. By now, Danny was friendly and relaxed, making clear that he liked Miles's company and attention.

During the second afternoon the old man wanted to talk. 'Yesterday,' he said, 'that creep LaRocca said you know a lot about money.'

'He tells everybody that.' Miles explained about his hobby and the interest it aroused in prison.

Danny asked more questions, then announced, 'If you don't mind, I'd like my own money now.'

'I'll get it for you. But I'll have to lock you in again.'

'If you're worrying about the booze, forget it. I'm over it for this time. A break like this does the trick. Could be months before I'll take a drink again.'

'Glad to hear that.' Miles locked the door, just the same.

When he had his money, Danny spread it on the bed, then divided it into two piles. The new twenties were in one, the remaining, mostly soiled, assorted notes in another. From the second grouping, Danny selected three ten-dollar notes and handed them to Miles. 'That's for thinking of some little things, son – like taking care of my teeth, the shave, the sunlamp. I appreciate what you did.'

'Listen, you don't have to.'

'Take it. And by the way, it's real stuff. Now tell me something.'

'If I can, I will.'

'How did you spot that those twenties were homegrown?'

'I didn't to begin with. But if you use a magnifier, some of the lines on Andrew Jackson's portrait show up blurred.'

Danny nodded sagely. 'That's the difference between a steel engraving, which the government uses, and a photo-offset plate. Though a top offset man can come awful close.'

'In this case he did,' Miles said. 'Other parts of the notes are close to perfect.'

There was a faint smile on the old man's face. 'How about the paper?'

'It fooled me. Usually you can tell a bad note with your fingers. But not these.'

Danny said softly, 'Twenty-four-pound coupon bond. Hundred per cent cotton fibre. People think you can't get the right paper. Isn't true. Not if you shop around.'

'If you're all that interested,' Miles said, 'I have some books about money across the hall. There's one I'm thinking of, published by the US Secret Service.'

'You mean *Know Your Money*?' As Miles looked surprised, the old man chuckled. 'That's the forger's handbook. Says what to look for to detect a bad note. Lists all the mistakes that counterfeiters make. Even shows pictures!'

'Yes,' Miles said. 'I know.'

Danny continued chortling. 'And the government gives it away! You can write to Washington – they'll mail it to you. There was a hot-shot counterfeiter named Mike Landress who wrote a book. In it he said *Know Your Money* is something no counterfeiter should be without.'

'Landress got caught,' Miles pointed out.

'That was because he worked with fools. They had no organization.'

'You seem to know a lot about it.'

'A little.' Danny stopped, picked up one of the good notes, one of the counterfeits, and compared them. What he saw pleased him; he grinned. 'Did you know, son, that US money is the world's easiest to copy and to print? Fact is, it was designed so that engravers in the last century couldn't reproduce it with the tools they had. But since those days we've had multilith machines and high resolution photo-offset, so that nowadays, with good equipment, patience, and some wastage, a skilled man can do a job that only experts can detect.'

'I'd heard some of that,' Miles said. 'But how much of it goes on?'

'Let me tell you.' Danny seemed to be enjoying himself, obviously launched on a favourite theme. 'No one really knows how much queer gets printed every year and goes undetected, but it's a *bundle*. The government says thirty million dollars, with a tenth of that getting into circulation. But those are government figures, and the only thing you can be sure of with *any* government figure is that it's set high or low, depending on what those in government want to prove. In this case they'd want it low. My guess is, every year, seventy million, maybe closer to a billion.'

'I suppose it's possible,' Miles said. He was remembering how much counterfeit money had been detected at the bank and how much more must have escaped attention altogether.

'Know the *hardest* kind of money to reproduce?'

'No, I don't.'

'An American Express traveller's cheque. Know why?'

Miles shook his head.

'It's printed in cyan-blue, which is next to impossible to photograph for an offset printing plate. Nobody with any knowledge would waste time trying, so an Amex cheque is safer than American money.'

'There are rumours,' Miles said, 'that there's going to be new American money soon with colours for different denominations – the way Canada has.'

378

''Tain't just rumour,' Danny said. 'Fact. Lots of the coloured money's already printed and it's stored by the Treasury. Be harder to copy than anything made yet.' He smiled mischievously. 'But the old stuff'll be around a bit. Maybe as long as I am.'

Miles sat silent, digesting all that he had heard. At length he said, 'You've asked me questions, Danny, and I answered them. Now I've one for you.'

'Not saying I'll answer, son. But you can try.'

'Who and what are you?'

The old man pondered, a thumb stroking his chin as he appraised Miles. Some of his thoughts were mirrored on his face: a compulsion to frankness struggled against caution; pride mingled with discretion. Abruptly Danny made up his mind. 'I'm seventy-three years old,' he said, 'and I'm a master craftsman. Been a printer all my life. I'm still the best there is. Besides being a craft, printing's an art.' He pointed to the twenty-dollar notes still spread out on the bed. 'Those are my work. I made the photographic plate. I printed them.'

Miles asked, 'And the drivers' licences and credit cards?'

'Compared with printing money,' Danny said, 'making those is as easy as pissing in a barrel. But, yep – I did 'em all.'

thirteen

In a fever of impatience now, Miles waited for a chance to communicate what he had learned to Nolan Wainwright, via Juanita. Frustratingly, though, it was proving impossible to leave the Double-Seven and the risk of conveying such vital intelligence over the health club's telephone seemed too great.

On Thursday morning – the day after Danny's frank revelations – the old man showed every sign of having made a full recovery from his alcoholic orgy. He was clearly enjoying Miles's company and their chess games continued. So did their conversations, though Danny was more on guard than he had been the day before.

Whether Danny could hasten his own departure, if he chose to, was unclear. Even if he could, he showed no inclination and seemed content – at least for the time being – with his confinement in the fourth-floor cubicle.

During their later talks, both on Wednesday and Thursday, Miles had tried to gain more knowledge of Danny's counterfeiting activities and even hinted at the crucial question of a headquarters location. But Danny adroitly avoided any more discussion on the subject and Miles's instinct told him that the old man regretted some of his earlier openness. Remembering Wainwright's advice – '*don't hurry, be patient*' – Miles decided not to push his luck.

Despite his elation, another thought depressed him. Everything he had discovered would ensure the arrest and imprisonment of Danny. Miles continued to like the old man and was sorry for what must surely follow. Yet, he reminded himself, it was also the route to his own sole chance of rehabilitation.

Ominsky, the loan shark, and Tony Bear Marino were both involved with Danny, though in precisely what way was still not clear. Miles had no concern for Russian Ominsky or Tony Bear, though fear touched him icily at the thought of their learning – as he supposed they must eventually – of his own traitorous role.

Late on Thursday afternoon Jules LaRocca appeared once more. 'Gotta message from Tony. He's sending wheels for ya tomorra morning.'

Danny nodded, but it was Miles who asked, 'Wheels to take him where ?'

Both Danny and LaRocca looked at him sharply without answering, and Miles wished he hadn't asked.

That night, deciding to take an acceptable risk, Miles telephoned Juanita. He waited until after locking Danny in his cubicle shortly before midnight, then walked downstairs to use a public phone on the club's main floor. Miles put in a dime and dialled Juanita's number. On the first ring her voice answered softly, 'Hello.'

The phone was a wall type, in the open near the bar, and Miles whispered so he would not be overheard. 'You know who this is. But don't use names.'

'Yes,' Juanita said.

'Tell our mutual friend I've discovered something important here. Really important. It's most of what he wanted to know. I can't say more, but I'll come to you tomorrow night.'

'All right.'

Miles hung up. Simultaneously, a hidden tape recorder in the club basement, which had switched on automatically when the phone receiver was lifted, just as automatically switched off.

fourteen

Some verses from *Genesis*, like subliminal advertising, flashed at intervals through Roscoe Heyward's mind: *Of every tree of the garden thou mayest freely eat: But of the tree of the knowledge of good and evil, thou shalt not eat of it; for in the day that thou eatest thereof thou shalt surely die.*

In recent days, Heyward had worried at the question: had his illicit sexual affair with Avril, which began that memorable moonlit night in the Bahamas, become his own tree of evil from which he would harvest the bitterest of fruit? And was all that was happening adversely now – the sudden, alarming weakness of Supranational, which could thwart his own ambition at the bank – intended as a personal punishment by God?

Conversely: if he severed all ties with Avril decisively and at once, and expunged her from his thoughts, would God forgive him? Would He, in acknowledgement, restore strength to Supranational and thereby revive the fortunes of His servant, Roscoe? Remembering *Nehemiah . . . Thou art a God ready to pardon, gracious and merciful, slow to anger, and of great kindness . . .* Heyward believed He might.

The trouble was, there was no way to be sure.

Also, weighing against severance from Avril was the fact that she was due in the city on Tuesday, as they had arranged last week. Amid his current mélange of problems, Heyward longed for her.

Through Monday and early Tuesday morning in his office, he vacillated, knowing he could telephone New York and stop her. But at mid-morning Tuesday, aware of flight schedules from New York, he realized it was too late and he was relieved that no decision could be taken.

Avril phoned in late afternoon, using the unlisted line which rang directly on his desk. 'Hi, Rossie! I'm at the hotel. Suite 432. The champagne's on ice – but I'm hot for you.'

He wished he had suggested a room instead of a suite, since he would be paying. For the same reason, champagne seemed needlessly extravagant and he wondered if it would be ungracious to suggest sending it back. He supposed it would.

'I'll be with you shortly, my dear,' he said.

He managed a small economy by having a bank car and chauffeur take him to the Columbia Hilton. Heyward told the man. 'Don't wait.'

As he entered Suite 432, her arms went around him immediately and those full lips hungrily ate at his own. He held her tightly, his body reacting at once with the excitement he had come to know and crave. Through the cloth of his trousers he could feel Avril's long slim thighs and legs, moving against him, teasing, shifting, promising, until all of him seemed concentrated in a few square inches of physique. Then after several moments, Avril released herself, touched his cheek, and moved away.

'Rossie, why don't we get our business arrangements out of the way? Then we can relax, not worry any more.'

Her sudden practicality jolted him. He wondered: was this the way it always happened – the money first, before fulfilment? Yet he supposed it made sense. If left until afterwards, a client – his urgency gone and appetite sated – might be disinclined to pay.

'All right,' he said. He had put two hundred dollars in an

envelope; he gave it to Avril. She took the money out and began counting it, and he asked her, 'Don't you trust me?'

'Let me ask *you* something,' Avril said. 'Suppose I took money to your bank and paid it in, wouldn't someone count it?'

'They certainly would.'

'Well, Rossie, people have as much right as banks to look out for themselves.' She finished counting and said pointedly, 'This is the two hundred for me. As well as that, there's my air fare plus taxis, which comes to a hundred and twenty; the rate on the suite is eight-five; and the champagne and tip were twenty-five. Why don't we say another two hundred and fifty? That should cover everything.'

Staggered by the total, he protested, 'That's a lot of money.'

'I'm a lot of woman. It's no more than Supranational spent when they were paying, and you didn't seem to mind then. Besides, if you want the best, the price comes high.'

Her voice had a direct, no-nonsense quality and he knew he was meeting another Avril, shrewder and harder than the yielding, eager-to-please creature of a moment before. Reluctantly, Heyward took two hundred and fifty dollars from his wallet and handed it over.

Avril placed the full amount in an interior compartment of her purse. 'There! That's business finished. Now we can attend to loving.'

She turned to him and kissed him ardently, at the same time moving her long, deft fingers lightly through his hair. His hunger for her, which had briefly flagged, began to revive.

'Rossie, sweetie,' Avril murmured, 'when you came in, you looked tired and worried.'

'I've had a few problems lately at the bank.'

'Then we'll get you loosened. You'll have champagne first, then you can have me.' Dexterously she opened the bottle, which was in an ice bucket, and filled two glasses. They sipped together, this time Heyward not bothering to mention his teetotalism. Soon, Avril began to undress him, and herself.

. When they were in bed she whispered to him constantly, endearments, encouragement . . . 'Oh, Rossie! You're so big and strong!' . . . 'What a man you are!' . . . 'Go slow, my dearest;

383

slow' ... 'You've brought us to Paradise' ... 'If only this could last for ever!'

Her ability was not only to arouse him physically, but to make him feel more a man than ever before. Never, in all his desultory couplings with Beatrice, had he dreamed of this all-encompassing sensation, a glorious progression towards fulfilment so complete in every way.

'Almost there, Rossie' ... 'Whenever you tell me' ... 'Yes, darling! *Oh, please, yes!*'

Perhaps some of Avril's response was acting. He suspected that it might be, but it no longer mattered. What did, was the deep, rich, joyous sensuality he had discovered, through her, in himself.

The crescendo passed. It would remain, Roscoe Heyward thought, as one more exquisite memory. Now they lay, sweetly languorous, while outside the hotel the dusk of early evening turned to darkness and the city's lights winked on. Avril stirred first. She padded from the bedroom to the suite living-room, returning with filled glasses of champagne which they sipped while they sat in bed and talked.

After a while Avril said, 'Rossie, I want to ask your advice.'

'Concerning what?' What girlish confidence was he about to share?

'Should I sell my Supranational stock?'

Startled, he asked, 'Do you have much?'

'Five hundred shares. I know that isn't a lot to you. But it is to me – about a third of my savings.'

He swiftly calculated that Avril's 'savings' were approximately seven times greater than his own.

'What have you heard about SuNatCo? What makes you ask?'

'For one thing, they've cut back a lot on entertaining, and I've been told they're short of money, and they aren't paying bills. Some of the other girls were advised to sell their shares, though I haven't sold mine because they're trading at a lot less than when I bought.'

'Have you asked Quartermain?'

'None of us have seen him lately. Moonbeam ... You remember Moonbeam?'

384

'Yes.' Heyward was reminded that Big George offered to send the exquisite Japanese girl to his room. He wondered how it would have been.

'Moonbeam says Georgie has gone to Costa Rica and may stay there. And she says he sold a lot of his own SuNatCo shares before he went.'

Why hadn't he sought out Avril as a source of information weeks ago?

'If I were you,' he said, 'I'd sell those shares of yours tomorrow. Even at a loss.'

She sighed. 'It's hard enough to earn money. It's harder still to keep it.'

'My dear, you have just enunciated a fundamental financial truth.'

There was a silence, then Avril said, 'I'll remember you as a nice man, Rossie.'

'Thank you. I shall think of you in a special way too.'

She reached out to him. 'Try again?'

He closed his eyes in pleasure while she caressed him. She was, as always, expert. He thought: both of them accepted that this was the last time they would meet. One reason was practical: he couldn't afford Avril any more. Beyond that was a sense of events stirring, of changes imminent, of a crisis coming to a head. Who knew what would happen after?

Just before they made love, he remembered his earlier concern about the wrath of God. Well, perhaps God – the father of Christ who acknowledged human frailty, who walked and talked with sinners and died with thieves – would understand. Understand and forgive the truth – that in Roscoe Heyward's life a few sweet moments of his greatest happiness had been in the company of a whore.

On leaving the hotel, Heyward bought an evening paper. A two-column heading, half-way down the front page, attracted his attention.

SUPRANATIONAL CORP DISQUIET
HOW SOLVENT IS GLOBAL GIANT?

fifteen

No one ever knew what specific event, if any, provoked the final collapse of Supranational. Perhaps it was one incident. Or it could have been the accumulated weight of many, causing gradual shifts in balance, like a growing strain on underpinning, until suddenly the roof falls in.

As with any financial débâcle involving a big public company, isolated signs of weakness had been evident for weeks and months beforehand. But only the most prescient observers, such as Lewis D'Orsey, perceived them as a pattern and communicated warnings to a favoured few.

Insiders, of course – including Big George Quartermain who, it was later learned, sold most of his shares through a nominee at SuNatCo's all-time high – had more warning than anyone and bailed out early. Others, tipped off by confidants, or friends returning favour for favour, had similar information and quietly did the same.

Next in line were those like Alex Vandervoort – acting for First Mercantile American Bank – who obtained exclusive information and swiftly unloaded all SuNatCo stock they had, hoping that in any later confusion their action would not be probed. Other institutions – banks, investment houses, mutual funds – seeing the stock price slide and knowing how the insider system worked, soon sized up the situation and followed suit.

There were federal laws against insider stock trading – on paper. In practice, such laws were broken daily and were largely unenforceable. Occasionally in a flagrant case, or as a whitewash job, an accusation might be levelled with a petty penalty. But even that was rare.

Individual investors – the great, hoping, trusting, naïve, beaten, suckered public – were, as usual, the last to know that anything was wrong.

The first public intimation of SuNatCo's difficulties was in an AP newswire story, printed in afternoon newspapers – the same news story which Roscoe Heyward saw on leaving the

Columbia Hilton. By the following morning a few more details had been garnered by the press and amplified reports appeared in morning papers, including *The Wall Street Journal*. Even so, details were sketchy and many people had trouble believing that anything so reassuringly sizeable as Supranational Corporation could be in serious trouble.

Their confidence was soon assailed.

At 10am, at the New York Stock Exchange, Supranational shares failed to open for trading with the rest of the market. The reason given was 'an order imbalance'. What this meant was that the trading specialist for SuNatCo was so swamped with 'Sell' orders that an orderly market in the shares could not be maintained.

Trading in SuNatCo did reopen at 11am when a big 'buy' order of 52,000 shares crossed the tape. But by then the stock, which had traded at 48½ a month before, was down to 19. By the afternoon closing bell it was at 10.

The New York Stock Exchange would probably have halted trading again the following day, except that overnight the decision was taken from its hands. The Securities and Exchange Commission announced that it was investigating the affairs of Supranational and, until its enquiry was completed, all trading in SuNatCo shares would be suspended.

There ensued an anxious fifteen days for the remaining Su-NatCo shareholders and creditors, whose combined investments and loans exceeded five billion dollars. Among those waiting – shaken, nervous, and nail-biting – were officers and directors of First Mercantile American Bank.

Supranational did not, as Alex Vandervoort and Jerome Patterton hoped it might, 'hang on for several months'. Therefore the possibility existed that late transactions in SuNatCo shares – including the big block sale by FMA's trust department – might be revoked. This could come about in one of two ways – either by order of the SEC following a complaint, or by purchasers of the shares bringing suit, claiming that FMA knew the true condition of Supranational, but failed to disclose it when the shares were sold. If that happened, it would represent an even greater loss to trust clients than they already faced, with the bank almost certainly liable for breach of trust.

There was one other possibility which had to be faced – and it was even more likely. First Mercantile American's fifty million dollar loan to SuNatCo would become a 'write-off', a total loss. If so, for the first time in FMA history the bank would suffer a substantial operating loss for the year. It raised the probability that FMA's own next dividend to shareholders would have to be omitted. That, too, would be a first.

Depression and uncertainty permeated the higher councils of the bank.

Vandervoort had predicted that when the Supranational story broke, the press would start investigative reporting and First Mercantile American would be involved. In this, too, he was right.

News reporters, who in recent years had been motivated by the example of the *Washington Post*'s Watergate heroes, Bernstein and Woodward, bored in hard. Their efforts were successful. Within several days, newspeople had developed sources inside and outside Supranational, and exposés of Quartermain's sleight-of-hand began emerging, as did the conglomerate's shady 'Chinese accounting'. So did the horrendously high figure of SuNatCo's indebtedness. So did other financial revelations, including FMA's fifty-million-dollar loan.

When the Dow Jones news service tapped out the first reference linking FMA with Supranational, the bank's public relations chief, Dick French, demanded and was granted a hastily summoned top-level conference. Present were Jerome Patterton, Roscoe Heyward, Alex Vandervoort, and the burly figure of French himself, the usual unlighted cigar in a corner of his mouth.

They were a serious group – Patterton glowering and gloomy, as he had been for days; Heyward seeming fatigued, distracted, and betraying nervous tension; Alex with a mounting inner anger at being involved in a disaster he had predicted, and which need never have happened.

'Within an hour, maybe less,' the PR vice-president began, 'I'm going to be hounded for details about our dealings with

SuNatCo. I want to know our official attitude and what answers I'm to give.'

Patterton asked, 'Are we obliged to give any ?'

'No,' French said. 'But then no one's obliged to commit hara-kiri either.'

'Why not admit Supranational's indebtedness to us,' Roscoe Heyward suggested, 'and leave it at that ?'

'Because we won't be dealing with simpletons, that's why. Some of the questioners will be experienced financial reporters who understand banking law. So their second query will be: how come your bank committed so much of its depositors' money to a single debtor ?'

Heyward snapped, 'It was not to a single debtor. The loan was spread between Supranational and five subsidiaries.'

'When I say it,' French said, 'I'll try to make like I believe it.' He removed the cigar from his mouth, laid it down, and drew a note pad towards him. 'Okay, give me details. It'll all come out anyway, but we'll look a lot worse if we make this painful, like a tooth extraction.'

'Before we go on,' Heyward said, 'I should remind you we're not the only bank to whom Supranational owes money. There's First National City, Bank of America, and Chase Manhattan.'

'But they all headed consortiums,' Alex pointed out. 'That way, any loss is shared with other banks. So far as we know, our bank has the greatest individual exposure.' There seemed no point in adding that he had warned all concerned, including the board of directors, that such a concentration of risk was dangerous to FMA and possibly illegal. But his thoughts continued to be bitter.

They hammered out a statement admitting First Mercantile American's deep financial involvement with Supranational and conceding some anxiety. The statement then expressed hope that the ailing conglomerate could be turned around, perhaps with new management which FMA would press for, and with losses minimized. It was a wan hope and everybody knew it.

Dick French was given some leeway to amplify the statement if he needed to, and it was agreed he would remain sole spokesman for the bank.

French warned, 'The press will try to contact all of you individually. If you want our story to stay consistent, refer every caller to me, and caution your staffs to do the same.'

That same day, Alex Vandervoort reviewed emergency plans he had set up within the bank, to be activated in certain circumstances.

'There's something positively ghoulish,' Edwina D'Orsey declared, 'about the attention that gets focused on a bank in difficulties.'

She had been leafing through newspapers spread around the conference area of Alex Vandervoort's office in FMA Headquarters Tower. It was a Thursday, the day after the press statement by Dick French.

The local *Times-Register* bannered its page one story:

LOCAL BANK FACES HUGE LOSS
IN WAKE OF SUNATCO DEBACLE

With more restraint, *The New York Times* informed its readers:

FMA BANK DECLARED SOUND
DESPITE SOUR LOAN PROBLEMS

The story had been carried, too, on last night's and this morning's TV network news shows.

Included in all reports was a hasty assurance by the Federal Reserve that First Mercantile American Bank was solvent and depositors need have no cause for alarm. Just the same, FMA was now on the Fed's 'problem list' and this morning a team of Federal Reserve examiners had quietly moved in – clearly the first of several such incursions from regulatory agencies.

Tom Straughan, the bank's economist, answered Edwina's observation. 'It isn't ghoulishness, really, that excites attention when a bank's in trouble. Mostly, I think, it's fear. Fear among those with accounts that the bank might be forced out of business and they'd lose their money. Also a wider fear that if one bank fails, others could catch the same disease and the entire system fall apart.'

'What *I* fear,' Edwina said, 'is the effect of this publicity.'

390

'I'm equally uneasy,' Alex Vandervoort agreed. 'It's why we'll continue to watch closely to see what effect it has.'

Alex had called a mid-day strategy meeting. Among those summoned were heads of departments responsible for branch bank administration, since everyone was aware that any lack of public confidence in FMA would be felt in branches first. Earlier, Tom Straughan had reported that branch withdrawals late yesterday and this morning were higher than usual, and deposits lower, though it was too early yet to be sure of a definable trend. Reassuringly, there had been no sign of panic among the bank's customers, though managers of all eighty-four FMA branches had instructions to report promptly if any were observed. A bank survives on its reputation and the trust of others – fragile plants which adversity and bad publicity can wither.

One purpose of today's meeting had been to ensure that actions to be taken in event of a sudden crisis were understood, and communications functioning. Apparently they were.

'That's all for now,' Alex told the group. 'We'll meet tomorrow at the same time.'

They never did.

At 10.15 next morning, Friday, the manager of the First Mercantile American branch at Tylersville, twenty miles upstate, telephoned Headquarters and his call was put through immediately to Alex Vandervoort.

When the manager – Fergus W. Gatwick – identified himself, Alex asked crisply, 'What's the problem ?'

'A run, sir. This place is jammed with people – more than a hundred of our regular customers, lined up with passbooks and chequebooks, and more are coming in. They're withdrawing everything, cleaning out their accounts, demanding every last dollar.' The manager's voice was that of an alarmed man trying to stay calm.

Alex went cold. A run on a bank was a nightmare any banker dreaded; it was also – in the last few days – what Alex and others in top management had feared most. Such a run implied public panic, crowd psychology, a total loss of faith. Even worse, once news of a run on a single branch got out, it could sweep through others in the FMA system like a flash fire, impossible to put out, becoming a catastrophe. No banking institution -- not even the biggest and most sound -- ever had enough liquidity to repay the majority of its depositors at once, if all demanded cash. Therefore, if the run persisted, cash reserves would be exhausted and FMA obliged to close its doors, perhaps permanently.

It had happened before to other banks. Given a combination of mismanagement, bad timing, and bad luck, it could happen anywhere.

The first essential, Alex knew, was to assure those who wanted their money out that they would receive it. The second was to localize the outbreak.

His instructions to the Tylersville manager were terse. 'Fergus, you and all your staff are to act as if there is nothing out of the ordinary. Pay out *without question* whatever people ask for and have in their accounts. And don't walk around looking worried. Be cheerful.'

'It won't be easy, sir. I'll try.'

'Do *better* than try. At this moment our entire bank is on your shoulders.'

'Yes, sir.'

'We'll get help out to you as quickly as we can. What's your cash position?'

'We've about a hundred and fifty thousand dollars in the vault,' the manager said. 'I figure, at the rate we're going, we can last an hour, not much more.'

'There'll be cash coming,' Alex assured him. 'Meanwhile get the money you have out of the vault and stack it up on desks and tables where everyone can see it. Then walk among your customers. Talk to them. Assure them our bank is in excellent shape, despite what they've been reading, and tell them everyone will get their money.'

Alex hung up. On another phone he immediately called Straughan.

'Tom,' Alex said, 'the balloon's gone up at Tylersville. The branch there needs help and cash -- fast. Put Emergency Plan One in motion.'

sixteen

The municipality of Tylersville, like many a human being, was engaged in 'finding itself'. It was a neo-suburb – a mixture of bustling market town and farmland now partially engulfed by the encroaching city, but with enough of its origins remaining to resist, for a while, exurban conformity.

Its populace was a hybrid assortment of the old and new – conservative, deep-rooted farming and local business families and freshly resident commuters, many of the latter disgusted with decaying moral values of the city they had left, and seeking to absorb – for themselves and growing families – something of peaceful, rustic mores before these disappeared. The result was an unlikely alliance of real and would-be ruralists, mistrusting big business and city-style manoeuvrings, including those of banks.

Unique, too, in the case of the Tylersville bank run, was one gossipy postman. All day Thursday, while delivering letters and packages, he had also handed out the rumour, 'Did you hear about First Mercantile American Bank going bust? They say anyone who has money in there and doesn't get it out by to-morrow is going to lose everything.'

Only a few who heard the postman believed him implicitly. But the story spread, then was fuelled by news reports, including those of evening television. Overnight, among farm folk, trades people and the new migrants, anxiety grew so that by Friday morning the consensus was: why take a chance? Let's get our money now.

A small town has its own jungle telegraph. Word of people's decisions circulated rapidly and, by mid-morning, more and more of the populace was heading for the FMA branch bank.

So, out of small threads, are large tapestries woven.

At FMA Headquarters Tower, some who had scarcely heard of Tylersville were hearing of it now. They would hear more as the chain of events in Vandervoort's Emergency Plan One went forward quickly.

On instructions from Tom Straughan, the bank's computer was consulted first. A programmer tapped the question on a keyboard: What are the totals of savings and demand deposits at Tylersville Branch? The answer was instantaneous – and up to the minute since the branch was on-line to the computer.

SAVINGS ACCOUNTS	$26,170,627.54
DEMAND DEPOSITS	$15,042,767.18
TOTAL	$41,213,394.72

The computer was then instructed: Deduct from this total an allowance for dormant accounts and municipal deposits. (It was a safe assumption that neither of these would be disturbed, even in a run.)

The computer responded:

DORMANT & MUNICIPAL	$21,430,964.61
BALANCE	$19,782,430.11

Twenty million dollars more or less which depositors in the Tylersville area could, and might, demand.

A subordinate of Straughan's had already alerted Central Cash Vault, a subterranean fortress below the FMA Tower. Now the vault supervisor was informed, 'Twenty million dollars to Tylersville Branch – rush!'

The amount was still more than might be needed, but an objective – decided on during advance planning by Alex Vandervoort's group – was to make a show of strength like running up a flag. Or, as Alex expressed it, 'When you fight a fire, make sure you have more water than you need.'

Within the past forty-eight hours – anticipating exactly what was happening now – the normal money supply in Central Cash Vault had been augmented by special drawings from the Federal Reserve. The Fed had been informed of, and had approved, the FMA emergency plans.

A Midas fortune in currency and coin, already counted and in labelled sacks, was loaded on to armoured trucks while an array of armed guards patrolled the loading ramp. There would be six armoured trucks in all, several recalled by radio from other duties, and each would travel separately with police escort – a precaution because of the unusual amount of cash involved. However, only three trucks would have money in them. The others would be empty – dummies – an extra safeguard against hold-up.

Within twenty minutes of the branch manager's call, the first armoured truck was ready to leave Headquarters and, soon after, was threading through downtown traffic on its way to Tylersville.

Even before that, other bank personnel were en route by private car and limousine.

Edwina D'Orsey was in the lead. She would be in charge of the support operation now under way.

Edwina left her desk at the main downtown branch at once, pausing only to inform her senior assistant manager and to collect three staff members who would accompany her – a loan officer, Cliff Castleman, and two tellers. One of the tellers was Juanita Núñez.

At the same time, small contingents of staff from two other city branches were being instructed to go directly to Tylersville where they would report to Edwina. Part of over-all strategy was not to deplete any branch seriously of staff in case another run should begin elsewhere. In that event, other emergency plans were ready, though there was a limit to how many could be managed at once. Not more than two or three.

The quartet headed by Edwina moved at a brisk pace through the tunnel connecting the downtown branch with FMA Headquarters. From the lobby of the parent building they took a lift down to the bank's garage where a pool car had been assigned and was waiting. Cliff Castleman drove.

As they were getting in, Nolan Wainwright sprinted past, heading for his own parked Mustang. The security chief had been informed of the Tylersville operation and, with twenty million dollars cash involved, intended to oversee its protection personally. Not far behind him would be a station wagon with a half-dozen armed security guards. Local and state police at Tylersville had been alerted.

Both Alex Vandervoort and Tom Straughan remained where they were, in FMA Headquarters Tower. Straughan's office near the Money Trading Centre had become a command post. On the thirty-sixth floor, Alex's concern was to keep close tab on the remainder of the branch system, and to know instantly if fresh trouble erupted.

Alex had kept Patterton informed and now the bank president waited tensely with Alex, each mulling the unspoken questions: could they contain the run in Tylersville? Would First Mercantile American make it through the business day without a rash of runs elsewhere?

Fergus W. Gatwick, the Tylersville branch manager, had expected that his few remaining years until retirement would pass unhurriedly and uneventfully. He was sixtyish, a chubby apple of a man, pink-cheeked, blue-eyed, grey-haired, an affable Rotarian. In his youth he had known ambition but shed it long ago, deciding wisely that his role in life was supportive; he was a follower who would never blaze a trail. Managing a small branch bank ideally suited his ability and limitations.

He had been happy at Tylersville, where only one crisis had marred his tenure until now. A few years ago a woman with an imagined grudge against the bank rented a safe deposit box. She placed in the box an object wrapped in newspaper, then departed for Europe leaving no address. Within days, a putrid odour filtered through the bank. At first, drains were suspect and examined, to no effect, while all the time the stench grew greater. Customers complained, staff were nauseated. Eventually suspicion centred on the safe deposit boxes where the awful smell seemed strongest. Then the crucial question arose – which box?

It was Fergus W. Gatwick who, at duty's call, sniffed his way around them all, at length settling on one where the malodour was overpowering. After that, it took four days of legal proceedings before a court order was obtained permitting the bank to drill the box open. Inside were the remains of a large, once-fresh sea bass. Sometimes, even now in memory, Gatwick still sniffed traces of that ghastly time.

But today's exigency, he knew, was far more serious than a fish in a box. He checked his watch. An hour and ten minutes since he had telephoned Headquarters. Though four tellers had been paying out money steadily, the number of people crowding the bank was even greater, with newcomers pouring in, and still no help had come.

'Mr Gatwick!' A woman teller beckoned him.

'Yes?' He left the railed management area where he normally worked and walked over to her. Across a counter from them both, at the head of a waiting line, was a poultry farmer, a regular bank customer whom Gatwick knew well. The manager said cheerfully, 'Good morning, Steve.'

He received a cool nod in return while silently the teller showed him cheques drawn on two accounts. The poultryman had presented them. They totalled $23,000.

'Those are good,' Gatwick said. Taking the cheques, he initialled both.

In a low voice, though audible across the counter, the teller said, 'We haven't enough money left to pay that much.'

He should have known, of course. The drain on cash since opening had been continuous with many large withdrawals. But the remark was unfortunate. Now there were angry rumblings among those in line, the teller's statement being repeated and passed back. 'You hear that! They say they don't have any money.'

'By Christ!' The poultry farmer leaned wrathfully forward, a clenched fist pounding. 'You just better pay those cheques, Gatwick, or I'll be over there and tear this goddamn bank apart.'

'There's no need for any of that, Steve. Not threats or shouting either.' Fergus W. Gatwick raised his own voice, striving to be heard above the suddenly ugly scene. 'Ladies and gentlemen, we are experiencing a temporary cash shortage because of exceptional demands, but I assure you a great deal more money is on the way and will be here soon.'

The last words were drowned by wrathful shouts of protest. 'How come a bank runs out of money?' . . . 'Get it now!' . . . 'Forget the bullshit! Where's the cash?' . . . 'We'll camp here till this bank pays what it owes.'

Gatwick held up his arms. 'Once again I assure you . . .'

'I'm not interested in your sleazy assurances.' The speaker was a smartly dressed woman whom Gatwick recognized as a newish resident. She insisted, 'I want my money out now.'

'Damn right!' a man behind her echoed. 'That goes for all of us.'

Still others surged forward, voices raised, their faces revealing anger and alarm. Someone threw a cigarette package which hit Gatwick in the face. Suddenly, he realized, an ordinary group of citizens, many of whom he knew well, had become a hostile mob. It was the money, of course; money which did strange things to human beings, making them greedy, panicked, at times sub-human. There was genuine dread, too – the possibility, as some saw it, of losing everything they had, along with their security. Violence, which moments ago appeared unthinkable, now loomed close. For the first time in many years, Gatwick felt physical fear.

'Please!' he pleaded. 'Please listen!' His voice disappeared under growing tumult.

Abruptly, unexpectedly, the clamour lessened. There seemed to be some activity in the street outside which those at the rear were craning to see. Then, with a bravura flourish, the bank's outer doors flung open and a procession marched in.

Edwina D'Orsey headed it. Following her were Cliff Castleman and the two young women tellers, one of them the petite figure of Juanita Núñez. Behind was a phalanx of security guards shouldering heavy canvas sacks, escorted by other protective guards with drawn revolvers. A half dozen more staff who had arrived from other branches filed in behind the guards. In the wake of them all – a vigilant, wary Lord Protector – was Nolan Wainwright.

Edwina spoke clearly across the crowded, now near-silent bank. 'Good morning, Mr Gatwick. I'm sorry we all took so long, but traffic was heavy. I understand you may require twenty million dollars. About a third of it just arrived. The rest is on the way.'

While Edwina was speaking, Cliff Castleman, Juanita, the guards and others continued through the railed management area to the rear of the counters. One of the newly arrived relief staff was an operations man who promptly took charge of incoming cash. Soon, plentiful supplies of crisp new bills were being recorded, then distributed to tellers.

The crowd in the bank pressed around Edwina. Someone asked, 'Is that true? Do you people have enough money to pay us all?'

'Of course it's true.' Edwina looked over heads around her and spoke to everyone. 'I'm Mrs D'Orsey, and I'm a vice-president of First Mercantile American Bank. Despite any rumours you may have heard, our bank is sound, solvent, and has no problems which we cannot handle. We have ample cash reserves to repay any depositor – in Tylersville or anywhere else.'

The smartly dressed woman who had spoken earlier said, 'Maybe that's true. Or maybe you're just saying so, hoping we'll believe it. Either way, I'm taking my money out today.'

'That's your privilege,' Edwina said.

Fergus W. Gatwick, watching, was relieved at no longer being the focus of attention. He also sensed that the ugly mood of moments earlier had eased; there were even a few smiles among those waiting as increasing amounts of money continued to appear. But less obdurate mood or not, a purposefulness remained. As the process of paying out continued briskly, it was clear that the run on the bank had not been halted.

While it continued, once more like Caesar's legionaries, the bank guards and escort who had returned to their armoured trucks outside, marched in again with still more loaded canvas sacks.

No one who shared that day at Tylersville would ever forget the immense amount of money eventually displayed on public view. Even those who worked at FMA had never seen so much assembled at a single time before. On Edwina's instructions and under Alex Vandervoort's plan, most of the twenty million dollars brought to fight the bank run was out in the open where everyone could see it. In the area behind the tellers' counter, every desk was cleared; from elsewhere in the bank more desks and tables were moved in. On to them all, great stacks of currency and coin were heaped while the extra staff who had been brought in somehow kept track of running totals.

As Nolan Wainwright expressed it later, the entire operation was 'a bank robber's dream, a security man's nightmare'. Fortunately, if robbers learned of what was happening, they learned too late.

Edwina, quietly competent and with courtesy to Fergus W. Gatwick, supervised everything.

It was she who instructed Cliff Castleman to begin seeking loan business.

Shortly before noon, with the bank remaining crowded and a lengthening line outside, Castleman carried a chair forward and stood up on it.

'Ladies and gentlemen,' he announced, 'I'd like to introduce myself. I'm a loan officer from the city, which doesn't mean a lot except that I have authority to approve loans for larger amounts than are normally dealt with at this branch. So if any of you have been thinking of applying for a loan and would like a fast answer, now's the time. I'm a sympathetic listener and I try to help people who have problems. Mr Gatwick, who is busy doing other things right now, has kindly said I can use his desk, so that's where I'll be. I hope you'll come and talk to me.'

A man with a cast on his leg called out, 'I'll be right over, soon's I get my other money. Guess if this bank's going bust I should grab a loan. I'd never have to pay it back.'

'Nothing's going bust here,' Cliff Castleman said. He enquired, 'What did you do to the leg?'

'Fell over in the dark.'

'From the sound of you, you're still in the dark. This bank is in better shape than either of us. What's more, if you borrow money you'll pay it back or we'll break the other leg.'

There was some laughter as Castleman climbed down from his chair, and later a few people drifted over to the manager's desk to discuss loans. But withdrawals continued. The panic eased, but nothing, it seemed – neither a show of strength, assurances or applied psychology – would stop the bank run at Tylersville.

By early afternoon it appeared, to despondent FMA officials, that only one question still remained: how long would it take for the virus to spread?

Alex Vandervoort, who had talked several times by telephone with Edwina, left for Tylersville himself in mid-afternoon. He was now even more alarmed than this morning when he had hoped the run could be terminated quickly. Its continuance meant that, over the week-end, panic among depositors would spread, with other FMA branches certain to be inundated Monday.

So far today, while withdrawals at some other branches had been heavy, nothing comparable to the Tylersville situation had occurred elsewhere..But clearly that same luck could not hold for long.

Alex went by chauffeured limousine to Tylersville and Margot Bracken rode with him. Margot had concluded a court case earlier than she expected that morning and joined Alex at the bank for lunch. Afterwards at his suggestion she stayed on, sharing some of the tensions by then pervading the tower's thirty-sixth floor.

In the car Alex leaned back, savouring the relaxed interval which he knew would be brief.

'This year has been hard for you,' Margot said.

'Am I showing the strain?'

She reached over, running a forefinger across his forehead gently. 'You've more lines there. You're greyer at the temples.'

He grimaced. 'I'm also older.'

'Not that much.'

'Then it's a price we pay for living with pressures. You pay it too, Bracken.'

'Yes, I do,' Margot agreed. 'What matters, of course, is which pressures are important and if they're worth the part of ourselves we give to them.'

'Saving a bank is worth some personal strain,' Alex said sharply. 'Right now if we don't save ours, a lot of people will be hurt who shouldn't be.'

'And some who should?'

'In a rescue operation you try to save everybody. Any retribution can come later.'

They had covered ten of the twenty miles to Tylersville.

'Alex, are things really that bad?'

'If we have an unstoppable run on Monday,' he said, 'we'll have to close. A consortium of other banks may then get together to bail us out – at a price – after which they'll pick over what's left, and in time, I think, all depositors would get their money. But FMA as an entity would be finished.'

'The most incredible part is how it can happen so suddenly.'

'It points up,' Alex said, 'what a lot of people, who ought to, don't fully understand. Banks and the money system, which includes big debts and big loans, are like delicate machinery. Monkey with them clumsily, let one component get seriously out of balance because of greed or politics or plain stupidity, and you imperil all the others. And once you've endangered the system – or a single bank – and if word leaks out as usually happens, diminished public confidence does the rest. That's what we're seeing now.'

'From what you've told me,' Margot said, 'and from other things I've heard, greed is the reason for what's happening to your bank.'

Alex said bitterly, 'That and a high percentage of idiots on our board.' He was being franker than usual but found it a relief.

There was a silence between them until Alex exclaimed, 'God! How I miss him.'

'Who?'

'Ben Rosselli.'

Margot reached out for his hand. 'Isn't this rescue operation of yours exactly what Ben would have done himself?'

'Maybe.' He sighed. 'Except it isn't working. That's why I wish Ben were here.'

The chauffeur let down the dividing window between the front seat and his passengers. He spoke over his shoulder. 'We're coming into Tylersville, sir.'

'Good luck, Alex,' Margot said.

From several blocks away, they could see a line-up of people outside the branch. New arrivals were joining it. As their limousine pulled up outside the bank, a truck screeched to a halt across the street and several men and a girl jumped out. On the side of the truck in large letters was WTLC-TV.

'Christ!' Alex said. 'That's all we need.'

Inside the bank, while Margot looked around her curiously, Alex talked briefly with Edwina and Fergus W. Gatwick, learning from both that there was little if anything more that anyone could do. Alex supposed it had been a wasted journey but had felt the need to come. He decided it would do no harm, and might even help, if he chatted with some of those waiting. He began to walk down the several lines of people, quietly introducing himself.

There were at least two hundred, a sizeable cross-section of Tylersville – old, young, middle-aged, some well-to-do, others obviously poorer, women with babies, men in work clothes, some carefully dressed as if for an occasion. The majority were friendly, a few not, one or two antagonistic. Almost everyone showed some degree of nervousness. There was relief on the faces of those who received their money and left. An elderly woman spoke to Alex on the way out. She had no idea he was a bank official. 'Thank heaven that's over! It's been the most anxious day I ever spent. This is my savings – all I have.' She held up a dozen or so fifty dollar bills. Others left with much larger or smaller sums.

The impression Alex got from everyone he talked to was the same: maybe First Mercantile American Bank was sound; maybe it wasn't. But no one wanted to take a chance and leave their money in an institution which might collapse. The publicity linking FMA with Supranational had done its work. Everyone knew that First Mercantile American was likely to lose a huge amount of money, because the bank admitted it. Details didn't matter. Nor did the few people to whom Alex mentioned Federal Deposit Insurance trust that system either. The amount of federal insurance was limited, a few pointed out, and FDIC funds were believed to be inadequate in any major crunch.

And there was something else, Alex realized, perhaps even more profound: people didn't believe any more what they were told; they had become too accustomed to being deceived and lied to. In the recent past they had been lied to by their President, other government officials, politicians, business, industry. Lied to by employers, by unions. Lied to in advertising. Lied to in financial transactions, including the status of stocks and bonds, stockholder reports and 'audited' corporate statements. Lied to at times – through bias or omission – by communications media. The list was endless. Deception had been piled on deception until lying – or, at best, distortion and failure to make full disclosure – had become a way of life.

So why should anyone believe Alex when he assured them that FMA was not a sinking ship and their money – if they left it there – was safe ? As the hours slipped by and afternoon waned, it was clear that no one did.

By late afternoon Alex had become resigned. What would happen would happen; for individuals and institutions, he supposed, there came a point where the inevitable must be accepted. It was about that time – near 5.30, with dusk of the October evening closing in – that Nolan Wainwright came to him reporting a new anxiety in the waiting crowd.

'They're worried,' Wainwright said, 'because our closing time is six o'clock. They figure in the half hour that's left we can't deal with everybody.'

Alex wavered. It would be simple to close the Tylersville branch bank on schedule; it would also be legal, and no one could seriously object. He savoured an impulse born of anger and frustration; a spiteful urge to say, in effect, to those still waiting: *You've refused to trust me, so sweat till Monday, and the hell with you !* But he hesitated, swayed by his own nature and a remark of Margot's about Ben Rosselli. What Alex was doing now, she had said, was 'exactly what Ben would have done himself'. What would Ben's decision have been about closing ? Alex knew.

'I'll make an announcement,' he told Wainwright. First he sought out Edwina and gave her some instructions.

Moving to the doorway of the bank, Alex spoke from where he could be heard by those inside and others still waiting on the street. He was conscious of TV cameras directed at him. The first TV crew had been joined by a second from another station,

404

and an hour ago Alex made a statement for them both. The TV crews stayed on, one of their people confiding they were getting extra material for a week-end news feature since 'a bank run doesn't happen every day'.

'Ladies and gentlemen' – Alex's voice was strong and clear; it carried easily. 'I am informed that some of you are concerned about the time of our closing tonight. You need not be. On behalf of the management of this bank I give you my word that we will remain open here in Tylersville until we have attended to you all.' There was a murmur of satisfaction and some spontaneous handclapping.

'However, there is one thing I urge on all of you.' Once more, voices quietened as attention returned to Alex. He went on, 'I strongly advise that over the week-end you do not keep large sums of money on your person or in your homes. It would be unsafe in many ways. Therefore I urge you to select another bank and deposit there whatever you withdrew from this one. To help you in this, my colleague Mrs D'Orsey is at present telephoning other banks in this area, asking them to remain open later than usual in order to accommodate you.'

Again there was an appreciative hum.

Nolan Wainwright came to Alex, whispered briefly and Alex announced, 'I am informed that two banks have already agreed to our request. Others are still to be contacted.'

From among those waiting in the street a male voice called, 'Can you recommend a good bank ?'

'Yes,' Alex said. 'My own choice would be First Mercantile American. It's the one I know best, the one I'm surest of, and its record has been long and honourable. I only wish that all of you felt that way too.' For the first time there was a hint of emotion in his voice. A few people smiled or laughed halfheartedly, but most faces watching him were serious.

'Used to feel that way myself,' a voice behind Alex volunteered. He turned. The speaker was an elderly man, probably nearer eighty than seventy, wizened, white-haired, stooped, and leaning on a cane. But the old man's eyes were clear and sharp, his voice firm. Beside him was a woman of about the same age. Both were tidily dressed, though their clothing was old-fashioned and well worn. The woman held a shopping bag which, it could be seen, contained packages of currency. They had just come from the bank counter.

'The wife and me, we've had an account at FMA for more'n thirty years,' the old man said. 'Feel kinda bad taking it away now.'

'Then why do it?'

'Can't ignore all them rumours. Too much smoke for there not to be some truth somewhere.'

'There is some truth and we've admitted it,' Alex said. 'Because of a loan to Supranational Corporation, our bank is likely to suffer a loss. But the bank can withstand it, and it will.'

The old man shook his head. 'If I was younger and working, maybe I'd take a chance on what you say. But I ain't. What's in there' – he pointed to the shopping bag – 'is pretty well all we got left until we die. Even that ain't much. Them dollars don't go half as far as when we worked and earned 'em.'

'That's for sure,' Alex said. 'Inflation hits good people like you hardest. But, unfortunately, changing banks won't help you there.'

'Let me ask you a question, young fellow. If you was me and this here was your money, wouldn't you be doing the same as I am now?'

Alex was aware of others closing in and listening. He saw Margot a head or two away. Just behind her, TV camera lights were on. Someone was leaning forward with a microphone.

'Yes,' he admitted. 'I suppose I would.'

The old man seemed surprised. 'You're honest, anyways. Just now I heard that advice you gave about getting to another bank and I appreciate it. I guess we'll go to one and put our money in.'

'Wait,' Alex said. 'Do you have a car?'

'Nope. Live just a piece from here. We'll walk.'

'Not with that money. You might be robbed. I'll have someone drive you to another bank.' Alex beckoned Nolan Wainwright and explained the problem. 'This is our chief of security,' he told the elderly couple.

'No sweat,' Wainwright said. 'Be glad to drive you myself.'

The old man didn't move. He stood looking from one face to the other. 'You'd do that for us? When we've just moved our money out of your bank? When we've good as told you we don't trust you any more?'

'Let's say it's all in our service. Besides,' Alex said, 'if you've been with us thirty years, we ought to part as friends.'

Still the old man paused uncertainly. 'Maybe we don't have to. Let me ask you one more question, man to man.' The clear, sharp, honest eyes regarded Alex steadily.

'Go ahead.'

'You told me the truth once already, young fellow. Now tell me it again, remembering what I said about being old and knowing what them savings mean. Is our money safe in your bank? *Absolutely safe?*'

For measurable seconds Alex weighed the question and all its implications. He knew that not only the old couple was watching him intently, but many others, too. The omnipresent TV cameras were still turning. He caught a glimpse of Margot; she was equally intent, a quizzical expression on her face. He thought of the people here, and of others elsewhere affected by this moment; of those relying on him – Jerome Patterton, Tom Straughan, the board, Edwina, more; of what might happen if FMA failed, of the wide and damaging effect, not just at Tylersville but far beyond. Despite all this, doubt rose. He thrust it down, then answered crisply and confidently, 'I give you my word. This bank is absolutely safe.'

'Aw shucks, Freda!' the old man told his wife. 'Looks like we been barkin' up a tree about nothing. Let's go put the damn money back.'

In all the post-mortem studies and discussions over the following weeks, one fact stayed undisputed: the bank run at Tylersville effectively ended when the old man and his wife turned back into the FMA branch and redeposited the money from their shopping bag. People who had been waiting to withdraw their own money, and who witnessed the exchange between the old man and the bank executive either avoided each other's eyes or, if they didn't, grinned sheepishly and turned away. Word passed speedily among the remainder of those outside and in-side; almost at once the waiting lines began dispersing, as quickly and mysteriously as they had formed. As someone said later: it was the herd instinct in reverse. When the few remaining people in the bank were dealt with, the branch closed only ten minutes later than was normal on a Friday night. A few FMA people, at Tylersville and in Headquarters Tower, had worried about Monday. Would the crowd return, the run begin again? In the event, it never did.

Nor, on Monday, did a run develop anywhere else. The reason – most analysts agreed – was an explicit, honest, moving scene involving an old couple and a good-looking, open, bank vice-president as it appeared on week-end television news. The film, when cut and edited, was so successful that stations used the item several times. It came through as an example of the intimate, effective *cinéma vérité* technique which TV can do so well, but seldom does. Many viewers were moved to tears.

During the week-end, Alex Vandervoort saw the TV film but reserved his comments. A reason was that he alone knew what his thoughts had been at the vital, decisive moment when he was asked the question: *Is our money . . . absolutely safe?* Another was that Alex knew the pitfalls and problems which still lay ahead for FMA.

Margot also said little about the incident on Friday night; nor did she mention it on Sunday when she stayed at Alex's apartment. She had an important question she wanted to ask but wisely decided that now was not the time.

Among First Mercantile American executives who watched the telecast was Roscoe Heyward, though he didn't see it all. Heyward turned on the TV after arriving home on Sunday night from a church vestry meeting but snapped it off in jealous anger part way through. Heyward had serious enough problems of his own without wishing to be reminded of a Vandervoort success. And quite apart from the bank run, several matters were likely to surface during the coming week which made Heyward highly nervous.

One other postscript developed from that Friday evening in Tylersville. It concerned Juanita Núñez.

Juanita had seen Margot Bracken arrive during the afternoon. She had recently debated whether or not to seek out Margot and ask advice. Now she decided to. But for reasons of her own, Juanita preferred not to be observed by Nolan Wainwright.

The opportunity Juanita had been waiting for occurred shortly after the bank run ended, while Wainwright was busy checking branch security arrangements for the week-end, and the day-long pressure on the staff had eased. Juanita left the counter where she had been assisting a regular branch teller and crossed to the railed management area. Margot was seated there alone, waiting until Mr Vandervoort could leave.

'Miss Bracken,' Juanita said, speaking softly, 'you once told me that if I had a problem I could come and talk to you.'

'Of course, Juanita. Do you have one now?'

Her small face creased in worry. 'Yes, I think so.'

'What kind of problem?'

'If you don't mind, could we talk somewhere else?' Juanita was watching Wainwright, near the vault on the opposite side of the bank. He seemed about to end a conversation.

'Then come to my office,' Margot said. 'When would you like to make it?'

They agreed on Monday evening.

seventeen

The reel of tape, retrieved from the Double-Seven Health Club, had been lying there on the shelf above the test bench for six days.

Wizard Wong had glanced at the tape several times, reluctant to wipe out what was on it, yet uneasy about passing on the information. Nowadays, recording *any* telephone conversation was risky. Even riskier was to play the recording back for some-one else.

Yet Marino, Wizard was certain, would very much like to hear a portion of that tape, and would pay well for the privilege. Whatever else Tony Bear Marino might be, he was generous about payment for good service, which was the one reason Wizard did work for him periodically.

Marino was a professional crook, he was aware. Wong himself was not.

Wizard (his real first name was Wayne, though no one who knew him ever used it) was a young, clever, second-generation Chinese-American. He was also an electronics-audio expert, specializing in the detection of electronic surveillance. His genius in the subject had earned him his name.

For a long list of clients, Wong provided guarantees that their business premises and homes were not bugged, their phones untapped, their privacy – from surreptitious electronics – inviolate. With surprising frequency he did discover planted listening devices and when it happened his clients were impressed and grateful. Despite official assurances to the contrary – including some recent presidential ones – bugging and wiretapping in the US continued to be widespread and flourishing.

Heads of industrial companies retained Wong's services. So did bankers, newspaper publishers, presidential candidates, some big-name lawyers, a foreign embassy or two, a handful of US senators, three state governors, and a Supreme Court justice. Then there were the other executives – the Don of a Mafia family, his *consigliori*, and various wheels at slightly lower level, of whom Tony Marino was one.

To his criminal clients Wizard Wong made one thing plain: he wanted no part of their illicit activities; he was making an excellent living within the law. However, he saw no reason for them to be denied his services, since bugging was almost always illegal, and even criminals were entitled to protect themselves by lawful means. This ground rule was accepted and worked well.

Just the same, his organized crime clients intimated to Wizard from time to time that any usable information he acquired as a result of his work would be appreciated and rewarded. And occasionally he *had* passed on titbits of knowledge in return for

410

money, yielding to that oldest and simplest of all temptations – greed.

He was being tempted by it now.

A week and a half ago, Wizard Wong had made a routine anti-bug survey of Marino's haunts and telephones. These included the Double-Seven Health Club where Marino had a financial interest. In course of the survey – which showed everything to be clean – Wizard amused himself by briefly bugging one of the club lines, a practice which he sometimes followed, rationalizing that he owed it to himself and his clients to maintain his own technical expertise. For the purpose he chose a public phone on the health club's main floor. For forty-eight hours Wizard left a tape recorder spliced across the public phone circuit, the recorder hidden in the basement of the Double-Seven. It was a type which switched itself on and off each time the phone was used.

Though the action was illegal, Wizard reasoned that it didn't matter since no one but himself would hear the tape played back. However, when he did play it, one conversation, especially, intrigued him.

Now, on Saturday afternoon, and alone in his sound lab, he took the tape from the shelf above the test bench, put it on a machine and listened to that portion once again.

A coin was inserted, a number dialled. The sound of dialling was on the tape. A ringing tone. One ring only.

A woman's voice (soft, with slight accent): Hello.

A male voice (whispering): You know who this is. But don't use names.

The woman's voice: Yes.

The first voice (still whispering): Tell our mutual friend I've discovered something important here. Really important. It's most of what he wanted to know. I can't say more, but I'll come to you tomorrow night.

A woman's voice: All right.

A click. The caller, in the Double-Seven Health Club, had hung up.

Wizard Wong wasn't sure why he thought Tony Bear Marino would be interested. He simply had a hunch, and his hunches had paid off before. Making up his mind, he consulted a private note book, went to a telephone and called a number.

Tony Bear, it transpired, could not see him until late Monday afternoon. Wizard made an arrangement for then and – having committed himself – set out to extract more information from the tape.

He rewound it, then carefully played it several times again.

'Judas Priest!' Tony Bear Marino's husky, thick features contorted in a savage scowl. His incongruous falsetto voice rose even higher than usual. 'You had that goddamn tape, and you sat on your goddamn ass a week before you came here!'

Wizard Wong said defensively, 'I'm a technician, Mr Marino. Mostly, the things I hear are none of my business. But after a while I got to thinking this one was different.' He was relieved in one sense. At least there had been no angry reaction because he had bugged a Double-Seven line.

'Next time,' Marino snarled, 'think faster!'

Today was Monday. They were at the trucking terminal where Marino maintained an office and, on the desk between them, was a portable table tape player which Wong had just switched off. Before coming here he had re-recorded the significant part of the original tape, transferring it to a cassette, then erased the rest.

Tony Bear Marino, in shirtsleeves in the stuffy, heated office, appeared physically formidable as usual. His shoulders were a prize-fighter's; his wrists and biceps thick. He overflowed the chair he sat in, though not with fat; most of him was solid muscle. Wizard Wong tried not to be intimidated, either by Marino's bulk or his reputation for ruthlessness. But, whether from the hot room or other reasons, Wong began to sweat.

He protested, 'I didn't waste all that time, Mr Marino. I found out some other things I thought you'd want to know.'

'Such as ?'

'I can tell you the number that was called. You see, by using a stop watch to time the length of each dial turn as recorded on the tape, then comparing it . . .'

'Cut the crap. Just give me the number.'

'There it is.' A slip of paper passed across the desk.

412

'You've traced it ? Whose number is it ?'

'I have to tell you, tracing a number like that isn't easy. Especially since this particular one is unlisted. Fortunately, I have some contacts in the phone company . . .'

Tony Bear exploded. He slammed a palm on the desk top, the impact like a gunshot. 'Don't play games with me, you little bastard! If you got information, give!'

'The point I'm making,' Wizard persisted, sweating even more, 'is that it costs. I had to pay off my phone company contact.'

'You paid a goddamn lot less than you'll squeeze out of me. Get on with it!'

Wizard relaxed a little, aware that he had made his point and Tony Bear would meet the price to be asked, each of them knowing there might be another time.

'The phone belongs to a Mrs J. Núñez. She lives at Forum East. Here's the building and apartment number.' Wong passed over another slip. Marino took it, glanced at the address, and put it down.

'There's something else might be of interest to you. The records show the phone was installed a month ago as a hurry-up job. Now normally, there's a long waiting list for phones at Forum East, but this one wasn't on the list at all, then all of a sudden it was put on at the top.'

Marino's growing scowl was part impatience, part anger at what he heard. Wizard Wong went on hastily, 'What happened was, some pressure was applied. My contact told me there's a memo in the phone company files showing it came from a guy named Nolan Wainwright who's head of security for a bank – First Mercantile American. He said the phone was needed urgently for bank business. Billing for it is going to the bank, too.'

For the first time since the audio technician's arrival, Tony Bear was startled. Momentarily the surprise revealed itself on his face, then vanished, to be replaced by a blank expression. Under it, his mind was working, relating what he had just learned to certain facts he already knew. The name Wainwright was the connection. Marino was aware of the attempt six months ago to plant a stoolie, a creep named Vic who, after they busted his balls, said 'Wainwright'. Marino knew of the bank dick by reputation. In that earlier series of events Tony Bear had been very much involved.

Was there another one now? If so, Tony Bear had a strong idea what action he was after, though there was a lot of other business through the Double-Seven he had no wish to see disclosed. Tony Bear did not waste time in speculation. The caller's voice, a whisper only, you couldn't tell. But the other voice – the woman's – had been traced, so whatever else was needed they could get from her. It did not enter his mind that the woman might not cooperate; if she was foolish, there were plenty of ways.

Marino paid Wong off quickly and sat thinking. For a while, he followed his usual cautious pattern, not rushing a decision and leaving his thoughts to simmer for several hours. But he had lost time, a week.

Later that night he summoned two musclemen. Tony Bear gave them a Forum East address and an order. 'Pick up the Núñez broad.'

eighteen

'If everything you just told me turns out to be true,' Alex assured Margot, 'I'll personally administer the biggest kick in the ass that Nolan Wainwright ever had.'

Margot snapped back, 'Of course it's all true. Why would Mrs Núñez invent it? In any case, how could she?'

'No,' he admitted, 'I don't suppose she could.'

'I'll tell you something else, Alex. I want more than your man Wainwright's head on a platter – or his ass. A whole lot more.'

They were in Alex's apartment where Margot had come a half hour ago, following her Monday-night talk with Juanita Núñez. What Juanita had revealed amazed and enraged her.

414

Juanita had nervously described the month-old agreement in which she had become the link between Wainwright and Miles Eastin. But recently, Juanita confided, she had begun to realize the risk she was running and her fears had grown, not just for herself but for Estela. Margot had gone over Juanita's report several times, questioning her on details, and at the end Margot went directly to Alex.

'I knew about Eastin going under cover.' Alex's face was troubled, as it had been so often recently; he paced the living-room holding an untasted scotch. 'Nolan told me what he planned. At first I opposed it and said no, then I gave in because the arguments seemed convincing. But I swear to you that no arrangement with the Núñez girl was ever mentioned.'

'I believe you,' Margot said. 'He probably didn't tell you because he knew you'd veto it.'

'Did Edwina know?'

'Apparently not.'

Alex thought peevishly: then Nolan was out of line there, too. How *could* he have been so shortsighted, even stupid? Part of the trouble Alex knew, was that department heads like Wainwright got carried away by their own limited objectives, forgetting the larger view.

He stopped pacing. 'A minute ago you said something about wanting "a whole lot more". What does that mean?'

'The first thing I want is immediate safety for my client and her child, and by safety I mean placing her somewhere where she's out of jeopardy. After that, we can discuss compensation.'

'Your *client*?'

'I advised Juanita tonight that she needs legal help. She asked me to represent her.'

Alex grinned and sipped his scotch. 'So you and I are now adversaries, Bracken.'

'In that sense, I suppose so.' Margot's voice softened. 'Except you know I won't take advantage of our private conversations.'

'Yes, I do. That's why I'll tell you privately we *will* do something – immediately, tomorrow – for Mrs Núñez. If it means sending her out of town for a while, to be certain she's safe, then I'll approve it. As to compensation, I won't commit us on that, but after I hear the whole story, and if it agrees with yours and hers, we'll consider it.'

What Alex left unsaid was his intention to send for Nolan Wainwright in the morning and order the entire undercover operation terminated. That would include safeguarding the girl, as he had promised Margot; also, Eastin must be paid off. Alex wished fervently he had stayed firm by his original judgement and forbidden the entire plan; all his instincts had been against it and he had been wrong in backing down under Wainwright's persuasion. The risks, in every way, were far too great. Fortunately it was not too late to remedy the error, since nothing harmful had occurred, either to Eastin or Núñez.

Margot regarded him. 'One of the things I like about you is that you're a fair man. So you do concede the bank has a liability to Juanita Núñez?'

'Oh, Christ!' Alex said, and drained his scotch. 'Right now we're liable for so much, what the hell is one thing more?'

nineteen

Only one more piece. Just one more needed to complete the tantalizing jigsaw. A single lucky break could yield it, and answer the question: where was the counterfeiter's base?

When Nolan Wainwright conceived the second undercover mission, he did not anticipate spectacular results. He considered Miles Eastin a long shot from whom some minor information might accrue, and even that could take months. But instead, Eastin had moved quickly from one revelation to another. Wainwright wondered if Eastin himself realized how outstandingly successful he had been.

On Tuesday at midmorning, alone in his plainly furnished office at FMA Headquarters Tower, Wainwright once more reviewed the progress made:

416

—The first report from Eastin had been to say 'I'm in' at the Double-Seven Health Club. In light of later developments that, in itself, had been important. Confirmation followed that the Double-Seven was a hangout for criminals, including the loan shark, Ominsky, and Tony Bear Marino.

—By gaining access to the illegal gambling rooms, Eastin had improved his infiltration.

—Soon after, Eastin had made a 'buy' of ten counterfeit $20 notes. These, when examined by Wainwright and others, proved to be of the same high quality as those circulating in the area over the past several months and were undoubtedly from the same source. Eastin had reported his supplier's name and the man was being watched.

—Next, a three-pronged report: the forged driver's licence; the licence number of the Chevrolet Impala which Eastin had driven to Louisville, apparently with a consignment of counterfeit money in the boot; and the counterfoil of the airline ticket given Eastin for his return journey. Of the three items, the airline ticket had proved the most useful. It had been purchased, along with others, with a Keycharge bank credit card, counterfeit. At last the bank security chief had a sense of closing in on his main objective – the conspiracy which had, and still was, defrauding the Keycharge system of huge amounts. The fake driver's licence confirmed the existence of a versatile, efficient organization to which there was now an additional lead – the ex-con, Jules LaRocca. The Impala, enquiry showed, had been stolen. A few days after Eastin's journey it was found abandoned in Louisville.

—Finally, and most important, had been identifying the counterfeiter, Danny, along with a cornucopia of information including the fact that the source of the counterfeit Keycharge credit cards was now known with certainty.

As Wainwright's knowledge had accumulated because of his pipeline from Miles Eastin, so had an obligation grown – to share what he knew. Therefore a week ago he had invited agents of the FBI and US Secret Service to a conference at the bank. The Secret Service had to be included because money counterfeiting was involved, and theirs was the constitutional responsibility for protecting the US money system. The FBI special agents who came were the same team – Innes and Dalrymple – who investigated the FMA cash loss and arrested Miles Eastin almost a year ago. The Secret Service men – Jordan and Quimby – Wainwright had not met before.

Innes and Dalrymple were complimentary and appreciative about the information Wainwright gave them, the Secret Service men less so. Their beef was that Wainwright should have notified them sooner – as soon as he received the first counterfeit notes from Eastin – and that Eastin, through Wainwright, ought to have advised them in advance about the Louisville journey.

The Secret Service agent Jordan, a dour, hard-eyed, runtish man whose stomach rumbled constantly, complained, 'If we'd been warned, we could have made an intercept. As it is, your man Eastin may be guilty of a felony, with you as an accessory.'

Wainwright pointed out patiently, 'I already explained there was no chance for Eastin to notify anybody, including me. He took a risk and knew it; I happen to think he did the right thing. As to a felony, we don't even know for sure there was counterfeit money in that car.'

'It was there all right,' Jordan grumbled. 'It's been surfacing in Louisville ever since. What we didn't know was how it came in.'

'Well, you do now,' the FBI agent Innes injected. 'And thanks to Nolan, we're all that much further ahead.'

Wainwright added, 'If you'd made an intercept, sure you might have got a batch of counterfeit. But not much else, and Eastin's usefulness would have been ended.'

In a way, Wainwright sympathized with the Secret Service point of view. The agents were overworked, harassed, their service under-staffed, yet the quantity of counterfeit money in circulation had increased by staggering amounts in recent years. They were fighting a hydra-headed monster. No sooner did they locate one source of supply than another sprang up; others remained permanently elusive. For public purposes the fiction was maintained that counterfeiters were always caught, that their kind of crime didn't pay. In reality, Wainwright knew, it paid plenty.

Despite the initial friction, a big plus from involving law enforcement agencies was recourse to their records. Individuals whom Eastin had named were identified and dossiers assembled against the time when a series of arrests could be made. The counterfeiter, Danny, was identified as Daniel Kerrigan, age seventy-three. 'Long ago,' Innes reported, 'Kerrigan had three arrests and two convictions for forgery, but we haven't heard of him in fifteen years. He's either been legit, lucky, or clever.'

Wainwright recalled and repeated a remark of Danny's – relayed by Eastin – to the effect that he had been working with an efficient organization.

'Could be,' Innes said.

After their first conference Wainwright and the four agents maintained frequent contact and he promised to inform them immediately of any new report from Eastin. All were agreed that the remaining key piece of information was the location of the counterfeiters' headquarters. So far, no one had any idea where that might be. Yet hopes of obtaining a further lead were high, and if and when it happened the FBI and Secret Service were ready to close in.

Abruptly, as Nolan Wainwright meditated, his telephone jangled. A secretary said that Mr Vandervoort would like to see him as soon as possible.

Wainwright was incredulous. Facing Alex Vandervoort, across the latter's desk, he protested, 'You can't be serious!'

'I'm serious,' Alex said. 'Though I have trouble believing you were, making use of the Núñez girl the way you have. Of all the insane notions . . .'

'Insane or not, it worked.'

Alex ignored the comment. 'You put the girl in jeopardy, consulting no one. As a result we're obligated to take care of her, and may even have a lawsuit on our hands.'

'I worked on the assumption,' Wainwright argued, 'that the fewer people who knew what she was doing, the safer she would be.'

'No! That's your rationalization now, Nolan. What you really thought was that if I had known, or Edwina D'Orsey, we'd have stopped you. *I* knew about Eastin. Was I likely to be less discreet about the girl ?'

Wainwright rubbed a knuckle along the surface of his chin. 'Well, I guess you have a point.'

'Damn right I do!'

'But that's still no reason, Alex, for abandoning the entire operation. For the first time in investigating Keycharge frauds we're close to a big breakthrough. Okay, my judgement was wrong in using Núñez. I admit it. But it wasn't wrong about Eastin, and we've got results to prove it.'

Alex shook his head decisively. 'Nolan, I let you change my mind once before. This time I won't. Our business here is banking, not crime busting. We'll seek help from law enforcement agencies and cooperate with them all we can. But we will *not* sustain aggressive crime fighting programmes of our own. So I tell you – end the arrangement with Eastin, today if possible.'

'Look, Alex . . .'

'I already have looked, and don't like what I see. I will not have FMA responsible for risking human lives – even Eastin's. That's definite, so let's not waste time in further argument.'

As Wainwright looked sourly despondent, Alex went on, 'The other thing I want done is a conference set up this afternoon between you, Edwina D'Orsey, me, to discuss what to do about Mrs Núñez. You can start considering ideas. What may be necessary . . .'

A secretary appeared in the office doorway. Alex said irritably, 'Whatever it is – later!'

The girl shook her head. 'Mr Vandervoort, Miss Bracken's on the line. She said it's extremely urgent and you'd want to be interrupted, whatever you were doing.'

Alex sighed. He picked up a phone. 'Yes, Bracken ?'

'Alex,' Margot's voice said, 'it's about Juanita Núñez.'

'What about her ?'

'She's disappeared.'

'Wait.' Alex moved a switch, transferring the call to a speaker phone so that Wainwright could hear. 'Go ahead.'

'I'm terribly worried. When I left Juanita last night, and knowing I was going to see you later, I arranged to telephone her at work today. She was deeply concerned. I hoped to be able to give some reassurance.'

'Yes?'

'Alex, she didn't get to work.' Margot's voice sounded strained.

'Well, maybe . . .'

'Please listen. I'm at Forum East now. I went there when I learned she wasn't at the bank and I couldn't get an answer on Juanita's home phone either. Since then I've talked to some other people in the building where she lives. Two of them say Juanita left her apartment this morning, at her usual time, with her little girl Estela. Juanita always takes Estela to nursery school on her way to the bank. I found out the name of the school and phoned. Estela isn't there. Neither she nor her mother arrived this morning.'

There was a silence. Margot's voice asked, 'Alex, are you still listening?'

'Yes, I'm here.'

'After that, I phoned the bank again and this time talked to Edwina. She's checked personally. Not only has Juanita not appeared, she hasn't phoned in, which isn't like her. That's why I'm worried. I'm convinced something's gone terribly, terribly wrong.'

'Do you have any ideas?'

'Yes,' Margot said. 'The same one you have.'

'Wait,' he told her. 'Nolan's here.'

Wainwright had hunched forward, listening. Now he straightened and said quietly, 'Núñez has been picked up. There isn't any doubt of it.'

'By?'

'By someone from that Double-Seven crowd. They're probably on to Eastin, too.'

'You think they've taken her to that club?'

'No. That's the last thing they'll do. She's somewhere else.'

'Do you have any idea where?'

'No.'

'And whoever it is has the child, too?'

'I'm afraid so.' There was anguish in Wainwright's eyes. 'I'm sorry, Alex.'

421

'You got us into this,' Alex said fiercely. 'Now, for God's sake, you've got to get Juanita and the kid out of it!'

Wainwright was concentrating, thinking as he spoke. 'The first thing is to see if there's a chance of warning Eastin. If we can get to him, and get him out, he might know something which could lead us to the girl.' He had a small black notebook open and was already reaching for another phone.

twenty

It happened so swiftly and was so totally unexpected that car doors had slammed, the big black limousine was moving, before she had a chance to cry out. By then Juanita knew instinctively it was too late, but screamed just the same – 'Help! Help!' – until a fist slammed savagely into her face, followed by a gloved hand clamped across her mouth. Even then, hearing Estela's shriek of terror alongside her, Juanita went on struggling until the fist hit hard a second time and vision blurred while sounds receded far away.

The day – a clear, fresh, early-November morning – had begun normally. Juanita and Estela were up in time to have breakfast, then watch the NBC *Today* news on their small black and white portable. After that, they hurried to leave as usual at 7.30, which allowed Juanita just enough time to accompany Estela to nursery school before catching a bus to downtown and the bank. Juanita always liked mornings, and being with Estela was a joyous way to start any day.

Coming out of the building, Estela had skipped ahead, calling back, 'Mommy, I'm missing all the lines,' and Juanita smiled because evading lines and cracks in the pavement was a game they often played. It was about then that Juanita took vague notice of the dark-windowed limousine parked just ahead, with its rear kerbside door open. She had taken more notice, though, as Estela neared the car and someone inside it spoke to her. Estela moved closer. As she did, a hand reached out and yanked the little girl inside. Instantly, Juanita had run to the car door. Then, from behind, a figure whom she hadn't seen closed in and shoved Juanita hard, making her trip and fall forward into the car, scraping her legs painfully. Before she could recover, Juanita was dragged inside and pushed to the floor with Estela. The door behind her slammed, also a door in front, and the car was moving.

Now, as her head cleared and full consciousness returned, she heard a voice say. 'For chrissakes, why ya bring the god-damned kid?'

'Hadda do it. If we don't, the kid's gonna make a big fat fuss, then some jerk hollers cops. This way we got away clear, fast, no sweat.'

Juanita stirred. Hot knives of pain, originating where she had been hit, surged through her head. She moaned.

'Listen, bitch!' a third voice said. 'Ya make trouble, y'll get hurt plenty more. And don't get ideas about anyone outside seein' in. This car's got one-way glass.'

Juanita lay still, fighting off panic, forcing herself to think. There were three men in the car, two on the back seat above her, one in front. The remark about one-way glass explained her earlier impression of a big car with dark windows. So what had been said was right: it was no good trying to attract attention. Where were she and Estela being taken? And why? Juanita had not the least doubt that the answer to the second question had something to do with her arrangement with Miles. What she had dreaded had come true. She was, she realized, in gravest peril. But, *Mother of God! – why Estela?* The two of them were sandwiched together on the car floor, Estela's body heaving in desperate sobs. Juanita moved, trying to hold and comfort her.

'There, *amorcito*! Be brave, little one.'

'Shaddup!' one of the men commanded.

Another voice – she believed the driver's – said, 'Better gag and blindfold 'em.'

Juanita felt movements, heard a cloth-like substance tear. She pleaded frantically, 'Please, no! I'll . . .' The remaining words were lost as a wide adhesive tape was slapped over her mouth and pressed down. Moments later a dark cloth covered her eyes; she felt it being fastened tightly. Next her hands were seized and tied behind her. Cords cut her wrists. There had been dust on the car floor which filled Juanita's nostrils; unable to see or move, choking under the gag, she blew frantically to clear her nose and breathe. From other movements beside her she sensed the same treatment was being meted out to Estela. Despair enveloped her. Tears of rage, frustration filled her eyes. *Damn you, Wainwright! Damn you, Miles! Where are you now? . . . Why had she ever agreed . . . made it possible . . . Oh, why? Why? . . . Mother of God, please help me! And if not me, save Estela!*

As time passed, with pain and helplessness increasing, Juanita's thoughts drifted. She was aware vaguely of the car moving slowly, stopping and starting as if in traffic, then of a long burst of speed followed by more slowness, twists, and turns. The journey, wherever it was to, seemed endless. After perhaps an hour – or was it much more or even much less? – Juanita felt the force of brakes applied fully. Momentarily the car's motor was louder, as if in a confined space. Then the motor stopped. She heard an electric hum, a rumble as if a heavy door was closing mechanically, a 'thunk' as the rumble stopped. Simultaneously the limousine's door clicked open, hinges creaked and she was pulled roughly to her feet and impelled forward. Juanita stumbled, striking her legs painfully again, and would have fallen, but hands seized her. One of the voices she had already heard ordered, 'Goddamnit – walk!'

With the blindfold still in place, moving clumsily, her fears remained centred on Estela. She was conscious of footsteps – her own, others – resounding on concrete. Suddenly the floor fell away and she stumbled, partly held, partly shoved down stairs. At the bottom, more walking. Abruptly she was pushed backwards off balance, her legs shooting out until the fall was stopped by a hard wooden chair. The same voice as before told someone, 'Take off the shade and tape.'

She felt the movement of hands, and fresh pain as the tape was pulled carelessly away from her mouth. The blindfold loosened, then Juanita blinked as darkness gave way to a bright light directed into her eyes.

She gasped only, '¡ *Por Dios* ! where is my . . .' when a fist struck her.

'Save the singing,' one of the car voices said. 'When we tell ya, y'll spill plenty.'

There were certain things which Tony Bear Marino liked. One was erotic sex – by his standards, erotic meant things women did to him which made him feel superior and themselves degraded. Another was cockfighting – the bloodier the better. He enjoyed detailed, graphic reports of gangland beatings and executions which he ordered, though he was careful to stay away from evidential involvement. Another, though milder, taste was for one-way glass.

Tony Bear Marino so liked one-way (or mirror pane) glass, which permitted him to observe without being seen, that he had it installed in multiple places – his cars, business premises, hangouts including the Double-Seven Health Club, and his secluded, guarded home. In the house, a bathroom and toilet which women visitors used had an entire wall of one-way glass. From the bathroom side it was a handsome mirror, but on the other was a small closed room in which Tony Bear would sit, enjoying a cigar and the personal privacies unknowingly revealed to him.

Because of his obsession, some one-way glass had been installed at the counterfeiting centre and though, out of normal caution, he seldom went there, it had proved useful occasionally, as was the case now.

The glass was built into a half-wall – in effect a screen. Through it he could see the Núñez woman, facing him and tied to a chair. Her face was bruised and bleeding, and she was dishevelled. Beside her was her child, secured to another chair, the little girl's face chalk white. A few minutes ago, when Marino learned the child had been brought in, he exploded angrily, not because he cared about children – he didn't – but because he smelled trouble. An adult could be eliminated, if necessary, with virtually no risk. But killing a child was something else. It would cause squeamishness among his own people, and emotion and danger afterwards if rumours leaked. Tony Bear had already made a decision on the subject; it related to the blindfold precautions taken while coming here. He was also satisfied to be out of sight himself.

Now he lit a cigar and watched.

Angelo, one of Tony Bear's bodyguards who had been in charge of the pick-up operation, leaned over the woman. Angelo was an ex-prize fighter who had never made the big time but was built like a rhino. He had thick, protruding lips, was a bully and enjoyed what he was doing. 'Okay, you two-bit hooker, start talkin'.'

Juanita, who had been straining to see Estela, turned her head towards him. '¿ De qué ? Talk, what about ?'

'Whassa name o' da guy who phoned ya from the Double-Seven ?'

A flicker of understanding crossed Juanita's face. Tony Bear saw it and knew it would be only a matter of time, not long at that, before they had the information.

'You bastard! ... Animal!' Juanita spat at Angelo. '¡ Canalla ! I know of no Double-Seven.'

Angelo hit her hard, so that blood ran from her nose and the corner of her mouth. Juanita's head drooped. He seized her hair, holding her face up while he repeated, 'Who's the guy who phoned you from the Double-Seven ?'

She answered thickly through swollen lips. '*Maricón,* I will tell you nothing until you let my little girl go.'

The broad had spirit, Tony Bear conceded. If she had been built differently he might have amused himself breaking her in other ways. But she was too scrawny for his taste – no hips worth a damn, half a handful of ass, and little peanut tits.

Angelo drew back his arm and punched her in the stomach. Juanita gasped and doubled forward as far as her bonds allowed. Beside her, Estela, who could see and hear, was sobbing hysterically. The sound annoyed Tony Bear. This was taking too long. There was a quicker way. He beckoned a second bodyguard,

Lou, and whispered. Lou looked as if he didn't like what he was being told, but nodded. Tony Bear handed over the cigar he was smoking.

While Lou stepped out past the partition and spoke in an undertone to Angelo, Tony Bear Marino glanced around him. They were in a basement with all doors closed, eliminating the chance of sounds escaping, though even if they did it wouldn't matter. The fifty-year-old house, of which this was part, stood in its own grounds in a high-class residential district and was protected like a fortress. A syndicate which Tony Bear Marino headed had bought the house eight months ago and moved the counterfeiting operation in. Soon, as a precaution, they would sell the house and move on elsewhere; in fact, a new location was already chosen. It would have the same kind of innocuous, innocent-appearing background as this one. That, Tony Bear sometimes thought with satisfaction, had been the secret of the long, successful run: frequent moves to quiet, respectable neighbourhoods, with traffic to and from the centre kept to a minimum. The ultra-caution had two advantages – only a handful of people knew exactly where the centre was; also, with everything buttoned down, neighbours weren't suspicious. They had even worked out elaborate precautions for moving from one place to the next. One of them: wooden covers, designed to look like household furniture, which fitted over every piece of machinery, so to a casual watcher all that was happening was a domestic move. And a regular house moving van, from one of the organization's outwardly legit trucking companies, was brought in for the job. There were even stand-by arrangements for an emergency, extra-fast trucking move if ever needed.

The fake furniture gimmick had been one of Danny Kerrigan's notions. The old man had had some other good ones, as well as proving a champion counterfeiter since Tony Bear Marino brought him into the organization a dozen years ago. Shortly before that time, Tony Bear heard about Kerrigan's reputation as a craftsman, and that he had become an alcoholic, skid row bum. On Tony Bear's orders the old man had been rescued, dried out, and later put to work – with spectacular results.

427

There seemed to be nothing, Tony Bear had come to believe, that Danny couldn't print successfully – money, postage stamps, share certificates, cheques, drivers' licences, Social Security cards, you name it. It had been Danny's idea to manufacture thousands of fake bank credit cards. Through bribery and a carefully planned raid, they had been able to obtain blank plastic sheets from which Keycharge cards were made, and the quantity was enough to last for years. Profit so far had been immense.

The only beef about the old man was that once in a while he went back to hitting the sauce and could be out of business for a week or more. When it happened there was danger of him talking, so he was kept confined. But he could be crafty and sometimes managed to slip away, as happened last time. Lately, though, the lapses had been fewer, mostly because Danny was happily stashing away his share of the dough in a Swiss bank account and dreamed of going there in a year or two to pick up his loot, then retire. Except that Tony Bear knew that was one move of the old drunk's which wouldn't happen. He intended to use the old man as long as he could function. Also Danny knew too much ever to be let go.

But while Danny Kerrigan was important, it had been the organization which protected him and made the most of what he produced. Without an efficient distribution system the old man would have been like most others of his breed – small time or a nothing. Therefore it was the threat to the organization which concerned Tony Bear most. Had it been infiltrated by a spy, a stool pigeon ? If 'yes', from where ? And how much had he – or she – learned ?

His attention swung back to what was happening on the other side of the one-way glass. Angelo had the lighted cigar. His thick lips were twisted in a grin. With the side of his foot he shoved the two chairs so the Núñez woman and her brat now faced each other. Angelo puffed on the cigar until its tip was glowing. Casually he moved to the chair where the child was seated and bound.

Estela looked up, visibly trembling, eyes wild with fright. Without hurrying. Angelo took her small right hand, lifted it, inspected the palm, then turned it over. Still slowly he removed the glowing cigar from his mouth and ground it, as if into an ashtray, on the back of her hand. Estela cried out – a piercing shriek of agony. Opposite her, Juanita, frantic, weeping, shouting incoherently, struggled desperately against her bonds.

The cigar was not out. Angelo puffed it into fresh redness then, with the same leisureliness as before, lifted Estela's other hand.

Juanita screamed, 'No, no, *déjela quieta*. I will tell you.'

Angelo waited, the cigar poised as Juantia gasped, 'The man you want . . . is Miles Eastin.'

'Who's he work for ?'

Her voice a despairing whisper, she answered, 'First Mercantile American Bank.'

Angelo dropped the cigar and ground it out with his heel. He looked interrogatively at where he knew Tony Bear Marino to be, then came around the screen.

Tony Bear's face was tight. He said softly, 'Get him. Go get that fink. Bring him here.'

twenty-one

'Milesy,' Nate Nathanson said with unusual grouchiness, 'whoever your friend is keeps phoning, tell him this place ain't run for the staff, it's run for members.'

'What friend ?' Miles Eastin, who had been away from the Double-Seven for part of the morning taking care of club errands, looked uncertainly at the manager.

'How in hell would I know ? Same guy's phoned four times, asking for you. Wouldn't leave a name; no message.' Nathanson said impatiently, 'Where's the deposit book ?'

Miles handed it over. Among his calls had been one to a bank to deposit cheques.

'Shipment of canned goods came in just now,' Nathanson

said. 'Cases in the storeroom. Check 'em against the invoices.' He handed Miles some papers and a key.

'Sure, Nate. And I'm sorry about the calls.'

But the manager had already turned away, heading for his office on the third floor. Miles felt some sympathy for him. He knew that Tony Bear Marino and Russian Ominsky, who owned the Double-Seven jointly, had been leaning hard on Nathanson lately with complaints about running of the club.

On his way to the storeroom, which was on the main floor at the rear of the building, Miles wondered about those phone calls. Who would be calling him? And insistently. As far as he knew, only three people connected with his former life were aware that he was here – his probation officer; Juanita; Nolan Wainwright. The probation officer? Highly unlikely. Last time Miles made his required monthly visit and report, the PO had been rushed and indifferent; all he seemed to care about was that he wouldn't be caused trouble. The probation man had made a note of where Miles was working and that was that. Juanita then? No. She knew better; besides, Nathanson had said a man. That left Wainwright.

But Wainwright wouldn't call either . . . *Or would he?* Might he not take the risk if it were something truly urgent . . . *like a warning?*

A warning of what? *That Miles was in danger? That he had been exposed as a spy, or might be?* Abruptly, icy fear seized him. His heart hammered faster. Miles realized: lately he had assumed an invulnerability, had taken his safety for granted. But in reality there was no safety here, never had been; only danger – even greater now than in the beginning, for now he knew too much.

Approaching the storeroom, as the thought persisted, his hands were trembling. He had to steady himself to put the key in the lock. He wondered: was he becoming frightened about nothing, reacting cravenly to shadows? Perhaps. But a sense of foreboding warned him – no. *So what should he do?* Whoever had telephoned would probably try again. But was it wise to wait? Miles decided: risk or not he would call Wainwright directly.

He had pushed the storeroom door open. Now he began to close it, to go to a public phone nearby – the one from which he had called Juanita a week and a half ago. At that moment he heard activity in the club's front lobby at the other end of the main floor corridor which ran from front to rear. Several men were entering from the street. They seemed in a hurry. Without knowing why, Miles reversed direction and slipped into the storeroom, out of sight. He heard a mix of voices, then one ask loudly, 'Where's that punk, Eastin?'

He recognized the voice. Angelo, one of Marino's bodyguards.

'Up in the office, I guess.' That was Jules LaRocca. Miles heard him say, 'What's with . . .'

'Tony Bear wants . . .'

The voices faded as the men hurried upstairs. But Miles had heard enough, knowing that what he feared had come true. In a minute, maybe less, Nate Nathanson would tell Angelo and the others where he was. Then they would be down here.

He felt his entire body quaking, yet forced himself to think. To leave by the front lobby was impossible. Even if he didn't encounter the men returning from upstairs, they had probably left someone on guard outside. The rear exit, then? It was seldom used and opened near an abandoned building. Beyond that was a vacant lot, then an elevated railway arch. On the far side of the rail line was a maze of small, mean streets. He could try dodging through those streets, though the chance of eluding a pursuit was slim. There could be several pursuers; some would have a car or cars; Miles had none. His mind flashed the message: *Your only chance! Don't lose more time! Go now!* He slammed the storeroom door closed and took the key; perhaps the others would waste precious minutes battering the door down, believing him to be inside.

Then he ran.

Through the small rear door, fumbling first with a bolt . . . Outside, stopping to close the door; no sense in advertising the way he had gone . . . Then down a lane beside the disused building . . . The building had been a factory once; the lane was littered with debris, old packing cases, cans, the rusty skeleton of a truck beside a caved-in loading bay. It was like running an obstacle course. Rats scampered away . . . Across the vacant lot, stumbling over bricks, garbage, a dead dog . . . Once Miles tripped and felt an ankle twist; it pained him sharply, but he kept on . . . So far he had heard no one following . . . Then as he reached the railway arch, with comparative safety of the streets ahead, there were running feet behind, a shout, 'There's the son of a bitch!'

Miles increased his speed. He was now on the firmer ground of streets and pavements. He took the first turning he came to – sharply left; then right; almost at once, left again. Behind him he could still hear the pounding feet . . . These streets were new to him but his sense of direction told him he was headed for the city centre. If he could only make it there he would disappear in midday crowds, giving him time to think, to telephone Wainwright, perhaps, and ask for help. Meanwhile he was running hard and well, his wind good. His ankle hurt a little; not too much. Miles's fitness, the hours spent on the Double-Seven handball court, were paying off . . . The sounds of running behind him receded, but their absence didn't fool him. While a car could not travel the route he had come – down the blocked lane and over the vacant lot – there were ways around. A detour of several blocks to cross the railway line would create delay. Not much, though. Probably, even now, someone in a car was trying to outguess him, head him off. He doubled left and right again, hoping, as he had from the beginning, for any kind of transportation. A bus. A taxi better still. But neither came . . . *When you needed a taxi badly, why was there never one around?* . . . *Or a cop.* He wished the streets he was passing through were busier. Running made him conspicuous, but he could not afford to slow down yet. A few people whom Miles passed looked at him curiously, but citizens here were used to minding their own business.

The nature of the area, though, was changing as he ran. Now it was less ghetto-like, showing signs of more prosperity. He passed several sizeable shops. Ahead were larger buildings still, the city skyline coming into view. But before getting there, two major intersecting streets would have to be crossed. He could see the first one now – wide, busy with traffic, divided by a central reservation. Then he saw something else – on the far side of the reservation a long black Cadillac with dark windows, cruising slowly. *Marino's.* As the car crossed the street which Miles was on, it seemed to hesitate, then speeded up, passing quickly out of sight. There had been no time to try to hide. Had he been seen? Had the car gone on to switch lanes and come back, or had he stayed lucky and been unobserved? Again fear struck him. Though he was sweating, Miles shivered but kept on. There was nothing else to do. He moved close to buildings, slowing his pace as much as he dared. A minute and a half later, with the intersection only fifty yards away, a Cadillac – the same car – nosed around the corner.

He knew that luck had run out. Whoever was in the car – most likely Angelo, for one – could not fail to see him, probably had already. So was anything to be gained by more resistance? Wouldn't it be simpler to give up, to allow himself to be taken, to let what was going to happen, happen? *No!* Because he had seen enough of Tony Bear Marino and his kind, in prison and since, to know what happened to people who incurred their vengeance. The black car was slowing. They *had* seen him. *Desperation.*

One of the shops Miles had noticed moments earlier was immediately alongside. Breaking his stride, he turned left, pushed open a glass door and went in. Inside, he saw it was a sporting goods shop. A pale, spindly clerk, about Miles's own age, stepped forward. 'Good day, sir. Is there something I can show you?'

'Er . . . yes.' He said the first thing that came into his head. 'I'd like to see bowling balls.'

'Certainly. What kind of price and weight?'

'The best. About sixteen pounds.'

'Colour?'

'Doesn't matter.'

Miles was watching the few yards of pavement outside the street door. Several pedestrians had gone by. None had paused or looked in.

'If you come this way, I'll show you what we have.'

He followed the clerk past racks of skis, glass cases, a display

433

of handguns. Then, glancing back, Miles saw the silhouette of a single figure, stopped outside and peering in the window. Now a second figure joined the first. They stood together, not moving from the shop-front. Miles wondered: could he get out through the back? Even as the thought occurred to him, he discarded it. The men who were after him would not make the same error twice. Any rear exit would already have been located and guarded.

'This is an excellent ball. It sells for forty-two dollars.'

'I'll take it.'

'We'll need your hand measurement for the . . .'

'Never mind.'

Should he try to phone Wainwright from here? But Miles was sure if he went near a phone the men outside would come in instantly.

The clerk looked puzzled. 'You don't want us to drill . . .'

'I said never mind.'

'As you wish, sir. How about a bag for the ball? Perhaps some bowling shoes?'

'Yes,' Miles said. 'Yes, okay.' It would help postpone the moment of returning to the street. Scarcely aware of what he was doing, he inspected bags put in front of him, chose one at random, then sat down to try on shoes. It was while slipping on a pair that the idea occurred to him. *The Keycharge card which Wainwright had sent through Juanita . . . the card in the name of H. E. Lyncolp . . . H-E-L-P.*

He motioned to the bowling ball, bag, and the shoes he had chosen. 'How much?'

The clerk looked up from an invoice. 'Eighty-six dollars and ninety-five cents, plus tax.'

'Listen,' Miles said, 'I want to put it on my Keycharge.' He took out his wallet and offered the LYNCOLP card, trying to stop his hands from trembling.

'That's okay, but . . .'

'I know, you need authorization. Go ahead. Phone for it.'

The clerk took the card and invoice to a glassed-in office area. He was gone several minutes, then returned.

Miles asked anxiously, 'Get through?'

'Sure. Everything's okay, Mr Lyncolp.'

Miles wondered what was happening now at the Keycharge Centre in FMA Headquarters Tower. Would it help him? Could *anything* help? ... Then he remembered the second instruction relayed by Juanita: after using the card, dawdle as much as possible. Give Wainwright time to move.

'Sign here, please, Mr Lyncolp.' A Keycharge account slip was filled in for the amount he had spent. Miles leaned over the counter to add a signature.

Straightening up, he felt a hand touch his shoulder lightly. A voice said quietly, 'Milesy.'

As he turned, Jules LaRocca said, 'Don't make no fuss. It won't do no good and you'll get hurt the worse.'

Behind LaRocca, their faces impassive, were Angelo and Lou, and a fourth man – another bruiser type – whom Miles hadn't seen before. The four moved around him, seizing him, pinioning his arms.

'Move, shitass.' The order was from Angelo, low-voiced.

Miles considered crying out, but who was there to help him? The flabby clerk, watching open-mouthed, could not. The hunt was ended. The pressure on his arms tightened. He felt himself propelled helpless towards the outer door.

The bewildered sales clerk ran after them. 'Mr Lyncolp! You've forgotten your bowling ball.'

It was LaRocca who told him, 'You keep it, buster. This guy don't even need the balls he's got.'

The black Cadillac was parked a few yards down the street. They pushed Miles roughly into it and drove off.

Business in the Keycharge authorization centre was near its daily peak. A normal shift of fifty operators was on duty in the semi-darkened auditorium-style centre, each seated at a keyboard with a TV-like cathode ray tube above it.

To the young operator who received the call, the H. E. LYN-COLP credit query was simply one of thousands dealt with routinely during a working day. All were totally impersonal. Neither she nor others like her ever knew where the calls they handled came from – not even which city or state. The credit sought might be to pay a New York housewife's grocery bill, provide clothing for a Kansas farmer, allow a rich Chicago dowager to load herself with unneeded jewellery, advance a Princeton undergrad's tuition fees, or help a Cleveland alcoholic buy the case of liquor which finally would kill him. But the operator was never told details. If really needed later, the specifics of a purchase could be traced back, though it seldom happened. The reason: no one cared. The money mattered, the money changing hands, the ability to repay the credit granted; that was all.

The call began with a flashing light on the operator's console. She touched a switch and spoke into her headset mike. 'What is your merchant number, please ?'

The caller – a sporting goods clerk attending to Miles Eastin – gave it. As he did, the operator typed the number. Simultaneously it appeared on her cathode ray screen.

She asked, 'Card number and date of expiry ?'

Another answer. Again, details on the screen.

'Amount of purchase ?'

'Ninety dollars, forty-three.'

Typed. On screen. The operator pressed a key, alerting a computer several floors below.

Within a millisecond the computer digested the information, searched its records and flashed an answer.

APPROVED.
AUTH. NO. 7416984
URGENT . . . EMERGENCY . . . DO NOT, REPEAT DO NOT,
ALERT MERCHANT . . . ADVISE YOUR SUPERVISOR . . .
EXECUTE IMMEDIATELY EMERGENCY INSTRUCTION 17 . . .

'The purchase is approved,' the operator told the caller. 'Authorization number . . .'

She was speaking more slowly than usual. Even before she began, she had flashed a signal to an elevated supervisors' booth. Now in the booth another young woman, one of six supervisors on duty, was already reading her own duplication of the cathode ray tube display. She reached for a card index, seeking emergency instruction 17.

The original operator deliberately stumbled over the authorization number and began again. Emergency signals were not flashed often, but when it happened there were standard procedures which operators knew. Slowing down was one. In the past, murderers had been caught, a kidnap victim saved, disappearances solved, stolen art treasures recovered, a son brought to his dying mother's bedside – all because a computer had been alerted to the possibility that a particular credit card might be used, and if and when it was, prompt action was essential. At such moments, while others took the needed action, a few seconds' foot-dragging by an operator could help significantly.

The supervisor was already implementing instruction 17 which informed her that N. Wainwright, v/p Security, was to be advised immediately by telephone that the special Keycharge card issued in the name H. E. LYNCOLP had been presented, and where. By depressing keys on her own keyboard, the supervisor summoned from the computer the additional information:

PETE'S SPORTING GOODS

and a street address. Meanwhile she had dialled the office number of Mr Wainwright who answered personally. His interest was instant. He responded crisply to the supervisor's information and she sensed his tension while he copied details down.

Seconds later, for the Keycharge supervisor, operator, and computer, the brief emergency was over.

Not so for Nolan Wainwright.

Since the explosive session an hour and a half ago with Alex Vandervoort, when he learned of the disappearance of Juanita Núñez and her child, Wainwright had been tensely and continuously on telephones, sometimes two at once. He had tried four times to reach Miles Eastin at the Double-Seven Health Club to warn him of his danger. He had had consultations with the FBI and US Secret Service. As a result the FBI was now actively investigating the apparent Núñez kidnapping, and had alerted city and state police with descriptions of the missing pair. It had been arranged that an FBI surveillance team would watch comings and goings at the Double-Seven as soon as the manpower could be spared, probably by this afternoon.

That was all that would be done concerning the Double-

Seven for the time being. As FBI Special Agent Innes expressed it, 'If we go in there with questions, we tip our hand about knowing the connection, and as for a search, we've no grounds to seek a warrant. Besides, according to your man Eastin, it's mostly a meeting place with nothing illegal – except some gambling – going on.'

Innes agreed with Wainwright's conclusion that Juanita Núñez and her daughter would not have been taken to the Double-Seven.

The Secret Service, with fewer facilities than the FBI, was working the hideout angle, contacting informers, probing for any scintilla of fact or rumour which might prove to be a lead the combined law enforcement agencies could use. For the moment, unusually, inter-force rivalry and jealousies were put aside.

When Wainwright received the Keycharge H. E. Lyncolf alert he promptly dialled the FBI. Special Agents Innes and Dalrymple were out, he was informed, but could be contacted by radio. He dictated an urgent message and waited. The reply came back: the agents were downtown, not far from the address given, and were on their way there. Would Wainwright meet them ?

Action was a relief. He hurried through the building to his car.

Outside Pete's Sporting Goods, Innes was questioning bystanders when Wainwright arrived. Dalrymple was still inside, completing a statement by the clerk. Innes broke off and joined the bank security chief. 'A dry hole,' he reported glumly. 'It was all over when we got here.' He related the little they had learned.

Wainwright asked, 'Descriptions ?'

The FBI man shook his head. 'The store guy who served Eastin was so shit scared, he's not sure if there were four men came in or three. Says it all happened so fast, he can't describe or identify anyone. And no one, inside the store or out, remembers seeing a car.'

Wainwright's face was drawn, the strain of anxiety and conscience showing. 'So what comes next ?'

'You were a cop,' Innes said. 'You know how it is in real life. We wait, hoping something else will turn up.'

438

twenty-two

She heard scuffling and voices. Now she knew they had Miles and were bringing him in.

For Juanita, time had drifted. She had no idea how long it was since she had gasped out Miles Eastin's name, betraying him, to end the horror of Estela's torture. Soon after that she had been gagged again and the bonds holding her to the chair were checked and tightened. Then the men left.

For a while, she knew, she had dozed – or, more accurately, her body had released her from awareness since any real rest was impossible, bound as she was. Alerted by the new noise, her constricted limbs protested agonizingly, so that she wanted to cry out, though the gag prevented it. Juanita willed herself not to panic, not to struggle against her bonds, knowing both would be futile and make her situation worse.

She could still see Estela. The chairs they were bound to had been left facing each other. The little girl's eyes were closed in sleep, her small head drooping; the noises which awakened Juanita had not disturbed her. Estela, too, was gagged. Juanita hoped that sheer exhaustion would spare her from reality for as long as possible.

Estela's right hand showed the ugly red burn from the cigar. Shortly after the men had left, one of them – Juanita had heard him addressed as Lou – came back briefly. He had a tube of ointment of some kind. Squeezing the tube, he covered Estela's burn, glancing quickly at Juanita as if to tell her it was the best he could do. Then he, too, had gone.

Estela had jumped while the ointment was being applied, then whimpered for a while behind her gag, but soon after sleep had mercifully come.

The sounds Juanita had been hearing were behind her. Probably in an adjoining room, and she guessed a connecting door was open. Briefly she heard Miles's voice protesting, then a thud, a grunt, and silence.

Perhaps a minute passed. Miles's voice again, this time more distinct. 'No! Oh, God, no! Please! I'll . . .' She heard a sound like hammer blows, metal on metal. Miles's words stopped, changing to a high-pitched, piercing, frenzied scream. The screaming, worse than anything she had ever heard, went on and on.

If Miles could have killed himself in the car, he would have done so willingly. He had known from the beginning of his deal with Wainwright – it had been the root of his fears ever since – that straightforward dying would be easy compared with what awaited an exposed informer. Even so, what he had feared was nothing beside the unbelievably awful, excoriating punishment being meted to him now.

His legs and thighs were strapped tightly, cruelly together. His arms had been forced down on to a rough wooden table. *His hands and wrists were being nailed to the table . . . nailed with carpenter's nails . . . hammered hard . . . A nail was already in the left wrist, two more in the wide part of the hand between the wrist and fingers, fastening it tightly down . . . The last few strokes of the hammer had smashed the bone . . . One nail was in the right hand, another poised to tear, to hack through flesh and muscle . . . No pain was ever, could be ever . . . Oh, God, help me ! . . . would be ever greater.* Miles writhed, screamed, pleaded, screamed again. But the hands holding his body tightened. The hammer blows, which had briefly paused, resumed.

'He ain't yelping loud enough,' Marino told Angelo, who was wielding the hammer. 'When you get through with that, try nailing down a couple of the bastard's fingers.'

Tony Bear, who was puffing on a cigar while he watched and listened, had not bothered concealing himself this time. There would be no possibility of Eastin identifying him because Eastin would soon be dead. First, though, it was necessary to remind him – and others to whom the news of what had happened here would filter out – that for a stool pigeon there was never any easy death.

'That's more like it,' Tony Bear conceded. Miles's agonized shrieks rose in volume while a fresh nail penetrated the centre finger of his left hand, mid-way between the two knuckles, and

440

was hammered home. Audibly, the bone in the finger split apart. As Angelo was about to repeat the process with the middle finger of the right hand, Tony Bear ordered, 'Hold it!'

He told Eastin, 'Stop the goddamn noise! Start singing.'

Miles's screaming turned to racking sobs, his body heaving. The hands holding him had been removed. They were no longer needed.

'Okay,' Tony Bear told Angelo, 'he ain't stopped, so go right ahead.'

'No! No! I'll talk! I will! I will!' Somehow Miles choked back his sobs. The loudest sound was now his heavy, rasping breathing.

Tony Bear waved Angelo back. The others in the room remained grouped around the table. They were Lou; Punch Clancy, the extra bodyguard who had been one of the four in the sporting goods shop an hour earlier; LaRocca, scowling, worried about how much he would be blamed for sponsoring Miles; and the old printer, Danny Kerrigan, ill at ease and nervous. Although this was normally Danny's domain – they were in the main printing and engraving shop – he preferred to keep out of the way at moments such as this, but Tony Bear had sent for him.

Tony Bear snarled at Eastin, 'So all the time you were a stoolie for a stinking bank?'

Miles gasped out, 'Yes.'

'First Mercantile?'

'Yes.'

'Who'd you report to?'

'Wainwright.'

'How much you found out? What'd you tell him?'

'About . . . the club . . . the games . . . who went there.'

'Including me?'

'Yes.'

'You son of a bitch!' Tony Bear reached over and slammed his clenched fist in Miles's face.

Miles's body sagged away with the force of the blow, but the strain tore at his hands and he pulled back desperately to the painful, bent-over position he was in before. A silence followed, broken only by his laboured sobs and groans. Tony Bear puffed his cigar several times, then resumed the questioning.

'What else you find out, you stinking turd?'

'Nothing . . . nothing!' Every part of Miles was shaking uncontrollably.

'You're lying.' Tony Bear turned to Danny Kerrigan. 'Get me that juice you use for the engravings.'

During the questioning until now, the old printer had been eyeing Miles with hatred. Now he nodded. 'Sure thing, Mr Marino.'

Danny crossed to a shelf and hefted down a gallon jug with a plastic cap. The jar was labelled NITRIC ACID: *Use for Etching Only*. Removing the cap, Danny poured carefully from the jar into a half-pint glass beaker. Being careful not to spill the beaker's contents, he carried it to the table where Tony Bear faced Miles. He put it down, then laid a small engraver's brush beside it.

Tony Bear picked up the brush and dipped it in the nitric acid. Casually he reached over and dabbed the brush down one side of Eastin's face. For a second or two, while the acid penetrated surface skin, there was no reaction. Then Miles cried out with a new and different agony as the burning spread and deepened. While the others watched in fascination, the flesh under the acid smouldered, turning from pink to brownish black.

Tony Bear dipped the brush in the beaker again. 'I'll ask you one more time, asshole. If I don't get answers, this goes on the other side. What else did you find out and tell?'

Miles's eyes were wild, like a cornered animal's. He spluttered, 'The counterfeit . . . money.'

'What about it?'

'I bought some . . . sent it to the bank . . . then drove the car . . . took more to Louisville.'

'And?'

'Credit cards . . . drivers' licences.'

'You know who made them? Printed the phoney money?'

Miles motioned his head as best he could. 'Danny.'

'Who told you?'

'He . . . told me.'

'And afterwards you spilled your guts to that cop at the bank?
He knows all that?'

'Yes.'

Tony Bear swung savagely to Kerrigan. 'You drunken stupid
fart! You're no better than him.'

The old man stood quaking. 'Mr Marino, I wasn't drunk. I
just thought he . . .'

'Shaddup!' Tony Bear seemed about to hit the old man, then
changed his mind. He returned to Miles. 'What else do they
know?'

'Nothing else!'

'Do they know where the printing's done? Where this place
is?'

'No.'

Tony Bear returned the brush to the acid and withdrew it.
Miles followed every movement. Experience told him the expected answer. He shouted, 'Yes! Yes, they know!'

'You told that bank security bum?'

Despairingly, Miles lied. 'Yes, yes!'

'How'd you find out?' The brush stayed poised above the acid.

Miles knew he had to find an answer. *Any* answer which
would satisfy. He turned his head to Danny. '*He* told me.'

'You're a liar! You lousy, stinking goddamned liar!' The old
man's face was working, his mouth opening and closing and jaw
quivering as emotion gripped him. He appealed to Tony Bear.
'Mr Marino, he's lying! I swear he's lying! It isn't true.' But
what he saw in Marino's eyes increased his desperation. Now
Danny rushed at Miles. 'Tell him the truth, you bastard! Tell
him!' Demented, knowing the potential penalty for himself, the
old man looked around him for a weapon. He saw the acid
beaker. Seizing it, he tossed the contents in Miles's face.

A fresh scream started, then abruptly stilled. As the odour of
acid and the sickly smell of burning flesh mingled, Miles fell
forward, unconscious across the table where his mangled, bleeding hands were nailed.

Though not wholly understanding what was happening to
Miles, Juanita suffered through his cries and pleadings and

443

finally the extinction of his voice. She wondered – dispassionately because her feelings were now dulled beyond the point where more emotion could affect her – if he were dead. She speculated on how long it would be before she and Estela shared Miles's fate. That they would both die now seemed inevitable.

Juanita was grateful for one thing: Estela had not stirred, despite the uproar. If sleep would only stay with her, perhaps she would be spared whatever awfulness remained before the end. As she had not done in many years, Juanita prayed to the Virgin Mary to make death easy for Estela.

Juanita was aware of new activity in the adjoining room. It sounded as if furniture was being moved, drawers opened and slammed, containers set down heavily. Once there was the jangle of metal cascading on cement and curses afterwards.

Then, to her surprise, the man she had come to recognize as Lou appeared beside her and began unfastening her bonds. She supposed she was being taken somewhere, exchanging one perdition for another. When he had finished, he left her where she was and started to untie Estela.

'Stand up!' he ordered both of them. Estela, coming awake, complied, though sleepily. She began crying softly, the sound muffled by her gag. Juanita wanted to go to her but could not yet move forward; she supported her weight against the chair, suffering as blood flowed through her cramped limbs.

'Listen to me,' Lou told Juanita. 'You got lucky because of your kid. The boss is gonna let you go. You'll be blindfolded, taken in a car a long ways from here, and then let out. You don't know where you've bin, so you can't bring nobody back. But *if* you blab, tell *anybody*, we'll find you wherever you are and kill your kid. Understand?'

Hardly able to believe what she was being told, Juanita nodded.

'Then get goin'.' Lou pointed to a door. Evidently it was not his intention to blindfold her yet. Despite her inertia of moments earlier, she found her normal mental sharpness coming back.

Part-way up a flight of concrete stairs, she leaned against the wall and wanted to be sick. In the outer room they had just

444

passed through, she had seen Miles – or what was left of him – his body slumped across a table, his hands a bloody pulp, his face, hair, and scalp burned beyond recognition. Lou had pushed Juanita and Estela quickly past, but not fast enough to prevent Juanita taking in the grim reality. She had also learned that Miles was not dead, though he was surely dying. He had stirred slightly and moaned.

'Move it!' Lou urged. They continued up the stairs.

The horror of Miles as she had seen him filled Juanita's mind. *What could she do to help him?* Clearly, nothing here. But if she and Estela were to be released, was there some way she could bring aid back? She doubted it. She had no idea where they were; there seemed no chance of finding out. Yet she must do *something*. Something to expiate – at least a little – her terrible sense of guilt. She had betrayed Miles. Whatever the motivation, she had spoken his name, and he was caught and brought here with the consequence she had seen.

The seed of an idea, not wholly thought out, came to her. She concentrated, developing the notion, blotting other things from her mind, even Estela for the moment. Juanita reasoned: it might not work, yet there was a slim chance. Success depended on the acuity of her senses and her memory. It was also important that she not be blindfolded until *after* getting in the car.

At the head of the stairway they turned right and entered a garage. With cement block walls, it looked like an ordinary two-car garage belonging to a house or business and, remembering the sounds she had heard on arrival, Juanita guessed they had come in this same way. There was one car inside – not the big car in which they had arrived this morning, but a dark green Ford. She wanted to see the licence number but it was beyond her view.

In a quick glance around, something puzzled Juanita. Against a wall of the garage was a chest of drawers of dark polished wood, but like no other chest that she had seen before. It appeared to have been sawn vertically in half, with the two halves standing separated and she could see the inside was hollow. Beside the chest was what looked like a dining-room sideboard cut in the same peculiar way, except that half the sideboard was being carried out of another doorway by two men, one shielded by the door, the other with his back to her.

Lou opened a rear door of the Ford. 'Get in,' he ordered. In his hands were two thick dark cloths – blindfolds.

Juanita entered first. Doing so, she tripped intentionally and fell forward, supporting herself by grabbing the back of the car's front seat. It gave her the opportunity she wanted – to look towards the front on the driver's side and read the odometer mileage. She had a second only to take in the figures: 25714.8. She closed her eyes, committing them – she hoped – to memory.

Estela followed Juanita. Lou came in after them, fastened the blindfolds and sat on the rear seat. He pushed Juanita's shoulder. 'Down on the floor, botha ya. Make no trouble, ya won't get hurt.'

Squatting on the floor with Estela close beside her, Juanita curled her legs and managed to keep facing forward. She heard someone else get in the car, the motor start, the garage doors rumble open. Then they were moving.

From the instant the car moved, Juanita concentrated as she had never done before. Her intention was to memorize time and direction – if she could. She began to count seconds as a photographer friend had once taught her. *A thousand* and ONE; a thousand and TWO; a thousand and THREE; a thousand and FOUR . . . She felt the car reverse and turn, then counted eight seconds while it moved in a straight line forward. Then it slowed almost to a stop. Had it been a driveway? Probably. A longish one? The car was again moving slowly, most likely easing out into a street . . . *Turning left. Now faster forward.* She recommenced counting. *Ten seconds. Slowing. Turning right . . . A thousand and* ONE; *a thousand and* TWO; *a thousand and* THREE . . . *Turning left . . . Speed faster . . . A longer stretch . . . A thousand* FORTY-NINE; *a thousand* FIFTY . . . No sign of slowing . . . *Yes, slowing now. A four-second wait, then straight on.* It could have been a traffic light . . . *A thousand and* EIGHT . . .

Dear God! For Miles's sake help me to remember!

. . . *A thousand and* NINE; *a thousand and* TEN. *Turning right . . .*

Banish other thoughts. React to every movement of the car. Count the time – hoping, praying that the same strong memory which helped her keep track of money at the bank . . . which once saved her from Miles's duplicity . . . would now save *him*.

. . . *A thousand* TWENTY; *One thousand and twenty dollars. No ! . . . Mother of God ! Keep my thoughts from wandering . . .*

A long straight stretch, smooth road, high speed . . . She felt her body sway . . . *The road was curving to the left; a long curve, gentle . . . Stopping, stopping.* It had been sixty-eight seconds . . . *Turning right.* Begin again. *A thousand and* ONE; *and a thousand* TWO . . .

On and on.

As time went by, the likelihood of remembering, of reconstructing, seemed increasingly less likely.

twenty-three

'This's Sergeant Gladstone, Central Communications Bureau, City Police,' the flat, nasal voice on the phone announced. 'Says here to immediately notify you people if Juanita Núñez or child Estela Núñez located.'

Special Agent Innes sat up taut and straight. Instinctively he moved the phone closer. 'What do you have, Sergeant ?'

'Car radio report just in. Woman and child answering description and names found wandering near junction of Cheviot Township and Shawnee Lake Road. Taken into protective custody. Officers bringing 'em to 12th Precinct now.'

Innes covered the mouthpiece with his hand. To Nolan Wainwright, seated across the desk at FBI Headquarters, he said softly, 'City police. They've got Núñez and the kid.'

Wainwright gripped the desk edge tightly. 'Ask what condition they're in.'

'Sergeant,' Innes said, 'are they okay ?'

'Told you all we know, chief. Want more dope, you better call the 12th.'

Innes took down the 12th Precinct number and dialled it. He was connected with a Lieutenant Fazackerly.

'Sure, we got the word,' Fazackerly acknowledged crisply. 'Hold it. Follow-up phone report just coming in.'

The FBI man waited.

'According to our guys, the woman's been beaten up some,' Fazackerly said. 'Face bruised and cut. Child has a bad burn on one hand. Officers have given first aid. No other injuries reported.'

Innes relayed the news to Wainwright who covered his face with a hand as if in prayer.

The lieutenant was speaking again. 'Something kind of queer here.'

'What is it?'

'Officers in the car say the Núñez woman won't talk. All she wants is pencil and paper. They've given it to her. She's scribbling like mad. Said something about things being in her memory she has to get out.'

Special Agent Innes breathed, '*Jesus Christ!*' He remembered the bank cash loss, the story behind it, the incredible accuracy of Juanita Núñez's circus freak memory.

'Listen,' he said. 'Please take this from me, I'll explain it later, and we're coming out to you. But radio your car right now. Tell your officers not to talk to Núñez, not to disturb her, help her in any way she wants. And when she gets to the precinct house, the same thing goes. Humour her. Let her go on writing if she wants. Handle her like she was something special.'

He stopped, then added, 'Which she is.'

Short reverse. From garage.
Forward. 8 secs. Almost stop. (Driveway?)
Turn left. 10 secs. Med. speed.
Turn right. 3 secs.
Turn left. 55 secs. Smooth, fast.
Stop. 4 secs. (Traffic light?)
Straight on. 10 secs. Med. speed.
Turn right. Rough road (short dist.) then smooth. 18 secs.
Slowing. Stop. Start immed. Curve to right. Stop – start. 25 secs.

Turn left. Straight, smooth. 47 secs.
Slow. Turn right . . .

Juanita's finished summation ran to seven handwritten pages.

They worked intensively for an hour in a rear room at the police station, using large-scale maps, but the result was inconclusive.

Juanita's scribbled notes had amazed them all – Innes and Dalrymple, Jordan and Quimby of the US Secret Service who had joined the others after a hurry-up call, and Nolan Wainwright. The notes were incredibly complete and, Juanita maintained, entirely accurate. She explained she was never confident that whatever her mind stored away could be recalled – until the moment came to do so. But once the effort had been made, she knew with certainty if her recollections had been correct. She was convinced they were now.

Besides the notes, they had something else to go on. Mileage.

The gags and blindfolds had been removed from Juanita and Estela moments before they were pushed from the car on a lonely suburban road. By contrived clumsiness and luck, Juanita had managed to catch a second glimpse of the odometer. 25738.5. They had travelled 23.7 miles.

But was it a consistent direction, or had the car doubled back, making the journey seem longer than it was, merely to confuse? Even with Juanita's summary, it was impossible to be certain. They did the best they could, working painstakingly backwards, estimating that the car might have come this way or that, turned here or there, travelled thus far on this road. Everyone, though, knew how inexact it was since speeds could only be guessed at and Juanita's senses while she was blindfolded might have deceived her so that error could be piled on error, making their present exercise futile, a waste of time. But there *was* a chance they could trace the route back to where she had been captive, or come close. And, significantly, a general consistency existed between the various possibilities worked out so far.

It was Secret Service Agent Jordan who made an assessment for them all. On an area map he drew a series of lines representing the most likely directions in which the car carrying Juanita

449

and Estela would have travelled. Then, around the origins of the lines, he drew a circle. 'In there.' He prodded with a finger. 'Somewhere in there.'

In the ensuing silence, Wainwright heard Jordan's stomach rumble, as on all the occasions they had met before. Wainwright wondered how Jordan made out on assignments where he had to stay concealed and silent. Or did his noisy stomach preclude him from that kind of work?

'That area,' Dalrymple pointed out, 'is at least five square miles.'

'Then let's comb it,' Jordan answered. 'In teams, in cars. Our shop and yours, and we'll ask help from the city police.'

Lieutenant Fazackerly, who had joined them asked, 'And what will we all be looking for, gentlemen?'

'If you want the truth,' Jordan said, 'damned if I know.'

Juanita rode in an FBI car with Innes and Wainwright. Wainwright drove, leaving Innes free to work two radios – a portable unit, one of five supplied by the FBI, which could communicate directly with the other cars, and a regular transmitter-receiver linked directly to FBI Headquarters.

Beforehand, under the city police lieutenant's direction, they had sectored the area and five cars were now criss-crossing it. Two were FBI, one Secret Service, and two from the city. The personnel had split up. Jordan and Dalrymple were each riding with a city detective, filling in details for the newcomers as they drove. If necessary, other patrols of the city force would be called for backup.

One thing they were all sure of: where Juanita had been held was the counterfeit centre. Her general description and some details she had noticed made it close to a certainty. Therefore, instructions to all special units were the same: look for, and report, any unusual activity which might relate to an organized crime centre specializing in counterfeiting. All concerned conceded the instructions were vague, but no one had been able to come up with anything more specific. As Innes put it: 'What else have we got?'

It was almost two hours since she and Estela had been set down abruptly, ordered to face away, and the dark green Ford had sped off with a screech of burned rubber. Since then Juanita had refused treatment – other than immediate first aid – for her badly bruised and cut face, and the cuts and lacerations on her legs. She was aware that she looked a mess, her clothing stained and torn, but knew too that if Miles was to be reached in time to save him, everything else must wait, even her own attention to Estela, who had been taken to a hospital for treatment of her burn and for observation. While Juanita did what she had to, Margot Bracken – who arrived at the police station shortly after Wainwright and the FBI – was comforting Estela.

It was now mid-afternoon.

Earlier, getting the sequence of her journey down on paper, clearing her mind as if purging an overburdened message centre, had exhausted Juanita. Yet, afterwards, she had responded to what seemed endless questioning by the FBI and Secret Service men who kept on probing for the smallest details of her experience in the hope that some unconsidered fragment might bring them closer to what they wanted most – a specific locale. So far nothing had.

But it was not details Juanita thought about now, seated behind Wainwright and Innes, but Miles as she had last seen him. The picture remained etched – with guilt and anguish – sharply on her mind. She doubted it would ever wholly disappear. The question haunted her: if the counterfeit centre was discovered, would it be too late to save Miles ? Was it already too late ?

The area within the circle Agent Jordan had drawn – located near the city's eastern edge – was mixed in character. In part, it was commerical, with some factories, warehouses, and a large industrial tract devoted to light industry. This last, the most likely area, was the segment to which the patrolling forces were paying most attention. There were several shopping areas. The rest was residential, running the gamut from regiments of box bungalows to a clutch of sizeable mansion-type dwellings.

To the eyes of the dozen roving searchers, who communicated frequently through the portable radios, activity everywhere was average and routine. Even a few out-of-the-ordinary happenings had commonplace overtones. In one of the shopping districts a man buying a painter's safety harness had tripped over it and broken a leg. Not far away a car with a stuck accelerator had crashed into an empty theatre foyer. 'Maybe someone thought it was a drive-in movie,' Innes said, but no one laughed. In the industrial tract the fire department responded to a small plant blaze and quickly put it out. The plant was making waterbeds; one of the city detectives inspected it to be sure. At a residential mansion a charity tea was beginning. At another, an Alliance Van Lines tractor-trailer was loading household furniture. Over amid the bungalows a repair crew was coping with a leaky water main. Two neighbours had quarrelled and were fistfighting on the pavement. Secret Service Agent Jordan got out and separated them.

And so on.

For an hour. At the end of it, they were no further ahead than when they started.

'I've a funny feeling,' Wainwright said. 'A feeling I used to get in police work sometimes when I'd missed something.'

Innes glanced sideways. 'I know what you mean. You get to believe there's something right under your nose if you could only see it.'

'Juanita,' Wainwright said over his shoulder, 'is there *anything*, any little thing you haven't told us ?'

She said firmly, 'I told you everything.'

'Then let's go over it again.'

After a while Wainwright said, 'Around the time Eastin stopped crying out, and while you were still bound, you told us something about there being a lot of noise.'

She corrected him, '*No, una conmoción.* Noise and activity. I could hear people moving, things being shifted, drawers opening and closing, that sort of thing.'

'Maybe they were searching for something,' Innes suggested. 'But what ?'

'When you were on the way out,' Wainwright asked, 'did you get any idea what the activity was about ?'

'*Por última vez, yo no sé.*' Juanita shook her head. 'I told you I

452

was too shocked at seeing Miles to see anything else.' She hesitated. 'Well there *were* those men in the garage moving that funny furniture.'

'Yes,' Innes said. 'You told us about that. It's odd, all right, but we haven't thought of an explanation for it.'

'Wait a minute! Maybe there is one.'

Innes and Juanita looked at Wainwright. He was frowning. He appeared to be concentrating, working something out. 'That activity Juanita heard ... Supposing they weren't searching for something but were packing up, preparing to move ?'

'Could be,' Innes acknowledged. 'But what they'd be moving would be machinery. Printing machines, supplies. Not furniture.'

'Unless,' Wainwright said, 'the furniture was a cover. *Hollow* furniture.'

They stared at each other. The answer hit them both at the same time. 'For God's sake,' Innes shouted. 'That moving van!'

Wainwright was already reversing the car, spinning the wheel hard in a tight, fast turn.

Innes seized the portable radio. He transmitted tensely, 'Strongthrust group leader to all special units. Converge on large grey house, stands back near east end Earlham Avenue. Look for Alliance Van Lines moving van. Halt and detain occupants. City units call in all cars in vicinity. Code 10–13.'

Code 10–13 meant: maximum speed, wide open, lights and siren. Innes switched on their own siren. Wainwright put his foot down hard.

'Christ!' Innes said; he sounded close to tears. 'We went by it twice. And last time they were almost loaded.'

'When you leave here,' Marino instructed the driver of the tractor-semi, 'head for the West Coast. Take it easy, do everything the way you would with a regular load, and rest up every night. But keep in touch, you know where to call. And if you don't get fresh orders on the way, you'll get them in LA.'

'Okay, Mr Marino,' the driver said. He was a reliable joe who knew the score, also that he would get a king-sized bonus for the personal risk he was running. But he had done the same thing other times before, when Tony Bear had kept the counter-feit centre equipment on the road and out of harm's way, moving it around the country like a floating crap game until any heat was off.

'Well then,' the driver said, 'everything's loaded. I guess I'll roll. So long, Mr Marino.'

Tony Bear nodded, feeling relief. He had been unusually antsy during the packing and loading operation, a feeling which had kept him here, overseeing and keeping the pressure on, though he knew he was being un-smart to stay. Normally he kept safely distant from the working front line of any of his operations, making sure there was no evidence to connect him in the event that something fouled up. Others were paid to take those kinds of risks – and raps if necessary. The thing was, though, the counterfeit caper, starting as chickenshit, had become such a big-time money-maker – in the real sense – that from once having been the least of his interests, it was now near the top of the list. Good organization had made it that way; that and taking *ultra*-precautions – a description Tony Bear liked – such as moving out now.

Strictly speaking, he didn't believe this present move was necessary – at least not yet – because he was sure Eastin had been lying when he said he had found out this location from Danny Kerrigan and had passed the information on. Tony Bear believed Kerrigan on that one, though the old fart *had* talked too much, and was going to have some unpleasant surprises soon which would cure him of a loose tongue. If Eastin *had* known what he said he did, and passed it on, the cops and bank dicks would have swarmed here long ago. Tony Bear wasn't surprised at the lie. He knew how people under torture passed through successive mental doors of desperation, switching from lies to truth, then back to lies again if they thought it was something their torturers wanted to hear. It was always an interesting game outguessing them. Tony Bear enjoyed those kinds of games.

Despite all that, moving out, using the emergency rush arrangements set up with the mob-owned trucking company, was the smart thing to do. As usual – ultra-smart. If in doubt, *move*.

And now the loading was done, it was time to get rid of what was left of the stoolie Eastin. Garbage. A detail Angelo would attend to. Meanwhile, Tony Bear decided, it was high time he got the hell away from here himself. In exceptional good humour, he chuckled. *Ultra*-smart.

It was then he heard the faint but growing sound of converging sirens and, minutes later, knew he had not been smart at all.

'Better move it, Harry!' the young ambulance steward called forward to the driver. 'This one doesn't have time to spare.'

'From the look of the guy,' the driver said – he kept his eyes directed ahead, using flashers and warbling siren to weave daringly through early rush hour traffic – 'from the look of him, we'd both be doing the poor bastard a favour if we pulled over for a beer.'

'Knock it off, Harry.' The steward, whose qualifications were somewhat less than those of a male nurse, glanced towards Juanita. She was perched on a jump seat, straining around him to see Miles, her face intent, lips moving. 'Sorry, miss. Guess we forgot you were there. On this job we get a bit case-hardened.'

It took her a moment to absorb what was said. She asked, 'How is he?'

'In bad shape. No sense fooling you.' The young ambulance steward had injected a quarter grain of morphine subcutaneously. He had a blood-pressure cuff in place and now was sloshing water on Miles's face. Miles was semiconscious and, despite the morphine, moaning in pain. All the time the steward went on talking. 'He's in shock. That can kill him, if the burns don't. This water's to wash the acid away, though it's late. As to his eyes, I wouldn't want . . . Say, what the hell happened in there?'

Juanita shook her head, not wanting to waste time and effort in talk. She reached out, seeking to touch Miles, even through the blanket covering him. Tears filled her eyes. She pleaded, uncertain she was being heard, 'Forgive me! Oh, forgive me!'

'He your husband?' the steward asked. He began putting splints, secured by cotton bandages, around Miles's hands.

'No.'

455

'Boyfriend?'

'Yes.' The tears were flowing faster. Was she still *his* friend? *Need* she have betrayed him? Here and now she wanted forgiveness, just as he had once asked forgiveness of her – it seemed long ago, though it was not. She knew it was no use.

'Hold this,' the steward said. He placed a mask over Miles's face and handed her a portable oxygen bottle. She heard a hiss as the oxygen went on and grasped the bottle as if, through her touch, she could communicate, as she had wanted to communicate ever since they had found Miles, unconscious, bleeding, burned, still nailed to the table in the house.

Juanita and Nolan Wainwright had followed the federal agents and local police into the big grey mansion, Wainwright having held her back until he made sure there was not going to be any shooting. There had been none; not even any resistance apparently, the people inside having decided they were outflanked and outnumbered.

It was Wainwright, his face more strained then she had ever seen it, who carefully, as gently as he could, pried loose the nails and released Miles's mangled hands. Dalrymple, ashen, cursing softly, held Eastin while, one by one, the nails came out. Juanita had been vaguely aware of other men, who had been in the house, lined up and handcuffed, but she hadn't cared. When the ambulance came she stayed close to the stretcher brought for Miles. She followed it out and into the ambulance. No one tried to stop her.

Now she began praying. The words came readily; words from long ago . . . *Acordaos, oh piadosisima Virgen Maria . . . that never was it known that anyone who fled to thy protection, implored thy help or sought thy intercession was left unaided. Inspired by that confidence I fly unto you . . .*

Something the ambulance steward had said, but she hadn't taken in played back in her subconscious. *Miles's eyes.* They were burned with the remainder of his face. Her voice trembled. 'Will he be blind?'

'The specialists will have to answer that. Soon's we get to Emergency he'll get the best treatment. There isn't a lot more I can do right here.'

Juanita thought: there wasn't anything she could do either. Except to stay with Miles, as she would, with love and devotion for as long as he wanted and needed her. That, and pray . . . *¡ Oh Virgen Madre de las vírgines ! . . . To thee I come, before thee I stand, sinful and sorrowful. O Mother of the World Incarnate, despise not my petitions but hear and answer me. Amen.*

Some colonnaded buildings flashed by. 'We're almost there,' the steward said. He had his fingers on Miles's pulse. 'He's still alive.'

twenty-four

In the fifteen days since official investigation was begun by the SEC into the labyrinthine finances of Supranational, Roscoe Heyward had prayed for a miracle to avert total catastrophe. Heyward himself attended meetings with other SuNatCo creditors, their objective to keep the multinational giant operating and viable if they could. It had proven impossible. The more deeply investigators probed, the worse the financial débâcle appeared. It seemed probable, too, that criminal charges of fraud would eventually be laid against some of Supranational's officers, including G. G. Quartermain, assuming Big George could ever be enticed back from his Costa Rican hideaway – at the moment an unlikely prospect.

Therefore, in early November, a petition of bankruptcy under Section 77 of the Bankruptcy Act was filed on behalf of Supranational Corporation. Though it had been expected and feared, the immediate repercussions were worldwide. Several large creditors, as well as associated companies and many individuals, were considered likely to go down the drain along with SuNatCo. Whether First Mercantile American Bank would be one of them, or if the bank could survive its enormous loss, was still an open question.

No longer an open question – as Heyward fully realized – was the subject of his own career. At FMA, as the author of the greatest calamity in the bank's one-hundred-year history, he was virtually finished. What remained at issue was whether he, personally, would be legally liable under regulations of the Federal Reserve, the Comptroller of the Currency, and the SEC. Obviously, there were those who thought so. Yesterday, an SEC official, whom Heyward knew well, advised him, 'Roscoe, as a friend, I suggest you get yourself a lawyer.'

In his office, soon after the opening of the business day, Heyward's hands trembled as he read *The Wall Street Journal*'s page one story on the Supranational bankruptcy petition. He was interrupted by his senior secretary, Mrs Callaghan. 'Mr Heyward – Mr Austin is here.'

Without waiting to be told, Harold Austin hurried in. In contrast to his normal role, the ageing playboy today merely looked an overdressed old man. His face was drawn, serious, and pale; pouches beneath his eyes were rings of age and lack of sleep.

He wasted no time in preliminaries. 'Have you heard *anything* from Quartermain ?'

Heyward motioned to the *Journal*. 'Only what I read.' In the past two weeks he had tried several times to telephone Big George in Costa Rica, without success. The SuNatCo chairman was staying incommunicado. Reports filtering out described him as living in feudal splendour, with a small army of thugs to guard him, and said he had no intention, ever, of returning to the United States. It was accepted that Costa Rica would not respond to US extradition proceedings, as other swindlers and fugitives had already proved.

'I'm going down the tube,' the Honourable Harold said. His voice was close to breaking. 'I put the family trust heavily into SuNatCo and I'm in hock myself for money I raised to buy Q-Investments.'

'What *about* Q-Investments ?'

Heyward had tried to find out earlier the status of Quartermain's private group which owed two million dollars to FMA in addition to the fifty million owing by Supranational.

'You mean you didn't hear ?'

Heyward flared, 'If I did, would I be asking?'

'I found out last night from Inchbeck. That son of a bitch Quartermain sold out all Q-Investments holdings – mostly stock in SuNatCo subsidiaries – when the group share prices were at their peak. There must have been a swimming pool full of cash.'

Including FMA's two million, Heyward thought. He asked, 'What happened to it?'

'The bastard transferred everything into offshore shell companies of his own, then moved the money out of them, so all Q-Investments is left with is shares in the shells – just worthless paper.' To Heyward's disgust, Austin began to blubber. 'The real money ... my money ... could be in Costa Rica, the Bahamas, Switzerland ... Roscoe, you've got to help me get it back ... Otherwise I'm finished ... broke.'

Heyward said tersely, 'There's no way I can help you, Harold.' He was worried enough about his own part in Q-Investments without concerning himself with Austin's.

'But if you hear anything new ... if there's any hope ...'

'If there is, I'll let you know.'

As quickly as he could, Heyward eased Austin out of the office. He had no sooner gone than Mrs Callaghan said on the intercom, 'There's a reporter calling from *Newsday*. His name is Endicott. It's about Supranational and he says it's important that he speak to you personally.'

'Tell him I have nothing to say, and to call the PR department.' Heyward remembered Dick French's admonition to the senior officers: *The press will try to contact you individually ... refer every caller to me.* At least that was one burden he need not bear.

Moments later he heard Dora Callaghan's voice again. 'I'm sorry, Mr Heyward.'

'What *is* it?'

'Mr Endicott is still on the line. He asked me to say to you: Do you wish him to discuss Miss Avril Deveraux with the PR department, or would you prefer to talk about her yourself?'

Heyward snatched up a phone. 'What is all this?'

'Good morning, sir,' a quiet voice said. 'I apologize for disturbing you. This is Bruce Endicott of *Newsday*.'

'You told my secretary . . .'

'I told her, sir, that I thought there were some things you'd prefer me to check with you personally, rather than lay them out for Dick French.'

Was there a subtle emphasis on the word 'lay'? Heyward wasn't sure. He said, 'I'm extremely busy. I can spare a few minutes, that's all.'

'Thank you, Mr Heyward. I'll be as brief as I can. Our paper has been doing some investigating of Supranational Corporation. As you know, there's a good deal of public interest and we're running a major story on the subject tomorrow. Among other things, we're aware of the big loan to SuNatCo by your bank. I've talked to Dick French about that.'

'Then you have all the information you need.'

'Not quite, sir. We understand from other sources that you personally negotiated the Supranational loan, and there's a question of when the subject first came up. By that I mean when did SuNatCo first ask for the money? Do you happen to remember?'

'I'm afraid I don't. I deal with many large loans.'

'Surely not too many for fifty million dollars.'

'I think I already answered your question.'

'I wonder if I could help, sir. Could it have been on a trip to the Bahamas in March? A trip you were on with Mr Quartermain, Vice-President Stonebridge, and some others?'

Heyward hesitated. 'Yes, it might have been.'

'Could you say definitely that it was?' The reporter's tone was deferential, but it was clear he would not be put off with evasive answers.

'Yes, I remember now. It was.'

'Thank you, sir. On that particular trip, I believe, you travelled in Mr Quartermain's private jet – a 707?'

'Yes.'

'With a number of young lady escorts.'

'I'd hardly say they were escorts. I vaguely recall several stewardesses being aboard.'

'Was one of them Miss Avril Deveraux? Did you meet her then, and also in the several days which followed in the Bahamas?'

'I may have done. The name you mentioned seems familiar.'

'Mr Heyward, forgive me for putting it this way, but was Miss Deveraux offered to you – sexually – in return for your sponsorship of the Supranational loan?'

'Certainly not!' Heyward was sweating now, the hand holding the telephone shaking. He wondered how much this smooth-voiced inquisitor really knew. Of course, he could end the conversation here and now; perhaps he should, though if he did he would go on wondering, not knowing.

'But did you, sir, as a result of that trip to the Bahamas, form a friendship with Miss Deveraux?'

'I suppose you could call it that. She is a pleasant, charming person.'

'Then you *do* remember her?'

He had walked into a trap. He conceded, 'Yes.'

'Thank you, sir. By the way, have you met Miss Deveraux subsequently?'

The question was asked casually. But *this man Endicott knew.* Trying to keep a tremor out of his voice, Heyward insisted, 'I've answered all the questions I intend to. As I told you, I'm extremely busy.'

'As you wish, sir. But I think I should tell you that we've talked with Miss Deveraux and she's been extremely cooperative.'

Extremely cooperative? Avril would be, Heyward thought. Especially if the newspaper paid her, and he supposed they had. But he felt no bitterness towards her; Avril was what she was, and nothing could ever change the sweetness she had given him.

The reporter was continuing. 'She's supplied details of her meetings with you and we have some of the Columbia Hilton hotel bills – your bills, which Supranational paid. Do you wish to reconsider your statement, sir, that none of that had anything to do with the loan from First Mercantile American Bank to Supranational?'

Heyward was silent. What could he say? *Confound* all news-

461

papers and writers, their obsession with invading privacy, their eternal digging, digging! Obviously someone inside SuNatCo had been induced to talk, had filched or copied papers. He remembered something Avril had said about 'the list' – a confidential roster of those who could be entertained at Supranational's expense. For a while, his own name had been on it. Probably they had that information, too. The irony, of course, was that Avril had not in any way influenced his decision about the SuNatCo loan. He had made up his mind to recommend it long before involvement with her. But who would believe him?

'There's just one other thing, sir.' Endicott obviously assumed there would be no answer to the last question. 'May I ask about a private investment company called Q-Investments? To save time, I'll tell you we've managed to get copies of some of the records and you are shown as holding two thousand shares. Is that correct?'

'I have no comment to make.'

'Mr Heyward, were those shares given to you as a pay-off for arranging the Supranational loan, and further loans totalling two million dollars to Q-Investments?'

Without speaking, Roscoe Heyward slowly hung up the phone.

Tomorrow's newspaper. That was what the caller had said. They would print it all, since obviously they had the evidence, and what one newspaper initiated, the rest of the media would repeat. He had no illusions, no doubts about what would follow. One newspaper story, one reporter, meant disgrace – total, absolute. Not only at the bank, but among friends, family. At his church, elsewhere. His prestige, influence, pride would be dissolved; for the first time he realized what a fragile mask they were. Even worse was the certainty of criminal prosecution for accepting bribes, the likelihood of other charges, the probability of prison.

He had sometimes wondered how the once-proud Nixon henchmen felt, brought low from their high places to be criminally charged, finger-printed, stripped of dignity, judged by jurors whom not long before they would have treated with contempt. Now he knew. Or shortly would.

A quotation from *Genesis* came to him: *My punishment is greater than I can bear.*

A telephone rang on his desk. He ignored it. There was nothing more to be done here. Ever.

Almost without knowing it, he rose and walked out of the office, past Mrs Callaghan who regarded him strangely and asked a question which he neither absorbed nor would have answered if he had. He walked down the thirty-sixth floor corridor, past the boardroom, so short a time ago an arena for his own ambitions. Several people spoke to him. He took no notice of them. Not far beyond the boardroom was a small door, seldom used. He opened it. There were stairs going upward and he ascended them, through several flights and turns, climbing steadily, neither hurrying nor pausing on the way.

Once, when FMA Headquarters Tower was new, Ben Rosselli had brought his executives this way. Heyward was one of them, and they had exited by another small door, which he could see ahead. Heyward opened it and went out, on to a narrow balcony almost at the building's peak, high above the city.

A raw November wind struck him with blustering force. He leaned against it and found it somehow reassuring, as if enfolding him. It was on that other occasion, he remembered, that Ben Rosselli had held out his arms towards the city and said: 'Gentlemen, what was once here was my grandfather's promised land. What you see today is ours. Remember – as he did – that to profit in the truest sense, we must give to it, as well as take.' It seemed long ago, in precept as well as time. Now Heyward looked downward. He could see smaller buildings, the winding, omnipresent river, traffic, people moving like ants on Rosselli Plaza far below. The sounds of them all came to him, muted and blended, on the wind.

He put a leg over the waist-high railing separating the balcony from a narrow, unprotected ledge. His second leg followed. Until this moment he had felt no fear, but now all of his body trembled with it, and his hands grasped the railing at his back tightly.

Somewhere behind him he heard agitated voices, feet racing

on the stairs. Someone shouted, 'Roscoe!'

His last thought but one was a line from *1 Samuel: Go, and the Lord be with thee.* The very last was of Avril. *O thou fairest among women . . . Rise up, my love, my fair one and come away . . .*

Then, as figures burst through the door behind him, he closed his eyes and stepped forward into the void.

twenty-five

There were a handful of days in your life, Alex Vandervoort thought, which, as long as you breathed and remembered anything, would stay sharply and painfully engraved in memory. The day – little more than a year ago – on which Ben Rosselli announced his impending death was one. Today would be another.

It was evening. At home in his apartment, Alex – still shocked from what had happened earlier, uncertain and dispirited – was waiting for Margot. She would be here soon. He mixed himself a second scotch and soda and tossed a log on the fire, which had burned low.

This morning he had been first through the door to the high tower balcony, having raced up the stairs after hearing worry expressed about Heyward's state of mind and deducing – from swift questioning of others – where Roscoe might have gone. Alex had cried out as he hurled himself through the doorway into the open, but was too late.

The sight of Roscoe, seeming to hang for an instant in air, then disappearing from view with a terrible scream which faded quickly, left Alex horrified, shaking, and for moments unable to speak. It was Tom Straughan, who was right behind him on the stairway, who had taken charge, ordering the balcony cleared, an order with which Alex had complied.

Later, in an act of futility, the door to the balcony had been locked.

Below, returning to the thirty-sixth floor, Alex had pulled himself together and gone to report to Jerome Patterton. After that, the rest of the day was a mélange of events, decisions, details, succeeding and merging with each other until the whole became a Heyward epitaph, which even now was not concluded, and there would be more of the same tomorrow. But, for today, Roscoe's wife and son had been contacted and consoled; police enquiries answered – at least, in part; funeral arrangements overseen – since the body was unrecognizable, the coffin would be sealed as soon as the coroner agreed; a press statement drafted by Dick French and approved by Alex; and still more questions dealt with or postponed.

Answers to other questions became clearer to Alex in the late afternoon, shortly after Dick French advised him that he should accept a telephone call from a *Newsday* reporter named Endicott. When Alex talked to him, the reporter seemed upset. He explained that just a few minutes earlier he had read on the AP wire of Roscoe Heyward's apparent suicide. Endicott went on to describe his call to Heyward this morning and what transpired. 'If I'd had any idea . . .' he ended lamely.

Alex made no attempt to help the reporter feel better. The moralities of his profession were something he would have to work out for himself. But Alex did ask, 'Is your paper still going to run the story ?'

'Yes, sir. The desk is writing a new lead. Apart from that, it will run tomorrow as intended.'

'Then why did you call ?'

'I guess I just wanted to say – to somebody – I'm sorry.'

'Yes,' Alex said. 'So am I.'

This evening Alex reflected again on the conversation, pitying Roscoe for the agony of mind he must have suffered in those final minutes.

On another level there was no doubt that the *Newsday* story, when it appeared tomorrow, would do the bank great harm. It would be harm piled on harm. Despite Alex's success in halting the run at Tylersville, and the absence of other visible runs else-

465

where, there had been a public lessening of confidence in First Mercantile American and an erosion of deposits. Nearly forty million dollars in withdrawals had flowed out in the past ten days and incoming funds were far below their usual level. At the same time, FMA's share price had sagged badly on the New York Stock Exchange.

FMA, of course, was not alone in that. Since the original news of Supranational's insolvency, a miasma of melancholy had gripped investors and the business community, including bankers; had sent stock prices generally on a downhill slide; had created fresh doubts internationally about the value of the dollar; and now appeared to some as the last clear warning before the major storm of world depression.

It was, Alex thought, as if the toppling of a giant had brought home the realization that other giants, once thought invulnerable, could topple, too; that neither individuals, nor corporations, nor governments at any level could escape for ever the simplest accounting law of all – that what you owed you must one day pay.

Lewis D'Orsey, who had preached that doctrine for two decades, had written much the same thing in his latest *Newsletter*. Alex had received a new issue in the mail this morning, had glanced at it, then put it in his pocket to read more carefully tonight. Now, he took it out.

Do not believe the glibly touted myth [Lewis wrote] that there is something complex and elusive, defying easy analysis, about corporate, national or international finance.

All are simply housekeeping – ordinary housekeeping, on a larger scale.

The alleged intricacies, the obfuscations and sinuosities are an imaginary thicket. They do not, in reality, exist, but have been created by vote-buying politicians (which means *all* politicians), manipulators, and Keynesian-diseased 'economists'. Together they use their witch doctor mumbo-jumbo to conceal what they are doing, and have done.

What these bumblers fear most is our simple scrutiny of their activities in the clear and honest light of commonsense.

For what they – the politicians, mostly – on one hand have created is Himalayas of debt which neither they, we, nor our great-great-great-grandchildren can ever pay. And, on the other hand, they have printed, as if producing toilet tissue, a cascade of currency, debasing our good money – especially the honest, gold-backed dollars which Americans once owned.

We repeat: It is all simply housekeeping – the most flagrantly incompetent, dishonest housekeeping in human history.

This, and this alone, is the basic reason for inflation.

There was more. Lewis preferred too many words, rather than too few.

Also, as usual, Lewis offered a solution to financial ills.

Like a beaker of water for a parched and dying wayfarer, a solution is ready and available, as it has always been, and as it always will be.

Gold.

Gold as a base, once more, for the world's money systems.

Gold, the oldest, the *only* bastion of monetary integrity. Gold, the *one* source, *incorruptible*, of fiscal discipline.

Gold, which politicians cannot print, or make, or fake, or otherwise debase.

Gold which, because of its severely limited supply, establishes its own *real*, lasting value.

Gold which, because of this consistent value and when a base for money, protects the honest savings of all people from pillaging by knaves, charlatans, incompetents and dreamers in public office.

Gold which, over centuries, has demonstrated:

–without it as a monetary base, there is inevitable inflation, followed by anarchy;

–with it, inflation can be curbed and cured, stability retained.

Gold of which Americans once stated proudly their dollar was 'as good as'.

Gold to which, some day soon, America must honourably return as its standard of exchange. The alternative – becoming clearer daily – is fiscal and national disintegration. Fortunately, even, now, despite scepticism and anti-gold fanatics, there are signs of maturing views in government, of sanity returning . . .

Alex put *The D'Orsey Newsletter* down. Like many in banking and elsewhere he had sometimes scoffed at the vociferous gold bugs – Lewis D'Orsey, Harry Schultz, James Dines, Congressman Crane, Exter, Browne, Pick, a handful more. Recently, though, he had begun wondering if their simplistic views might not after all be right. As well as gold, they believed in laissez-faire, the free, unhampered function of the market-place where inefficient companies were allowed to fail, and efficient ones succeed: devil take the hindmost. The obverse of the coin were the Keynesian theorists, who hated gold and believed in tinkering with the economy, including subsidies and controls, calling it all 'fine tuning'. Could the Keynesians be the heretics, Alex wondered, and D'Orsey, Schultz, et al, true prophets ? Perhaps. Prophets in other eras had been lonely and derided, yet some lived to see their prophecies fulfilled. One view Alex shared in totality with Lewis and the others was that grimmer times were close ahead. Indeed, for FMA they were already here.

He heard the sound of a key turning. The outer door of the apartment opened and Margot came in. She removed a belted camel's-hair coat and tossed it on a chair.

'Oh God, Alex. I can't get Roscoe out of my mind. How could he do it ? *Why ?*'

She went directly to the bar and mixed a drink.

'It seems there were some reasons,' he said slowly. 'They're beginning to come out. If you don't mind, Bracken, I don't feel like talking about it yet.'

'I understand.' She came to him. He held her tightly as they kissed.

After a while he said, 'Tell me about Eastin, Juanita, the little girl.'

Since yesterday Margot had masterminded arrangements concerning all three.

She sat facing him, sipping her drink. 'It's all so much; coming together . . .'

468

'Often things seem to happen that way.' He wondered what else, if anything, there would be before this day was done.

'Miles first,' Margot began. 'He's out of danger and the best news is that by a miracle he won't be blind. What the doctors believe is that he must have closed his eyes an instant before the acid hit, so the eyelids saved him. They're terribly burned, of course, like the rest of his face, and he'll be having plastic surgery for a long time.'

'What about his hands?'

Margot took a notebook from her purse and opened it. 'The hospital has been in touch with a surgeon on the West Coast – a Dr Jack Tupper in Oakland. He has the reputation of being one of the best men in the country for surgical repair of hands. He's been consulted by phone. He's agreed to fly here and operate the middle of next week. I assumed the bank will pay.'

'Yes,' Alex said. 'It will.'

'I've had a talk,' Margot continued, 'with Agent Innes of the FBI. He says that in return for Miles Eastin's testifying in court, they'll offer him protection and a new identity somewhere else in the country.' She put down her notebook. 'Has Nolan talked to you today?'

Alex shook his head. 'There hasn't been much chance.'

'He's going to. He wants you to use your influence in helping Miles get a job. Nolan says if necessary he'll pound on your desk to make you do it.'

'He won't need to,' Alex said. 'Our holding company owns consumer finance shops in Texas and in California. We'll find something for Eastin in one or the other.'

'Maybe they'll hire Juanita as well. She says wherever he goes, she's going with him. Estela, too.'

Alex sighed. He was glad there would be at least one happy ending. He asked, 'What did Tim McCartney say about the child?'

It had been Alex's idea to send Estela Núñez to Dr McCartney, the Remedial Centre psychiatrist. What mental harm, if any, Alex wondered, had befallen the little girl as a result of her kidnapping and torture?

But the thought of the Remedial Centre now was a dismal reminder to him of Celia.

'I'll tell you one thing,' Margot said. 'If you and I were as sane and balanced as little Estela, we'd both be better people. Dr McCartney says the two of them talked the whole thing out. As a result, Estela won't bury the experience in her subconscious; she'll remember it clearly – as a bad nightmare, nothing more.'

Alex felt tears spring to his eyes. 'I'm glad of that,' he said softly. 'Really glad.'

'It's been a busy day.' Margot stretched, kicking off her shoes. 'One of the other things I did was talk with your legal department about compensation for Juanita. I think we can work something out without taking you to court.'

'Thanks, Bracken.' He took her drink, and his own, to refill them. While he did, the telephone rang. Margot got up and answered it.

'It's Leonard Kingswood. For you.'

Alex crossed the living-room and took the phone. 'Yes, Len ?'

'I know you're relaxing after a rough day,' the Northam Steel chairman said, 'and I'm shook up about Roscoe, too. But what I have to say can't wait.'

Alex grimaced. 'Go ahead.'

'There's been a caucus of directors. Since this afternoon we've had two conference calls, with other calls between. A full meeting of the FMA board is being summoned for noon tomorrow.'

'And ?'

'The first order of business will be to accept the resignation of Jerome as president. Some of us demanded it. Jerome agreed. In fact, I think he was relieved.'

Yes, Alex thought, Patterton would be. He clearly had no stomach for the sudden avalanche of problems, along with the critical decisions needed now.

'After that,' Kingswood said with his usual blunt directness, 'you will be elected president, Alex. The appointment to take effect immediately.'

While talking, Alex had cradled the telephone against his

shoulder and lit his pipe. Now he puffed it while he considered. 'At this point, Len, I'm not sure I want the job.'

'There was a feeling you might say that, which is why I was elected as the one to call you. You could say I'm pleading, Alex; for myself and the rest of the board.' Kingswood paused, and Alex sensed he was having a hard time. Beseeching did not come easily to a man of Leonard L. Kingswood's stature, but he ploughed on just the same.

'We all know you warned us about Supranational, but we thought we were wiser. Well, we weren't. We ignored your advice and now what you predicted has come true. So we're asking you, Alex – belatedly, I admit – to help us out of this mess we're in. I might say that some of the directors are worried about their personal liability. All of us remember your cautioning about that, too.'

'Let me think a minute, Len.'

'Take your time.'

Alex supposed he should feel some personal satisfaction, a sense of superiority, perhaps, at being vindicated, able to say, *I told you so*; a conviction of power at holding – as he knew he did – trump cards.

He felt none of those things. Only a great sadness at the futility and waste, when the best that could happen for a long time to come, assuming he succeeded, was for the bank to regain the state in which Ben Rosselli left it.

Was it worth it? What was it all about? Could the extraordinary effort, deep personal involvement and sacrifice, the stress and strain, be justified? And for what? To save a bank, a money store, a money machine, from failure. Wasn't Margot's work among the poor and disadvantaged far more important than his own, a greater contribution to their times? Yet it wasn't all that simple because banks were necessary, in their way as essential and immediate as food. Civilization would break down without a money system. Banks, though imperfect, made the money system work.

Those were abstract considerations; there was a practical one. Even if Alex accepted the leadership of First Mercantile American at this late stage, there was no assurance of success. He

471

might merely preside, ignominiously, over FMA's demise or take-over by another bank. If so, he would be remembered for it, his reputation as a banker liquidated, too. On the other hand, if anyone could save FMA, Alex knew he was the one. As well as ability, he possessed the inside knowledge which an outsider would not have time to learn. Even more important: despite all the problems, even now, he believed that he could do it.

'If I accepted, Len,' he said, 'I'd insist on a free hand to make changes, including changes on the board.'

'You'd get your free hand,' Kingswood answered. 'I personally guarantee it.'

Alex drew on his pipe, then put it down. 'Let me sleep on it. I'll give you my decision in the morning.'

He hung up the phone and retrieved his drink from the bar. Margot had already taken hers.

She regarded him quizzically. 'Why didn't you accept? When both of us know you're going to.'

'You guessed what that was all about?'

'Of course.'

'Why are you so certain I'll accept?'

'Because you can't resist the challenge. Because your whole life is banking. Everything else takes second place.'

'I'm not sure,' he said slowly, 'that I want that to be true.' Yet it *had* been true, he thought, when he and Celia were together. Was it still? Possibly the answer was yes, as Margot said. Probably, too, no one ever changed his basic nature.

'There's something I've been wanting to ask you,' Margot said. 'This seems as good a time as any.'

He nodded. 'Go ahead.'

'That night in Tylersville, the day of the bank run, when the old couple with their life savings in that shopping bag asked you the question: *Is our money absolutely safe in your bank?* You answered yes. Were you really sure?'

'I've asked myself that,' Alex said. 'Right afterwards, and since. If I own up, I suppose I wasn't.'

'But you were saving the bank. Right? And that came first. Ahead of those old people, and all the others; ahead of honesty even, because "business as usual" was more important.' Suddenly there was emotion in Margot's voice. 'It's why you'll go on trying to save the bank, Alex – ahead of everything else. It's the way it was with you and Celia. And,' she said slowly, 'as it would be – if you had to make the choice – with you and me.'

Alex was silent. What could you say, what could anyone say, confronted with the naked truth ?

'So in the end,' Margot said, 'you aren't all that different from Roscoe. Or Lewis either.' She picked up *The D'Orsey Newsletter* with distaste. 'Business stability, sound money, gold, high share prices. All those things first. People – especially little, unimportant people – a long way after. It's the big gulf between us, Alex. It will always be there.' He saw that she was crying.

A buzzer sounded in the hallway beyond the living-room.

Alex swore. 'Goddamn the interruptions!'

He strode towards an intercom unit connecting with a doorman on the street floor. 'Yes, what is it ?'

'Mr Vandervoort, there's a lady here asking for you. Mrs Callaghan.'

'I don't know any . . .' He stopped. Heyward's secretary ? 'Ask if she's from the bank.'

A pause.

'Yes, sir. She is.'

'All right. Send her up.'

Alex told Margot. They waited curiously. When he heard the lift on the landing outside, he went to the apartment door and opened it.

'Please come in, Mrs Callaghan.'

Dora Callaghan was an attractive, well-groomed woman, nearing sixty. She had, Alex knew, worked at FMA for many years, at least ten of them for Roscoe Heyward. Normally she was poised and confident, but tonight she looked tired and nervous.

She wore a fur-trimmed suede coat and carried a leather briefcase. Alex recognized it as belonging to the bank.

'Mr Vandervoort, I'm sorry to intrude . . .'

'I'm sure you have a good reason for coming.' He introduced Margot, then asked, 'Could you use a drink ?'

'I really could.'

A martini. Margot mixed it. Alex took the suede coat. They all sat by the fire.

'You can speak freely in front of Miss Bracken,' Alex said.

'Thank you.' Dora Callaghan took a gulp of the martini, then put it down. 'Mr Vandervoort, this afternoon I went through Mr Heyward's desk. I thought there would be some things to clear, papers perhaps that should be sent to someone else.' Her voice thickened and stopped. She whispered, 'I'm sorry.'

Alex told her gently, 'Please don't be. There's no hurry.'

As her composure returned, she continued, 'There were some locked drawers, Mr Heyward and I both had keys, though I didn't use mine often. Today I did.'

Again a silence while they waited.

'In one of the drawers . . . Mr Vandervoort, I heard there would be investigators coming tomorrow morning. I thought . . . that you'd better see what was in there, that you'd know, better than I, what to do.'

Mrs Callaghan opened the leather briefcase and took out two large envelopes. As she handed them to Alex, he observed that both had been slit open previously. Curiously, he removed the contents.

The first envelope contained four share certificates, each for five hundred shares of Q-Investments common stock and signed by G. G. Quartermain. Though they were nominee certificates, there could be no doubt they had belonged to Heyward, Alex thought. He remembered the *Newsday* reporter's allegations of this afternoon. This was confirmation. Further proof would be needed, of course, if the matter were pursued, but it seemed certain that Heyward, a trusted, high-ranking officer of the bank, had accepted a sordid bribe. Had he lived, exposure would have meant criminal prosecution.

Alex's earlier depression deepened. He had never liked Heyward. They were antagonists, almost from the time that Alex was recruited into FMA. Yet never for an instant, until today, had he doubted Roscoe's personal integrity. It demonstrated, he supposed, that however well you thought you knew another human being, you never really did.

Wishing none of this was happening, Alex removed the contents from the second envelope. They proved to be enlarged photographs of a group of people beside a swimming pool – four women and two men in the nude, and Roscoe Heyward dressed. As an instant guess, Alex suspected the photos were a souvenir from Heyward's much-vaunted trip to the Bahamas with Big George Quartermain. Alex counted twelve prints as he spread them out on a coffee table while Margot and Mrs Callaghan watched. He caught a glimpse of Dora Callaghan's face. Her cheeks were red; she was blushing. *Blushing?* He'd thought no one did that any more.

His inclination, as he studied the photos, was to laugh. Everyone in them looked – there was no other word for it – ridiculous. Roscoe, in one shot, was staring fascinated at the naked women; in another he was being kissed by one of them while his fingers touched her breasts. Harold Austin exhibited a flabby body, drooping penis, and foolish smile. Another man, with his behind to the camera, faced the women. As to the women – well, Alex thought, some people might consider them attractive. For himself, he would take Margot, with her clothes on, any day.

He didn't laugh, though – out of deference to Dora Callaghan who had drained her martini and was standing up. 'Mr Vandervoort, I'd better go.'

'You were right to bring these things to me,' he told her. 'I appreciate it, and I'll take care of them personally.'

'I'll see you out,' Margot said. She retrieved Mrs Callaghan's coat and went with her to the lift.

Alex was by a window, looking out at the city's lights, when Margot returned.

'A nice woman,' she pronounced. 'And loyal.'

'Yes,' he said, and thought: whatever changes were made tomorrow and in ensuing days, he would see that Mrs Callaghan was treated considerately. There would be other people to think of, too. Alex would immediately promote Tom Straughan to Alex's own previous post as an executive vice-president. Orville Young could fill Heyward's shoes well. Edwina D'Orsey must move up to senior vice-president in charge of the trust department; it was a post Alex had had in mind for Edwina for some time, and soon he expected her to move higher still. Meanwhile she must be named, at once, a member of the board.

He realized suddenly: he was taking for granted that he himself would accept the bank presidency. Well, Margot had just told him that. Obviously she was right.

He turned away from the window and the outside darkness. Margot was standing at the coffee table, looking down at the photographs. Suddenly she giggled, and then he did what he had wanted to, and laughed with her.

'Oh, God!' Margot said. 'Funny-sad!'

When their laughter ended he bent down, collected the prints and returned them to their envelope. He was tempted to throw the package on the fire, but knew he mustn't. It would be destruction of evidence which might be needed. But he would do his best, he decided, to keep the photos from other eyes – for Roscoe's sake.

'Funny-sad,' Margot repeated. 'Isn't it all ?'

'Yes,' he agreed, and in that moment knew he needed her, and always would.

He took her hands, remembering what they had been speaking of before Mrs Callaghan came. 'Never mind any gulfs between us,' Alex urged. 'We have a lot of bridges, too. You and I are good for each other. Let's live together permanently, Bracken, starting now.'

She objected, 'It probably won't work, or last. The odds are against us.'

'Then we'll try to prove them wrong.'

'Of course, there *is* one thing in our favour.' Margot's eyes sparkled mischievously. 'Most couples who pledge "to love and to cherish, till death us do part", wind up in divorce courts within a year. Maybe if we start out not believing or expecting much, we'll do better than the rest.'

As he took her in his arms, he told her, 'Sometimes bankers and lawyers talk too much.'